JANE FEATHER

ZEBRA BOOKS
KENSINGTON PUBLISHING CORP.

ZEBRA BOOKS are published by

Kensington Publishing Corp.
850 Third Avenue
New York, NY 10022

10   9   8

Printed in the United States of America

LOVE IN HIDING

"Milord, you don't understand . . ."

"I understand perfectly," the earl interrupted curtly, still mindful of his bruised skin. "You have more layers of dirt on you than you have skin. Now, get those rags off and get in the tub." Hard hands grasped the boy's upper arms lifting him off the bed. As his feet touched the ground, Danny made a last desperate bid for the door.

"What in Hades is the matter with you?" Linton hissed furiously. He reached for the neck of the ragged shirt, and as Danny wrenched himself sideways, the threadbare material split with a harsh rending sound.

Total silence filled the room for a breathless moment. Justin, Earl of Linton, released his hold and stepped back, for once in his thirty-four years completely nonplussed.

"It seems I didn't understand," he murmured, pulling his eyes away from the enchanting view of bared flesh. He noticed absently that the girl—undoubtedly a girl—made no attempt to shield herself, merely stood, shoulders back, eyes glaring a challenge.

"So, milord, what do you choose to do with me now?"

He inhaled sharply, even more thoroughly taken aback.

"Your name, brat?" he demanded harshly.

"Danielle."

"Do not imagine, Mademoiselle Danielle, that I shall be satisfied with that," he warned softly. "But for now, I intend to proceed as I began. Are you going to take off those filthy britches, or am I?"

<u>BOOK YOUR PLACE ON OUR WEBSITE</u>
AND MAKE THE
<u>READING CONNECTION!</u>

We've created a customized website just for our very special readers, where you can get the inside scoop on everything that's going on with Zebra, Pinnacle and Kensington books.

When you come online, you'll have the exciting opportunity to:

- View covers of upcoming books
- Read sample chapters
- Learn about our future publishing schedule (listed by publication month *and author*)
- Find out when your favorite authors will be visiting a city near you
- Search for and order backlist books from our online catalog
- Check out author bios and background information
- Send e-mail to your favorite authors
- Meet the Kensington staff online
- Join us in weekly chats with authors, readers and other guests
- Get writing guidelines
- AND MUCH MORE!

**Visit our website at
http://www.zebrabooks.com**

Part I: The Chrysalis

Chapter 1

The tall elegant figure paused thoughtfully at the corner of the Fauborg St.-Honoré and cast a quick glance down the narrow paved alley on his left. He brushed an imaginary speck of dirt from his silver Mechlin lace peeping beneath a richly brocaded cuff before turning into the alley toward the sounds of altercation. It was not the Earl of Linton's custom to involve himself in street brawls, particularly in Parisian back alleys, but, if the truth were told, he was somewhat bored this fine spring afternoon and the disproportionate sizes of the antagonists offended his sense of fair play. A diminutive urchin, a mere scrap of humanity, was struggling manfully in the hold of an enormous bear of a man whose flour-dusted apron bore ample witness to his profession. The baker's attempts to wield a heavy leather belt were hampered by his intended victim, who, as slippery as an eel and with the teeth and claws of a wildcat, seemed, reflected the earl lazily, to be putting up a magnificent fight. So far his assailant was having too much trouble merely getting a grip on the squirming little figure to be able to use the belt as he so clearly intended. That, however, was only a matter of time given the indisputable physical facts. As if in confirmation of this thought an agonized yelp accompanied the loud crack as the weapon found its mark and the earl lengthened his stride. The language rending the street from both participants would not have been out of place on the quay at Marseille and the urchin seemed well able to hold his own in the verbal arena at least. The next minute he had sunk his teeth with desperate strength into the hand holding him, and the agonized yell this time came from the baker. The belt cracked viciously again and his lordship decided it was time to make his move.

The slender silver-mounted cane caught the brawny forearm as it swung back in preparation for another blow.

"Enough, I think," the earl said gently, catching the thick wrist between elegant fingers, squeezing with surprising strength until the astounded baker lost his grip on the belt and it fell to the mired cobblestones. The next instant the tiny figure, taking advantage of the suddenly slackened hold, drove a small fist upwards into his enemy's groin and the baker capitulated with a heavy groan, doubling over the excruciating pain rending his belly.

"*Mon Dieu*, but you fight dirty, *mon ami*," the earl murmured, reaching with an almost lethargic gesture to catch a bony arm as the creature turned to run. "If you run through the streets, *mon enfant*, you will be noticed and pursued."

His soft statement stilled the diminutive figure. An escaping urchin would most certainly be chased on the assumption that he was running from trouble.

"*When* you are caught," His Lordship emphasized calmly, "I am sure this gentleman here will enjoy his revenge. Some might even say he was entitled to it." He regarded the gasping, choking mountain with scant interest before turning back to his captive.

"He 'urt me," a mutinous voice muttered, a hand rubbing the small sore backside, "and jest for a crust o' yesterday's bread." The rebellious tone was belied by a sheen of unshed tears in the over-large brown eyes and a tiny defiant sniff accompanied the swift movement of a grimy, ragged forearm wiping a pert nose. The earl winced—the gesture seemed to have spread more dirt than it removed.

"Come, I think we should take ourselves away before your friend here recovers." With a grimace that was not lost on the urchin he seized a small grubby paw in an elegant, long-fingered hand and began to retrace his steps toward the broader thoroughfare.

"Tell me about yesterday's loaf," he invited, maintaining

his tight grip on the tiny hand struggling to pull away.

"Would only a' gone to the pigs," the voice mumbled. "Don't seem right when people are 'ungry."

"Quite so," His Lordship concurred smoothly. "And you, I take it, are hungry?" It was an unnecessary question—the tiny figure half running beside him was, for all its wiry strength, almost fleshless. Not unusual, of course, in this year of grace, 1789, and the Earl of Linton was well accustomed to the unpleasant facts of a social system that necessitated the poverty of the majority in order to provide for the greater comfort of the elite minority. But something about this filthy little bantam with a mouth as dirty as his person stirred an unusual interest in the normally hardened, disillusioned breast of this member of that elite. Probably boredom, the earl thought dismissively, heedless of the curious glances their progress brought. The sight of an immaculate aristocrat hand in hand with a backstreet waif was certainly unusual enough to provoke speculative interest.

"Where you takin' me?" A sudden tug on his hand brought him out of his reverie and he glanced down at the small anxious face peering up through its layers of grime. "I ain't done nothin' wrong."

"I find that hard to believe," he replied with a short laugh and then, seeing the sudden frightened appeal in those huge eyes, reassured, "I am just going to put some food in your belly." And get rid of that dirt, he added silently. But that part of the plan had best be kept to himself, at least for the time being. He rather suspected that soap and hot water would be considered as much an assault on this small body as the application of the baker's belt.

"What's your name, child?"

"Danny" came the prompt response.

"Danny what?"

"Jus' Danny."

He decided to let that go for the time being. "How old are you, Danny?"

"How old d'ya think?"

The earl frowned slightly at the aggressive tilt of the small chin. If they were to pursue their acquaintance this street-wise

9

waif was going to have to learn some manners. But maybe now was not an opportune moment—first things first.

"About twelve," he replied mildly.

"That'll do."

It was clearly going to have to, Linton mused as they reached the heavy double doors leading into the cobbled courtyard of the inn that had enjoyed the patronage of the house of Linton for many years.

The child hung back, digging the heels of his rough wooden clogs into the mud of the gutter. "Ain't goin' in there!"

"You most certainly are, my friend." A hard tug on the small hand and the unwilling body was pried loose from the mud and hauled willy-nilly into the courtyard.

"Take your cap off," the earl instructed smoothly as he pulled the reluctant urchin beside him into the cool, darkened passageway of the inn. When the boy showed no inclination to comply he took the ragged object between finger and thumb with a grimace of distaste and dropped it to the stone-flagged floor. His eyes widened in amazement at the haircut thus revealed, but he was prevented from immediate comment.

"Ah, Milord Linton, *j'espère que vous avez . . .*" The cheery greeting of the rotund landlord died as he caught sight of his guest's companion. The sharp blue eyes lost their superficial warmth, narrowed and hardened. *"Cochon!"* he hissed, moving steadily on the small figure. "You dare to come in here, you filthy little guttersnipe." He got no further. A small foot swung, catching him on the calf with a wooden sole and a tirade of backstreet abuse poured forth from the suddenly rigid, enraged youth.

"Tais-toi!" The earl jerked the hand in his with sufficient force to cause sharp pain in its owner's shoulders. Danny, with a gasp, fell silent.

"Your eyes, Monsieur Trimbel, must be becoming dim," Linton said coldly. "Can you not see that I have the child by the hand? He is here at my invitation."

"Mais, milord. Je m'excuse, mais . . ." Monsieur Trimbel stuttered, glancing over his shoulder, wondering miserably what his other guests would think of having their quiet, elegant haven sullied by the presence of this street urchin.

10

"You are excused," His Lordship said softly. "But just this once, you understand?"

The landlord's forehead almost reached his knees—no mean feat given the size of his belly—as he stammered his reiterated apologies. Linton made for the stairs, ignoring the groveling figure behind him until he became aware of the antics of his suddenly acquired charge. The little vagabond was prancing lightly on the balls of his feet, tongue out, thumb cocked on the tip of his nose at the enraged landlord.

"Good lord! I begin to suspect the baker knew what he was about—I should have left you to him, you outrageous brat!" He swung the child in front of him, laying a firm hand on the small buttocks propelling him upward. Danny's triumphant smirk died away as he heard his self-appointed guardian demand over his shoulder a tub of *very* hot water, soap, and towels immediately.

They reached the first landing and the earl struggled to maintain his grip on the suddenly desperate, squirming, wriggling body with one hand while he unlatched a wooden door with the other.

"Be still, you ridiculous infant," he demanded in exasperation pushing him into the room with an ungentle shove, kicking the door shut after them.

"I'm not going to hurt you," he began more gently and then swore violently as the urchin launched himself in full attack, nails and teeth searching for purchase as wooden shod feet flailed against Linton's immaculately clad legs.

"You hell-born brat!" Now totally exasperated and not a little anxious for his fine garments, not to mention his skin, the earl caught the spitting creature around an amazingly small waist lifting him high in the air, holding him at the full extent of his long arms. The shock of losing the ground beneath his feet temporarily stilled the wildly thrashing Danny, and in the manner of a true campaigner Linton took immediate advantage of his opponent's momentary disarmament and tossed him unceremoniously onto the bed.

"You move from there, brat, and I'll finish what the baker started!" he gritted, bending to brush the dust from the dove-colored silken stockings, rubbing against a bruised shin in the

11

process. It would indeed have gone ill with the urchin at that point had he attempted to move. However, although the brown eyes smoldered and the breath came quick and fast, the boy remained on the bed. If the earl had chanced to look, he would have seen a speculative, calculating gleam in the over-big eyes as Danny quieted himself, but a brisk knock on the door provided distraction.

"*Entrez.*"

A procession of serving wenches with jugs of hot water and two lackeys struggling beneath the weight of an enormous porcelain tub marched into the room. Danny watched their preparations, grim desperation in eyes that flicked wildly to the half-open door. But the tall figure of his erstwhile savior blocked the escape route. All gratitude for Milord's intervention in the fracas with the baker had now vanished, and if faced with the choice between the belt and the tub of water, there would have been no contest.

Steam rose from the bath as the last jug of water hissed to join its fellows and, with a bow, the procession left the chamber. The firm click of the door rang a knell in the boy's miserable ears.

"Milord," he began hesitantly. "You don't quite understand . . ."

"I understand perfectly," the earl interrupted curtly, still mindful of his bruised shin. "You have more layers of dirt on you than you have skin. God only knows when you last saw water! Now, get those rags off and get in the tub." Hard hands grasped the boy's upper arms lifting him off the bed. As his feet touched ground, Danny made a last desperate bid for the door.

"What in Hades is the matter with you?" Linton hissed furiously. "A little water won't harm you." He reached for the neck of the ragged shirt, and as Danny wrenched himself sideways, the threadbare material split with a harsh rending sound.

Total silence filled the room for a breathless moment. Justin, Earl of Linton, released his hold and stepped back, for once in his thirty-four years completely nonplussed.

"It seems I didn't understand," he murmured, pulling his eyes away from the enchanting prospect of two small but perfectly formed breasts, their rose coral tips jutting as defiantly, it seemed, as the small pointed chin above. He noticed absently that the girl—undoubtedly a girl—made no attempt to shield herself, merely stood, shoulders back, eyes glaring a challenge.

"So, milord, what do you choose to do with me now?"

He inhaled sharply, even more thoroughly taken aback. That was not the voice of a street urchin. She, whoever she was, had issued her challenge in the well accented, carefully modulated speech of a French aristocrat.

"Who are you?" he demanded harshly.

"My name is Danny" came the soft, determined reply.

"Not good enough, my child." Her refusal to cover herself suddenly irritated him. He was not used to being made to feel ridiculous. With a swift movement he seized the thin arms, pulling them away from her sides, his eyes deliberately raking the bare breasts.

"No Daniel carried quite such a sweetly adorned body." His words and eyes embedded their sharp insults like shards of steel in a spirit more vulnerable than he realized. Hurt darkened those deep velvet eyes sunk in the small, pinched, dirty face and he gave a sudden rueful sigh as he released her.

"Your name, brat?" he demanded, going over to the bath, running a hand through the water to test its temperature.

"Danielle."

"Do not imagine, Mademoiselle Danielle, that I shall be satisfied with that," he warned softly, turning back to the still figure. "But for now, I intend to proceed as I began. Are you going to take off those filthy britches, or am I?"

The look of horror flashing across the drawn face, hanging in the liquid pools of her eyes, convinced him of one thing. Whatever else she might be, this girl/waif was no wanton.

Deliberately he turned his back, crossed the sun-filled chamber to a small rosewood table by the mullioned casement, poured a glass of sherry from the decanter and, as deliberately, hooked a chair to face the window and sat, gazing with unwarranted interest at the street scene below.

Danielle looked at the averted back for no more than an instant before stripping off her remaining garments and sliding

13

into the hot water with a sigh of contentment that was not lost on her companion.

"Don't forget to wash your hair while you are about it," he remarked coolly. "What's left of it, anyway. I've a fancy to see what color it is under all that dirt."

Silence reigned for a very long time, disturbed only by the occasional splash of water and the soft murmur as the earl refilled his glass. The afternoon sun left the room and Danielle wrestled with the problem of how she was to get out of the bath while retaining what little modesty remained to her.

"Milord," she said eventually. The only response was a slight stiffening of those broad shoulders, but confident that she had his attention she continued. "Since you have torn my shirt I am in something of a puzzle as to how I should clothe myself. The water is becoming a little chilly, you see," she added in apologetic explanation.

"Those clothes of yours are fit only for the furnace" came the rumbled reply.

"In that case, milord, what do you suggest? Perhaps you wish me to remain naked for your pleasure?"

The insolently dulcet tones brought the hairs on his spine to prickly rigidity.

"*Mon enfant*, I most fervently suggest you watch your tongue. Unless, of course, you've a mind to add to your bruises." Rising swiftly, Linton strode with the hard-padded pace of a caged tiger across the room to the large cherrywood armoire. He selected a soft lawn shirt with lace edging to sleeves and neck and tossed it beside the tub. The small figure shrank beneath the scummy water as his eyes ran lazily over her.

"If you do not wish to come out as dirty as you went in, I also suggest that you get out now." He turned back to the window and with considerable relief Danielle hauled herself out of the disgustingly dirty water. It seemed that her savior/captor, whilst not averse to making certain physical threats appropriate to the treatment of a recalcitrant child, was not interested in molesting her as a woman. The realization, though it brought relief, also paradoxically brought a sense of pique that surprised and annoyed her. She had played the boy for so long

14

now it was ridiculous that she should be offended by this refusal to acknowledge what she had once been taught to accept were not inconsiderable charms.

She dried herself hastily, casting anxious glances at the averted back. She hadn't been this clean for months—a quick dip in a horse trough or a rough, freezing scrub under a backyard pump had been the best she could manage and she now inhaled deeply of the soapy clean fragrance of her warm dry limbs. The lawn shirt caressed her body with its unfamiliar soft fineness and her fingers fumbled with the delicate pearl buttons in her haste to cover herself before the figure at the window turned around. What had the landlord called him? . . . Ah, Milord Linton, that was it. An English name, surely? But his French was impeccable.

"Are you dressed?" the cool voice questioned.

"I would hardly describe it as such," Danielle snapped, conscious of the expanse of bare leg revealed beneath the shirt. She had been brought up to believe that the merest glimpse of an ankle denoted the height of immodesty—although why this should be so when one's décolletage left little of the bosom to the imagination had always been a puzzle.

The earl got up and strode toward her. "Your want of conduct, my ungrateful vagabond, is deplorable."

Danielle backed away hastily from the soft, almost gentle voice, but a hand caught the damp mop of curls and long fingers twined themselves firmly, forcing her to remain still. Her chin was taken between long fingers of his other hand and tipped remorselessly upward so that she could not evade the intent, frowning scrutiny of blue black eyes under well-shaped brows. Having no choice, she returned the look boldly, noting in her turn the wide, intelligent forehead beneath unpowdered black hair, firm curved lips, uncompromising jawline, and slim, aristocratic nose. It was a handsome face, albeit carrying a hint of cynicism about the mouth and eyes, a slightly bored, world-weary air.

The earl was examining a small, heart-shaped face dominated by a pair of enormous liquid brown eyes. The little nose

15

was impudent in the extreme and the delicate jaw, whose fragility he could feel beneath his fingers, carried an arrogant determination matched by the set of what was undoubtedly an adorable little mouth. The layers of dirt appeared to have done no damage to the ivory complexion, which flushed becomingly under his studied concentration.

"Are you quite satisfied, milord?" Danny attempted to pull her chin away, knowing she was playing with fire but unable to bear the scrutiny any longer.

Fortunately, His Lordship chose to ignore the sarcasm although his frown deepened and the fingers tightened on her chin.

"No, I'm not satisfied," he declared slowly. "Your features are very familiar, but I cannot for the moment place them. However, you shall help me on that score very soon." Abruptly the fingers left her jaw and hair and Danielle turned away hastily to hide a tremulous lip. He could not force her to declare her identity, to tell the story that she had buried deep in the recesses of her mind almost as effectively as she had buried the gently bred aristocrat under the layers of dirt. Or could he? For the first time she felt a twinge of doubt as to her ability to pursue the path she had set for herself after that night of horror. Could she have seen the earl's face at this moment, she might have felt slightly reassured. Watching the effort of this indomitable waif to keep her shoulders squared and back straight, Linton fell prey to a series of most unusual emotions—compassion, an overpowering desire to know the whole, and, most surprising of all, a need to help. How to rid her of the obstinate refusal to accept his help and to trust him was the puzzle.

"Danielle, I suggest you remove yourself to the darkest corner of the chamber while the room is set to rights again and our dinner is brought in." He made his voice deliberately brisk and was rewarded by her sudden whirl as she turned in surprise toward him. "You see," he added apologetically, "you bear no resemblance to the urchin I dragged in here. In fact, only a blind man would fail to recognize you for what you are in that garb."

A deep flush suffused the pale countenance but, without

comment, the small figure moved to the far side of the bed, seating herself on the low chair at its head, partially hidden by the brocade canopies of the tester. Linton gave a brief nod of satisfaction and tugged the bellpull.

His summons brought an army of servers into the room. The paraphernalia of the urchin's bath were removed swiftly as was the sad pile of discarded clothing with the brisk injunction to consign them to the furnace. The evening had become cool and a taper was placed to the fire laid ready in the hearth behind the round oak table now spread with snowy linen, heavy silver utensils, delicate china, and thick crystal.

Danielle remained in her corner throughout the bustle, her nostrils assailed by the savory aroma of hot food, her stomach cleaving to her backbone, the constant, gnawing rat of hunger now exploding into real pain under the miraculous possibility of imminent satisfaction. Her mouth ran with saliva and she swallowed convulsively, furious at her body's weak treachery. The door closed firmly behind the last servant, the last polite, "*Bon appétit*, milord," and the earl took his place at the table raising an inquiring eyebrow at the shadowy figure by the bed.

"You are served, *mon enfant*."

He watched the figure move slowly toward the table and regretted with deep sincerity what he was about to do.

"Before you eat, Danielle, I wish for some answers." A razor-sharp blade slid thinly through the oyster-stuffed capon, exuding a steamy aroma to entice even a well-fed stomach. The slight figure halted, turned, and sat resolutely on the bed.

"*Je n'ai pas faim.* I am not hungry," Danielle stated with a tiny shrug, forcing back the tears of desperate disappointment.

"What a pity," the earl murmured, taking a bite of his capon, which rapidly became ashes on his tongue. He had been moderately hungry, but now all appetite vanished. But if he was to win his objective the charade must be played through. Silence reigned, disturbed only by the sounds of one-half of the pair eating with apparent gusto.

"It seems, My Lord Linton, that you intend to keep me captive, seminaked and starved."

His head shot up in surprise. Danielle had spoken in perfect, barely accented English.

17

"No, I do not intend to starve you, infant," he replied in the same language and cut a large hunk of the baguette, poured water into a crystal goblet, and carried both to the bed. He put them down beside the rigid figure and returned to the table.

Danielle broke off a small piece of the bread, rolling it between thumb and forefinger, heedless of the flaky crust crumbs showering on the coverlet. This morning she had risked a beating for a crust of day-old bread half the size of this oven-warm chunk, but now could think only of the other offerings on the table. She took a slow sip of the ice-cold water and looked longingly through luxuriant sable eyelashes at the wine bottle from which the earl was helping himself in a totally cavalier, heartless fashion.

"Why don't we start with your age?" Linton sliced a piece of succulent breast, laying it carefully on the empty platter across from his, not looking at her as he did so.

Her age for a piece of capon—it didn't seem an unreasonable exchange. Whilst she continued to hesitate a spoonful of stuffing joined the meat.

"Then your full name," the voice continued softly. A spoonful of fresh baby peas sat beside the stuffing, followed by a mound of light, golden sautéed potatoes. The soft tinkle of ruby red wine filling a crystal goblet proved the last straw.

"Seventeen," Danielle murmured.

"Will you join me, mademoiselle?" The Earl of Linton rose politely, came around the table, pulled out the carved wooden chair, pushing it in as his urchin sat before the first plate of real food she had been offered in eight weeks.

"Eat slowly," he cautioned. "Your belly is not used to riches and I've no wish to spend the night holding your head over a bowl."

He need not have worried, he reflected, watching her as he twirled the slender stem of his wineglass between restless fingers. She was no more a glutton than she was a wanton. But he knew rather more about what she wasn't than about what she was, he remembered suddenly. It was time for further information.

"I hope you intend to play honorably, mademoiselle," he said softly. "You owe me your name, I think."

18

Danielle paused in her intent pursuit of green peas with the three-pronged fork. She had three choices: the lie direct, a careful half truth, or the truth.

"Only the full truth will suffice, *mon enfant*."

Her startled gasp at his uncanny reading of her thoughts was hopelessly revealing and, for a second, a pair of haunted brown eyes met curiously softened, curiously reassuring blue-black orbs.

"I am Danielle de St. Varennes," she stated with flat resignation. This man would not countenance a half story and would have the rest out of her now as easily as a tidal wave could sweep through a fragile dam.

A sudden fluke blaze of a green log in the hearth caught the tip of her mangled curls illuminating a pinkish tinge to the wheat-colored crop. The earl sighed as the elusive memory fell into place.

"You are Louise Rockford's daughter." It was a statement answered by a small nod and a soft, *"Ma mère."*

"You are, therefore, Danielle de St. Varennes, the granddaughter of Antoine, Duc de St. Varennes." Again a simple, inexorable statement, but this time the response surprised him.

"Was," his diminutive companion whispered, eyes bent resolutely to the plate in front of her. In spite of her concentration she was now eating nothing. He refilled her glass.

"Was?" The question hung in the air, dropped its oppressive umbrella over the two figures.

"He is dead."

"As I remember, Louise married the oldest son," the voice gently probed. "That makes you, *mon enfant*, the daughter of the Duc de St. Varennes."

"Mon père est mort."

The earl sipped his wine thoughtfully. So the duke was dead. The story had only just begun, of that he was sure, but the child needed time before she would be able or willing to tell the rest. The quick blink of hot tears had not gone unnoticed. But why, in the name of all that was good, was this daughter of one of the oldest and noblest families in France scratching a starvation existence in the back alleys of Paris?

"You learned your English from your mother?" He reached for the apple tart, cutting the crisp crust, slicing through the artistically arranged apple pieces under their glaze of raspberry jam. When had this child last seen a dessert, let alone eaten one? A small head shook a definite negative as he offered her a piece.

"Perhaps later, when you have unburdened yourself." He felt the most absurd urge to take the waif onto his lap, to cradle and comfort her until the full desolation of her secret had been revealed. Wisely he refrained. Whatever Danielle de St. Varennes had experienced it came under the panoply of adulthood and could not be wished away by nurseryland comfortings. Neither could the story be forced. The Earl of Linton was at a standstill when suddenly the soft voice began to speak.

"Use English, child," he interrupted with conscious briskness. "It will help to distance the reality."

A small accepting nod and the hesitant voice launched into a tale of black horror presaging the greater horror to come.

Chapter 2

"I was raised in Languedoc, on my grandfather's estates. You know, of course, the way these *'affaires'* are conducted?" A quick underlash glance ensured her of her audience's comprehension. "The tithes and taxes that the serfs must pay are at the discretion of their seigneur. He also has the right to use their land as and when La Chasse dictates. *Mon grandpère* . . . my grandfather . . . used his seigneural rights indiscriminately as did my father and my uncles. They also exercised their droit de seigneur over those virgins who interested them and also over those matrons who . . . who . . . challenged them. Or perhaps it was their husbands who challenged them?" The small chin now rested on the heel of a palm, elbow-propped on the table. The eyes held a dreamy, far-away look and the soft educated voice was almost a monotone, enlivened occasionally by a satirical note quite out of keeping with this fresh-faced innocent. The earl sat still and quiet, waiting for the revelation. So far he had heard nothing unusual.

"My sex was a disappointment to *grandpère*, and to my father. My uncles somehow could not manage to . . . to . . . persuade any sufficiently aristocratic family that they were fit husbands for their daughters. They bred many bastards on the estate, male ones at that, but they could hardly be recognized as the legitimate heirs to the dukedom." For an instant this afternoon's imp flashed across the intent face.

"You are perhaps shocked, milord, at my free speech?"

21

"No, brat, I am not. Pray continue." The earl's lips twitched despite his bone-deep knowledge that this seemingly light-hearted speech was but a preamble to a vast hellish chasm.

"I am . . . was . . . the only grandchild. Philippe would, of course, inherit after Lucien, *mon père*." A small shrug accompanied the statement. "You are aware how these matters are arranged. My role was, of course, the well-dowered marriage into the carefully chosen family." The bitter note of disillusionment crept apace into the soft-spoken monotone and the Earl of Linton reflected that such arrangements were sufficiently customary amongst his class as to make the brat's obvious contempt most unusual. But then, of course, she was Louise Rockford's daughter. He abstained from comment.

"*Maman* decided that I had a mind which should be educated beyond the usual requirements of a brood mare."

At that the earl inhaled sharply.

"Have I shocked you now, milord?"

"Just a little. But I must remember that you are Louise Rockford's daughter." He spoke aloud his earlier thought.

"You knew *Maman*?" The eager question and the sudden brightening of the eyes spoke volumes.

"A little, she is rather older than I," he said circumspectly. It seemed hardly appropriate to disclose that eighteen years ago Louise Rockford as a twenty-one-year-old disillusioned wife had initiated him at the age of sixteen into the joys and mysteries of love.

He let his mind drift. Louise must be thirty-nine now. She'd been whisked back to the seclusion of the Languedoc estates after that brief season in London and at the French court. The de St. Varennes were known as a reclusive, miserly lot, eschewing the debaucheries of Louis XVI's court in favor of the cheaper but infinitely satisfying excitements available on their estates. They were a hard-drinking, hard-riding group of look-alikes with an innate brutality that characterized them all.

Louise had been a dewy-eyed eighteen-year-old when Lucien, Vicomte de St. Varennes, had captured both her heart and her virginity. The Earl of March had yielded to his favorite daughter's entreaties and consented to a marriage that all his instincts and society rumor made abhorrent. By the time the

22

youthful Justin first succumbed to the charms of the young *vicomtesse*, Louise de St. Varennes had presented her lord with two stillborn sons in rapid succession. With a courage and fortitude extraordinary in a woman of her class she had banned Lucien from the marriage bed at the point of a dagger, demanding time for her body and spirit to recuperate before a fresh assault of pregnancy. The *vicomte* had given way, both because he still desired the svelte body and because the provision of an heir eventually was of paramount importance. He had also been not a little influenced by the dagger and the soft-spoken threat that an attempt at force would result in the death of his wife, or himself, or both.

The excursion into society was an attempt to placate and to ensure eventual compliance. Louise, in spite of her willingness to share discreetly the joys of the flesh with the young heir to the Earl of Linton, had honored her side of the bargain and returned without protest to exile in the wilds of Languedoc. This scantily clad, emaciated, spirited little vagabond opposite him was clearly the living result of that bargain.

"You appear, milord, to have lost interest in my story."

The earl's eyes narrowed at the sharp tone. Despite her predicament, Louise's daughter was clearly far from subdued.

"On the contrary, child," he said dryly. "My interest is merely piqued and awaits full satisfaction. Your mother was always a trifle unconventional, but I find it hard to believe she leant her countenance to this escapade of yours." To his dismay, two hot tears rolled slowly down the small face, were wiped away hastily by a firm thumb and the back of a small hand rubbed briskly across a damp nose. Silently cursing his thoughtless stupidity, his lordship drew a fine cambric handkerchief from a ruffled sleeve, passing it across the table with the brisk injunction, "Come, child, you are not on the street now."

Those liquid brown eyes flashed fire for the barest instant before Danielle took the offering and blew her nose vigorously.

"My mother is dead." Long restless fingers tore convulsively at the damp, flimsy material for a few moments before she scrunched it into a tight ball in her fist and raised a determined, defiant face.

The flat statement came as no surprise now and the earl reflected irritably that he should have known it from the beginning.

"I do apologize, Danielle," he said gently. "But I would like to know how and when."

It had been a brilliant February morning with a hard hoar frost glinting under the pale sun when Danielle de St. Varennes had sprung from her bed with all the eagerness of youth. There was a chill in the air, but in spite of the early hour someone had kindled a fire in the grate. She had no idea who and it wouldn't have occurred to her to ask. Apart from Old Nurse, who had cared for her from babyhood, her mother's maid, and a few of the upper servants, those who scurried around the enormous chateau making life pleasant for its owners were merely faceless bodies.

Once she had chanced upon her Uncle Eduard taking his pleasure in an embrasured window nook of one of the endless, draughty corridors. She had seen a pair of wide frightened eyes that for an instant locked with hers over the broad shoulder of her uncle, a pair of dumpy white legs in knee-length cotton stockings revealed under the simple peasant skirt now raised to the servant girl's waist. A soft voice had pleaded, "*Je vous emprie, milord. Je suis enceinte,*" and Danielle had ducked behind the arras half fascinated, half disgusted, watching as Eduard's ample buttocks in their tight hunting britches pumped vigorously before, with a deep grunt, he expended himself and without a word moved away, adjusting his dress carefully, heedless of the silent swooning fall of the figure he'd been holding rigid against the wall.

Danielle had slipped thoughtfully out of her hide, retracing her steps in search of her mother. She was not unfamiliar with the processes of mating and birth, growing up as she had in a careless, male-dominated environment where her predilection for roaming around the estate in a pair of britches astride a magnificent blood stallion had been viewed as perfectly reasonable. She had not, however, seen humans working in this way before—and it was work; that much she had learned

24

hanging around the breeding sheds, the kennels, and the fields. If caught at her observations by her uncles, her father, or grandfather an indulgent box on the ear was the most she could expect. But something told her that what she had just witnessed did not quite fall into the category of rutting animals. Or did it? Louise had informed her succinctly that it did and the twelve-year-old Danielle had learned an interesting lesson.

It was an unconventional upbringing for the daughter of one of France's aristocrats. Her father's only contribution to her education had been to toss his two-year-old infant onto the broad back of a supposedly placid mare. Since Lucien's idea of a placid horse was hardly congruent with the generally accepted reality, the tiny Danielle had tumbled from what child's eyes recognized as the highest peak of the universe. She had been instantly replaced, but this time, Lucien, with a rare flash of sense, had mounted behind her. By the time Danielle de St. Varennes was six there wasn't a horse in the stable she couldn't ride as long as someone was available to hoist her chubby little legs astride the saddle. Her Uncle Armand had taught her to shoot, Marc to fence, and her grandfather had instructed a willing mind in the intricacies of his wine cellar and the chessboard. But these attentions had been bestowed with a careless disregard for the developing girl beneath the quick, eager tomboy, and the child had realized early that she was interesting and worthy of notice only as long as she played the role of boy/heir to the dukedom.

Louise had exchanged her male relatives' right to educate her daughter in the way they would have done her son for the right to provide the child with an intellectual education befitting her quick mind. The village curé was a gentle, disillusioned man of great learning who took immense pleasure in training and immersing the girl's sharp wit in the disciplines of the classics, mathematics, and philosophy. From her mother she learned about the female role in this male-dominated world that was her birthright. By the time Danielle was sixteen she was a curious hodgepodge of a young woman whose understanding and experience of the gently bred world of an eighteenth-century virgin being prepared for the altar of

25

matrimony far exceeded respectable limits, a high spirited boy/girl who could outride, outshoot her male peers, whose prowess on the fencing piste was second to none, and whose exceptionally well-educated mind combined with a natural housekeeping ability to manage the intricacies of a nobleman's household.

That early February morning, the day after her seventeenth birthday, Danielle had pulled on her riding britches, splashed her face in the cold water in the ewer, and headed for the stables. Dom was saddled and ready for her, prancing on the cobbles of the stable-yard, the elegant velvety nose uplifted to the fresh scents of the dawn. Steamy breath filled the air from puckered nostrils as the stallion snorted his readiness for a headlong gallop. The girl laid her foot in the ready hand of the stableboy and swung her leg across the saddle as he threw her up.

Horse and rider made their way down the graveled driveway between the sweep of elegant lawns stretching into the distance on either side. The many-windowed château at their back stood tall, solid, magnificent, the epitome of a way of life that its enjoyers could never conceive ending. She had been riding for about an hour when the baying of hounds in the distance indicated the presence of the hunt and, eagerly, she pressed her heels into Dom's flank urging him forward. A gallop to hounds was an enticing prospect on this frosty morning and as long as she obeyed the rules of the field and could keep up, her presence would be permitted by her uncles.

They broke through the trees into a small clearing. Bitter nausea rose in Danielle's throat at the sight that met her horrified eyes. Hounds and horses milled around a small stone cottage, trampled heedlessly across the tiny garden and vegetable plot that would keep the cottage's owner just the right side of starvation. But it was not the wanton destruction that kept her sick and rigid—that happened all the time; the right of the seigneur to abuse his peasants' land in the pursuit of his pleasure was absolute and many a serf watched in stony faced desperation as hounds and horses carried La Chasse across his exiguous plot of land, sometimes even destroying an entire cornfield whose harvest represented the farmer's only

26

means of paying the heavy tithes demanded by His Lord. No, what held the girl horror-struck was the sight of an old man struggling naked in the hands of several huntsmen who were binding his wrists to a low overhanging branch of a massive oak tree. An old woman sobbed and pleaded on her knees before Armand who, with a swift movement of a heavy booted foot, kicked her aside.

Her uncle was in a towering rage. Danielle recognized the signs in the hard, narrowed eyes, the muscle twitching in a red face, the snarl of the thin lips. It was the face of de St. Varennes fury and she had learned to keep well away when any one of her male relatives carried that expression.

Suddenly a lash cracked across the frail back of the figure secured to the tree, leaving a bright line of blood along the thin flesh; the white withered buttocks tightened in agony. Heedless of the consequences, Danielle threw herself from her horse and hurtled across the clearing.

"Stop it! No, please, you must stop it, *mon oncle*, you'll kill him. *Je t'emprie.*" Her hands clutched at Armand's arm and the furious face bent astounded toward her.

"What the devil are you doing here, you interfering whelp!" Armand hissed. "Get back to the house, where you belong. Unless, of course, you've a mind to watch." Hard hands gripped her upper arms so that she cried out in pain. Terror filled her as she read the determination in the cruel face. He was quite capable of forcing her, child though she still was, to witness the barbaric murder of an old man at the hands of his henchmen—and Danielle knew it would be murder. The ancient was too frail and weak to survive the punishment still being meted out behind her. Accepting defeat she managed a wordless shake of the head and, when abruptly released, ran, blinded by tears, back to Dom, head averted from the oak tree, trying to shut out the agonized groans accompanying the hiss and snap of the lash.

She rode herself to exhaustion, heedless of the day's passing and the rumbling pangs of hunger, and it was only when Dom stumbled wearily that she returned heartsick to home.

She had never been ignorant of the cruelties imposed by her family on their serfs, who had no redress either practically or

27

under the law. But she had never seen anything before. She had heard, of course, the screams of village girls accompanying the riotous drunken carouses of her uncles in the great dining room of the château, but her mother had always whisked her upstairs or sent her to the curé so her knowledge of what took place on these occasions was necessarily hazy.

In the great marble-paved hall of the mansion Louise de St. Varennes paced restlessly. Her daughter had not been seen all day and whatever she had done to offend Armand had thrown her father into a passion. It would be as well for Danielle if Louise could catch her before she came to the attention of either Armand or Lucien. They were all drunk tonight and Louise had thankfully instructed the majordomo to serve the men as they pleased but to provide dinner for herself and Danielle in her own rooms abovestairs. But where was the child? It was high time that she grew up and stopped these unchaperoned excursions in that indecorous costume. An attempt to get her to ride sidesaddle had resulted in a true de St. Varennes tantrum and, as usual, Lucien, backed up by his brothers, had laughed and said the brat was a bruising rider and he saw no harm in her riding astride. Louise sighed now, as she wondered for the thousandth time how she was to find a suitable husband for an overeducated tomboy who had but once left the rural wilds of Languedoc. She must approach both the duke and Lucien again on the vital necessity to take Danielle to court in the next year. But even if she were to prevail in that quarter there was no guarantee that Danielle would behave with decorum in the rigidly structured, etiquette-governed life of Louis XVI's Versailles.

These melancholy reflections led her to react with unusual anger when her daughter eventually came through the great front door, and Louise failed to notice the drooping shoulders or the dragging step that replaced Danielle's customary impetuous, bouncing progress.

"Where on earth have you been, child? Have you no sense or consideration?" she railed, shaking the slim shoulders. "Dear God, you reek of the stable! Get upstairs and take a bath and if you've a care for your skin, you'll keep away from your father and your uncles!" She pushed her toward the stairs.

Only as Danielle disappeared without a word up the broad, curving flight did her unusual meekness strike Louise.

Danielle soaked in the hot tub before her bedroom fire, feeling its warmth ease her weary limbs and provide some comfort for her numb, deadened spirit. If the truth be told, she had heard almost nothing of her mother's angry words which had washed off her like water on an oiled skin.

She was never sure quite what it was that first brought the goose bumps prickling on the back of her neck. It was as if a curious expectant silence hung over the house, but it was a silence bristling with menace rather than anticipation. Then a strange rumble filled the air. Danielle pulled a robe over her barely dried body, little knowing that the next bath she took would be many weeks later in a Parisian inn at the insistence of an English earl.

She gazed in bewilderment at the scene below her window on the gravel sweep. Her eyes could not take in the reality of the vast mob advancing slowly across the beautifully tended park, mowing down her mother's beloved flowers under rough boots, wielding heavy cudgels, pitchforks, tree branches, and brandishing flaming torches. They all seemed to have the same face—heavy peasant faces set in lines of grim determination under the flickering torchlight. But it wasn't what she saw that lifted her scalp and sent cold shafts of terror shuddering through her slight frame so much as the sound, a low menacing murmur that seemed to swell as the wave of humanity reached the front steps. Gently she cracked her casement. "St. Varennes, St. Varennes," the voices rumbled as one, filling her ears, her head, becoming a part of her.

Suddenly the great doors were thrown wide as the irate family, headed by the old duke, pushed out onto the steps to confront the now still but not silent mob. Cruel they most certainly were, blinded to the needs of their less fortunate fellowmen certainly, but no de St. Varennes could be accused of cowardice.

Danielle watched in hypnotized horror as her grandfather began to harangue the throng. She could imagine his own bewilderment and disbelief—that they, the de St. Varennes, were being threatened by their own serfs. The duke gestured suddenly behind him and a group of henchmen from the house joined Antoine and his sons, training muskets on the crowd. For a second there was utter silence and the girl at the window held her breath, sensing that the confrontation could go either way at this stage. Numbers were on the side of the mob, but the traditional habits of obedience and the fear inspired by the show of armed force was on the side of their lords—until Louise de St. Varennes decided to play the last role of her life. In a flurry of velvet skirts she brushed roughly through the line of henchmen, pushed past her husband and father-in-law addressing the mob in cool, measured tones, sweeping away Lucien's restraining hand with all the contempt for him that the last twenty years had wrought. Her hands opened in appeal to the crowd and she began to walk down the broad shallow flight of stone steps toward them. As she reached the gravel a large man brandishing a thick staff made a move toward her— whether in aggression or truce no one was ever to discover. Shots rang out from the steps and Danielle watched in disbelief the bright blood spreading from a tiny spot between her mother's shoulder blades to a wide stain covering the narrow back as Louise slipped in slow motion to the driveway. She was not the only casualty of the nervous, quick-fingered firing which now became totally uncontrolled, and figures in the front ranks fell under the hail of bullets. Suddenly the murmur changed, became a great, unanimous shout: "*Les aristos! Tuez! Tuez!*"

Danielle saw little else, just an image of blood and tumbled limbs scorched into her retina. She whirled as the door to her chamber opened and Old Nurse, white-faced, the old myopic eyes glazed in shock, ran to her, dragging her away from the window, muttering incoherently as she pushed the britches and the damp, grubby shirt she had been wearing all day into the girl's hands.

"*Vite, vite, mon enfant,*" the cracked voice repeated desperately, and, without understanding, the bemused Danielle obeyed. "The back stairs . . . you must go to the curé, he will help you, quickly, child!" The crone seized Danielle's hand, tugging her out of the room.

"No wait, Belledame." Danielle stopped suddenly in the

corridor, her senses returning sharply at the sounds of breaking glass and splintering wood coming from below. A great roar of satisfaction bellowed through the house, and she thought with a strange detachment, "They have killed *Grandpère.*"

"No, milady, please. You must leave now," the ancient pleaded in terror, but Danielle pulled her arm free and ran down the corridor to her mother's room. She knew exactly where the case was kept, at the back of the shelf of the wardrobe behind Louise's finest gowns—those she rarely had occasion to wear in Languedoc. With feverish haste the girl, standing on tiptoe, pulled the intricately carved chest toward her, catching it with a grunt as it toppled off the high shelf and into her arms. It was more awkward than heavy and she had little difficulty maintaining a swift pace down the back stairs, through a kitchen now silent and deserted and filled with the acrid stench of scorching meat as the baron of beef rested neglected over the blazing fire, no permanent pot boy sitting in its heat to turn the spit. It occurred to her as she ran into the kitchen courtyard, instinctively seeking the shadow of the high wall, that she had eaten nothing since the night before, and an empty belly was an inauspicious beginning to a desperate flight that would take her God only knew where.

It was a five-mile walk to the curé's house in the village. She dared not risk detection by taking a horse. In their orgy of blood and destruction the mob might well forget the youngest member of the house of de St. Varennes and she could not afford to prod their memories. But she was young and strong after a life spent mostly out of doors, and one day's fast was unlikely to make too many inroads on a usually healthy well-fed body. So it proved, and although weary from the need for both speed and stealth and the added burden of the wooden chest, Danielle arrived at the curé's humble abode little the worse for wear. A tentative tap at the firmly closed back door brought no response. She risked a louder knock. There were sounds of movement inside, but her friend and mentor showed no inclination to open up. She slipped around the house, peering through the grimy windows for a sign of life. There was an eerie silence in the village, even the animals seemed

31

unwilling to make their usual barnyard noises. It occurred to her that the entire population was probably rampaging around the chateau at this moment and on that basis decided to risk a heavier knock and a fairly loud identifying, *"C'est moi, mon père; c'est Danielle."*

Heavy bolts creaked in their rusted well-worn hinges and the door swung open the tiniest crack.

"Thank God you are safe. Inside, child, quickly!" A hand seized her arm, pulling her into the sparsely furnished single room of the cottage.

Danielle remembered little of the remainder of that night. The curé shared his scanty supper of vegetable broth enhanced by a lump of salt pork and a crust of black bread, agreed to take charge of the chest and, with trembling fingers, reached under the mattress for a piece of cloth which, when unwrapped, revealed a small hoard of silver coins—all of the money Louise had managed to pay him in recompense for the education of her daughter. He offered the whole to Danielle, but she refused with an adamant headshake, accepting out of sheerest necessity only four of the smaller coins.

"Keep *Maman's* jewels, *mon père*, and I will return to claim them. Then you shall be well rewarded for your kindness, I promise." She did not refuse, out of the same necessity, the small loaf of bread and the half bottle of wine, and set off in the very early dawn on foot toward Paris.

Danielle did not elaborate on the privations of that journey as she recounted her tale to Justin, Earl of Linton, and was unaware that the quiet, expressionless individual opposite had filled in the gaps for himself without difficulty. He was astounded at the fortitude of this diminutive scrap and filled with a sick horror at her story. But, unlike many of his peers, he was not surprised. The tidal wave of blood and destruction that would soon sweep through France had just begun in the isolated parts of the country, not yet recognized for what it was—a vast rebellion of an entire population against the cruelties and injustices of generations of tyranny perpetrated by the few on the many.

"One question, Danielle." He broke the silence that followed what she clearly considered to be the end of the story.

"You say you have been in Paris now for four days?" The earl selected a pear from the fruit bowl and began to peel it with careful deliberation. He received a short assenting nod as answer.

"Who stands godfather to you?"

"The Vicomte de St. Just." The brown eyes darted suspiciously at him through the long eyelashes.

The earl sliced the pear into symmetrical quarters and leaning over placed the fruit on the child's dessert plate. She had eaten nothing during her narrative but now bit deep into the juicy flesh with an eagerness that revealed all too clearly the deprivations of the past two months.

"Then why, *mon enfant*, have you not sought his protection?"

For a second there was silence and then to his utter amazement an imp of mischief sparkled in those previously haunted eyes. "Why, milord," the soft voice proclaimed innocently, "I had no desire to be flogged from his scullery door!"

The Earl of Linton grinned. There was no other way to describe the sheer delight that curved the well-shaped lips and had any of his friends or acquaintances seen the expression they would have doubted the evidence of their eyes.

"Your point is well taken, brat." A walnut cracked between the pressure of his long fingers, was peeled deftly, and placed beside the remains of the pear.

"However, I am certain that the disadvantages of your . . . uh . . . earlier disreputable costume can now be remedied. St. Just shall receive you in the morning."

"No!" The flat negative hung in the air and the earl's eyebrows disappeared into his scalp.

"I beg your pardon?" he inquired gently, too gently, and a slight flush mantled the girl's ivory complexion.

"You do not understand, milord."

"Clearly not and since you were correct when you informed me of that fact earlier this evening I await your explanation."

His reminder of that embarrassing confrontation deepened her flush but his lordship had already decided that this indomitable creature's manners required mending and he

33

ruthlessly quieted his conscience.

"I have not the intention of remaining in France, milord. I shall make my way to Calais and from there to England. My mother's family are in Cornwall. I visited once with *Maman*—they were very kind to me." The soft voice sank slightly and Linton again forced himself to push the softer emotions aside.

"And just how, pray, do you intend to cross the Channel?"

"I shall work my way on a *paquet*," Danielle declared, her small chin tilting in angry defiance at this rude catechism.

"Idiot child!" the earl exclaimed. "Your disguise would be penetrated immediately and the only way you would work your passage would be on your back!"

This brutal declaration produced none of the maidenly horror to be expected of a well-bred virgin. Danielle merely nodded.

"In that case I shall stow away."

"You will be discovered and the consequences the same."

"Nevertheless, Lord Linton, I shall take my chance as I have done in recent weeks. You cannot stop me and, indeed, have no right to do so."

The earl raised his gold quizzing glass and examined the small, determined face. "No?" he inquired with interest.

"No," Danielle stated definitely. "You are not my guardian, sir."

"This may come as something of a surprise to you, brat, but in the absence of any other, I assumed that role, albeit unwillingly, some time ago."

Danielle half rose from the table, face set and eyes blazing. "I do not accept that, milord."

"You may accept it or not, as you choose," Linton said calmly, opening an exquisite lapis lazuli snuff box and taking an insouciant pinch. "The fact remains, however. Now, I suggest you resume your seat before I am obliged to encourage you to do so."

He waited until the reluctant, furious figure had obeyed before continuing. "If you will not seek the protection of your godfather you will have to endure mine. Why do you not wish to remain in France?"

"I *hate* France," the mutinous voice spat. "You forget,

perhaps, milord," she layed sarcastic stress on the title, "that I have lived here both as an aristocrat and as a starving peasant. I wish to pursue neither role again. Besides," the rebellious note of an aggrieved child left the soft voice suddenly to be replaced by a thoughtful consideration, "the role of 'aristo' is going to be a dangerous one across the land in a short time—only those idiots do not realize it!"

"I will not argue with you on that score." Linton sat back, legs extended beneath the table as he regarded this troublesome acquisition. He had never been one for the infantry, although his sister's children unfortunately seemed not to be aware of this fact as they lavished unwanted attentions on their favorite uncle. But this frequently ill-mannered brat carried an air of practical and intellectual sophistication totally at odds with her aggressive manner, though perhaps not so much at odds with her near unbelievable success at survival. Not for the first time, it occurred to the earl that once her safety was ensured the horrors she had lived through would surface in all their grisly detail. But Danielle de St. Varennes appeared to have an adamantine will and a sense of humor to match. With the right care she would come through. Whether the Earl and Countess of March were the right people to deal with the break when it came was a moot point. Kind and gentle to a fault, they would undoubtedly receive their granddaughter with open arms, but a strong hand would be needed to hold the reins. Linton was unaware of the deep frown drawing his thick arched eyebrows together as he pondered the situation until Danielle spoke again with quiet dignity.

"Lord Linton, I am, as I'm sure you are aware, at something of a disadvantage. I have no clothes."

"I would hardly dignify what you *were* wearing by that name," her companion said with an amused quirk of an eyebrow.

"Perhaps not. However, they did cover me. This"—she indicated the shirt contemptuously—"would hardly service me on the street."

"Indeed not," he concurred smoothly, giving not an inch.

"You do not think, perhaps, that you have an obligation to replace those you so roughly tore from my back?" A sweet smile accompanied the question.

"I accept the obligation, infant, but also the right to provide what I see fit."

They were fencing now and Danielle's eyes narrowed slightly. "I think, sir, that if you cannot return my original garments you have the obligation to replace them with their like. I am sure the landlord could be of service, for a consideration, and any expenses you may incur would, of course, be reimbursed once I reach my grandparents' house, so you need have no fear of being out of pocket."

The earl's eyes gleamed appreciatively. "A hit, infant!"

"So, what is your answer, milord?"

"My answer is very simple. Are you suggesting that having scooped their granddaughter from the gutters of Paris I could with any honor face the Earl and Countess of March if, after a meal, a bath, and some new clothes, I simply returned her from whence she came?"

That aspect of the situation had been lamentably absent from Danielle's well-planned scheme.

"I do see that it might be a problem," she began with careful understanding. "You do not think you could . . . forget . . . that we met?"

"Forget you, Danielle de St. Varennes! What an absurd idea! Once met, my child, I fear you will engrave yourself into the memory of every unfortunate who happens into your path."

"That, sir, does not sound altogether complimentary. Danielle bit a suddenly tremulous lip.

"I'm not sure it was intended to be so," the earl said with a rueful grimace. "Come, child, you have had enough for one day, if not for many weeks. Into bed with you and we will work out a plan to suit both you and my self-appointed guardianship in the morning."

"But where am I to sleep?" Danielle's eyes widened in horror-struck amazement.

"There's a bed behind you," her companion informed her evenly.

"And you?" It was barely a whisper.

"You are quite safe, infant. I could no more face your grandparents with honor having breached your maidenhead

36

han I could having tossed you back into the gutter."

"No, I suppose you could not," she said matter-of-factly, totally reassured by his logic and just as much unaware of the devastating effect her prosaic agreement had on the Earl of Linton's sang-froid.

"But where will *you* sleep?" The question carried only interest. "Those chairs do not look very comfortable."

"I do not intend to spend an uncomfortable night," Linton reassured on a choke of laughter. "I do, however, suggest that you do as you are bid. You may sleep until you wake."

That was an almost forgotten luxury, as were the feather mattress and the soft, well-laundered sheets. Linton tucked the small, exhausted figure into the large bed with an unexpected efficiency that should have been born of practice—except that it wasn't—and it was a rather puzzled man who drew the curtains around the bed and pulled the bell cord for the ready servants. He remained in the room as the remnants of dinner were removed, ignored the occasional inquisitive glances toward the enclosed bed, and, when finally the tapers had been lit and the room was at rights again, went over to his ward. She was unconscious in a deep and, it was to be hoped, healing sleep. Linton quietly left the chamber, turning a heavy key in the lock outside and pocketing it before making his way into the night-darkened streets of Paris. He hoped the child would not wake and try the door. His intention was not to frighten her; the lock was to keep inquisitive souls out rather than his urchin in.

Chapter 3

The lanes were unusually quiet as the earl, sunk in thought,
picked his way carefully, avoiding the slime running in the
gutters and the piles of filth sullying even the broader streets.
A brooding, restless atmosphere seemed to permeate the city as
its inhabitants awaited the arrival of deputies from across the
land to attend, as representatives of the Commons (the Third
Estate), the States General, summoned by Louis XVI for the
first time in over a century and a half. High hopes that this
meeting of parliament would both address and redress the evils
of poverty and injustice under which the peasant population of
France labored were mingled with a sense of helplessness.
When the peasant representatives were outvoted two to one
by the nobility and the clergy was it reasonable to hope for
change? The Earl of Linton thought not. Danielle's story of the
uprising in Languedoc was one of several that had filtered
through into the towns. Panic and rumor were beginning to
spread, foreshadowing the "grande peur" that would sweep the
country by July.

A sudden movement to his left caught his eye. It seemed
innocent enough—a figure disappearing into an alleyway just
ahead of him—but his well-honed instincts for danger were
instantly aroused. He gave no sign, however, unless one could
see the sudden tightening of the slender fingers around the
silver-mounted cane. As he reached the opening to the alley
Linton moved outward into the middle of the street, thus
ensuring open space at his back and room for maneuver that he

39

would not have had in the shadow of the high courtyard wall bordering the narrow paved street. As the three men jumped out of the dark alley he swung to face them, raising the cane which was now a deadly weapon, a wicked sword blade flashing at its tip. A swift movement and one of his assailants fell back, clutching an arm which seemed split from shoulder to wrist by an ugly, bleeding gash. A cudgel cleaved the air above the earl's head and came down harmlessly as he sidestepped with the quick dancing movement of an expert swordsman. His opponent, caught off balance, could not evade the blade as it sank deep into his shoulder and he fell groaning into the dirt. The third man, after one look at his disabled companions and the calm, expressionless face of their intended victim who was quite clearly not the easy mark they had thought him, decided that discretion was decidedly the better part of valor and fled. Linton wiped his blade on the jacket of the man at his feet, an expression of distaste curling the fine lips. The sword stick became a cane again and he continued toward his destination.

"Ah, my friend, I had almost given you up." The Comte de Mirabeau turned to greet Linton as he was ushered by a blue-liveried lackey into a luxurious, book-lined library on the first floor of a stylish Parisian town house, set behind high walls on the rue de Richelieu.

"The streets are becoming a trifle dangerous, Mirabeau," the earl commented calmly, accepting a glass of claret.

The other man nodded. "They will be even more so if the States General proves as ineffective as I fear it may."

Linton sipped his wine with an appreciative nod. "You still intend to sit with the Third Estate?"

"I do and Orléans also. But what brings you here, my friend. Your message was unspecific, to say the least."

"A little unofficial information-gathering," the earl replied, reposing his powerful frame in a small, exquisitely carved chair, crossing one smooth silk-stockinged leg over the other. "Traveling without one's valet is damnably inconvenient," he murmured, examining the unblemished sheen of a buckled shoe through his quizzing glass. "Do you not think the left buckle is just the merest bit tarnished, Mirabeau?"

The count laughed. "Play the dandy with someone else,

Justin. I am not to be fooled. What information are you after?"

The earl lowered his quizzing glass with a regretful sigh. "There is much concern in my government about your affairs, *mon ami*. Our two countries are separated, after all, by only the narrowest strip of water. What happens in France touches us nearly. Pitt is a man who likes to be forewarned."

"Ah yes—he is a man of sound judgment, your prime minister," Mirabeau observed. "If only France were as lucky."

"We too have had our Civil War, our revolution," Linton reminded him gently.

"True enough," the other man agreed. "So you are here to carry back firsthand your impressions and what information you can gather?"

"Correct. So far, I have only a black picture. I was hoping you might relieve it a little."

"Alas, Justin, I cannot. You have heard tales of the 'jacquerie' beginning in the villages?"

"I have heard firsthand of one today." The earl told Danielle's story, omitting only the identity of his source and the fact that at this moment that source was soundly sleeping in his bed at the Inn of the Rooster.

"The de St. Varennes, one cannot help feeling, have received only their just desserts," Mirabeau commented with a heavy sigh. "And they are not the only ones. But the whole family, did you say?"

"As far as I know," Linton replied. The lie was smooth and, for the moment, necessary. Danielle's survival would be revealed much later, when she was safely ensconced with her relatives in Cornwall. Her adventures must at all costs be kept secret if her reputation was to survive untarnished. Society, even in the face of catastrophe, remained hypocritically censorious and there would be neither understanding nor acceptance for a maiden who had roamed the byways of France as a half-starved beggar in boy's clothes.

The two men talked for another hour before Linton rose to take his leave. "One small favor, my friend?" he asked suddenly.

"Anything" was the ready response.

"I need a suit of clothes for a servant lad, a very small boy,

41

about this tall." The earl gestured with a considering frown.

"What a very strange request." Mirabeau laughed in puzzlement. "If I did not know you as well as I do, my friend, I would assume you had developed some . . . um . . . odd predilections!"

Lord Linton laughed too, but without much humor. "I can assure you that the case is quite the opposite. Somewhere in your household you must have a servant who could be relieved, for a consideration of course, of his second best suit of clothes."

Mirabeau rang a small gold handbell and explained his friend's needs to the inscrutable footman who had instantly responded to the summons. The extraordinary request was carried into the far depths of the vast mansion and within a remarkably short time the earl was presented with a packet and an apologetic explanation that the household contained no one quite as small as His Lordship had described but it was hoped that these would suffice. Coins exchanged hands as Linton assured the lackey, after a quick examination, that they would do quite well. A chair was summoned, the earl having decided that he did not wish to risk another such incident as had occurred on his way by again walking alone through the streets, and he was borne in relative comfort and all but immoderate speed by strong-armed carriers back to the Inn of the Rooster.

Mine Host, in nightshirt, was hovering to receive his returning guest and responded with a deep bow to the demand for a truckle bed in My Lord's chamber. His place was not to question the whims of nobility and if Milord Linton chose to share his apartments with a backstreet waif that was his business. It was certainly interesting, though, and an explanation similar to that hinted earlier by the Comte de Mirabeau flashed through his mind.

The earl, well aware of his host's suspicions, went upstairs, silently bemoaning the slur on his reputation. The chamber was quiet as he entered, lit dimly by a single taper and the embers of a dying fire. A quick glance behind the bed curtains assured him that his urchin was still deeply asleep. She appeared by her position not to have stirred in his absence.

42

Sitting at the writing desk, sharpening a quill with quiet concentration, Linton began a letter to the Earl of March, pausing only to bid entrance to the servants with the truckle bed, instructing them to set it up in the far corner of the chamber. Alone again, he sanded the two sheets of paper covered in close black script and read the missive through. Unwilling to go into too much detail, he had described the incident at Languedoc in bald, unadorned phrases, stated simply that he would bring their granddaughter to them as fast as traveling conditions permitted, and enjoined his lordship's absolute secrecy until he could explain the situation in full and in person. It would have to do, although it would undoubtedly give rise to more questions than it satisfied. A messenger traveling alone on horseback would accomplish the journey several days faster than the earl and his charge could and the Earl and Countess of March would at least be alerted to their granddaughter's arrival. He left the letter on the desk. Time enough to find a messenger in the morning.

Linton prepared himself for sleep, turning back the covers on the truckle bed before drawing aside the bed curtains. Danielle lay curled on her side, facing away from him. Very gently he pulled back the covers and then swore under his breath. The shirt had become tangled around her waist revealing the soft curves of quite the prettiest little bottom. Grim-faced, Linton hastily disentangled the material, pulling it down to cover the entrancing sight before sliding his arms beneath the still sleeping figure. As he lifted her, Danielle's eyes shot open and she gazed in shock and fear at the impassive face above her. For one petrifying moment she had no idea where she was until a calm remembered voice spoke with brisk reassurance.

"Do not be afraid, child. I'm going to put you into another bed. It's a little small for me," he added dryly. "And I do not see why I should spend the night with my feet hanging over the end."

The large brown eyes closed again instantly and he felt an absurd urge to kiss the paper thin, blue-veined lids. Resolutely he bent and laid the sleeping figure on the narrow cot, pulling the covers over her. She flipped instantly onto her side again,

43

drawing her knees up to her chin. Trying very hard not to think of what must have happened to the shirt as a result of that maneuver, Justin, Earl of Linton, took himself to his body-warmed, rumpled bed.

The arrival of his shaving water and the heady aroma of strong coffee heralding the coming of breakfast awoke him after what seemed like a very short night. Once the bustle in the chamber had died away, he pushed aside the bed curtains and got yawning to his feet. The mound on the truckle bed stirred.

"Are you awake, Danny?"

"No" came the muffled response.

"Good. Then perhaps you would stay that way until I'm dressed." A slight smile tugged fleetingly at his lips as he drew on the fine hose and perfectly tailored buckskin riding britches. He must remember to ensure in their future resting places that the room was equipped with a dressing screen.

Padding shirtless on stockinged feet he went over to the dresser. Seating himself before the mirror and his shaving water he carefully sharpened the broad blade of the razor on the leather strop before beginning to remove his overnight beard.

"Why are you traveling without your valet?" The sudden question startled him and he nicked his chin, closing his mouth on the oath that had sprung readily to his lips.

"You are supposed to be asleep," he declared irritably. "Don't you know better than to talk to someone whilst they are shaving?"

"Well, you see, I have never seen anyone shaving before," Danielle apologized.

The earl wiped his face with a dampened towel and turned around. His observer was sitting up in bed, hugging her knees, regarding him with mischievous interest.

"And I suppose you've never seen a man without his shirt before," Linton muttered.

"Oh no, I have seen that often," she assured him cheerfully. "On the estate, you know? Particularly in the summer."

"Well, that's very fortunate," His Lordship observed dryly. "I should hate to shock your maidenly sensibilities."

"Do you really think I have any?" the voice gurgled merrily.

"Quite frankly, no." He completed his dressing under the unnervingly curious stare of those melting brown eyes, tying the snowy cravat with the intent concentration of a nonpareil. The bright polish to his top boots did not meet his exacting standards, but in the absence of Petersham they would have to do.

"You didn't answer my question—about your valet," the urchin persisted, uncannily tuning into his thoughts.

"You can be thankful I *am* traveling alone," he commented shortly. "If Petersham were with me I would have handed you over to him to scrub yesterday."

There was a short silence as Danielle absorbed this unpalatable piece of information. "But why isn't he?"

"You are the most persistent child! He is not with me because my business on this occasion necessitates the minimum of fuss and the maximum of speed. I wished to travel without ceremony. And if you are thinking of asking me about my business, I'd advise you to save your breath." Linton drew the second boot over his slim muscled calf and, standing, reached for the blue velvet coat that slipped over the lawn and lace of his shirt with an ease belied by a fit so perfect it could have been moulded to his shoulders.

"Come and have some breakfast, brat, and I will tell you how we are going to proceed." He poured coffee into two cups and broke into a fragrant, steaming brioche.

"I do not need *you* to tell me how we are to proceed," Danielle said indignantly. "I have my own plans and if they do not suit you, we must go our separate ways."

The earl disdained to respond to this blunt statement. He merely continued calmly with his meal under the now baleful eye of his ward.

"If you are intending to eat, child, I suggest you do so. We are in somewhat of a hurry this morning."

"I do not wish for your charity," Danny declared stubbornly.

"Please yourself." Linton shrugged, pulling the bell rope. Danielle watched crossly as breakfast was removed. He could at least have attempted to persuade her!

"It is fortunate that you are accustomed to hunger," the earl remarked casually, coming over to the little bed, "because I do not intend that we should break our journey until dinner-time."

"What journey?" she exclaimed.

"Why, to Calais, of course," he said smoothly. "Isn't that where you wished to go?"

Danielle was, for once, silenced.

"Come along now," her mentor instructed brusquely. "I have to go out for about an hour. In my absence you will please me by dressing yourself in the clothes on the chair." A casual wave indicated the previous night's package. "And you will pack up my things. The portmanteau is by the window."

"I am not your servant!" Danielle gasped indignantly.

"You will be traveling in that guise," Linton stated flatly. "And, since you have just said that you do not wish for my charity, you should be glad of the opportunity to earn your keep."

The girl leapt from the bed in a flurry of bedclothes, hastily pulling the shirt to her knees as she faced him. "You, milord, are the most pompous, insufferable, arrogant . . . bastard!"

She got no further. The earl seized her chin between hard, tapering fingers and Danny found herself looking into a pair of flinty eyes, the sculpted lips narrowed in a grim line.

"I warned you yesterday about that tongue of yours," Justin said with soft menace. "You have one hour, and if you are not ready by the time I return, I shall dress you myself." With that he turned on his heel and left the chamber with Danielle still standing openmouthed in the middle of the room. The sound of the key turning in the lock brought her back to a sense of reality and a wave of frustrated helplessness surged through her. How dared he? She began pacing the room with long angry strides, tears of rage prickling her eyelids. But slowly the fury subsided as cold common sense reasserted itself. Why on earth was she fighting him? Under his protection she could cross the Channel in a degree of safety and comfort. Time enough, once they reached Dover, to effect her escape and make her own way to Cornwall. She had lived on her wits for many weeks now; it was foolish to allow them to desert her now, simply out

46

of pride.

During these calming reflections she had begun absently to examine the pile of clothing on the chair. They were the strong, warm, serviceable clothes of the servant of a wealthy and considerate master—corduroy britches, worsted hose, a linen shirt, and woolen jacket. The small clothes were clean if somewhat mended in places. The linen was not of the best quality certainly, but was an immeasurable improvement on her rags of recent weeks. She poured some water from the ewer into the basin and washed her face thoughtfully before stripping off the shirt and sponging her body. It was such luxury to feel clean again and the water, whilst not as hot as it had been, was blissful compared to the icy jets of a backyard pump.

Once dressed in a stranger's clothes she sat down to pull on the soft leather boots. Her feet, after weeks of wooden pattens, felt constricted, although the boots were clearly made for something bigger than the small, slender, high-arched feet of a de St. Varennes. Danielle examined herself critically in the mirror. She would pass, although without the dirt her disguise was not nearly as effective. The corduroy cap pulled low over her eyes certainly helped and at least it covered her roughly chopped curls. Tossing the cap onto the bed, she turned to survey the room. The earl was a tidy, well-ordered man and packing his possessions in the large portmanteau was a simple task, even for someone who, until two months ago, had never so much as thought of picking up after herself—that had been a task accomplished automatically by someone from the ranks of the family retainers. Not for the first time in recent weeks, Danielle wished that she had known the identity of that busy, faceless someone.

She had just closed the portmanteau and was feeling a degree of satisfaction at a task well done when the key grated in the lock and the heavy door swung open. Linton made no comment as he took in the orderly scene, and for that she was grateful. Clearly he was gracious in victory.

"Come here, child. I must do what I can with that mangled hair. Who the devil cut it?"

"I did," she muttered uneasily, noticing for the first time

47

the large pair of scissors he carried.

"Well, it is fortunate you have no aspirations toward barbering. I don't either, as it happens, but anything has to be an improvement. Sit over here." He gestured imperatively toward the chair in front of the mirror. With a slightly mutinous thrust of her bottom lip Danielle warily took her seat. Her protector draped a towel over her shoulders and began with a deep frown to tidy the much abused crop.

"You're cutting it all off," she wailed despairingly, watching the wheat-colored curls fall in profusion to her shoulders and onto the floor at her feet.

"Of course I'm not, you ridiculous infant. But to return any semblance of order to this mess I have to cut it very short."

Danielle subsided and for a long time the only sound in the room was the click-click of the scissors.

"That should do." The earl stood back surveying his handiwork critically. "What did you do with my comb?"

"I packed it, as instructed, milord," Danielle answered demurely.

Linton's eyes narrowed slightly but he said nothing, merely retrieved the article from the portmanteau and proceeded with unnecessary vigor to tug the curly mop so that it came to resemble somewhat a masculine style. Danielle's eyes were watering when he at last pronounced himself satisfied.

"Now put this on, and let us have a look at you." Her cap sailed through the air, catching her unawares to fall at her feet. Biting back an angry retort, she bent to pick it up and crammed it on her head.

"Well, milord?" She couldn't keep the taunting note out of her voice as she stood, feet apart, hands on hips, facing his inspection. Just like some banty little rooster, Linton thought, as he examined her with quivering lip.

"If you keep your eyes down, the cap low, and your mouth shut we might brush through this ridiculous affair quite tolerably" was his only response. "Can you carry that portmanteau? It will look a little peculiar if I carry it myself with a servant on hand."

Danielle inhaled sharply, but stalked across the room and seized the piece of luggage with angry determination. It was very heavy and only with the most supreme effort at self control was she able to refrain from staggering under its weight.

The earl watched her with some amusement. "At least, while you have that in charge I won't have to worry about your running away."

The portmanteau hit the floor with a resounding thump as she turned to face him. "I will *not* run away, Lord Linton."

"No?" An eyebrow lifted quizzically.

"Word of a de St. Varennes," the small, rigid figure spat.

Linton bowed his acknowledgment. "In that case, my little vagabond, our journey should be a great deal pleasanter for both of us than I had anticipated." He moved past her out of the door as befitted the master and seemed to pay no mind to the slight figure behind struggling with the heavy weight.

Monsieur Trimbel bowed low as his guest reached the foot of the stairs. His Lordship's reckoning had been paid and generous douceurs distributed amongst the staff. It was indeed a pleasure to serve Milord Linton—even if he was on occasion somewhat unconventional. Mine Host covertly observed the small servant staggering in his master's wake. Cleaned of his dirt he looked positively respectable, but the memory of the kick and the virulent abuse still rankled and, with malevolent intent, the landlord stretched a foot casually in the boy's path as he reached the bottom stair.

Concentrating as she was on her efforts and the tug on her straining muscles, Danielle was blind to all else. Her foot caught against the obstacle and she tripped, falling in an ungainly heap after the portmanteau on the hard stone-flagged floor of the passageway. She bounced to her feet as if the floor were a trampoline and turned her pent-up fury and frustration on the well-fed, complacent landlord in a torrent of animadversions on his parentage and on his virility, all the while kicking and clawing at the rotund belly, the short, fat legs in their leather britches, and the florid, well-wined face.

Linton had reached the courtyard door as chaos broke out behind him and he turned swiftly with a muttered oath. Having no idea what had happened to throw his brat into this fury he did the only thing possible. One hand at the collar of the woolen jacket, the other at the seat of the corduroy britches, he pulled her off the enraged landlord cowering under the assault.

"'E tripped me—'E did it a' purpose!" Danny shrieked, struggling in the invincible hold.

"I don't give a damn what he did, you ragamuffin," the earl gritted in utter exasperation, still maintaining his grip. "Get that put into the carriage." He released his hold on the britches to jerk an imperious thumb toward both Monsieur Trimbel and the portmanteau and then propelled Danielle de St. Varennes by the scruff of the neck out of the inn, across the courtyard to the waiting coach. The hand again grasped the seat of her pants and she was lifted bodily off the ground to be tossed in an unceremonious heap upwards and into the vehicle. The portmanteau was stowed on top and the earl gave quick-fire instructions to both coachman and postillions before mounting the footstep, seating himself on the leather-squabbed seat and shutting the carriage door with a definitive slam.

"What the devil did you think you were doing? You're conspicuous enough as it is, without asking for notice, you little alley cat!"

Danielle, nursing both a bruised dignity and a bruised body, shifted on the seat opposite, contenting herself with a muttered stream of invective directed at landlords in general and one Monsieur Trimbel in particular. Linton's annoyance faded as his sense of humor got the better of him. How the devil had he allowed his exquisite, peaceful, well-ordered existence to crumble into ashes under the cataclysmic arrival of this outrageous wretch? What had happened to his usually utterly reliable sense of self-preservation when he'd decided on a whim to save a street urchin from what was probably well-deserved punishment? Not probably, indisputably, he decided caustically, as he regarded his urchin, still mumbling and muttering opposite.

The coach bumped and swayed its way through the narrow cobbled streets. It was as well-sprung as one could expect of any hired traveling coach but nevertheless was unable to cushion its passengers from the jolting, jarring effects of their progress. Linton, resigned to discomfort, held a supporting strap and stretched his long legs as far as was feasible in the cramped space. His companion, however, seemed impervious to the discomfort. Compared with her usual mode of travel recently this was luxury, bearing only the most favorable comparison to the back of a hay wagon or the soles of her wooden shod feet.

Paris passed under the intent scrutiny of a fascinated child peering through the small window in the door. Danielle's exposure to urban living had consisted only of a few days in Paris as a very small child on her way to England and her grandparents, and the last four days when she'd been scratching for a crust of bread in the back streets, earning the odd bowl of watery broth by sweeping out stores or running errands. Now, from the shelter of this private coach she could view the city with the holistic eye of an observer rather than through the myopic vision of a starved urchin.

They left the crowded, fetid narrowness of the inner city behind and began to move through the environs—still urban, still poor, but the air smelled cleaner. They passed through the North Gate and were out in the countryside, their progress slowed by a farmer's wagon, lumbering slowly ahead as it returned emptied of its produce that had, as usual, fetched barely a subsistence price in the market that morning.

The day wore on. Two hours outside the city they stopped at an inn to change the horses. It was now well past noon and Danielle's stomach was beginning to rebel against her impetuous, prideful decision to go breakfastless. She had had nothing but a sip of water since the previous evening and although her belly was no stranger to hunger, its satisfaction last night seemed quite unaccountably to have created expectations of regular satisfaction. As her hunger blossomed her stomach growled with annoyance and Danielle lost all pleasure in the scenery and the novelty of the journey in her embarrassment and irritation.

Linton watched her through half-closed eyes for a while before deciding that she had paid adequate penalty for her earlier obstinacy. Bending, he drew a small hamper out from beneath the seat.

"Here, child. This journey is quite tedious enough without the cacophonous demands of your empty belly."

Danielle took the basket with a dignified thank-you, but her eager fingers betrayed her as she opened it. A chicken leg, a meat pasty, half of a baguette, a large chunk of ripe cheese, and a strawberry tart nestled in the checkered napkin beside a bottle of lemonade. She raised her eyes to meet His Lordship's amused regard.

"Will you eat with me, milord?"

"Thank you, no, infant. If you remember, I broke my fast earlier."

Danielle abstained from comment although a pink tinge bloomed on the ivory skin. She returned her attention to the contents of the basket and with the ease and recovery of youth consumed every last scrap, washed down with the refreshingly bittersweet taste of the lemonade.

In spite of her obvious hunger she ate with all the daintiness the earl had noticed the previous evening and—her repast ended—she wiped both face and fingers fastidiously before returning the napkin to the basket and the basket to the floor beneath her seat. Hot midafternoon sun filled the confined space and Linton drew the curtains across the windows. They kept out the blaze, but an airless stuffiness filled the coach and Danielle felt the sticky trickle of sweat between her breasts and under her arms. With a restless movement she tugged off the woolen jacket. Linton averted his eyes from the outline of those perfect breasts pressed against her shirt as she drew her shoulders back in her attempt to wriggle out of the tight garment. It was so much easier to forget this budding womanhood when his charge played the role of street waif. The next ten days or so were going to be a sore trial, he reflected gloomily, unless he could maintain a distance between them. He could do that only by treating her as a child. She would assuredly resent that, but any conflict that ensued would be a great deal easier to manage than this overpowering arousal that swept through him at the indications, albeit unconscious on her part, of her very obvious attractions.

Without the heavy jacket, Danielle felt immeasurably more comfortable. The regular motion of the vehicle, the warmth of its interior and the fullness of her stomach all conspired to produce a wonderful feeling of lethargy creeping slowly through her body. She did not identify the main cause of this relaxation—that for the first time in an eternity, it seemed, she was safe and not obliged to keep her wits about her even in sleep as she planned her next move or reacted with instinctive wariness to whatever dangers her situation might hold from moment to moment. Since that February night of horror, she had lived on a knife-edge of fear and danger, and her constant watchfulness had become second nature as had the readiness to attack first and ask questions later. But now the presence of her large, lazy-eyed companion stretched at his ease across from her strangely made such wariness unnecessary. Her head nodded as her long lashes fluttered. With an effort she jerked awake again, glancing guiltily at Linton, but his own eyes appeared to be closed. With a soft sigh of contentment Danielle gave herself up to sleep.

The carl, despite appearances, was actually wide awake, watching the girl through half-closed eyes. The coach jolted violently over a pothole and he moved swiftly, catching the unconscious figure as it threatened to slip to the floor. With a reluctant smile he moved to the seat beside her, sliding a supporting arm around the slight figure. Danielle's head instantly found a resting place on a broad, velvet-covered shoulder. Reflecting ruefully on the speculation such a sight would give rise to, Milord resigned himself to a few cramped hours.

It was late in the afternoon when the coach halted for a second change of horses. Linton, gently disengaging himself, alighted into the small yard in front of a pretty country inn. Having requested a tankard of ale he was stretching his muscle-locked limbs when Danielle climbed sleepily from the coach, looking around her purposefully.

"What can I do for you, infant?" he asked with a smile. The coachman and postillions were refreshing themselves in the inn and no one was about to note this curious manner of addressing a servant lad.

"Actually, milord, you can do nothing for me. This is something I must do for myself." Shooting him a cheeky grin Danielle made her way down the garden path at the side of the building in the direction of the small, noisome outhouse at the rear.

The earl chuckled, wondering how Society would receive this most unusual candor. He found it immensely refreshing but suspected that his reaction would be shared by only a small minority. The girl was going to need a very firm hand guiding her path through the intricacies of life amongst the ton. In spite of her orphaned state she would not be dowerless—the Earl of March was a very wealthy man, well able to provide for his granddaughter, and his countess was one of the leaders of London society. The child's birth was impeccable and an excellent *parti* should be no problem to find—unless, of course, the story of her adventures became known to the gossips. Linton frowned, well aware that the most scandalous aspect of her escapades so far was his protection and their present mode of travel. She was hopelessly compromised by his companionship and its absolute necessity would be considered no excuse. There was but one acceptable solution and it was one he strongly suspected would be pressed most ardently by the Earl of March.

They resumed their journey. Danielle, refreshed by her nap and relieved by their halt, seemed disposed to conversation. But hers was a far cry from the artless prattle of the young girls of Linton's acquaintance. He found himself in the presence of an exceptionally well-informed mind whose interests ranged far and wide across the gamut of philosophy, the arts, horse-breeding, and, most particularly, politics. Her knowledge and insight about what was happening in her country both amazed and informed him. In fact, Linton reflected, she would probably be of more use to William Pitt at this time than he. He had gleaned some information and impressions during his brief stay but Danielle was considerably better informed, and her wanderings amongst the populace had given her an invaluable opportunity to gauge the mood of the people—an opportunity that she appeared to have used to best advantage. If it could be arranged without revealing too much of her personal story and endangering her reputation, a meeting between Danielle de St. Varennes and William Pitt, Earl of Chatham, could prove most enlightening to the latter.

When at long last they reached their day's destination some

forty miles south of Calais they were both heartily sick of the carriage. Danny, in particular, was tired, hungry, irritable, and not disposed to accept with equanimity the earl's brisk instructions that she say nothing and do exactly as she was bid. Her self-appointed guardian, however, was equally irritable and not inclined to brook argument. A pithy description of the consequences of any disturbances similar to those at the Inn of the Rooster was sufficiently convincing to ensure a rather sullen compliance, and she followed Milord, in the manner of an obedient servant, across the courtyard and into the inn.

Mine Host, with much bowing and scraping, assured milord of the best bedchamber, a private parlor, and a superb dinner. His offer to provide the lad with a bed in the attic with his own servants was politely refused.

"The boy can be wild on occasion," the earl explained blandly. "I prefer to keep him under my eye—a cot in my chamber will suffice."

The landlord shot Danny an interested look—the lad didn't look wild, just rather sulky and effeminate. However, appearances were frequently deceiving, and with a shrug, he dismissed the matter and went off to his cellar to bring up a bottle of the best burgundy for his discriminating guest.

"Come," the earl directed over his shoulder and began to mount the stairs after the serving wench deputed to show him to his chamber.

As there was no option, Danielle followed. The large airy room was pronounced satisfactory, the portmanteau bestowed under the window, and steaming jugs of water placed on the dresser. Left to themselves again, Linton put up his quizzing glass and surveyed his charge.

"You do look the most complete urchin, Danny. I think—yes I really think we must contrive a change of clothes. If only one day's travel can reduce you to that state of disorder I dread to think what a week will do."

Danielle flushed crossly. "It's hardly my fault."

"I do not remember saying that it was," Linton clipped with a frown. "Do you think you could manage to stay out of trouble for an hour whilst I ponder the question and get out my own dirt."

Danny glared at him in soundless fury, then turned on her heel and whisked out of the room, slamming the heavy door resoundingly. She had gone no more than three steps before it was flung open and Milord's suddenly very soft voice arrested her.

"Come back here and shut this door properly." She bit her lip in frustration, but hesitated for only a second before turning to comply. Linton had returned to the chamber insultingly sure of her obedience, leaving the door opened wide. She closed it gently and made her way downstairs and out into the cool remnants of daylight.

Linton, furious with himself for having provoked her unnecessarily, stripped, washed, and changed his clothes. It was amazing what a clean shirt and a fresh cravat could do for a man's temper and, in a much improved frame of mind, he went in search first of his urchin and then of the burgundy. He ran his quarry to earth in the large stone-flagged kitchen addressing a bowl of milk and a huge chunk of cheese whilst regaling the motherly landlady with some distinctly ribald stories.

The woman's fat cheeks shook with laughter as she stirred the aromatic contents of a pot on the vast range. "Oh, you ought to be ashamed of yourself, young man," she protested halfheartedly. "Such stories on the tongue of a babe!"

"Now what have you been up to, brat?" Linton lounged in the kitchen doorway.

Danny leapt instantly to her feet, her own temper much restored by the satisfaction of the inner self. "Oh, Milord, just imagine. Madame here was so sorry to hear of the loss of my cloakbag that she has offered me a suit of her youngest son's clothing. He's grown out of them, you see."

"Well, that is indeed kind of madame," the earl murmured, his eyes glinting with amusement—trust this indomitable creature to solve her own problems. "Perhaps you would like to change, then. I shall require you to wait at table when I dine."

"You come on back to the kitchen afterwards, then, lad," madame said warmly, "and you can have your supper with our lads. We've a good rabbit stew waiting."

Danielle did not care for rabbit stew at the best of times, and

56

particularly not when compared with the delicate repast being prepared for his lordship's delectation. However, she need not have worried. Linton had no intention of allowing Danielle de St. Varennes to spend the evening in the company of stablehands and pot boys, whatever her experiences in recent weeks.

"You are too kind, madame," he broke in smoothly, "but the boy remains with me. He may dine at my table when I have finished. We must make an early start in the morning and I wish him to have a clear head."

The landlady looked surprised but approving. Such concern for the health and morals of very youthful servants was unusual but gratifying.

"I'll fetch those clothes for you then, m'dear, and you bring those you're wearing back down here and I'll have them good as new by the morning." She bustled off leaving the earl to reflect that his vagabond could clearly charm the birds off the trees if she put her mind to it. In fact, the charming of farmers' wives was one of Danielle's stocks in trade, learned as a lonely child roaming the vast estates, frequently from sunup to sundown. She'd shared many a peasant meal over the years, repayed with coin or kind, whatever happened to be available to her at the time.

The landlady's son was clearly a lot fatter than Danielle and the britches showed an alarming reluctance to stay up over the slender hips. Frowning, she rummaged through the portmanteau—the Earl of Linton obviously did not have such problems; there was nothing remotely resembling a belt or cord. With a resigned shrug she broached the stack of snow-white cravats, twisted one into a strip with a rough brutality that would have made its owner wince, and tied it securely around the waist of the offending garment. Hardly elegant, but it would have to do.

Her arrival in the private parlor caused his lordship a moment of acute pain as he wrestled with laughter, amazement at her ingenuity and irritation that she should so calmly have rifled his possessions.

"You might have asked, Danny," he expostulated. "That is a most hideous abuse of a perfectly good cravat!"

57

"Would you have had me come down in my small clothes to do so, milord?" she retorted.

That was an image Linton preferred to put from his mind. "Well, at least you are clean and relatively tidy again," he conceded, seating himself at the laden table. "I have informed our host that I do not wish to be disturbed unless I ring, so I think you may safely come to table."

The meal was simple, a single course, as was to be expected in a country inn, but the wild mushrooms in the *mousse aux champignons* reverberated on the palate, the delicate texture of the dish of artichokes pleased the eye as much as the taste buds and provided perfect accompaniment to the succulent river trout swimming in butter, crisped with almonds. Danielle surveyed the haunch of venison and shook her head regretfully as her companion offered her a slice. The rich, cheesy gratin of thinly sliced potatoes was also rejected, prompting the earl to remark, "Those britches will never fit you if you continue to eat so circumspectly."

"Last night, my lord, you were cautioning me to eat sparingly. My belly, as you said, is not used to riches. I would hate to subject you to a night of nursing."

"You are an incorrigible wretch, Danielle de St. Varennes. Have you ever been short of an answer?" Linton sat back in the carved chair, sipping his wine as he regarded her with interest.

"I am not normally required to look for them quite so hard, milord," Danielle replied sweetly.

The earl gave a shout of laughter. He would like to spend the rest of the evening fencing with this sharp tongue, this quick wit, this exquisite creature whose beauty at this moment was barely hidden by the ridiculous clothes. Those enormous eyes danced with the readiness to respond to challenge and something else that he did not want to see right now—a naturally flirtatious awareness of her femininity. The full lips of that adorable mouth curved in impish anticipation of his response and a soft glow suffused the delicate ivory of her cheeks.

"If you've finished your dinner, brat, I should be obliged if you would seek your bed."

The heart-shaped face fell. Hurt, quickly masked, flashed in the velvet depths of her eyes as Danielle rose instantly. "As you command, milord." With a mock leg she left the room, leaving Justin to his melancholy reflections. He had not intended to be so abrupt, but in the face of his unbidden arousal it was the only response possible. She was a child, for God's sake! Just a child! But, of course, she was not. Had he met her in any other circumstances, the careful pursuit of an eligible maid would have been quite in order. But she had given him her trust and was as yet unaware of her own sexuality or the power of another's, or, indeed, of her ability to arouse that power.

It was very late before he repaired to his bed, conscious that he had imbibed more than he had intended of Mine Host's excellent cognac. He was far from under the hatches, but just a little more concerned than was his custom. There was a rigidity about the heap of bedclothes on the cot that declared his ward's wakefulness, but he refrained from comment, preparing for bed behind the dressing screen before blowing out the single, flickering candle and climbing thankfully into the feathered comfort of his enclosed bed.

The unearthly shriek brought him upright, wide awake, feeling for the silver-mounted pistol under his pillow. He sat blinking in the darkness, poised, ready for he knew not what. Mumbled, incoherent words came from outside the tent of the bed curtains and slowly he drew them back, sliding to the floor crouched in a position of attack. The room was in pitch darkness, only the strange keening moans penetrated the silence of the night. Linton, no longer expecting an intruder, crossed the room barefoot to light the candle on the mantel. Danielle was tossing restlessly on the cot, moaning, mumbling incoherently a desperate dream tale of confusion and terror.

So, it was happening already, he thought, crossing to the writhing figure. For a long while he stood vigil until the deep, gasping sobs of grief replaced the dream terror. Then he knelt by the narrow cot, soft nonsense words of comfort on his lips as he stroked the damp forehead, pushed back the matted curls.

"Alone, so alone," the broken voice repeated until it became almost a chant and Linton gave up the struggle. Lifting the small figure in the sweat-soaked shirt he moved back to his bed, not releasing his tight hold as he slid beneath the covers. Danielle was aware only of a warm body against her own shivering one, of strong arms cradling her, holding off the terror. Deep black, dreamless unconsciousness beckoned its promise and was welcomed.

Chapter 4

Danielle awoke in a strange, darkened world. Her legs were pinioned to the mattress by a heavy weight, her head held in a tight grip against an expanse of finest linen. Something was rhythmically causing a gentle rise and fall of the curls on her bent head. She lay very still, resisting the urge to leap in panic from her curious situation until she had decided exactly where she was and how she had got there. The darkness was created by bed curtains, and whatever was holding her legs down was definitely hairy. Something of last night's nightmare came back to her and she realized that not only was she in the same bed as Justin, Earl of Linton, she was clamped to his side and it was the even in and out of his sleeping breath that lifted her hair. His legs, heavy with relaxation, held her captive unless she chose to wake him. Strangely, she was not afraid. Surely he could not have taken her virginity without her knowing? Breaching the maidenhead was supposed to be painful—she could not have slept through such an experience!

"Sweet Jesus!" The Earl of Linton, with a convulsive heave, shook off his burden roughly and bolted upright, blinking in dazed half-remembrance. What had seemed a perfectly reasonable action in his not entirely sober state in the middle of the night struck him now in the cold light of dawn as a piece of the most sentimental, utter foolishness. His aching head was yet another reminder of his stupidity. If it hadn't been for this troublesome chit he would not have overindulged in the cognac and certainly would not be in this ridiculous position now. He turned the full force of his anger on Danielle.

"Get out of this damned bed! In fact, get dressed and get out of the room altogether!"

"But what have I done?" Those huge eyes widened in distress and bewilderment.

"What do you mean, what have you done? You have somehow contrived to get yourself into my bed, that's what!" he thundered.

"But I didn't; *you* put me here," she protested. "I was asleep."

"You were *not* asleep. You were in the middle of some damn nightmare. Oh, the devil take it!" The earl ran a frustrated hand through his unpowdered locks. "Just dress and go downstairs while I try to pull myself together."

Danielle got off the bed, pulling aside the curtains. As she stood up an early ray of sunlight flashed across the room and her body under the fine lawn of his shirt was suddenly silhouetted against the light, the dark tips of her breasts pressing against the thin material, the soft curve of buttocks and long length of leg as transparently revealed as if she were naked. His loins stirred, throbbed in time with his aching temples, and Linton groaned, sinking back onto the pillows. He could still feel the slight, warm body against his and began seriously to question his ability to deliver Danielle de St. Varennes virgo intacta to her grandparents if there were to be any more nights like the last.

"Milord?" There was an almost pleading note in the soft voice.

"Well?"

"Nothing . . . I mean . . . nothing happened, did it?" The words came out in a rush.

"No child." With an effort he sat up, remembering that this was a seventeen-year-old who in the last two months had undergone more terrifying experiences than most people endured in a lifetime. "I am angry with myself, not with you. It is very hard for a . . . a . . . normal man to spend the night as we did. I am suffering for it this morning."

"Oh?" Interest quickened in her eyes. "How are you suffering?"

Why the devil had he started this? Linton wondered irritably if there were any insanity in his family. "You'll find out when you are married," he said dismissively.

"Oh, but I would much rather know now. It's better to be prepared, don't you think? Could you not explain?"

"No, I could not!" the earl roared, closing his eyes against the sharp stab of pain. "Just get out of here, would you? And tell them to bring up my shaving water and I'll breakfast in an hour."

"Yes, milord." Danielle sketched him a sardonic curtsy and turned behind the dressing screen. "The water's cold," she complained.

"Well, since you have managed without it altogether for I don't know how many weeks, you should be grateful for what there is" was the callous reply.

She pulled a face in the direction of the bed, but washed as best she could and pulled on the landlady's son's clothes. If she was to spend another day in that horrid coach it didn't matter if she started out looking scruffy. She would save her rather more respectable suit for more public occasions.

The kitchen was filled with the wonderful smells of fresh baking when she reached it. "*Bonjour, madame.*" Her cheery greeting brought the landlady around from the bread oven, a batch of crescent-shaped rolls steaming golden brown on the flat wooden paddle between her hands.

The plump face, rosy from the oven, beamed at Danny. "It's going to be a beautiful one, lad. How's your master this morning?"

"Wants his shaving water."

"The kettle's hot on the range," Madame instructed brightly. "Jug's on the dresser." She was too busy arranging a second batch of rolls on the paddle to notice Danny's indignant, startled expression. So, she was supposed to do it herself, was she?

"You can take the clean linen up with you," the landlady continued. "Your own clothes are there, too—all pressed and as good as new."

Danielle muttered to herself as she filled the jug with the dipper from the iron cauldron on the range. The jug was very

63

heavy and she crammed the clean laundry under one arm before picking it up by an uncomfortably warm handle and staggering for the door.

"Come back down for your breakfast," the cheerful voice called after her.

Danielle aimed a warning kick at the door of the chamber before setting down her burden and reaching for the latch. The door, however, swung open and a startled Earl of Linton stood there, splendid in a long robe of brocaded silk.

"It's heavy," she mumbled in half-apologetic explanation.

"I see," he responded dryly, bending to lift the jug.

"I thought inns were supposed to have their own servants." She followed him into the room with the pile of laundry.

"So they do," her exasperating companion concurred blandly. "But since I have a perfectly good one of my own, I'm sure Madame Bonnet considers it unnecessary to employ hers on my personal needs."

"I suppose you'd like me to shave you as well?"

"I do not think, brat, that I would trust you with a razor," His Lordship chuckled, examining the clean linen with a sudden frown. "You do appear to have creased my cravat. That's the second one you've ruined."

"I've only got two hands, you know," Danielle snapped.

"Well you could always have made two journeys. Or didn't that occur to you?"

Danny gobbled at him in wordless fury and His Lordship, with infuriating calm, said, "If you have something to say, infant, do so quickly. I wish to get dressed."

Those brown eyes threw daggers at him before she turned on her heel with an impudent twitch of her small rear that aroused in the earl two quite conflicting urges and flounced out of the room.

"Shouldn't wonder if His Lordship's got quite a head on him this morning," Madame Bonnet remarked casually as she half filled a bowl with hot creamy milk, added strong black coffee, and set it on the table before Danny.

"Why?" Danny mumbled through a mouthful of honeycomb and hot, fresh bread.

"Dipped deep into the cognac last night," her informant

stated matter-of-factly. "Must have something on his mind."

Danielle pondered this information in silence. She was well accustomed to the aftereffects of a heavy night on the imbiber—her father and uncles had given her ample opportunities for observation of that condition. It would certainly explain Milord's irascibility.

The imperative peal of a bell from within had Madame Bonnet clucking over to the range for the coffeepot. "That'll be His Lordship wanting his breakfast. Hurry along, lad." She thrust a laden tray toward Danny, who was about to announce that she'd finish her own meal first, but thought better of it.

Her protector, apart from a slight heaviness around the eyes, was looking his usual immaculate self, the black hair drawn into a neat queue at his neck, snowy lace at throat and wrists beneath a brown cloth coat over a short waistcoat of the same material. Buckskin britches and top boots encased the shapely legs.

Danny placed the tray on the table, regarding him solicitously. "Perhaps, milord, you should take a powder for your headache. It might make you feel more the thing."

"What headache?" His Lordship demanded suspiciously.

"In my experience, sir, when one gets foxed it is the usual consequence." She smiled innocently.

"What the devil do you mean, brat? I was *not* foxed! And what do you know about it, anyway?" But he was talking to empty air. Danielle had whisked herself from the room. Furiously he tugged the bellpull again and within seconds the door opened and the impish face of his urchin appeared around it.

"Yes, milord?"

"Bring me a tankard of ale," he growled.

"Is that wise, sir? After the cognac, I mean."

"Danny, I'm warning you . . ." Linton took an infuriated step toward the door. The tip of a small pink tongue peeped between rosy lips for a second and she was gone again leaving the earl torn between reluctant amusement and considerable annoyance.

When she returned with the foaming pewter tankard there was nothing about her demeanor to annoy and Linton, examining her through his glass, observed, "Judging by whatever it is you have on your nose, you have already breakfasted."

"I haven't finished it yet," she retorted. "And I do not have anything on my nose." The back of her hand went up to wipe the offending feature, but her companion moved swiftly, catching her wrist.

"How many times do I have to remind you that you are not now on the street, urchin? Hold still." He scrubbed her face vigorously with his napkin. "It's honey, you sticky brat."

"I am not a sticky brat." Danny moved backward from his ignominious ministrations. "I don't know how I'm to be expected to eat properly when I have to keep leaping up to answer your bell!"

"Well, when you've filled your belly you can pack up my things. I wish to leave in half an hour." Linton sat down at the table and addressed himself to his own breakfast, effectively dismissing Danielle from his presence.

Her task completed, twenty minutes later Danny went out of the kitchen and into the sunny stableyard. The ostlers were busy putting the horses to the heavy coach and watching them she didn't hear the soft footsteps behind her until her cap left her head and a rough voice mocked, "What little bantam is this?"

She whirled to face a brawny stablehand whose little eyes in a pudgy face glinted spitefully. "Can't imagine what you're good for," her tormentor continued, grabbing her upper arm and pinching it painfully.

Danny wrenched herself free. "Gimme my cap." She stretched for it, but the youth merely held it higher.

"Got to jump for it," he taunted.

"*Cochon!*" Danny spat, leaping at his arm.

He laughed maliciously and tossed the cap onto the high wall surrounding the yard.

"Betch can't climb either, runt."

Danny knew that she should leave the cap and walk away, but she had never been able to run from a fight—it was not the de St. Varennes way. She was also as agile as a monkey and the wall uneven with plenty of foot and handholds. In no time she

66

had retrieved the article and crammed it back onto her head, making to walk out of the yard. But the bully was not finished yet. He grabbed the cap, seizing a painful handful of the hair beneath as he dragged it off again. It sailed through the air to land again on the wall.

"This time, bantam, you're gonna 'ave to fight fer it!" Two sledgehammer fists went up. Danielle thought rapidly. She was no physical match for this oaf who quite clearly intended for some reason to do her considerable damage, but he was all brawn. With a swift dancing movement she aimed a kick at his shin. It was unlikely to cause him much pain, but, as she had hoped, it enraged him mightily. Prancing backward, just out of reach of those treetrunk arms, she delved into her wide vocabulary of insults, producing a tirade that drew reluctant admiration from the circle of interested spectators who had appeared instantly it was known that Jacques was out to teach the snob servant of Milord a lesson or two. She didn't know it, but she had Linton to thank for this unprovoked attack. His refusal to allow her to eat in the kitchen the previous evening had been misinterpreted as a high and mighty gesture of the servant's rather than the edict of the master.

She had attained her goal when she delivered the coup de grace—the pithy comparison of her assailant's male organ with a pig's bladder. Jacques lunged for her with all the blindness of an enraged bull. With all the daintiness of a toreador, Danielle sidestepped neatly and her pursuer went headfirst into the horse trough that had been behind her. She was about to deliver a few more well-chosen epithets at the discomfitted Jacques's upturned rear when Linton's voice cut through the laughing throng.

"Danny! *Viens-ici!*" She turned to see him standing well to one side of the suddenly silenced group, now shuffling awkwardly on the cobblestones. Why he should be looking so furious, she couldn't imagine. She had not exactly been responsible for this little fracas.

The earl told her in very few words when she reached him. "What the devil did you think you were doing?" The voice was very, very soft. "Once that lout had his hands on you, how long do you imagine it would be before he discovered exactly *what* you are? Do you think a wench masquerading as a lad with a mouth as dirty as yours would get any consideration from that lot?" He gestured toward the group, now melting discreetly away. "They'd have you on your back with your britches down and your legs spread before you could open your mouth to scream!"

Danielle seemed to be taking an inordinate interest in her boots throughout this short, deliberately brutal speech and a deep flush crept over the fragile pillar of her bent neck.

"Just remember that, the next time you decide to embroil yourself in a stableyard scrap," the earl finished, resisting the sudden urge to run his finger along that sweet column, turning away abruptly instead, striding across the yard. He reached the dripping Jacques, who had just extricated himself from the trough. Linton's left fist, by way of the bully's chin, returned Master Jacques to his trough without so much as a whimper. Retrieving the cap from the wall he returned to his charge, who, embarrassment forgotten, was dancing in gleeful triumph at her enemy's downfall.

"You knocked him down!" she exclaimed. "That, milord, is a punishing left you have."

"What do you know of such things?" The earl sighed, replacing the cap on the small head. It was a silly question—this brat knew altogether too much of the most unsuitable subjects. How on earth had Louise allowed her daughter to have such an unconventional upbringing? But then, he reflected grimly, if she had not, the child would not be here now. She would never have survived the last weeks.

The earl proved a poor traveling companion that day, spending the greater part of the journey with his eyes closed in an attempt to soothe his raw eyeballs and placate the persistent throb of his temples. Danielle, well versed in the advisability of maintaining a low profile in these circumstances, kept her counsel and endured the tedium of the journey in silence, relieved only by the ample contents of the picnic hamper thoughtfully provided by Madame Bonnet. Linton shook his head with a grimace of distaste when she tentatively offered to share her repast and attempted to shut out the sounds of someone enjoying a hearty meal, wincing slightly as she scrunched into a large, very crisp apple.

They reached the small port of Calais in the late afternoon and Danielle gazed eagerly through the grimy window at the harbor crowded with elegant yachts and not so elegant fishing boats.

"What ship will we take, milord?" she ventured, unable to contain herself a moment longer.

"My own—the *Black Gull*," he replied briefly.

"That sounds like a pirate sloop," Danny commented.

"Well she's not," was the uncompromising reply.

A small sigh escaped her and the earl relented. It really was not just to take his own tedium and ill temper out on her. She had certainly contributed to his discomforts earlier in the day but since then had behaved with impeccable consideration. He leant toward the window.

"Look over to the left, amongst that group of yachts beside the pier. You see the white one with the black trim? That's the *Black Gull*."

"Oh, she's beautiful," Danielle exclaimed. "Are we to go aboard immediately?"

"It is my intention to sail with the evening tide," His Lordship informed her. "The sooner I get you out of France," and off my hands, he thought, "the happier I shall be."

The coach drew up at the pier. Its weary passengers prepared to disembark.

The earl paused for a moment, one hand on the door. "Do you know the meaning of the word inconspicuous, brat?"

"Of course I do," she affirmed indignantly.

"Well, you must admit I have had cause to wonder."

Danielle wrinkled her nose at the sarcasm, but Linton was continuing. "My sailors are good seamen but they *are* sailors and I want no trouble on this voyage. You will oblige me by remaining in your cabin for the duration. If you are obliged to say anything speak only French. Is it understood?"

"I must stay below *all* the time?" Her eyes widened in disappointment.

"*All* the time, Danny," His Lordship stressed firmly.

She shrugged in resignation and followed her mentor onto the quay.

"Button your jacket," Linton whispered suddenly. "You may not have much to display, but sailors have sharp eyes."

Danny hissed with indignation but did as he bade her, pulling her cap low over her eyes as she walked behind him along the pier, casting covert glances at the fascinating scene around her.

Forster, captain of the *Black Gull*, came forward to greet its master as they crossed the gangplank. "Ah, my lord, so you have made it in time. I received your message this morning and we are ready to sail with the tide." He gave the small figure standing meekly behind the earl only a cursory glance before examining the salmon-tinged sky.

"We may be in for some dirty weather, my lord. Looks like a squall or two up there."

Linton gave a brief nod. "Do you advise we wait for the morning?"

"Nah!" The captain spat contemptuously over the deck rail. "The *Gull* can handle a bit o' wind."

"Good. Have my luggage stowed below. The lad has the small cabin next to mine."

Danielle watched wistfully as her protector strode off along the deck.

"Look sharp then, lad. We don't have all day, you know." The captain's brusque tone brought her head up and the sailor surprised a flash of annoyance in those big brown eyes. He'd seen that look on many a young cabin boy at the start of his first voyage. It didn't last long, though, he reflected with grim satisfaction—not under the command of Captain Forster.

He rapped out a sharp order to a seaman hovering nearby who, with an imperative jerk of his head toward Danny, moved off with a curious swinging gait to the companionway. She followed silently, seething with indignation at the earl's cavaliar disappearance, and soon found herself in a tiny cabin whose only furnishings were a narrow bunk with a thin pallet and blanket, a table and chair both bolted to the floor, and a chamber pot. There was little room for anything else and no space at all for moving around. The door closed behind the departing sailor and she sat miserably on the bunk, tired, dirty, and hungry. The cabin was close and airless and she thought longingly of the fresh breeze on deck, listening to the sounds of activity above her, the creak and rattle of chains, shouted orders, and scurrying feet.

After a while the door opened again abruptly to admit a boy of about twelve with a tray which he set down on the table while examining Danny curiously but not unkindly.

"'Is Lordship says as 'ow yer to eat yer vittles in 'ere and Cap'n says yer to stay below 'till we reaches Dover." He paused, clearly waiting for some response, but received only a puzzled frown and a murmured, "*S'il vous plaît?*"

"Oh, yer one 'o them froggies wat can't speak the King's English," the boy said in disgusted comprehension and left the cabin and Danny to her solitary meal and her cheerless thoughts.

It was neither an elegant nor comforting meal—cold meat, cheese, unfresh bread that clearly had been baked that morning, washed down with a cup of unpleasantly warm water. But at least it was food and her memories of real hunger were still too recent for her to turn up her nose. Once finished, Danny put the tray outside the door concluding, on the basis of past experience, that whoever came to retrieve it would otherwise barge into the cabin without so much as an alerting knock. In the absence of any diversion she lay down on the hard bunk feeling the yacht rock gently beneath her. She didn't think they had taken up the anchor yet—they didn't seem to be moving anyway—and soon her suspicions were confirmed as a tremendous rattling noise beneath the cabin floor, louder instructions above, and pounding feet indicated the *Black Gull's* readiness to leave Calais.

She dozed and then slept, lulled by the gentle motion as the yacht sailed out of the shelter of the harbor and into the English Channel. The crash as the tin chamber pot rolled across the floor and slammed into the door brought her wide awake and upright in one movement. Dear God! What was happening? The cabin would not keep still, the low ceiling seemed to duck toward her before rising again as the floor came up to meet her petrified eyes. Her stomach followed these gyrations with slavish obedience and with the sudden, absolute knowledge that she was going to be very sick Danny bolted for

71

the door, wrenched it open, and made a panic-stricken dash for the companionway, her only thought the need for air, to get out of this claustrophobic environment where the walls closed in and the ceiling descended and the floor rose. But the hatchway at the top of the steps was bolted down. With a strength born of desperation she wrenched the bolts back, skinning her hands in the process, flinging back the hatch, gasping for the fresh air above. As she dragged herself up her horrified eyes encountered an enormous, dark green, foam-flecked wall racing toward the craft. Running, shouting figures hung onto the ropes securing them around the waist to the deckrail, and the next minute the ground left her feet as the hatchway crashed shut behind and a rock-hard arm caught her against a wet, slippery oilskin, holding her with desperate strength as the green wall crashed over them. For a moment she was trapped in a roaring, suffocating bubble, her body an object in a tug of war between the iron band around her waist and the almost overpowering pull of the water as it fought for possession. For a moment Danielle was convinced she was about to meet her maker and when she raised her eyes into the furious black ones of the man holding her almost wished she had.

"You disobedient, stubborn, hell-born little fool," the earl raged. "Are you trying to get yourself drowned?"

"But the ship's sinking, and I'm going to be sick," Danielle whimpered.

"The ship is *not* sinking, and if you're going to be sick be so in your cabin. Now, get below!"

Bending, Linton wrenched open the hatchway and pushed her roughly onto the top step. "For God's sake hurry! Before the next one!"

Danielle half fell down the steps as the hatch crashed shut over her head and bolted for her cabin, reaching the chamber pot just as her dinner finally decided to part company with her stomach.

By the time the earl was satisfied that his presence was no longer needed on deck her lunch and breakfast had joined her supper and she was lying in a soaked and shivering heap on the cabin floor, clutching the chamber pot as if it were her only lifeline.

Linton, still in his oilskins, paused in the doorway before, with a muttered oath, taking the half step necessary to reach her. As he attempted to pry her hands loose from the pot she gasped out a protest, clutching it tighter.

"For goodness sake, child, let go! There's no room in here for any more." Taking advantage of a break between waves he pried open the porthole and emptied the contents into the storm, thankful that the cabin was on the lee side.

Danielle reached for the pot with pleading hands and he gave it back before grimly beginning to remove her wet clothes. Dimly realizing what was happening she struggled feebly, mumbling incoherent protests.

"Stop it, will you?" Linton gritted. "Unless you wish to be soundly smacked to add to your discomforts!"

He sounded so much like Old Nurse that she gave up her struggles and, indeed, as renewed spasms of nausea wracked her, ceased to care altogether. She was wrapped cocoonlike in the blanket and deposited on the bunk still clutching her lifeline, although by now her retching body had nothing left to give. Linton left the cabin, returning in a very few minutes with a lidded jug and a bottle of brandy. Dipping a towel in the water in the jug, he bathed her face before holding the bottle to her lips. Danny gasped and choked as the spirit burned its way down her raw throat to curl in her stomach. It didn't stay there very long, but he doggedly repeated the process until she had kept enough down for it to have some effect. The yacht was still pitching and rolling, but not as violently as before, when her eyes closed and the convulsive grip on the chamber pot slackened. Satisfied that his charge would sleep out the tail end of the storm, the earl sought dry clothes and his own bed.

Sunlight and a miraculous lack of motion greeted Danielle's slowly opening eyes. For a moment she lay bemused, conscious of a rough, prickly sensation on her skin whose source she eventually identified as the tightly wrapped blanket around her naked body. A hot flush crept slowly over her as the memories of last night flooded back in all their unwelcome detail. Gingerly she sat up, loosening the constricting cover slightly, and looked around. Her wet clothes were nowhere to be seen.

Sliding off the bunk, she took a step toward the porthole and then sat down again hastily. Her legs had taken on the consistency of marshmallow.

A brisk rap on the door was followed instantly by the entrance of the Earl of Linton looking enviably fresh, bright eyed, and as immaculate as ever.

"How do you feel, infant?" He laid her more respectable suit of clothes on the chair before putting up his glass and subjecting her to that minute, unnerving scrutiny.

"My legs feel funny."

"That's only to be expected. It will wear off soon. You need food," he responded matter-of-factly.

Danielle took a deep breath, plucking nervously at the blanket before managing to ask, "What happened?"

"You had one of the worst bouts of seasickness it has ever been my misfortune to witness," she was informed calmly. "You should not, however, feel badly about it," the earl continued kindly. "You were in good company last night, half the crew were suffering to some degree or another."

"But not you." A bitter note sounded in the flat statement.

"No, I never have. But I'm in the minority, I assure you. Now get dressed; there's water in the jug, and when you're ready come next door for some breakfast." On that, Linton turned and left the cabin.

Wondering uneasily if she were safe from intrusion, Danny unwound the blanket and staggered over to the table. The water in the jug was cold but felt wonderful on her skin where salt and sweat seemed to have dried into an almost visible crust. Her movements were slow and fumbling at first, but as her legs began to feel more like themselves she was able to perform her ablutions with something approaching her usual efficiency.

A brisk "*Entrez*" greeted her tentative knock on the adjoining door. The master cabin was a far cry from the narrow space she had occupied. There was even a Turkey carpet on the shiny floorboards and the large bed bore no resemblance to a bunk. The earl rose from the breakfast table as she came in, and looking at the woebegone little face and huge sunken eyes a smile softened his usually impassive features.

74

"Poor brat, you *have* had a rough time," he said compassionately. "Come and eat."

It was a very un-French breakfast—no light meal of bread, rolls, jam, honey, and coffee this. Looking at the plate of crispy bacon, the mound of fluffy eggs, the pink ham and the huge sirloin, all thoughts of last night fled as Danielle sat eagerly in the plush-covered chair the earl held for her.

"What may I serve you, Danielle?"

"Everything, I think, milord, except perhaps the beef," she responded politely, reaching for the silver coffeepot.

"Milk first," Linton stated firmly, filling a large mug to the brim with thick, creamy liquid and placing it before her. "It lines the stomach, and yours, *mon enfant*, I strongly suspect needs some lining."

The earl finished his meal well in advance of his ward and sat, sipping his tankard of ale, pondering a means by which on their way to Cornwall, he could contrive a meeting with William Pitt for both himself and Danielle. Her information and opinions were too valuable to waste at this point and would, he knew, be eagerly received by the prime minister. But how to accomplish this, without revealing her identity and disguise?

"Does something trouble you, milord?" The soft-spoken question broke into his frowning reverie. She had such a pretty, musical voice when not haranguing landlords and stableboys in the language of the gutter. The sooner Danielle de St. Varennes donned her petticoats again the better! That thought gave rise to another and a plan glimmered in His Lordship's mind. It would need refining certainly, but just might serve the purpose.

"Milord?" Danielle was regarding him anxiously and he forced a light smile.

"Nothing troubles me, infant. I was wondering if you felt strong enough to ride today."

"Instead of traveling boxed up in one of those horrid coaches?" Her eyes shone.

"Exactly."

"Oh, I should like it of all things. But where shall we find horses?"

"We shall hire them in the village." A slightly pained look passed across His Lordship's countenance. "They will be hacks, of course, but I daresay we can contrive to make do."

Danny clapped her hands in delight. "I have not been on the back of a horse since February."

His Lordship felt a twinge of doubt. "How well do you ride, brat?"

The look of withering scorn he received informed him all too clearly that that was a question better not to have been asked.

"Certainly as well as you, sir, if not better" was the very dignified response.

Linton sighed. "Danielle, you really must learn to guard your tongue. Such sharp responses to relatively innocent questions will not endear you to the ton."

"I cannot imagine why I should wish to endear myself," she bristled. "I have no intention of being introduced to the ton."

The earl frowned, opened his mouth on a sharp retort, and then thought better of it, saying only, "I rather think your grandparents will have a different view of the matter. I am going to see to the horses. Do you care to accompany me?"

This prospect was sufficiently diverting to put out of mind the uneasy feelings provoked by their exchange and Danielle was far too accustomed to pursuing her own course to be long troubled by the idea of opposition to a path she had decided upon when her flight began.

She gazed around her with great interest as they came up on deck. The famous white cliffs of Dover were as awe-inspiring as she remembered from her childhood journey and the small sea-side village bustled under the early morning sun. The Pelican Inn stood back from the quay, the gleaming, white-washed brick and sparkling mullioned casements ample evidence of its prosperity.

In the clean, orderly stableyard behind the inn the earl surveyed the five available horses critically.

"Do you have a preference, Danny?"

She clearly took the question very seriously and he watched with interest and growing respect her thorough examination of the candidates. Sensitive fingers explored tendons, checked the broad backs for a hint of concealed saddle-soreness, lifted

76

thick velvety lips to reveal yellow, tombstone teeth.

"The piebald gelding and the gray mare. They're not pretty." Two enchanting dimples peeped in the thin cheeks. "But they have the most stamina. The black will be blown after twenty miles, the bay is swaybacked, and the roan fit only for a child in leading strings."

Linton nodded, having reached much the same conclusion himself. The two she had selected were certainly rawboned jobbing horses but quite the best on offer.

"See that they are saddled then. I'll be in the coffee room."

Danielle watched him go into the inn, reflecting that this role of servant was not becoming less irksome with practice. Soon she would have to face the uncomfortable task of informing her self-appointed guardian that she had rescinded her promise made in Paris. Having pledged the word of a Varennes she could not, in honor, break it, so the promise must be openly withdrawn first.

She saddled the mare herself while a stableboy performed the same office for the gelding and then, mounting without assistance, took the piebald's rein and rode to the front of the inn. Linton swung himself into the saddle and the portmanteau was strapped securely behind. Danny, he noticed, sat the large gray as if she were an integral part of the animal, its personality a mere extension of her own.

"We take the London road," he declared briskly. "I hope to do sixty miles today."

"Why London?" Danielle frowned in puzzlement. "As I recall, we did not pass through London on the way to Cornwall when I came with *Maman*."

"I have some business to transact first."

"Oh?" His inquisitive charge raised a pair of inquiring eyebrows and Linton decided that now was probably as good an opportunity as any other to broach some part at least of his plan.

Danielle heard him out in interested reflective silence. "But in what guise am I to meet your Monsieur Pitt?"

"He is Milord Chatham, actually," Linton corrected her. "As to your question, I am in something of a puzzle as how to contrive for the best. But I daresay something will occur

77

to me."

They made good speed, stopping only twice to rest the horses and take refreshment at the inns liberally scattered along this busy post road. It was late afternoon when they clattered into the stableyard of the Red Lion, some twenty miles outside London. Danielle showed no obvious signs of fatigue and if it hadn't been for her ordeal of the previous night, Linton would have been tempted to complete the journey that evening. But, in spite of the straight back and easy seat, there were drawn lines around the purple-smudged eyes and a pallid tinge to the ivory complexion.

"Gad, Linton! Is it indeed you? Well, 'pon my soul, what brings you here, Justin?"

Danny, gazing wide-eyed at the author of this exclamatory speech, missed the look of annoyance that flashed across her companion's features which were instantly schooled to their customary impassivity.

"Good day to you, Julian. My dinner, as it happens," the earl replied calmly, reaching down a slender hand to take his cousin's beringed fingers.

Danielle had never seen anyone quite so magnificent as Lord Julian Carlton. A coat of claret velvet with silver lacing, dove-colored britches clasped at the knee with sapphire buckles, white silk stockings, and diamond-heeled shoes encased a frame quite as powerful as her guardian's. Sapphires gleamed in the lace at his throat and his own hair was hidden beneath a magnificent *perruque* whose curls fell artlessly on the broad forehead of a surprisingly boyish face.

"Then, m'boy, you are in luck," Lord Julian boomed jovially. "I have already bespoken a dinner to gratify even your exacting tastes, and Mine Host has assured me of the excellence of his '67 claret." A cerulean blue eye suddenly fell on His Lordship's mount. "Lud, Justin," he murmured in awe, "what the devil are you doing racketing around the countryside on that boneshaker?"

"It has stamina, Julian," His Lordship observed blandly, "although, I confess, little claim to grace."

He swung easily to the ground and turning toward Danny surprised the look of ill-concealed admiration on a face that suddenly looked too feminine for comfort.

"Your manners appear to have left you with your wits, boy." He spoke harshly in rapid French as he handed her the reins of his gelding.

Lord Julian, for the first time, noticed his cousin's companion and his eyebrows shot up at the most un-servantlike look of indignation that the lad flashed at his master before, with an almost defiant gesture, snatching the reins from His Lordship's hand and turning the horses toward the stables. Any comment he might have made, however, was forestalled by Linton who, laying a friendly arm over his shoulders, moved him toward the inn with a polite inquiry as to his presence on the road to Dover.

Justin was actually very fond of his young cousin whose guardianship he had relinquished some four years previously when the orphaned Lord Julian came of age, but at this moment he wished him at the devil. Nothing could be more unfortunate than this unexpected meeting. Julian, for all his dandified affectations, carried sharp eyes and a good head on those broad shoulders and he could place no reliance on Danielle's powers of discretion. In fact, he strongly suspected that she didn't know the meaning of the word. It looked as if he was facing a most uncomfortable evening that would not be compensated even by the Red Lion's best dinner and the '67 claret.

His worst fears were confirmed by Danny's somewhat precipitate entrance some minutes later into the private parlor that he had perforce agreed to share with Julian. Both men turned in surprise as the door burst open with a lamentable lack of ceremony.

"It is customary to knock on a closed door, brat," Linton said in that soft voice that Danielle had come to recognize as denoting annoyance.

"Well, I'm sorry, milord, I'm sure—I jest come for me orders." She had reverted to her backstreet French but her whole body radiated challenge and her eyes kept sliding toward Lord Julian. "I seen to the 'orses and if you'll not be wantin' me agin, I'll go fer me dinner."

Linton sighed. His cousin's presence obliged him to respond

to the challenge. If he let it pass Lord Julian's curiosity would be piqued even further—he was already gazing in startled amazement at this extraordinary display of impudence from a mere servant lad.

The earl crossed the room. "You are insolent, boy," he said gently, the handle of his riding whip catching the urchin's chin, pushing it upwards to meet his narrowed eyes. "I do not tolerate insolence, as you will discover if you are not very careful. Is it understood?"

The brown eyes sparked fire, but the earl had placed himself between Danny and his cousin, effectively blocking the latter's view. "You will go to my chamber," he continued as gently as before. "Unpack my portmanteau and lay out my clothes for the evening. I shall require hot water and your presence when I come up myself in about fifteen minutes."

A look of uncertainty crossed the small heart-shaped face as Danielle wondered uneasily if this time she had perhaps gone too far. She murmured a meek "Yes, milord," and on being released beat a hasty retreat.

"'Pon my soul, Justin, that's an engaging scapegrace! Not your usual style though. Where'd you acquire him?"

His Lordship examined his cravat minutely in the mirror above the mantel, making an imperceptible adjustment to a fold before replying lazily, "It was a vast error on my part, Julian, I must confess. I yielded, would you believe, to a moment of pity and intervened in a brawl between that vagabond and a mountain of a baker. It was the odds, you see," he added with a weary sigh. "They were really not entirely fair and I felt an unaccountable urge to even them. It was an impulse I have since had cause to regret on many occasions."

"Gad, Justin!" Lord Julian's shoulders were shaking. "No one is going to believe that, moved by such an energetic emotion as compassion, you of all people have saddled yourself with an impudent whelp."

"I do beg of you, Julian, that you will not feel the urge to try our friends' powers of belief. It is a tale I prefer kept secret." Arched eyebrows lifted, and Lord Julian, realizing that he had in some way been issued an order, made haste to ensure his cousin that his lips were sealed.

"What do you intend doing with him, though? You'll hardly keep him beside you. I'd lay a thousand guineas to see Petersham's reaction!"

The earl shuddered slightly. He could well imagine the reaction of that august personage to the incorrigible Danny.

"I shall send him to Danesbury," he replied with a bland disregard for the truth. "The lad has a way with horses, he'll do well enough in the stables, and John will knock him into shape."

Julian nodded his agreement. The head groom at Linton's Hampshire estates had been responsible for knocking more than stable-boys into shape over the years. He himself had spent some uncomfortable moments under that rough tutelage.

Linton found his urchin in an unusually subdued frame of mind when he entered the large, sun-filled chamber some minutes later. He bent a stern eye on the small figure curled up in a large chair by the window.

"Your hot water is here, milord, and I unpacked your toilet articles, but I did not know what you wished to wear this evening," she murmured placatingly, dropping her eyes under that unrelenting gaze.

"Danielle, you should know by now that I do not expect you to play the role of servant when we are private, but if we are to brush through this ridiculous charade with any degree of success, you must maintain your part in public. That ill-conceived performance you have just put on for my cousin's benefit was foolish beyond tolerance. Do you choose to spend your life a social outcast immured in the depths of Cornwall? Because, make no mistake, my girl, that is exactly what will happen if any part of this escapade of yours becomes common knowledge!"

"You made me cross and I . . . I sometimes don't think very clearly when I am cross." It didn't sound much of an explanation even to Danny's ears and her guardian was clearly unimpressed.

"If by that you mean my attempt to bring you to your senses in the stableyard then you are even more foolish than I thought. You were looking at Julian with the doe eyes of a

81

heartsick debutante—hardly an appropriate expression for a servant lad!"

"He is very handsome," Danielle muttered and the earl shot her a startled look, surprised by a curious stab of a most unusual emotion—not jealousy, surely? Of course, his cousin was much closer in age to this disreputable vagabond than he, who was undoubtedly viewed as an irritatingly dictatorial guardian. He shrugged slightly. In both their interests it was a role he must maintain to the hilt, at least until he could hand the charge over to the Earl of March.

"He may be handsome, brat, but he is also a rake, as you will no doubt discover when you make your debut," he declared curtly, turning to his portmanteau for a change of shirt and cravat.

"My plans, milord, do not include making my debut," Danielle said steadfastly, deciding that since Linton was already out of temper now was as good a moment as any other to make her declaration.

"Now what the devil do you mean by that?" Linton went impatiently behind the dressing screen. "Of course you will make your come-out, unless you intend to marry some clod of a country squire and bury yourself amongst the cows in Cornwall."

"My lord, I should tell you that the promise I made in Paris must be withdrawn. I can no longer accept your protection."

If she had expected an explosion, she was disappointed. His lordship merely said, in a tone of polite interest, "Now why should that be, brat?"

"I have plans, milord, that I do not think you will approve. I am sure I can count on my grandfather's assistance, but I am afraid you will attempt to dissuade him."

This disengenuous statement brought a smile to the Earl of Linton's lips. "If they are anything like your usual plans, infant, I am sure you are right. Am I to know what they are?"

"I may be foolish, milord, but I am not an imbecile," Danielle stated with dignity. An involuntary shout of laughter came from behind the screen.

"However," she went on, disregarding this unseemly reaction as utterly contemptible, "I will not leave you until we

82

have met your Lord Chatham. I will help there in any way I can."

"Well, brat, I am obliged to you for informing me of these new developments. However, I should inform you that you will not be leaving me at all before I hand you into the charge of your grandfather." The earl reemerged, a new man in fresh linen and snowy lace, and reached for a soft silk coat of midnight blue, easing it over his shoulders, making minute adjustments to the ruffs at cuffs and throat before inserting a large diamond in the latter.

"I do not think, milord, that you will succeed in preventing me," Danielle pronounced stoutly.

At that His Lordship's eyebrows rose. "Oh come now, child, that is truly idiotish, if not imbecilic. I am only sorry that you wish to put me to the test, for it will add most considerably to the tedium of our journey, I do assure you. However, we must hope between here and London that you will come to your senses, for you are really not stupid at all," he added kindly, taking snuff from a pretty enameled box.

Danielle glowered at him in wordless indignation. She was strongly tempted to launch one of her tirades of abuse at this insufferably arrogant individual but that was a lesson she had learned well and wisely decided to keep her own counsel.

"I will not insist you remain abovestairs this evening," Linton continued thoughtfully, "although I do recommend it. You must certainly seek your bed at an early hour, however. You had little enough sleep last night and a long ride today. Shall I have your dinner sent up?"

"No, indeed not," Danny declared. "I will take my meal in the kitchen as befits the public role of a mere servant."

"As you wish," the earl said calmly, refusing to rise to the challenge. "You will stay out of trouble, though, won't you, brat?" He pinched her cheek carelessly before leaving the chamber to seek his dinner and his cousin in the private parlor.

The gesture for some reason infuriated Danielle. She muttered crossly as she used what water her companion had left to cleanse herself of the worst of her travel dust before making her own way to the kitchen and what proved a very convivial evening. Her ready wit and easygoing friendliness

83

endeared her rapidly to the large group of servers, wenches, and stablelads crowding the long kitchen table. Mrs. Jarvis, the innkeeper's lady, was a motherly soul who instantly decided that this scrawny lad was much in need of feeding and piled the wooden trencher in front of her with mounds of floury boiled potatoes and thick slices of mutton. Danny didn't particularly care for the taste of ale but the foaming pitchers passed back and forth down the table and, in the absence of anything more palatable, she sipped circumspectly, carefully hiding the involuntary moue of distaste.

Supper over, the group repaired to the stableyard to enjoy the first and last half hour of leisure their long working day afforded. Rising before the dawn, working without respite until the dinner hour, they would all seek their pallets by sundown. Thus it was that the Earl of Linton, strolling with Lord Julian after an excellent meal and a claret that was all and more than the landlord had promised, came across a sight that filled him with a black rage.

Danielle de St. Varennes, granddaughter of the Duc de St. Varennes and the Earl and Countess of March, was sitting astride a low wall alongside the well-kept stables, a foaming pewter tankard in her hand, regaling a laughing circle of louts in exaggeratedly broken English with some of the riper stories she had picked up in her wanderings.

The earl was beyond careful thought. Striding through the group who, one look at the dark face and blazing eyes, fell back hastily, he reached the startled figure of his ward. The tankard crashed to the ground, splashing its contents on all and sundry and the next minute Danielle was reeling on her perch, hands clapped to a pair of tingling ears.

"How dare you drink that!" her mentor hissed.

"But . . . but all the lads do," she protested in a shocked whisper.

The earl's face came very close to hers. "You, Danielle de St. Varennes, are *not* one of the lads, do you understand me?"

She shrank away from the naked fury in those black eyes and the hard, narrow line of his lips, managing only a wordless nod as the tears filling her eyes threatened to spill in a hot flood down her cheeks.

A pair of large hands caught her under the arms and she was swung through the air to land with a jolt on the cobblestones.

"Get to bed!" The earl turned on the curt command and strode back to where Lord Julian was standing in amazed wonder at the scene he had just witnessed. He had never seen his cool, deceptively lazy cousin lose his temper, let alone strike a servant.

"Gad, Justin! What was all that about? The lad was doing no harm, 'pon my soul."

"He's far too young to be drinking ale and has an insolent tongue to boot," Justin spat, struggling with the extraordinary emotions shaking him—fury at Danielle for her lack of conduct, but more so at himself and a deep regret for his violent reaction.

Lord Julian shrugged and suggested peaceably that they sample Mine Host's excellent port over a hand of piquet before retiring. My Lord concurred. He needed time to calm himself and for Danny to get to bed before he attempted to repair the damage. Lord Julian, however, found him an abstracted companion and achieved the unheard-of success of rising from the table a hundred guineas ahead.

"Lud, Justin, but you've windmills in your head tonight. You gave me that last hand, I swear."

"Probably, Julian, probably. I cannot imagine how else you should have succeeded in taking such a sum from me. You play as abominably as ever."

"That's the outside of enough, Linton. I take every hand from you and you insult my skill."

The earl laughed softly. "Come out of the boughs, Julian. You find me somewhat distracted tonight."

A sharp look crossed the heavy-lidded eyes as Julian refilled his glass. "Nothing to do with that lad of yours, coz, I suppose?"

"I cannot imagine why it should be," Linton murmured dismissively. "No, I must see Pitt tomorrow and the news I have of France will not please him."

The red herring worked as well as he had hoped and all thoughts of the strange waif his cousin had in tow left Lord Julian as he questioned with an intelligent eagerness belied by

85

the slightly vacuous look he cultivated.

It was considerably later, when, his cousin's curiosity satisfied, My Lord took his candle and made his way to bed. A soft knock eliciting no response, he unlatched the door gently and entered the dark chamber. Danielle had extinguished all the tapers before retiring to her cot in the corner—a gesture that could have been interpreted as unfriendly had the earl not strongly suspected she required the cover of darkness in which to lick her wounds. He placed his own candle beside the bed and lit the tapers above the mantel before crossing to the cot and examining the diminutive mound under the covers. His urchin was definitely asleep, but the tear-streaked cheeks and sticky lashes bore witness to the outburst of emotion that had preceded sleep. Linton sighed, bending to pull the disarrayed cover over the slight shoulders before blowing out the candles on the mantel and making his own preparations by the single, dim, flickering light by the bed.

Chapter 5

The Earl of Linton woke to an empty chamber and a countryside shrouded in that fine English mizzle that made the seasons in this damp land so hard to differentiate. It was definitely not riding weather and he reconciled himself to completing the last leg of the journey to London by post chaise.

The parlor, in which a bright fire now glowed, was also empty of everything except his breakfast. He had not expected to find his cousin, for whom the matutinal hours before ten o'clock were supposed not to exist, but he had expected some indication of his urchin's whereabouts. An inquiry of the wench who served him his coffee produced the information that Danny had been seen by Mrs. Jarvis at around six o'clock but not since.

The earl frowned at his sirloin, wondering if Danny had thought better of her agreement to remain with him until London, but he dismissed the suspicion as unworthy. The child quite clearly had a very rigid code of honor and even if she were laboring under a sense of injustice would not break her word.

In fact, the subject of his thoughts was making her damp way back across the fields after a sorely needed period of quiet reflection. She had awoken before the first bird song and making her way to the kitchen had found that hub of the hostelry already seething with life. She had been bidden to the breakfast table by the motherly Mrs. Jarvis but had accepted instead a meat pasty and an apple and set off on a long trudge across the surrounding countryside. Her reflections had been

87

gloomy and the steady drizzle had done nothing to spark her usual optimism. Milord appeared to take his guardianship much more seriously than she had thought, as last evening's episode so clearly demonstrated. It seemed to encompass far more than a simple concern for her physical welfare. That being the case he would, without doubt, do his possible to prevent the furtherance of her plans once she reached Cornwall. She had hoped, she now realized naively, that once she had effected her escape from his protection that apparent careless lethargy of his would persuade him to put the entire episode out of mind. His fears for her safety, now she was out of France, must surely be considerably allayed and he would know that a simple and relatively short journey across England would be easily accomplished by one who as a fugitive had made the infinitely longer and more hazardous trip from Languedoc to Paris. But he seemed to have some strange and most exasperating notions about the manner in which Danielle de St. Varennes should proceed both now and in the future.

Pausing, she threw her apple core into a small stream, watching the circle of ripples widen on the rain-pitted surface of the sluggish brown water. She had ceased to think of herself as Danielle de St. Varennes since that February night, had concentrated only on a plan that required the identity of "Danny" to carry it through. But the Earl of Linton seemed only to acknowledge Danielle and his constant reminders of this person were disturbing, forcing her out of hiding in the deep recesses of the mind of Danny. Now she seemed to slip with bewildering rapidity from urchin to aristocrat and the only fact of which she was absolutely convinced was Linton's determination that she assume the latter role permanently, at the earliest possible moment.

Maybe her grandparents, whom she remembered as a gentle, kindly couple, would share Linton's view of the matter and be much less amenable to persuasion than she had anticipated? But she could not return to France without their help—or someone's at least—and return she must, albeit for as brief a stay as possible. She had a task to complete and not all the Earls of Linton should stand in her way. She had reached this rousing decision as she attained the courtyard of the Red Lion to come face to face with her protector who was about to sally forth in search of his errant ward.

"Good morning, Danny," His Lordship murmured courteously, stepping aside to allow her entrance into the inn.

"Morning." She made to brush past him, but a lazy hand took her wrist.

"You appear to be rather wet, brat."

"It's raining."

"Yes, I had noticed," he concurred silkily. "I think you had better change your clothes before we continue our journey."

"Why? I shall only get wet again." Danielle was painfully aware that she sounded like a sulky child but somehow could do nothing to alter her tone.

"Ah, but you see, you won't," the earl said gently, flipping open his silver snuff box and one-handedly taking a delicate pinch. "We shall travel today by post chaise."

Danny wrinkled her nose disgustedly. "But it's only twenty miles and a little rain hurt no one."

"It will hurt me, my child. I am sorry to inconvenience you, but I really must insist." The long fingers tightened for an instant around the fragile bones of her wrist. "I would like to leave within the quarter hour so you would oblige us both by making all speed to don some dry clothes. Of course," he added pleasantly, "should you find yourself in difficulties in this matter, I should be most happy to assist you."

Danielle twitched her wrist out of the immediately relaxed hold. "Your assistance, my lord, will not be necessary," she stated frigidly and went off with as much dignity as she could muster in the direction of their bedchamber.

Linton looked after her with quivering lip. She was definitely going to be more than the Earl of March and his countess could manage alone. His suspicion that the peaceful pattern of an existence ruled only by his own desires and comforts had been permanently destroyed on that sunny April afternoon in Paris was rapidly becoming a certainty.

The post chaise was light and well sprung—an infinite improvement on the heavy conveyance that had accommodated them through France—and they made the twenty-mile journey in three hours reaching My Lord's town house in

Grosvenor Square soon after the noon hour. Danielle forgot her aggrieved sullens as they clattered through the London streets. The sights, sounds, and smells of this seething metropolis entranced her. So different was the atmosphere here from the dreariness of Paris with its sense of brooding menace hanging in the narrow, fetid alleys. There was squalor and poverty here too, and the gutters ran malodorously with the soil of the city's inhabitants in the crowded houses rising alongside the cobbled streets, at times almost seeming to touch their opposite neighbor, forming an archway over the narrow lanes. But there was elegance too and Danielle gazed open-mouthed at the quiet squares with their tall mansions, the constant traffic of barouches, landaus, phaetons, curricles passing down the broader thoroughfares, their exquisite passengers bowing and smiling to acquaintances. She gazed longingly at the riders, briefly glimpsed behind the railings of Hyde Park, and for the first time in months felt an unaccountable urge to be rid of her boy's clothes. But, however did women manage to walk in those wide hooped skirts, those enormous panniers at the side? And the coiffures! Enormous powdered creations, adorned with waving ostrich plumes, stuffed birds, and even more exotic articles. The isolated life of Languedoc had not required the extravagances and fripperies of the fashionable city and indeed was many years behind in fashion—a fact which her mother had frequently lamented but had never repined over. Or if she had, Danielle frowned suddenly, had certainly kept it to herself.

Her companion, guessing fairly accurately at what was passing through his ward's mind, watched her open delight and wide-eyed wonder with amusement and a degree of pity. It had been an act of near criminal negligence to keep this enchanting scion of a noble family from her birthright, immured in the fastnesses of a wild, uncivilized backcountry.

The chaise drew up outside Linton House and instantly the enormous front door swung open. A liveried footman let down the steps, opened the door, and bowed his lordship and the disheveled scrap of humanity behind him onto the pavement. Danielle hung back, suddenly shy, but the earl took her hand in a warm, reassuring grip.

"You have nothing to fear. These are my people. Just say nothing and do exactly as you are bid."

For once that instruction provided comfort rather than irritation. She followed her guardian up the flight of well-scrubbed steps into an enormous high-ceilinged hall with a wide curving flight of shallow stairs rising gracefully to the floors above.

"Welcome, my lord." A most elegant, black-clad figure moved sedately with measured tread across the gleaming tiled floor to greet them. His gaze flicked across Danielle but the shocked surprise in those calm gray eyes was instantly extinguished.

"Thank you, Bedford. I shall be in town only one night to transact some business. The lad is to have the Blue Room. Have it prepared and hot water for a bath sent up. I will also require Petersham in about fifteen minutes and if Mr. Haversham is in the house please ask him to wait on me in my bookroom in one hour. You may bring some Madeira into the library." Still holding Danielle's hand, the earl turned briskly and went through the door held by an impassive footman into the luxurious book-lined saloon on one side of the hall, facing the street.

Danielle looked around appraisingly. She was not awed by the magnificence of the Aubusson carpet, the delicate Sheraton and Chippendale furniture, the heavy brocaded curtains at the long windows. The de St Varennes château, albeit in the wilds, had commanded all the elegancies of life. Neither was she intimidated by Milord's servants, although they carried themselves with a deal more consequence than would have been tolerated under the feudal regime operating in Languedoc. But she was very interested in His Lordship's life-style. He was clearly a man of considerable wealth.

A discreet knock at the door was followed immediately by Bedford with a silver tray on which reposed a cut glass decanter and two crystal wineglasses. No one was to know the anguish that had wracked this austere gentleman as he wondered whether he was to provide a glass for His Lordship's extraordinary companion. To do so could be an unforgivable solecism but there was something about the way the earl had been holding the lad's hand, a sort of proprietorial possessiveness that caused his butler to opine that a lack of courtesy to this unusual guest might be an even more unforgivable solecism. He was much relieved, therefore, when His Lordship made no comment on the contents of the tray.

"Would Your Lordship care for a nuncheon?" Bedford inquired.

"I think not, but you may have a tray sent up to the Blue Room." Linton poured the golden wine and handed his brat a glass, waiting until the butler had left the room before raising his own in a toast.

"Let us drink to the end of this masquerade, *mon enfant.* A few more days will see the finish. It is unfortunate that your grandparents have remained in the country for the Season, otherwise I could have restored you to them within the hour."

Danielle was not convinced that this was an unfortunate circumstance but kept her reflections to herself, merely sipping her wine appreciatively, surprising His Lordship with an informed comment on the vintage.

"You know wine, child?"

"My grandfather's cellar was renowned throughout France. I was interested, so he taught me," she said carelessly. "I am thought to have an excellent palate. *Grandpère* always trusted my judgment at the tastings."

Linton wondered how many more surprises this brat had up her sleeve. He strongly suspected that he had but glimpsed the tip of the iceberg.

"I am going to leave you for a few hours, Danielle." He held up his hand as she began a dismayed protest. "You will be quite safe. No one will disturb you, I promise. You may take a long bath, have some nuncheon, rest, read a book maybe?"

At his last words her eyes lit up. "I haven't seen a book since February. May I look now?"

"My library is at your disposal, infant."

Danielle roamed the shelves in an absorbed silence, commenting only, "They are well catalogued, my lord."

"I have an excellent secretary." Her choice fascinated him—a copy of Pliny's essays and Montaigne for, he presumed, a little light relief.

"If you are sure you have enough to occupy you for an hour or so, perhaps you would like to go to your chamber." His voice shook slightly and Danny gave him a suspicious look.

"Does something amuse you, sir?"

"Not at all," he denied hastily. "But tell me, do you ever read novels?"

"They have rarely come my way," she replied simply.

My Lord preceded her up the stairs, wondering yet again at the effect this wine connoisseur and bluestocking was going to have on London society. Next Season was going to be most interesting, of that he was in no doubt.

The Blue Room was a haven of warmth and comfort. A fire blazed in the hearth and candles glowed softly, chasing away the dank, dark afternoon glowering outside the long windows facing the square. A maid servant rose hastily from her knees beside the large porcelain tub at their entrance and bobbed a curtsy.

"I hope everything is to your satisfaction, my lord. And if the young gentleman should need anything he has only to ring."

"Thank you." The earl smiled. "It's Molly, isn't it?"

The rosy cheeks blushed scarlet as the girl bobbed another curtsy. "Yes . . . yes, my lord, it is," she stammered in confusion, quite overset by this unlooked for and most unusual recognition. The door closed on her somewhat precipitate retreat and Danielle looked approvingly at Linton.

"That was well done, indeed, milord. Do you know all your servants by name?"

"Alas no, infant," he confessed ruefully. "I cannot claim that credit, merely lucky chance in this instance. The girl is the granddaughter of my housekeeper and as such was once presented to me."

"But you remembered. I have been wishing just recently that I had taken the trouble to learn something of our servants in Languedoc." There was a dispirited note in the soft voice which the earl made haste to dispel.

"You know what they say about spilt milk, Danielle." He examined the linen-covered tray on the table. "You have a most delicious nuncheon, brat. I suggest you address yourself

93

to it without delay."

Danielle peered at the baked egg, the bread and butter, roasted chicken wing, and custard tart. A glass of sherry and a pot of tea accompanied the repast. "I think your advice is sound, sir." Her eyes gleamed mischievously. "You may safely leave me to my own devices, milord. I look forward to a few hours of luxurious solitude."

Linton laughed. "I will fetch you something to wear after your bath." To her amazement he left through a door in the far wall and she heard an unfamiliar voice from the neighboring room before the earl returned with a velvet robe over one arm.

"You will be quite lost in this, I fear. But it will have to serve in the absence of anything more suitable."

"Who is in there?" Danielle gestured to the half-open door.

"Petersham, my valet."

"That is your chamber, then?"

"Yes." He frowned at her concerned face and then, as comprehension dawned, smiled reassuringly. "I wished you near me, child. I thought perhaps you might be more comfortable too, knowing I was within calling distance. Was I mistaken?"

Danielle shook her head slowly. "No, milord. I find the thought of your proximity most reassuring. This is all a little unfamiliar, you see."

"I do see, infant. Now, you need have no fear that you will be disturbed unless you so choose and I must attend to my business." Yielding to a sudden impulse he laid a gentle finger under her chin, tipping her head and dropping a light kiss on the upturned nose. Danielle looked startled, but made no attempt to draw back. Such caresses had rarely come her way, the de St Varennes not being given to displays of affection, but she decided that this salute was infinitely preferable to her boxed ears of the previous evening.

"You are going to be a most beautiful woman one day, Danielle de St Varennes," the earl said softly. "I am amazingly eager to see the transformation."

The next instant she was alone, one finger absently rubbing the tip of her nose where his lips had just rested.

With immense relief the earl once more placed himself in

Petersham's able hands, doing his best to ignore the hurt, disapproving sniffs that accompanied that gentleman's ministrations. The valet's pride had been sorely wounded by his master's refusal to allow him to accompany him on his journey to France and since he was also to be left behind when Linton journeyed into Cornwall, His Lordship deemed it sensible to do nothing to soothe the ruffled feathers at this point. He would only have to repeat the process on his return.

He emerged from his bathing chamber much refreshed and nodded his approval of the coat of blue superfine with silver buttons that Petersham had laid ready on the bed.

"The *perruque à bourse*, I think," he decided firmly, sitting at the dresser mirror to tie the cravat reverently handed to him. Whilst traveling, particularly without his valet, he preferred not to be bothered with the wigs and powder considered de rigueur in Society but in the comfort of home bowed to the edicts of fashion and concealed his own black locks beneath a variety of wigs. As he was adjusting one of these creations with careful fingers under the anxious gaze of Petersham the most unusual sound drifted through the room. The earl's fingers stilled for an instant and the valet's eyes widened. Someone was singing. A pretty, lilting voice, quite unmistakably female, trilled the melody of a very familiar French folk song.

After the barest hesitation, Linton continued his toilette. "I have often remarked, Petersham," he observed calmly, "that one of your most priceless qualities is a certain gift of deafness—selective deafness. You understand me, I'm sure." His eyes met those of the other man in the mirror.

"Perfectly, my lord." The valet bowed and handed the earl his snuffbox.

Justin made his way down the stairs, reflecting with amused exasperation that he must inform his ward that singing in her bath was, on this occasion at least, a somewhat indiscreet activity.

"Ah, Peter, I am returned to plague you, I fear." He greeted the somber-suited young man, who rose instantly from the desk at his entrance to the book room.

Peter Haversham, the younger son of an impoverished baronet, considered himself very fortunate to have found

95

employment as secretary to the Earl of Linton. Not only was His Lordship a most considerate employer, he was also deeply involved in his country's political activities, particularly those overseas. This involvement was known to few, the earl preferring to cultivate for more public consumption the demeanor and life-style of a leader of the ton, but for the young man with strong political ambitions no better patron could be found. So it was with very genuine disclaimers that Mr. Haversham responded to My Lord's greeting.

"Your business in Paris was successful, I hope, Lord Linton?"

"Depressing, Peter, very depressing—and unexpectedly fatiguing," Linton added with a slight smile. "Will you take a glass of Madeira, dear boy?"

He poured the wine before seating himself behind the large carved desk. "I have a task for you, Peter, admirably suited to your talents—in particular to your gift for tact and discretion."

The young man bowed, wondering with interest what his employer was about to demand of him.

"A letter to Pitt," Linton went on calmly, "requesting a meeting, most urgently, for this evening. At a time that will be convenient to him, of course, but if you could manage to convey that a relatively early hour would be most convenient for me, I should be obliged to you." An eyebrow lifted questioningly.

"Of course, my lord."

"You are a prince amongst secretaries," Linton murmured. "You will explain to Pitt that I shall have a companion—a young lady—who has some information that he will find invaluable. I see you look startled, Peter?"

"Not at all, sir." The young man made haste to deny the charge.

"You will also convey that this young lady's identity must be kept secret, for reasons of her own, but that I will vouch for the truth of her story and the reliability of her information. I beg his indulgence in this regard. . . . You will understand how to put the matter, I am sure, Peter."

"I shall do my best, my lord."

"Yes, I know you will, dear boy. I shall be going into the country tomorrow for a se'enight, maybe longer, so if there are any matters requiring my immediate attention perhaps we could deal with them now." The earl sipped his Madeira thoughtfully, regarding the inscrutable countenance of the young man with a degree of well-concealed amusement. He could well imagine the speculation going on behind that broad, intelligent brow.

"You are going to Danesbury, my lord? There are some small matters of the estate that need your attention."

"No, Peter, my destination, I fear, is not to be Danesbury," Linton said uninformatively.

"In that case, sir, there is nothing but some invitations to which I will send your regrets. Do you expect to return for the Duchess of Devonshire's ball?"

The earl frowned. "No, I think, Peter, that I shall contrive to be out of town on that day. Regretfully, of course."

"Of course." A gleam of amusement flickered in the cool green eyes. Peter Haversham was well aware of his lordship's bored distaste for the "squeezes" of the Season.

"I will leave you to your work, then. Would you inform Bedford that I shall dine at six o'clock in my apartments. He should lay covers for two? One course will suffice as I will not wish to be disturbed."

Peter bowed, imagining the consternation and havoc this message would wreak in the kitchen where its master was already joyously involved in preparations for a magnificent repast to welcome His Lordship's return. His artistry had little enough opportunities for creative fulfillment during the earl's absences.

A smart curricle stood at the door to Linton House, a wiry lad holding the heads of a pair of beautifully matched blood chestnuts, as Justin emerged into the sullen afternoon. It was no longer raining, but an overcast gray sky hung low over the town.

"They look fresh, Tomas," His Lordship observed, climbing into the curricle and taking the reins between his gloved hands.

"Beggin' your pardon, me lord, but they've the devil in 'em.

97

Been eatin' their 'eads off for the last week," the tiger replied.

Justin only laughed. "Stand away then."

The lad released their heads and the pair sprang forward, hardly giving the agile figure time to leap up behind. Linton steadied them with a barely perceptible movement of his wrists and the magnificent equipage set off at a well-controlled trot out of the square, totally unaware of the pair of envious brown eyes watching from a second-floor window.

Madame Lutèce, alerted by a wide-eyed servant girl, hurried into her shop as the Earl of Linton, with the brisk injunction to Tomas to walk the horses as he'd not be above a half hour, descended from the curricle outside her Bond Street establishment.

"My lord, this is indeed an honor. How can I be of service?" The beautifully gowned figure swept a curtsy, hiding her sharp-eyed speculative look beneath lowered lashes.

The earl brushed a speck of dust from an immaculate forearm before replying. "I wish for an afternoon gown for a young lady, madame."

"Might I ask how young, milord?"

"Very young," Linton informed her succinctly. "Also rather small."

Madame schooled her features. If the Earl of Linton was setting up his mistress from amongst the infantry that was no concern of hers, although reliable rumor had it that Linton's tastes ran to the more sophisticated members of the demimonde.

"Something . . . demure . . . perhaps, milord?"

"We understand each other perfectly, madame."

A shrill stream of orders was issued to the waiting girls hovering in the background and within minutes a selection of crisp muslins, some sprigged, some figured, all in the first style of elegance was being paraded before His Lordship's knowledgeable eyes.

"That, I think." He pointed to a delicate pale green gown, sprigged with flowers in a darker shade with deep green velvet knots adorning the sleeves and a taffeta sash of the same color. It would be worn with a modest white fichu at the neck and a slight hoop.

"About fittings?" Madame inquired tentatively.

"There will be none." The earl took snuff, snapping the box and replacing it in the deep pocket of his coat before looking around the group of girls surrounding Madame. "You, child." He beckoned and the smallest member of the group stepped forward hesitantly. "Would you oblige me by trying the gown?" A warm smile accompanied the request, lightening Milord's somewhat intimidating countenance.

The child was a little fuller in the bosom than Danielle and a little shorter, but apart from that of very similar size. He gave madame his instructions regarding these matters coolly before continuing with the quiet request that she procure all the necessary garments to accompany the gown.

"Everything, my lord?" The astounded modiste could not keep the astonishment out of her voice.

The earl did not reply, merely raised his glass and examined her with haughty indifference until those sharp eyes dropped and a slight discomfited flush tinged the sallow cheeks.

"Do you find yourself in difficulties over this, madame?"

"No, no, not at all, my lord. I will send one of the girls to the milliners for . . . for everything. You . . . you will require slippers also?"

"Everything. Also a warm cloak and a veiled bonnet. Is it quite clear?" He smiled pleasantly.

"Quite clear, my lord. When will you be requiring the articles?" Madame Lutèce struggled for composure. Never had she received such a request in all her years as unrivaled modiste to the ton. She was to scour the town for petticoats, chemises, pantalettes, stockings—everything!

"Have them delivered by five-thirty, if you please."

Madame gasped. It was now three o'clock. But Justin, Earl of Linton, was a customer whose value could never be overrated. One day he would surely marry and his countess would then most certainly repay Madame's establishment for this minor inconvenience. Another deep curtsy saluted His Lordship's departure and with a piercing stream of invective directed at her luckless apprentices Madame Lutèce gave vent to her injured dignity and furious frustration at the task facing her.

Blithely unaware of the dismayed furor his visit had caused,

Linton continued on his way. A visit to his bankers, another to a well-known jewelers on Bond Street, and another to a discreet establishment where he procured toilet articles necessary to the comfortable travel of a young lady and he returned well satisfied to Grosvenor Square.

"Ah, my lord." Peter Haversham hurried across the hall at his entrance. "The prime minister will be happy to receive you at eight o'clock this evening. He has to be in the House for a vote at eleven o'clock but hopes this will be convenient."

"Perfectly, Peter." The earl preceded the secretary into the library. "I must ask you for one other small favor, I think . . . Ah, thank you, Bedford. Yes, you may pour me a glass of the claret."

"What would you wish done with the packages from Madame Lutèce's establishment, my lord?" The butler handed his master a glass, keeping both face and voice bland.

"Have them taken to my apartments and inform Petersham that I shall not require his services until later tonight. I shall not be changing for dinner."

"Yes, my lord." Bedford left the library, now firmly convinced that His Lordship was more than a little mad, unless he had been dipping very deep, which would be easier to understand but equally unlikely.

"Just so, Peter, just so," the earl observed coolly, seeing the broad grin on the young man's normally well-disciplined face. "Poor Bedford! I am sure he is convinced I have windmills in my head. Of course, he may be right," Linton added reflectively. "I begin to wonder myself."

"My lord!" Haversham was deeply shocked, but Justin just laughed.

"If I have, Peter, they are remarkably enchanting ones. Now, I shall be traveling by post tomorrow, so please see to it, will you?"

"You wish me to hire you a chaise, sir?"

The earl raised his glass. "That is what I said, I think," he commented gently.

"You will not be using your own coach, then?" the secretary mumbled lamely.

"Well, it might be a little difficult to travel in two carriages simultaneously, don't you agree?"

"I will see to it right away, Lord Linton." The young man bowed stiffly. "You wish for hired postillions?"

"Indeed. But I will take two of my own riding horses, should the chaise become *too* uncomfortable a mode of conveyance." A sweet smile accompanied the soft statement.

The earl's apartments consisted of his bedchamber, dressing room and bathing chamber, and a well-appointed paneled sitting room. It was to the latter that he now repaired. A table was laid for dinner *à deux* before the glowing hearth and a footman drawing the heavy crimson velvet curtains against the unwelcoming dusk turned at his entrance.

"Do you wish to be served, my lord?" he asked expressionlessly.

"No, you may leave everything on the sideboard. I shall serve myself." Linton went through to his bedchamber. Madame Lutèce's packages covered the bed and with a slight smile he rapped briskly on the door connecting this room to the Blue Room.

"Oui?" The soft voice sounded hesitant.

"May I come in, Danny?"

"Bien sûr, milord."

Danielle was curled on the chaise longue under the window, completely enveloped in the dark brown velvet robe. She looked gratifyingly pleased to see him.

"I was feeling excessively lonely, milord. It is very strange to be locked in a strange room in a strange house when you can hear so many things going on around and you have no part in them."

"But you were not locked in, Danny?" Linton picked on what he decided to be the central point in this swift-spoken speech.

"Well, I might just as well have been," she stated flatly. "I cannot imagine that your household would have appreciated my appearance if I floated through the hallways in this robe—like Lady Macbeth!"

"I am sure you're right, brat." His lips twitched at the image thus created. "Come now, I have a surprise for you."

"A surprise!" The small figure leapt to her feet, gathering up

101

the voluminous folds of the robe as she stumbled across the room toward him. "I have never had a surprise, milord. At least," she added ingenuously, "not a nice one."

This matter-of-fact declaration had a strange effect on My Lord Linton, creating a most odd sensation in his throat.

"Well, infant, I trust you will find this one pleasing," he commented dryly, repressing the unwelcome emotion and bowing her ceremoniously into his bedchamber.

Danielle gazed wide-eyed at the parcels and bandboxes. "But what are they, milord?"

"Would you have me spoil the surprise, child? Open them."

With that total lack of inhibition or embarrassment that no longer surprised him although continued to entrance him, Danielle tore open the packages and with exuberant delight began to prance around the room, holding the delicate garments against her, rubbing her cheek against the soft fragrance of the finest linen. She seemed as delighted with the frilled pantalettes as she was with the gown and the dainty kid slippers.

"Am I to wear them, milord?"

"That was certainly my intention," he remarked gravely. "Unless you have an alternative suggestion."

Two dimples peeped. "Idiot!"

"Do not be impudent, brat," he chided with mock severity. "Go and dress yourself. Our dinner awaits and I have an inordinate dislike of cold food."

Danielle gathered up the clothes and then, under his startled gaze, her face fell in a look of almost comical dismay.

"Whatever is it, Danny?"

"Well . . . well . . . you see, milord, I have never dressed myself before."

"Odd's breath!" Why had he not thought of that? Of course, until her flight she would never have had the need and since then had worn nothing but britches—much easier to manage than the bewildering array of ribbons, buttons, and laces that were the necessary accompaniments to female attire. In the circumstances he could hardly summon a maidservant to assist her and the Earl of Linton resigned himself to the inevitable.

"I will help you, child. I am becoming increasingly accustomed to new roles these days. Do what you can and call me when you need assistance."

Danielle looked rather doubtful but accepted his offer without demur and returned to the Blue Room where she struggled doggedly with the myriad of tiny buttons at the back of the soft lawn chemise. Her violent expletive reached His Lordship and he entered her room without ceremony.

"This is quite absurd," she declared roundly. "How can one be expected to fasten buttons at the back when one does not have eyes at the back of one's head and one's hands face the wrong way?"

"Quite impossible, brat," he said soothingly, moving behind her, trying not to notice that the unbuttoned chemise left most of her breasts exposed. He had undressed her the other night, but his only thought on that occasion had been to rid a desperate, nausea-wracked scrap of humanity of a burden of sodden clothing as quickly as possible. This, however, was very different. In the silken stockings and white pantalettes she looked as feminine and as desirable as any one of the many women he had seen in a similar state of undress. Fortunately for them both, Danielle seemed quite unaware of her charms and in fact had become so accustomed to the intimate presence of the Earl of Linton that she would have been astounded could she have read his thoughts at this moment.

"Thank you, sir." With a totally unselfconscious gesture she adjusted the now fastened garment over her breasts and picked up the corset with a look of distaste. "Is this really necessary, do you think?"

"I fear so," he said solemnly. "The gown will not fit properly without it. But we need not, I think, lace it too tightly. You have a naturally small waist."

That did bring a tinge of color to the creamy cheeks but she said nothing, merely held the offending garment to her front and gave him her back.

Linton smiled to himself as he fastened the laces with deft fingers, resisting the urge to run his hands over the soft curve of her neat little bottom.

"You appear, milord, to have had a deal of practice in these

103

matters. You have had, I suppose, many mistresses?" Danielle moved away from him, stepping daintily into the first of her three petticoats.

"That, Danielle, is *not* a subject for polite conversation," he said repressively.

"Well, I hardly think this is an arena for polite conversation." Her eyes twinkled mischievously and those dimples danced again.

His lips twitched. "Perhaps not, but I do beg you will confine such remarks to the privacy of our own company. I may not find them improper, but others will."

Danielle pulled a face which expressed all too clearly what she thought of those "others" and which filled the earl with a sense of foreboding.

Danielle surveyed the hoop as if it were a rather dangerous member of the animal kingdom. "Just how, milord, is one supposed to walk through doors with that?"

"It is a very small hoop, infant. You will have no difficulty and will soon learn to deal quite well with much wider ones and panniers too. Now let us hurry. I am exceedingly sharp set and our dinner cools whilst you argue. We have an appointment with Pitt at eight o'clock."

"Oh, so that is why I am to be dressed in this way. Is your prime minister to know my identity?" This speech was somewhat muffled as her head disappeared inside the flounces of the gown which the earl dropped over her.

"No. And he will not see your face either." She was turned briskly as her self-styled maid hooked the gown at her back. "You will speak only French and answer only those questions asked of you. There will be no necessity to volunteer information as Pitt will know exactly what he wishes to find out. Now, turn around and let us take a look at you."

She turned slowly to face him, suddenly quite unaccountably shy. The clothes felt very strange and uncomfortably constricting and it had been so long since she had seen herself dressed as a girl that she could not imagine how she looked.

The earl put up his glass and examined the small figure. The gown was a perfect fit and the soft swell of her bosom, uplifted by the stays beneath, rose tantalizingly at the neck.

"I was quite wrong," he said slowly, "when I said you would be a most beautiful woman one day. You are already quite enchanting, milady."

Color mounted to the roots of the neat, short cap of pink-tinged curls. "Truly, sir?"

"Truly, Danielle. Look in the glass if you do not believe me." He took her shoulders, turning her to face the long pier glass, and she saw a young woman in a soft green gown that accentuated the ivory skin and deep brown eyes. Slender forearms and dainty wrists emerged from the froth of lace at the sleeves and the tiny waist was outlined by a broad sash. Small feet in pale green kid slippers peeped beneath a ruffled hem.

Linton left her for a moment, returning with a small box bearing the insignia of the jewelers he had visited that afternoon. Taking the dainty white fichu from the bed, he arranged it in the neck of the gown, covering her semi-exposed bosom. "Until you are out, child, you must maintain true maidenly modesty." He smiled.

"You once told me I did not have much to display," she accused, peering down at his skillful fingers.

"Did I really? How very indelicate of me," the earl murmured. "You must have annoyed me exceedingly." He opened the box and took out a small brooch of tiny diamonds and seed pearls, fastening it carefully in the fichu at her breast.

"Oh, how pretty!" Danielle breathed, fingering the delicate object. "Thank you for letting me wear it, milord. I promise I will take very good care of it."

"It is yours, Danny."

"But, my lord, I cannot. I . . . I have already taken so much from you," she stammered, flushing with dismay.

"Now you are being foolish again and quite ridiculously missish. I expect you to be awkward, stubborn, argumentative, and thoroughly disobliging, but not to be missish—a quality of the very young which I find both exasperating and boring!" she was informed roundly. "You will accept the brooch graciously and I will hear no more of this nonsense. Is it understood?"

"Perfectly, milord." Danielle sank into a beautifully

executed curtsy of just the right depth, extending a small, long-fingered hand as she rose. The earl received the tapered fingers in his, raising them to his lips as he bowed gracefully.

"Well done, Lady Danielle," he said approvingly. "I see that you *have* had an education in the finer points of etiquette."

"But of course, sir," she exclaimed. "Did you imagine I had not?"

"Most reprehensible of me," he murmured apologetically, "but you see, I have only, until now, encountered a grubby, sharp-tongued urchin of fearsome pride and independence, who rides, walks, talks, curses, and dresses like a veritable vagabond."

"I do not ride like a vagabond," she protested indignantly, seizing on that as the only part of his speech she could dispute.

"True, but I have not yet seen you ride as a lady," he reminded gently.

"Yes, well, that is something I do not care to do. If I may not ride astride I will not ride at all."

"In that case, my child, you will, I fear, be doing very little riding in the future."

Those eyes blazed at him. "What I do in the future, my lord, will be no concern of yours."

"How very wrong you are," he sighed. "Come now, Danielle, let us not quarrel tonight. You are looking far too adorable—it quite puts me at a disadvantage, and I know you believe in playing fair."

At that her mouth curved in a thoroughly impish grin, two deep dimples appearing in cheeks which were certainly less thin than they had been a few days ago.

"You mean, sir, that when I am dressed in this manner you find yourself unable to make threats against my person?"

"If you behave in a manner befitting your attire, I will find it quite unnecessary to do so. So, let us cry peace for a few hours."

The small head bowed a graceful acknowledgment. "Shall we dine, milord?"

Linton, with a slight bow, crooked his arm invitingly and, laying her hand on the fine cloth, she allowed him to escort her to the table.

The artist in the kitchen had had a bad time since receiving Bedford's relayed orders that afternoon, but nothing in the meal arranged in chafing dishes on the sideboard gave any indication of the tantrums that had shaken the lower regions of the mansion. Danielle did ample justice to the large carp in parsley sauce, a dish of buttered crab, and a saddle of mutton with mint sauce, but, to the earl's astonishment, rejected the dish of pastries and the rhenish cream in favor of a piece of stilton and an apple that he peeled for her with his tiny silver dessert knife.

"I have not a sweet tooth, you see," she informed him seriously. "*Grandpère* said it would ruin my palate and I daresay he was right. Anyway, I have not been in the habit of eating puddings, so do not miss them."

Linton hid a smile, wondering what this unusually sophisticated creature would do when faced with her first glass of ratafia, considered the only fit drink for young ladies. He must endeavor to be on hand when it happened, he decided— her reaction, if not forestalled, would inevitably be less than polite.

"I wonder what your household must think of all this disturbance and secrecy," Danielle remarked suddenly, taking an appreciative sip of her claret.

"I do not pay my staff to think," His Lordship replied dismissively. "Neither do I pay them to speculate on my activities."

"I am sure you do not," she retorted sharply, "but I cannot imagine that that will prevent them."

"Not so sharp, Danny, if you please," he warned mildly. "Your point is well taken, but it could have been made with more courtesy."

"You were a little sharp yourself, sir."

"My humble apologies, ma'am. If you have finished your dinner, I think we should leave."

The earl managed to get himself and his charge installed in the light town carriage bearing the Linton arms on its panels with only the smallest difficulty—Danielle having taken an inordinate dislike to the thickly veiled straw bonnet provided by Madame Lutèce. For a moment it had looked as if their earlier accord was in jeopardy until His Lordship had had the happy notion of concealing the offending hat under the capacious hood of the heavy velvet cloak. He refused to be budged on the subject of the veil, however, and eventually, with a martyred sigh, Danielle had capitulated, recognizing the common sense behind the need for secrecy whilst bemoaning the fact that, shrouded as she was, no one could see her finery. This small flash of vanity had pleased rather than annoyed her guardian, giving him grounds for hope that his urchin might accept with pleasure the eventual permanent resumption of her female role.

William Pitt, Earl of Chatham, now in his thirtieth year and his first term as prime minister after six years of steering his nation through a troubled sea of domestic strife, political reform, and overseas conquest, received them in his bookroom in the tall house near Westminster. He bowed the veiled figure to a chair beside the hearth before turning with raised eyebrows to her companion. "So, Linton, what news do you bring?"

"Depressing, sir," the earl replied, accepting a glass of port with a smile of thanks. "You will find Mademoiselle a more accurate informant than I, however. Her English is quite fluent, but I have asked her to speak only French. There is a need for discretion, sir. Her situation is somewhat delicate."

The prime minister bowed. "I am most grateful to you, mademoiselle, for allowing me this opportunity to talk with you. May I offer you some refreshment?"

"Since, sir, I must put up my veil in order to take it and I am not permitted to do so, I am afraid I must decline your kind offer."

A pained look crossed the Earl of Linton's face at this and Pitt's eyes widened in astonishment, but he said only, "Quite so, ma'am. It was a thoughtless suggestion."

"Oh dear," the soft voice murmured contritely. "It was not at all thoughtless but most kind in you, sir. I have a lamentable tongue when I am out of humor and milord is now looking very annoyed. If you will ask me your questions I will attempt to redeem myself for, I can assure you, sir, that it can be most uncomfortable when milord is cross with one." This disingenuous statement brought a choke of laughter to the lips of William Pitt and caused the earl to wish most fervently that he were alone with his brat. He was, however, obliged to hold his tongue and temper in check under the interested gaze of the prime minister.

"Would you tell me, mademoiselle, what you know of the States General?"

"Do you mean its structure, sir, its purpose, or how its efficacy is viewed by the people?"

"The structure as I understand it, mademoiselle, is made up of the three estates—the nobility, the clergy, and the commons. The first two outvote the third two to one?"

"That is correct, sir. Also, the commons must elect deputies to represent their interests and therefore vote indirectly, whereas the nobility and the clergy may vote directly. As to its purpose— The king is responding to a crisis in the old way by summoning parliament. Unfortunately there is some confusion. It has been over one hundred and fifty years since this body has been called into use and the system is not well understood by those presently responsible."

"And the people of France, mademoiselle. How do they react?"

"As far as I could gather, sir, with mixed feelings. There is a sense of hope—more so in the villages than in the towns. The townspeople are perhaps a little more cynical?"

Pitt nodded, his almost colorless eyes resting thoughtfully on the small, straight-backed figure. "You said feelings were mixed?" he prompted into the short silence.

"Oh, yes." Danielle recollected herself hastily. This interrogation was proving more difficult than she had imagined. Too many buried memories were being forced to the surface. "There is a degree of hope, but also of hopelessness and great anger—an anger born of desperation; the most dangerous kind, I fear, Milord Chatham." She glanced through her veil at the prime minister whose erect, concentrated posture was curiously at odds with his somewhat slovenly, negligent appearance. Receiving a short, affirmative nod she continued.

"At the moment the people still appear to trust their king

and to revere him. But for the Austrian there is only hate! She is seen as the author of all their misfortunes and the corruptor of their monarch."

"Do you also view Marie Antoinette in this light, mademoiselle?"

"'Toinette is a very foolish woman. She has no understanding of the responsibilities of her position, only of its advantages. While the people of France starve, their queen creates playgrounds for herself and her favorites, squandering the nation's bankrupt resources in full view of those who must choose between their own starvation or that of their children. Whilst Marie Antoinette plays milkmaid in the Petit Trianon, France weeps under a burden of tyranny and poverty that only the blood of its perpetrators will assuage." Danielle's voice remained evenly pitched throughout this speech, but the passion and emotion underlying her words were powerfully felt by both members of her audience.

"You are very sure of this, mademoiselle." The half question, half statement forestalled Linton as he was about to ask Danny if she would prefer to close the interview.

"I speak only of what I have heard and seen, sir. My own family were typical of the worst of their kind and have already suffered the fate that will overtake the rest if the States General achieves nothing. There are some members of the nobility who understand the dangers—the Comte de Mirabeau and the Duc d'Orléans, for instance. They, it is understood, will sit with the Commons and vote as representatives of the people and not of the nobility. The people's hopes rest with them and on the assumption that Louis XVI has their best interests at heart. He may well have, but his interpretation of their best interests is, I fear, at variance with the peoples'." This last was said with a sardonic cynicism that startled Linton although he realized that he should have expected it. This quiet, controlled individual seemed to bear no resemblance to the impish brat he had reluctantly assumed responsibility for. That brat had lived through and learned from a series of horrendous experiences that would have broken a lesser spirit. The woman who was just beginning to emerge from this

110

childish chrysalis would be special indeed. But Pitt was continuing.

"Mademoiselle, I understand and accept the need for discretion, but can you tell me nothing of your own story?"

"I am quite willing, sir, to tell you the whole. It is Milord Linton who has the so delicate notions of propriety."

"Oh, infamous, Danielle!" Linton murmured, offering his snuff box to the Earl of Chatham before himself taking a pinch.

"I can assure you of my absolute discretion, Linton." Chatham bowed carelessly in his direction.

"I do not doubt it, sir. You may put up your veil, brat, and tell what you choose."

The small figure rose instantly, casting aside the heavy velvet cloak and removing the despised bonnet and veil with a gesture of ill-concealed relief.

"I was like to roast in those swaddling clothes," she announced cheerfully, standing on tiptoe before the mirror above the mantel to adjust her disordered curls in a gesture so utterly feminine that Linton was hard put to keep a straight face. "Now, sir, I will take that refreshment, if I may?" She turned a dazzling smile on William Pitt, who bowed hastily and turned to the decanter. Whatever he had been expecting under the layers of disguise, it was not this sparkling creature in a gown of the first style of elegance.

"Would you perhaps prefer a glass of lemonade, mademoiselle, or perhaps ratafia?" He hesitated, decanter in hand.

"Not at all. If that is port, I should like it of all things."

"It is an excellent port, Danny," Linton assured her gravely. "Perhaps I should perform formal introductions. May I present the Earl of Chatham to the Lady Danielle de St. Varennes?"

"My lord." Danielle sank gracefully into her curtsy, rising as Pitt took her hand with a low bow.

"*Enchanté*, milady. You are, of course, Louise Rockford's daughter," he continued with a smile. "There is a strong resemblance, but the mouth and nose are pure de St. Varennes. Do you not agree, Linton?"

"Absolutely, Pitt."

111

Danielle took a sip of her port, frowned slightly, then gave a short approving nod. "It is indeed an excellent port, sir. Now, I will tell you my story and you will understand perfectly, *n'est-ce pas?*"

William Pitt the younger was not at all sure that he would ever understand anything perfectly again but he merely bowed courteously.

"Do, pray, be seated, sir. I will remain standing as I find it easier to think if I walk around." Danny gave him that dazzling smile again and Linton wondered uneasily if she were being deliberately coquettish. Those petticoats seemed to have wrought the damndest changes in his urchin.

She told her tale, however, with a quiet, articulate objectivity that held both men spellbound. The few questions that Pitt posed were answered pertinently with a deep frown of concentration as she sought the right words, using both English and French with the same ease.

"And then, sir, Milord Linton rescued me from a nasty baker who had most unpleasant designs upon my person and there the story ends."

"You have much courage, milady," Pitt said heavily, "but your impressions and information fill me with the deepest foreboding."

"That is only to be expected of a realistic mind, sir," she responded simply. "I do not know what is to be done, though."

"Your people will have many sympathizers in this country. Their struggles will be seen by some idealists as a great example."

"Fox, of course," Linton said thoughtfully.

"Of course, and Burke."

"*Mais, d'accord*, milord," Danielle said briskly. "But will they support the vengeance?"

"You anticipate much blood, Danielle?" Only Linton seemed aware that Pitt had used her first name as if he had known her from the cradle.

"I have seen the power of the mob, sir," she reminded him gently.

At that Linton rose gracefully. "If you have no further questions, Chatham, I think it is time Danielle sought her bed.

112

We have a long journey ahead of us."

"Indeed." Pitt chewed his lip thoughtfully before turning to Danielle. "Do you care to refresh yourself, Danielle, before you leave?"

"You are suggesting, I think, that I absent myself for a while, sir?" A slight curtsy and those peeping dimples accompanied the soft statement. "If you wish to be private with My Lord Linton you have only to say so."

"Oh, Danny," the earl sighed. "Such want of conduct, child!"

"I fail to see why the truth should be considered want of conduct," she declared stoutly. "If you will show me to your library, sir, I will endeavor to amuse myself."

When she had left, Pitt refilled both their glasses. "You will call on me, Linton, should you require any assistance when Danielle takes her place in Society?"

"I think it is Society who will require the assistance," Linton responded dryly.

Pitt laughed softly. "She is an extraordinary child, but sponsored by March will have all the right entrées." He gave his companion a shrewd look. "You, I imagine, will continue to hold the reins?"

"It seems my destiny," the earl replied calmly.

"It will require all your skill, my friend, and the lightest hand on the strongest curb!"

"Just so, Pitt."

"Well, you know I stand her friend and yours. Now, did you meet with Mirabeau?"

The earl sat in frowning silence as the light chaise made its way through the night streets of London prompting Danielle to inquire tentatively, "Are you still cross with me, milord?"

He sat up suddenly. "Cross with you? Why should I be, child?"

"Well, I do not really know, but . . . but . . . my want of conduct, perhaps?"

"Well, as I have had occasion to remark in the past, that is certainly deplorable," he replied briskly. "However, we shall

113

have some months to work on that particular problem before your come-out next Season." Ignoring Danielle's suddenly opened mouth, he continued coolly. "I am sorry if I appear abstracted, Danny. Your information and my subsequent discussion with Pitt have created some uncomfortable reflections. I will share them with you on our journey to Mervanwey—it is too late tonight."

With that she was obliged to be satisfied and in all honesty was far too fatigued either to question his blithe assumption about her future or to enter into any further political discussions.

The night porter bowed them into the hall of Linton House and the earl accompanied Danielle to the Blue Room where she was summarily unlaced, unbuttoned, and dismissed to her bed with the firm injunction that she refrain from bursting into song at her ablutions and be prepared to be up betimes in the morning.

That morning dawned bright and clear and Danny was awakened by the servant, Molly, who brought her hot chocolate, hot water, and her boy's clothes freshly laundered and pressed. Even the boots carried a shine that had taken the boot boy an hour to achieve.

"Breakfast, sir, will be served in the parlor behind the dining room." Molly bobbed a curtsy as she turned from drawing back the curtains and Danny buried her face in the pillows not at all anxious to be viewed in the full light of day by this young woman who was all too close to her in age. As the door closed behind the girl a dreadful thought struck her and she shot upright in the bed. What had happened to her clothes of the night before? She remembered only stepping out of them. It had not occurred to her to put them away. But they were nowhere to be seen and their absence only added to the curious dreamlike memories of the previous evening. Once dressed in her usual garments she became Danny again and indeed felt as if she had never been anyone else. Her task now was to evade the protection of the Earl of Linton at the earliest moment and proceed with her original scheme. The nagging doubts as to her ability to pursue this course she dismissed as an attack of morning megrims and having forced her curls into their rather unconvincing masculine style set off to find the breakfast parlor. In this she was ably assisted by a watchful footman and was ushered into the small room at the back of the house where Milord was already breaking his fast with a degree of enthusiasm.

"Ah, good morning, brat," he greeted her without ceremony. "You slept well, I trust?"

"Very well, thank you, sir." She took her place and examined the deviled kidneys, mushrooms, eggs, and ham with considerable appetite.

"May I carve you some ham?" the earl asked politely.

"If you please, milord. It is amazing how easy I find it to become accustomed to this English breakfast," she confided, pouring coffee. "In France it would be considered barbaric to begin the day with meat."

Linton's lips quivered slightly, but he maintained his composure as she piled her plate and silence reigned for some considerable time.

"Oh, milord?" Danielle suddenly looked up. "Do you know what happened to my clothes last night? I was most afraid Molly would see them this morning."

"I find I have an unexpected talent as lady's maid," Linton informed her dryly.

"Oh." Danielle absorbed this in thoughtful silence.

"You will find a portmanteau in your room. It contains those clothes and toilet articles for the journey," he went on calmly. "Within three days, I intend that you shall put on your petticoats permanently."

"Milord, I have told you . . ."

"Yes, I am well aware of what you have told me. I, however, have also told you certain things. We shall see whose plans prevail. If you are quite finished, I suggest we start for Cornwall."

"May . . . may we not discuss this, milord?" Danielle decided on one last try, an attempt at mature, dignified reasoning.

"There is nothing to discuss, Danny. You will endure my guardianship until I can give you into the charge of your grandparents. I quite understand that you find that fact

115

unpalatable and your position irksome. However, I should warn you that if you throw down the glove, I shall most certainly take it up. Shall we go?"

Tranquilly, Linton pulled out her chair and held the door for her and Danielle, the wind quite taken out of her sails, had no choice but to comply.

Just how difficult her guardian was going to be was revealed all too clearly when she emerged into the quiet·square. The hired chaise stood at the steps, an enchantingly pretty dappled mare, unsaddled, tied to the back, whilst His Lordship was standing at the stirrup of a magnificent glossy black.

"In you get, Danny," he instructed calmly.

"But you are riding!" she protested.

"I am."

"May I not also ride?"

"Not until we have left the town. I do not underestimate your resourcefulness, you see," he murmured almost apologetically. "And the opportunities for escape will be many in the streets. They are so crowded and narrow, you understand." A gentle smile accompanied the soft words. "Should you, of course, wish to renew your promise . . ."

Danielle responded to this with a cross sniff and climbed disgustedly into the chaise, leaving Linton to mount his horse, unsure whether the desire to kiss or to spank her was uppermost.

The next four hours passed for Danielle in lonely tedium and she clambered down with relief at their first changing post. The earl gave instructions for the mare to be saddled and ushered her into the inn. He made no attempt to explain her presence to the innkeeper judging that since he was traveling incognito, unless he had the misfortune to meet an acquaintance, speculation could harm neither of them. He put her himself into the saddle of the mare before mounting the black and then, to Danielle's momentary speechless indignation, reached across to take hold of the leading rein attached to the mare's bridle.

"You . . . you cannot!" she managed to gasp at last.

"Cannot what, brat?"

"Cannot lead my horse as if I were a baby!"

116

"You do not imagine, Danny, that I would be so foolish as to put you up on one of my horses without taking *some* precautions?" The note of polite incredulity brought an angry flush to her cheeks. "Of course," he continued mildly, "you may prefer to continue your journey in the chaise."

"Infinitely," Danny stated and without another word swung easily to the ground and returned to the stuffy discomforts of the carriage.

That night she ate her dinner in their chamber under the calm eye of her guardian who, once she had finished, bade her a polite good night and went to his own meal in the private parlor, locking the door behind him. He had bespoken a room on the third floor—not nearly as comfortable as the spacious chamber urged by the landlord, but one whose small window offered no chance for escape. Danny toyed only momentarily with the idea of knotted bedsheets—it was a device that she strongly suspected worked only between the pages of romances. By midmorning of the next day she was ready to exchange the coach for the hated leading rein and after three hours of this mortification decided that she was in no wise going to evade Justin, Earl of Linton. She would reach Mervanwey at the end of a leading string or riding independently, but he would be beside her.

"Milord?"

"Yes, Danny." He turned immediately toward her with that unfailing politeness.

"I will renew my promise."

The earl said nothing, merely leant sideways to unfasten the rein.

Danny looked speculatively at the broad green turf bordering the rather narrow road. "I should like to gallop, sir, and unless I much mistake this pretty lady would enjoy it also." The mare raised her head, sniffing the wind eagerly as if she understood and Linton laughed.

"Come then, child, let us try the lady against the stallion." Danielle was off almost before the words were out of his mouth, leaning low over the mare's neck as she encouraged the spirited filly to lengthen her stride. The black thundered behind them, drawing level, nostrils flaring at the excitement

117

of the race. For a while they kept pace, but Danny knew that her mare had not the chest of the earl's stallion and while she had the spirit to push herself to exhaustion must not be allowed to do so. As soon as she sensed the animal beneath her had reached her limit she drew back on the rein allowing the other to forge ahead, murmuring soft words of approval and encouragement as their pace slowed to one easily within the comfortable capacity of her mount. Linton, realizing what had happened, checked his stallion and she soon drew level again.

"You know your horse, Danielle," he observed.

"But of course. What rider does not?"

The earl kept his caustic response to himself. Danielle was clearly one of those riders for whom a lack of skill was quite incomprehensible. How she was going to accept a docile trot in Hyde Park in habit and sidesaddle, he did not know. Quite clearly some compromise must be found, but that was just another of those complications to add to the already long list he had formed.

Chapter 6

They reached Mervanwey on the afternoon of the third day. Their route took them by way of the coast road and Danielle was entranced by the contrast between the gentle green and gold countryside glowing under the soft spring sunshine and the awesome gray cliffs rising from a wild froth of surf as the dangerous blue green sea crashed against their wild, rocky foundations. They passed through small hamlets and fishing villages receiving only cursory interest from their inhabitants—the Cornish folk being a reclusive race, preferring to mind their own business rather than that of others and assuming the rest of the world would follow suit.

Mervanwey stood, a long, low house of mellow gray stone, atop a tall cliff overlooking the sandy beach of a rocky bay. The child Danielle had spent an idyllic summer running wild over the beaches and fields, exploring the rocks and winning her way into the hearts of the taciturn villagers and fisherfolk. Her cheerful conversation died as they took the steep road toward the house—those memories were too full of her mother to be welcome or comfortable ones and for the first time she wondered uneasily how her grandparents would receive her unorthodox and utterly unexpected arrival.

"Your grandparents are expecting you, child." Linton's quiet voice broke into her reverie, echoing her thoughts, and she looked at him in wonder.

"But how, milord?"

"I wrote to them from Paris," he replied calmly. "The

119

messenger will have arrived several days ago. He was instructed to make all speed."

"Do they also expect you?" she inquired hesitantly.

"I certainly hope so."

"And . . ., about . . . about *Maman*?"

"They know."

Relief washed through her and gratitude toward her self-appointed guardian who had foreseen and forestalled the unenviable task of informing the Earl and Countess of March of the violent, untimely death of their only, beloved daughter.

Lavinia, Countess of March, was in her rose garden overlooking the cliff road when the small procession wound its way up the steep path to the house. Her pruning sheers fell unheeded to the ground and, gathering the skirt of the faded gown she wore for gardening, she hastened toward the house, crossing the broad terrace to enter her husband's library by way of the open French doors.

"Charles, they are coming."

Instantly the Earl of March left his book and his chair to hold his wife for a brief moment before taking her arm and moving with her into the cool, flagged hallway and out into the warm sun of the circular sweep before the front door. Two riders were coming toward them some way ahead of the coach with its postillions and outriders lumbering up the steep drive.

"Is that Danielle, Charles?" Lavinia gazed in shocked amazement at the slight, boyish figure astride the dappled mare riding beside the unmistakable figure of Justin, Earl of Linton.

"She was always a tomboy, Lavvy," her husband remarked gently. "Like Louise, if you remember? I am sure Linton will explain all—there is bound to be a good reason."

The two riders reached them and the Earl of Linton swung easily from the large, black stallion, turning to lift Danielle's suddenly motionless figure from her own mount.

"As promised, March, I have brought you your grand-daughter," he said quietly. "Lady Lavinia." He made a magnificent leg toward the still stunned figure of the countess.

Black spots danced in the sunlight before Danielle's eyes, her heart and head began to pound painfully, and cold, clammy sweat broke out on her palms and forehead as panic quite unaccountably and unexpectedly swept through her. Gasping suddenly to draw breath from a tightly constricted chest she turned automatically in unspoken appeal toward the one person whose strength she had come to rely on unconsciously but absolutely.

Linton took the outstretched hand in a grip that crushed her fingers. "Quite so, Danielle," his voice reassured from a vast distance. "It is always strange to reach journey's end, particularly after such a journey as yours."

The Countess of March was a woman blessed with both common sense and wisdom. The look Linton bent on her granddaughter was one she recognized—she had seen it in her husband's eyes on many occasions and had been warmed to the depths of her soul by its love and tenderness. She wondered fleetingly if Danielle also recognized the look for what it was and suspected not—the child's eyes carried only trust and appeal.

Swiftly she moved forward, gathering the small figure to her ample bosom, enfolding her in loving arms, stroking and patting the narrow back with hands that still carried the soil of the rose garden beneath her fingernails.

"There, there, child. You are home now," she whispered softly against the wind-tangled curls. "No one will ever harm you again." Her eyes met those of her husband over the bent head and the Earl of March moved to enfold both wife and granddaughter in his own strong arms. At last Lavinia drew herself upright as practical necessities began to occur.

"We must get you out of those clothes, child," she declared briskly. "Do you have any others?" The question was ostensibly asked of Danielle, but she looked automatically at Linton.

"In the chaise, ma'am," he said calmly.

"Good. See to things, will you, Charles? If we move quickly we'll have Danielle looking respectable again before the household realizes what has happened. The less talk the better, even this far from London."

"My thoughts exactly, Lady Lavinia," Linton concurred with a smile and watched with considerable relief as his charge was whisked into the house by the energetic countess.

121

Charles gave quick orders as to the disposal of the luggage before extending his hand to Linton. "Come, Justin, we shall take a glass of sherry on the terrace. We owe you more than we can ever repay."

"You owe me nothing, Charles," Linton demurred quietly. "But the sherry I will accept with pleasure. The story, if you please, should wait for the return of the ladies. It is long and involved and bears telling only once."

"Indeed," March concurred gracefully and ushered his guest through the house and onto the flagged terrace overlooking the front lawn which stretched to the very edge of the cliff top.

They had taken but one sip of the dry wine when Danielle's outraged tones pierced the reflective quiet. Linton looked up with a frown. The sound floated across the garden from an open upstairs window overlooking the terrace.

"No! You may not take them. They are mine!" Her voice was rising alarmingly.

"What the devil?" March gazed in astonishment at Linton who put his glass down on a small table.

"I think, if you will excuse me, March, my presence is required upstairs before Danielle regales your entire household with some of the choicer epithets in her lamentably extensive vocabulary."

Linton strode swiftly through the house and up the stairs, following the sounds that seemed dangerously close to hysteria, entering the chamber from whence they came without ceremony. Danielle, in chemise and petticoat, was standing in the middle of the room seemingly engaged in a tug of war with an elderly woman who bore all the marks of an old and trusted retainer. The countess stood to one side, looking on helplessly as her granddaughter appeared on the verge of strong hysterics for no immediately explainable reason. She welcomed Linton's arrival with only relief, forgetting the impropriety of a gentleman's presence in a young lady's bedchamber, particularly when the young lady in question was clad only in her undergarments.

In another minute Danielle was going to be beyond control and Linton didn't hesitate. He reached her in two long strides

122

and gripped the slim shoulders with fingers that bit into the smooth, bare skin. "Danielle, you will cease this unseemly display immediately! Do you hear me?"

The firm level voice reached her through the rising panic and desperation and slowly the wild, almost feral look in the brown eyes faded, a tinge of color returned to the deathly white cheeks, and the rigidity left her body.

The countess turned away to hide a slight smile. Quite clearly, the Earl of Linton had more than one way of dealing with her granddaughter's complex personality.

"I'm sorry," Danielle whispered, "but please, milord, tell them they must not take away my clothes. I . . . I may need them again, if something happens again and I . . . I have to run away again."

Compassion flooded the earl as he realized what was happening. It was far too soon for Danielle to accept security, to put behind her the thought that she needed to be prepared for any eventuality. Her boy's clothes were utterly necessary to her peace of mind.

"No one will take them away, brat," he said gently. "But you can surely do without them whilst they are laundered."

Slowly she released her convulsive grip on the britches and jacket, allowing the maid to take them before the storm of weeping overwhelmed her. Linton took the shaking figure in his arms and, sitting on the bed, settled her on his lap cradled against his chest until the racking sobs slowed and at long last ceased. The Countess of March herself sat on the broad window seat feeling in some vague way that she should remain as chaperone but also that it was both too late and quite unnecessary. There was an intimacy between these two that had been forged in some extraordinary situation that she was certain had been as inevitable as it had been improper.

"I'm all right now," Danielle whispered, struggling to sit up, wiping her bare arm across her wet eyes and running nose.

"Oh, Danny! When will you stop doing that?" Linton chuckled softly, pulling out his handkerchief and wiping her face himself. "Blow your nose, now."

She gave him a watery smile and obeyed vigorously. "Why did that happen?"

"You have been holding a great deal inside in recent weeks." He set her on her feet and rose himself. "Get dressed now. I'll leave you in the competent hands of your grandmama."

Lady Lavinia followed him out of the room, pulling the door half shut behind her. "You do not think, Linton, that perhaps a draught of laudanum and her bed might not be the best course?"

Justin frowned and then shook his head. "No, I think not. She is remarkably resilient, ma'am. I think that outburst will probably have done more good than any opiate. She will want to tell you her story herself and also has some further plans which I am hoping she will reveal without too much delay." His lips curved in a slight smile. "She has informed me that I will not approve of them, and, I think, hopes to persuade you and March to accede to her wishes without my interference."

"A forlorn hope, I gather, Justin?" Her Ladyship smiled.

"Quite."

The countess nodded in brief satisfaction and returned to the bedchamber.

The muslin gown earned her immediate approval. "It has the mark of Lutèce, unless I am much mistaken."

"Milord bought it for me," Danielle informed her, adjusting the fichu carefully.

"Then it is undoubtedly Lutèce," the countess averred.

"He also gave me this brooch, ma'am. Do you think it was perhaps improper of me to accept it?" Danielle looked anxiously at her grandmother, who could not resist smiling.

"My love, I suspect that that gift is about the only 'proper' thing that has happened to you in months. It is quite unexceptionable, just right for a young girl. But Linton's taste is always as impeccable as his judgment in these matters. You have minded him well, I hope."

"I have not had very much choice, Grandmama," Danielle replied tartly. "My Lord Linton is most persuasive!"

Her Ladyship had no difficulty in believing this, but merely suggested mildly that they repair to the drawing room.

They kept country hours when in Conwall and dinner was announced soon after the ladies had arrived downstairs. Linton had exchanged his riding clothes for a plain but superbly tailored coat of brown cloth and fawn knee britches—

more morning dress than evening but Lord March had informed him that they stood on no ceremony when at Mervanwey. They dined with a degree of informality but their dinner, in quantity and quality, would not have disgraced any London table. Once the covers had been removed, however, and the port decanter placed at Lord March's elbow, the servants were dismissed and March suggested that they dispense with the formality of the ladies' withdrawal and hear Danielle's story in the privacy and comfort of the dining room.

Danielle looked askance at the port decanter which showed no inclination to move in her direction and Justin smiled slightly.

"It is not considered the thing, Danny, for ladies, particularly very young ladies, to partake of port after dinner."

At her rather crestfallen look, her grandfather gave a low chuckle. "We are quite private, Linton, and the child is half French after all. If she is used to taking it I cannot see that it will do any great harm. However, miss, in company it will not do at all, so you must accustom yourself to two standards." He filled her glass, casting a twinkling glance at his wife, who was looking most disapproving.

Danielle told her story for the third time to an audience as attentive as her two previous ones, finding that with repeated telling the horror seemed to recede somewhat. On this occasion she included much more detail of her life and that of her mother and of events leading to the massacre, providing her listeners with an explanation and a description that shocked them considerably more than it did her. As before, she ended her narrative at the point where she had met the Earl of Linton.

A heavy silence hung over the table as she concluded and she was not to know that the thought uppermost in all three of her listeners' minds was how to put Danielle de St. Varennes on the conventional tracks again after such a life and such an experience. Justin had already decided how this was to be done and watched with secret amusement the cogitations of his hosts, knowing that sooner rather than later they would reach his conclusion. He hoped, however, that they would not blurt this out in front of Danielle; it was a task he preferred to keep for himself.

But neither the earl nor his countess were foolish, and having raised a family of two sons and one very high-spirited, self-willed daughter, were well aware of the dangers inherent in a premature announcement to the mercurial Danielle as to her future.

"And what of your subsequent journey, Justin?" March refilled his glass and passed the decanter to his guest.

"One beset with alarums and excursions, sir," Linton said with a rueful half smile. "But I think we contrived to keep Danielle's identity a secret from the world—except for Pitt." He explained their sojourn in London and the meeting with the prime minister. "Pitt has promised both his discretion and his friendship, so I think we need have no fears in that quarter."

"Danielle traveled as a boy all that time?" Lady Lavinia spoke for the first time in a tone of shocked incredulity.

"Yes, ma'am. As my servant, actually. Although it is not a role she is particularly adept at," Linton murmured.

Danielle took a deep breath into the sudden silence before speaking with some difficulty. "I realize, milord, that I have not always appeared sensible of your many kindnesses and that perhaps I might have seemed ungrateful for your protection . . ."

"Danny!" the earl exclaimed, interrupting this fumbling beginning. "You are not about to thank me, are you? If you do so, I shall begin to think your experiences have quite overset your reason!"

"I was intending to apologize, as it happens," she replied acidly. "Whilst I was not grateful for your interference, I could perhaps have been a little more amenable."

The earl's eyes danced. "You were certainly an unpredictable traveling companion."

"Yes, well I should not have teased you about your headache when you were foxed in France, and then got into a fight with that *bête* Jacques," Danielle continued doggedly, determined to rid herself of this unpleasant confession and thus missing Linton's warning look. "And then I came up on deck when you had said not to and nearly got swept overboard and then was horribly seasick and you had to look after me and

126

then I made Lord Julian notice me and . . ."

"I think, Danielle, that we do not need a catalog of your indiscretions," Justin broke in very softly. "Your grandparents will not find them edifying."

Silenced, she glanced at her grandparents, who were both looking thunderstruck at the chasm of impropriety revealed by her artless recitation.

"Lord Linton is quite right, child," Lavinia said hastily. "Those few days you spent in his company had best be buried as deep as possible. Although, I must confess to feeling a degree of compassion for you, Justin."

"Not necessary, ma'am, I assure you," he demurred with a smile.

"Well, we must think now of how best we can brush through this affair," March declared firmly. "I think, my dear, that Linton and I should discuss this alone."

"Yes, of course." Lady Lavinia rose instantly. "Come, Danielle, I have asked Hannah to sort through some clothes that we might be able to alter for you, until we can have your wardrobe made up. Let us go and see what she has discovered."

"No!" Danielle exclaimed suddenly. "You do not understand—none of you understands. I cannot remain here."

Only Linton showed no surprise at this impassioned statement. He took snuff and with great deliberation flicked a speck from his sleeve with a lace handkerchief before saying, "Enlighten us, Danny."

"I have to return to Languedoc before the situation in France becomes so bad that all travel is impossible. We have perhaps two months, no more, and maybe less if the States General produces confrontation." She was talking quietly, desperately now, turning to her stunned grandfather. "I have it all planned, sir, but I will need some funds and passage to France. If you still have Dream Girl, I can sail to Brittany and make my way on horseback, traveling as a factor, perhaps, on a journey to oversee his master's estates. I have not quite worked that out, but it will serve, I think. I can travel in relative comfort and safety in that guise."

"Why?" Linton sat up, resting his elbows on the table, looking closely at the pale, set face opposite.

"You would not understand," she said quietly, turning her head away.

"That seems to be a favorite accusation of yours, brat. I suggest you put me to the test."

"All I have left is there." Her voice sank to barely a whisper. "I must bring back *Maman*'s jewels and do something for the curé and . . . and . . . find out what has happened to the château and the bodies of my family. It is not finished otherwise."

The Earl of March opened his mouth and was instantly silenced by a quick frown from his guest.

"Do you trust me, Danielle?" Linton asked what seemed to Danny a complete non sequitur and she gazed at him blankly.

"But of course, milord. What an idiotish question!"

"It is not idiotish and it is most certainly not courteous of you to speak in that fashion." This down-to-earth rebuke in the face of Danielle's extraordinary scheme had the effect of returning reality to the dining room. The Earl and Countess of March relaxed once again, more than willing to leave this matter in the clearly capable hands of the Earl of Linton.

"I will make the journey for you," he continued coolly. "You will furnish me with a letter for the curé, maps, and all relevant information. Whilst I am gone, you will remain here and practice some of the gentler arts of being a lady. Is that a fair exchange?"

"It will be dangerous, milord, and the danger should be mine not yours," she responded with quiet dignity.

"You will, however, allow me to assume that danger for you. I can accomplish the task with much more facility than you, and much more speed. Is it agreed?"

Danielle struggled with herself for long moments. Her pride rebelled against allowing someone else to take on such an unpleasant and difficult task for her. She had expected total opposition and the assumption that even to wish for such a thing was quite out of the question. Instead, Linton had not questioned her wishes or her reasons, merely presented an alternative mode of execution that would most certainly be more efficient. She did not doubt but that he would accomplish his objective and that perhaps she would not.

"I shall be forever in your debt, my lord," she said softly.

"Fustian!" My Lord declared brusquely. "You will repay me by learning to ride sidesaddle and by banishing from your memory those words and expressions usually found on the tongues of sailors and fishwives."

"You strike a hard bargain, milord." Danielle suddenly gave him that dazzling smile that had so struck him during their evening with Pitt.

Lady Lavinia's eyes widened. She had not seen this before and had had neither the time nor the opportunity to speculate on the more feminine traits of her granddaughter. The child had seemed well enough looking, certainly, but with that ridiculous haircut and the overly intense expression she wore constantly was not immediately to be perceived as a beauty. Now, however, she saw a diamond of the first water under the tomboy facade. A quick glance at Linton assured her that he too saw it—probably always had done, she thought suddenly. She nodded to herself, pursing her lips in a gesture her husband knew well as denoting happy decision. They would pull the coals out of this fire most satisfactorily.

"So, Linton, how do you suggest we proceed?" March rose from the table once the ladies had withdrawn and went thoughtfully over to the long window overlooking the terrace. The sun was sinking slowly behind the cliff top, filling the sky with a soft pink glow that promised another beautiful day for the morrow.

"With all speed," Linton replied briefly, reaching for the decanter. "A period of mourning will, of course, be necessary, but I think not a full year. The circumstances of her family's death are sufficiently extreme and the timing unknown by all save ourselves that I feel sure a September wedding would cause no censure. It is possible to be . . . uh . . . uninformative . . . about the finer details, I think."

"Quite so, Justin." The Earl of March was in no wise surprised by his guest's matter-of-fact statement. It had not occurred to him that a shotgun would be necessary in this delicate affair.

"I think it would be as well to give the impression that Danielle has been with you for some considerable period— certainly since before her parents' death. It will cause no remark and you have been out of town for some time?"

"Since October," March replied. "We shall put it about that Danielle has been paying us an extended visit in preparation for her debut next Season. Perhaps Louise has been in failing health and therefore unable to sponsor her daughter herself?" A slight sigh escaped him—he and his wife had mourned their daughter in the days since receiving Linton's letter, but now the living required their undivided attention.

"That will serve well, sir." Linton looked at the older man, compassion in his eyes as he understood his thoughts. "I shall drop this information into a few, carefully chosen ears in both London and Paris—the gossips will have it in no time and if news of Languedoc has already reached the French court it will explain the matter of Danielle's survival most satisfactorily."

"And the wedding . . . ?" March queried, raising one eyebrow.

"In London, I think, at the start of the Season. We do not wish any appearance of a hole-in-the-corner affair, any undue haste or secrecy," Linton said slowly. "A quiet ceremony attended only by family in St. George's, Hanover Square, will do very well—Danielle's and your recent tragic loss will explain the lack of pomp. It will be quite unexceptionable."

"And how, Justin, do we explain to my granddaughter that she is to become the Countess of Linton?" March could not resist a soft chuckle as he put this so-important question.

"I think you may safely leave that to me," Justin declared coolly. "On my return will be soon enough. My brat needs some healing time before she is presented with any more shocks." ,

"She is remarkably quick-witted," March murmured, avoiding Linton's eye. "I am sure she will quickly grasp the principles of a marriage of convenience."

"You mistake the matter, Charles," Justin said gently. "This is to be no marriage of convenience. I will wed Danielle de St. Varennes because I choose to do so, not to preserve my honor or hers."

130

"Is this to be a love match, then?"

"I have loved your granddaughter since the first evening I met her" was the calm reply. "She is, of course, quite unaware of this fact. I could hardly take advantage of her situation, so have played the part of dictatorial guardian." He shrugged slightly. "She is not, I think, indifferent to me but the woman in her still sleeps. I look forward to the very pleasant task of awakening her." He smiled suddenly. "Have no fear, March. Danielle will come to no harm from me."

"I have no such fear, Justin. We will take good care of her in your absence."

"That I don't doubt," Linton said with a short laugh, "but I think it time she stopped running wild and began to make some excursion into Society."

"Lavinia will arrange that with great enthusiasm, unless I am much mistaken. There are several families in the area who will provide quite unexceptionable contacts for the child so long as she does not develop some 'tendre' for the squire's son."

"I shall return with all due haste, March." Linton laughed. "But Danielle, for all her childishness, has a deep core of sophistication that will not, I suspect, allow her to fall prey to the dubious charms of some callow youth."

When Danielle descended to the breakfast parlor very early the next morning she found only Linton. She was not to know that this had been arranged at his request when he had taken leave of his hosts the previous evening and came forward eagerly, her hands full of papers.

"I am glad to find you alone, milord. I have written to *Monsieur le Curé* and have drawn up some maps. Shall I explain them to you?"

"Certainly." He smiled. She was wearing a rose silk wrapper over her nightgown and looked entrancingly feminine in spite of the short, slightly rumpled curls—except that she was barefoot.

"Where are your shoes, brat?" He raised his glass, subjecting her pink toes to an interested scrutiny.

"Oh, I couldn't find them," she declared airily, apparently

131

unmoved by his examination. The earl sighed and gave up the attempt to bring her to a proper sense of confusion and recognition of this solecism.

"This is a map of the village." Danielle stood at his shoulder, leaning over to put the paper beside his plate. "This is the lane from the château." It was a beautifully drawn map, cartography clearly being another of her many and varied skills, he reflected distractedly, trying not to react to the sweet fragrance of her skin, the soft pressure of her breast under the thin silk as she leant against his arm.

"Danielle, it is quite impossible for me to eat my breakfast with your arm in the way," he declared suddenly, taking her by the waist and drawing her onto his knee. "There, that is much better. Now I can eat with one hand and we can put the map to the side, like so. Pray continue."

Danielle stiffened momentarily as a most odd sensation washed over her. His hand was light and warm around her waist, his shoulder firm and supportive at her back, the thighs in their buckskin britches taut and hard-muscled beneath her buttocks. She had never been so powerfully aware of another physical presence.

"I . . . I could sit in the chair beside you, milord," she murmured.

"You could," he agreed cheerfully, spearing a kidney with his fork. "But I am quite comfortable. Are you not?"

She was very comfortable, too comfortable for comfort, but her companion was continuing with his breakfast as if their seating arrangement were the most natural thing in the world. Danielle went on with her explanation.

Afterward, she accompanied him outside to his waiting horse and the post chaise. "Why, milord, where is the mare?"

"I am leaving her for you, brat." He smiled. "But you will ride her sidesaddle—are we agreed?"

The small nose wrinkled. "I will undertake to learn, milord, but I cannot promise never to ride astride."

"I am satisfied, Danielle." He took the reins of the black in one hand and smiled down at her, a look in his eye that she had never seen before and that puzzled her mightily—it was almost as if he was seeing someone else; he had certainly never looked at his brat in that way. His next words reassured her slightly. "You will be good now, won't you?"

"Assuredly, sir, for I know what to look forward to on your return if I am not," she murmured demurely, lowering her eyes meekly beneath the long lashes.

"Minx!" A long, gloved finger caught her chin, tipping it upward. "Do not be too sure of anything, *mon enfant*. I am not known for my predictability." The dark head bent, those firm, curved lips brushed hers in a featherlike caress so light she wondered afterward if it had ever happened, and the Earl of Linton mounted and without a backward glance rode off down the driveway.

Danielle gathered up the skirt of her wrapper and ran across the dew wet grass to the cliff top, watching the procession out of sight behind the bend in the steep path. Her hand, raised in farewell, dropped to her side as she scrunched her bare toes in the damp, rough crabgrass, feeling forlorn and bereft and wondering why.

Chapter 7

Time passed rapidly and Danielle's thin cheeks and skinny body filled under the application of good food, rest, fresh air, and an abundance of love and kindness. She found her excursions into Cornish society tedious in the extreme, the young people boring, ill-educated, and with a sense of humor that she could not help but castigate as puerile and totally unamusing, their elders complacent, smug, stay-at-homes with no understanding of or interest in the world outside their farms, their shooting, and the whisk table. But she tried hard to bridle her impatient tongue and swallow the hasty, sarcastic comments that rose all too frequently to her lips. Her efforts were viewed with sympathy and understanding by her grandparents and her occasional lapses drew no more than the mildest reproof.

Lavinia found to her amazement that this girl/woman was most knowledgeable about the finer points of running a household. With her easy manners and obvious competence she became quickly accepted as a trusted member of the family who could always be relied upon to untangle a knotty domestic problem whether it be the unexplainable disappearance of three pairs of the best bed sheets, a discrepancy in the kitchen accounts, or the awkwardness arising from the housekeeper's niece having inadvertently insulted Lady Lavinia's dresser.

Lord March found an educated mind, a quick brain at the chessboard, and a very skilled cardplayer and soon resigned himself to losing at piquet or chess at least twice as often as he

135

won. When she was discovered in the cellar advising the butler on the readiness of the '73 burgundy he privately decided that for all her unconventional ways she would make Linton a very lucky husband. This was no schoolroom miss who would fritter away her allowance and her time and bore him with vapid inanities on the rare occasions she chose his company above that of her society friends.

But Danielle was not truly happy. She kept herself occupied because it was not in her nature to repine, but her thoughts were too often with a dark-haired, black eyed, soft-spoken individual. In a strange way she felt him looking over her shoulder and began to judge her actions and words according to how she knew he would react—the amused smile, the approving nod, the slightly raised eyebrow, the brisk rebuke, or the so gently pronounced warning.

They heard no news. May 5, the date set for the meeting of the States General, came and went. Danny fretted and fumed, and took to riding out astride the dappled mare from sunup to sundown across the flat countryside and the long deserted beaches.

It was the first week of June before the messenger arrived bearing a short, uninformative note from Linton stating simply that he would arrive at Mervanwey within three days of their receipt of this communication and he hoped he would find them well.

"But he doesn't even say if he reached Languedoc, or what has happened at Versailles . . . or anything!" Danielle exclaimed in frustration and a fair degree of pique that the terse note had carried no special message for her.

"Patience, my love. You will hear all from Linton himself in just a short time. You are twisting those ribbons into a veritable bird's nest," Lady Lavinia scolded gently. "I will instruct Betsy to make haste with the green silk—it will be just the thing for you to wear to greet His Lordship."

Danielle, however, had other ideas—ideas that were fortunately not imparted to Lady Lavinia who might otherwise have succumbed for the first time in her sensible life to a fit of the vapors.

Thus it was that in the late afternoon of the third day, Justin,

Earl of Linton, traveling this time in the comfort of his own well-sprung coach, was startled out of a deep and exceedingly pleasant reverie concerned with the awakening of the tenderer emotions in the bosom of one Danielle de St. Varennes by the crack of a pistol shot, an alarmed yell from his coachman, and the sudden, violent halt of the conveyance. A quick thought for the wooden box beneath his seat and his own pistol was in his hands as he reached for the door handle. The next instant, a very familiar voice reached his ears.

"For God's sake, man! You are quite cow-handed. Look to your horses before the leader throws a trace. They would not have plunged like that if you had not jabbed at them in such an idiotish fashion!"

Replacing his pistol in the small pocket of his waistcoat the earl let down the window and regarded the slight figure, still castigating the clumsy coachman, with considerable exasperation.

"Danny, you incorrigible wretch! Come over here this instant."

He couldn't see her face, hidden as it was behind a black silk loo mask, but his eyes were riveted to the still smoking flintlock pistol in her hand.

"How dare you, Danny! Give me that pistol."

Danielle pulled off her mask showing him a pair of brightly laughing eyes. "It is quite all right, milord. I am considered an excellent shot, you should know." And with total ease she slid the pistol back into her belt. "I have been used to handling firearms forever, and if your idiot of a coachman had not reacted so foolishly there would have been no discomfort to anyone. Did you get sadly jolted, sir? I really did not intend for that to happen. I fired well over their heads."

Linton, rendered momentarily speechless, merely looked at her and slowly the laughter faded from her eyes.

"I see you are cross now, milord. It was just a prank, something *un peu amusant, n'est-ce-pas?*"

"It was not at all amusing," His Lordship informed her bluntly.

"Oh." Her bottom lip disappeared between her teeth. "It seemed so when I thought of it—to hold you up for my own

137

property. You do have it, do you not, milord?"

Laughter welled deep in Lord Linton's powerful chest b
was severely repressed. "I have the property of the La
Danielle de St. Varennes, nothing that belongs to a hoyde
who considers playing at highwayman '*un peu amusant*.' I sha
expect to meet with Danielle de St. Varennes within the ha
hour."

"Perhaps within the hour, sir?" A pair of slender eyebrow
arched delicately.

"Certainly no longer."

Danielle tugged her cap down over her eyes, gave him a gri
of pure mischief, and turned the dappled mare, riding low ove
the saddle as they disappeared into the trees bordering th
path. "All right, George. If the horses are quieted, pray let u
continue."

The coachman leant from from his box peering around th
side of the coach. "Just let me get my hands on that lad," he
muttered direly. "I'll dust his jacket for him!"

"I know the feeling, George," His Lordship sighed, and
pulled up the window again as the coach moved forward.

Lady Lavinia greeted him with pleasure not unmixed with
consternation as she confided that Danielle had not been seen
all day. "She has been very restless these last weeks—I think
the lack of news has bothered her greatly," she explained,
taking his arm and leading him into the drawing room.

"I am confident, ma'am, that she will make an appearance
very shortly," he replied easily and Her Ladyship was instantly
soothed, although she could not imagine why.

Meanwhile, Danielle was tearing off her riding clothes,
throwing out a bewildering series of commands to the placid
girl assigned to wait on her.

"The pink and white taffeta, Hetty, quickly. No, no, the
striped one with the cherry velvet knots. You must do my hair
like you did the other night, with the curls over the ears, but I
must bathe. Oh, but there is no time, damnation! Why did I
have that so stupid idea?" Naked, Danielle strode to the
porcelain tub and began swiftly to scrub herself, dipping
briefly under the water before holding out imperative hands
for the towel.

Hetty had long since become used to her young mistress's immodesty in prancing around the chamber in her bare skin, heedless of the sensibilities of a servant girl who believed firmly that bathing was a dangerous business at the best of times and when utterly necessary should be pursued only when clad in an undervest. One did not see oneself naked, let alone allow others to do so! However, waiting on the Lady Danielle was not an arduous task and indeed provided considerable amusement, and she was a considerate and most generous mistress who rarely allowed her own low spirits to affect those around her.

It was just within the hour set by the earl when Danielle appeared in the drawing room. Her hair, while still unfashionably short, had grown considerably in the last weeks and was now dressed in soft ringlets caught up over her ears and falling softly to the nape of her neck. A cherry red ribbon threaded its way through the wheat-colored curls adding to the look of demure innocence created by a simple but beautifully cut gown whose low neck was somehow both concealed and accentuated by a lacy collar that slipped over a pair of creamy sloping shoulders to fall in a froth of wide sleeve at her elbow. A lace-edged petticoat peeked tantalizingly from the hem of the gown, drawing the eye to pink and white satin slippers exactly matching the stripes of the dress. Linton's glass went up with his eyebrows before he turned to Lady Lavinia.

"My compliments, ma'am. You have indeed wrought a transformation."

"Well, of all things!" Danielle exclaimed indignantly. "Am *I* to receive no credit?"

"When I am assured that your conduct has undergone a similar transformation, most certainly you will," His Lordship replied dampeningly.

"Danielle, your curtsy, child!" Lady Lavinia spoke hastily in shocked reproof and Danielle, remembering her manners belatedly, sank with a swish of her skirts into a deep salute receiving a most magnificent leg in exchange.

"Why, milord," she twinkled roguishly, "you have never done that to me before."

"I only bow to ladies" was the cool response. "Hoydenish

minxes receive other treatment."

A pink tinge stole into her cheeks and the brown eyes held an appeal he could not resist. "Very well, we will say no more about it, brat. I will put it down to the effects of the full moon which must have run away with your wits."

"Whatever are you talking about?" the countess said in bewilderment.

"Nothing of any consequence, ma'am," Linton replied easily and then turned at a gasp of delight from Danny. She had opened the carved box resting on the small mahogany table under the window and was now holding a magnificent diamond necklace to her throat.

"The St. Varennes diamonds," she whispered reverently. "Are they not magnificent? *Maman* always said that not even 'Toinette had such stones as these." She struggled with the clasp at the back of her neck but Linton forestalled her, taking the necklace gently but firmly from her hands.

"You may not wear these, Danielle, or the emeralds," he said quietly. "Not until you are a married lady—they are quite unsuitable for a debutante."

"Oh, pshaw!" Danny expostulated. "What nonsense. They are mine after all."

"That is not under dispute." Linton drew out a simple strand of flawless pearls. "Turn around. You may wear these as often as you choose, also the topaz and the turquoise set. The rest must go to the bank for safekeeping."

"But then I shall never wear them," she declared stoutly, "for I shall never be married."

Justin's eyes met those of the Earl and Countess of March over the bent head as he fastened the pearls around her neck. "Now you are being idiotish, Danielle. You will most certainly marry."

"If you are that certain, sir, then perhaps you will also tell me whom I am to marry." She turned, delivering her acid challenge with angry eyes and squared shoulders.

"Why me, of course." The earl spoke calmly, opening his snuff box with deliberation.

There was a short stunned silence and then Danielle stammered, "But . . . but you cannot wish to marry me."

140

"Why ever not, brat?" He smiled.

"Well *that*, for one reason," she said, recovering herself somewhat. "People do not marry people they call 'brat' and all sorts of other uncomplimentary names. You are forever telling me what to do and being most unpleasant when I have other ideas, and you have threatened to beat me I don't know how many times . . . and . . . and you even boxed my ears once!" She delivered the coup de grace with the full force of her suddenly remembered indignation.

"Yes, well that was indeed a little hasty of me," the earl said thoughtfully, "but you must admit the provocation was great."

"I do not admit it," Danny cried. "I was not drinking the ale—I find the taste *most* disagreeable!"

"I appear to be out of my depth here." March broke in suddenly. "What has ale to do with anything?"

"Quite a lot, it seems," Linton murmured. "Come, Danny, if I undertake never to do such a reprehensible thing again will you at least listen to what I have to say?"

Danielle chewed her lip, that deep frown of concentration drawing her delicate brows together, giving her that fierce, serious expression she had worn habitually in her vagabond days. "I think, milord, that your so delicate notions of propriety compel you to offer for me," she began slowly. "It is not at all necessary, you know. My reputation was already hopelessly compromised before you rescued me from the baker. You are perhaps unaware that I have known this for very many weeks, since before I met you, and everything I have done, both before and since, has been in the full knowledge of the consequences. That is why I have said that I will not make my come-out. I shall be quite content to remain here."

This simple speech had a profound effect on her listeners and Lady Lavinia turned away, feeling for the handkerchief tucked in the lace at her bosom.

"I seem always to be underestimating you, Danielle," Linton said quietly. "But there remains one thing, of more importance than any other in this affair, that you do not yet understand."

141

She gave him a serious, inquiring look and he bowed deeply. "Milady, will you do me the very great honor of joining me in a turn about the garden?"

For a second she remained motionless and then, to his everlasting delight and astonishment, unfurled her fan, holding it up to her face so only her eyes were visible as she swam into a curtsy.

"La, sir, but I must protest. It is you who do me too much honor."

Taking her hand as she rose gracefully he tucked it firmly under his velvet-covered arm, inclined his head briefly in the direction of the Earl and Countess of March, and escorted Danielle through the open doors onto the terrace.

March passed a hand expressively across his brow. "You know, m'dear, I do not know whether to offer Linton my condolences or my felicitations."

"The latter, my love," his wife said with a sniff into her handkerchief. "They will deal extremely together. They already know each other a great deal better than most couples starting along that road and Linton loves her as much for her unconventional ways as despite them, I suspect."

The earl at that point was plunged in thought, debating how best to convince the silent figure at his side that his offer of marriage was made through much more than chivalry. Then it occurred to him that Danielle was such a direct, honest person herself that a simple statement would most likely be believed. The main problem would be to achieve her acceptance.

They had reached the rose garden. Danielle moved toward the low stone wall separating this fragrant spot from the cliff road. The evening air was heavy with the scent of June roses and a soft breeze from the sea wafted the fresh tang of salt and seaweed across the cliff top.

"I would like to sit on the wall, milord," she announced calmly, breaking the long silence. The earl did not respond, merely rested his forearms on the mellow stone, looking intently but unseeing down the road.

"Milord?"

He turned with an abstracted smile.

"I would like to sit on the wall."

"Then do so, child."

"If I were dressed otherwise, sir, I could manage myself, but these—" she gestured to her gown—"give me some difficulty."

He laughed then, picking her up by the tiny waist and lifting her onto the stonework. "It is most indecorous of you to be sitting on walls and, besides, you will dirty your gown, but I daresay such considerations do not weigh with you, my brat."

"Not in the least," she concurred cheerfully. "Now that we are comfortable, sir, you have something you wish to say to me?"

Her hands disappeared into a firm warm clasp. "Danielle, you have said that you trust me, you must therefore believe me when I say that I have loved you for these many weeks. I have not behaved as a lover but, as you have already proved once today, you are sufficiently aware of the facts of life to understand why."

Her response to this blunt statement surprised him. She did not question his statement, but instead asked with quiet interest, "When did you start to love me, milord?"

"It's a little difficult to be exact." He frowned thoughtfully. "But I think it all began that moment when you stood like some little Amazon with those entrancing breasts bared, daring me to take advantage of you. In fact," he added with a rueful smile, "I felt merely ridiculous and at a great disadvantage."

"You did not appear so, sir." She laughed. "You were quite horrid to me and made me feel most uncomfortable."

"For that, I apologize." Justin laid a firm finger over her lips, continuing seriously, "I wish you to be my wife, milady."

"I do not know a great deal about the love between husband and wife, sir. *Maman*, I fear, had little experience. In the beginning there was some love, I think, but it lasted only a very short time. You understand that I talk not about the physical aspects of marriage, milord, but of the spirit?"

He nodded gravely. What an extraordinary creature she was.

"Of the former, I perhaps know more than I should." Her dimples danced. "But that will not surprise you."

"Not at all," he concurred, suppressing a smile.

143

"But of the latter—you will teach me, milord, *n'est-ce pas?*"
She held out her arms to him in a completely unself-conscious
gesture of trust and invitation.

"I will teach you of both, Danielle," he said softly, lifting
her off the wall. "You cannot truly know of what you have
never experienced."

He continued to hold her by the waist, looking seriously into
those big brown eyes regarding him with a gravity to equal his
own.

"Would it be most improper of you to kiss me, milord?"

"I do not think I should pay much attention to the
proprieties if it were." His hands left her waist, cupping the
heart-shaped face as his lips very gently touched hers. She held
herself still and breathless, eyes open, waiting for she knew not
what. The pressure on her lips increased as his thumbs began
to trace her cheekbones, fingers to explore the softness of her
shell-like ears.

Justin raised his head for a moment. "Close your eyes, brat.
This is an exercise in sensation, not observation."

The long lashes dropped instantly and his lips twitched
before returning to their original position, but now they began
to demand as his tongue flicked, darted between her lips,
forcing entry. In the dark world behind her closed eyes
crimson flashes of panic sparked as, for a second, she fought
the intrusion, tried to draw her head back. But the grip
tightened and suddenly the sensation of violation disappeared.
Her mouth opened and he was inside her head, a strong,
muscular presence exploring the softness of her mouth,
becoming a part of her as it became familiar with the contours
of her cheeks, the roof of her mouth, slid across her teeth,
drawing from her something she did not know she possessed.
Tentatively her own tongue began to move, to fence with the
other, stroking and curling as a tightness began to build deep
within her and her body moved involuntarily against his. One
hand left her face, the fingers stroking the taut skin of her
throat before heat exploded through her body as it found the
soft swell of her breast beneath the lace collar of her gown.
Long fingers slipped inside the neck, reaching further and, to
her utter confusion and embarrassment, she felt the tips of her

144

breasts take on a life of their own, beginning to burn as they hardened, pressing against the taffeta bodice.

"No, no, milord, please!" She pulled back desperately and was instantly released, whirling away from him, one hand unconsciously on her breasts, the other touching her warmed, swollen lips.

"Danny?" Hands held her shoulders, slipped down to seize her own as it plucked at her bodice.

"You don't understand," she whispered.

"No, child, this time I understand; it is you who do not."

"But what happened?"

"Your body, my little love, was responding quite naturally and most pleasingly to my caress. It is right that it should do so."

She was turned gently but inexorably to face him, her downcast face lifted by a firm finger to meet his amused but understanding regard.

"You are not out of countenance, are you?" His voice mocked gently. "Not my indecorous litte vagabond, surely?"

A slight smile touched her eyes. "It is truly normal for that to happen, milord?"

"Quite normal. Did your *maman* tell you nothing of such things?"

"A little, but, as you said, sir, one cannot truly know of what one has never experienced."

"I think that should conclude the lesson for today." Linton straightened the lace at her bosom with efficient fingers. "Your grandparents will be wondering what has become of us."

Danielle peered over her shoulder, dusting the back of her dress impatiently. "Have I grass stains on my skirt, sir? The wall is a little mossy, I fear."

"You were warned," he observed mildly, turning her around, brushing her down briskly. His hand slowed suddenly, and yielding to impulse he allowed it to rest on the curve of her buttocks, his fingers caressing the firm flesh beneath the layers of skirt and petticoat.

"Sir!" she squeaked indignantly, jumping away from him.

Linton laughed softly. "You have an adorable little bottom,

145

my love. I have long thought so."

"You should not say such things!" she exclaimed, a deep flush suffusing the ivory complexion.

"Perhaps we should have the second lesson today, also." He was smiling at her, but there was a hint of gravity in the black eyes. "It is a most important one. Whatever is said or done between two people during their loving can never be wrong. Do you understand that, Danielle?"

She regarded him thoughtfully. "I think, milord, that I shall perhaps understand it better when I experience more of these things you refer to."

"You have much wisdom under those curls." He pinched her cheek lightly. "Let us go back to the house."

The announcement of the forthcoming marriage between the Lady Danielle de St. Varennes and Justin Earl of Linton made its appearance in the *Gazette* at the end of June, just in time to provide the last *on dit* of the Season before the ton deserted London's heat and dust and the disease-laden air of summer to continue their round of pleasures either at Bath or on their country estates.

The news was received with curiosity, much speculation, and not a little chagrin by those mamas who had continued to hold out hopes that Linton would forsake his bachelordom for the charms of one of their daughters. Nothing was known of his affianced bride except that she was, of course, a Rockford, and even though her father's family were viewed with a degree of caution by high sticklers her lineage was unimpeachable and not even the most malicious tongue could say that the earl was to make a bad match in this regard. Her age, however, was another matter altogether. Linton had never evinced the slightest interest in girls in their first Season and the little de St. Varennes was surely barely out of the schoolroom? But Society's curiosity was not to be satisfied throughout the summer as Lord Linton remained in Cornwall engaged in the very pleasant task of awakening the sleeping woman in his erstwhile brat.

They received little news of the events in France during this time, and that little was grim. On June 17, the Commons at the States General declared themselves the *Assemblée Nationale—*

the only representative body of the nation—and thus denied the claims of the privileged orders, the nobility and the clergy, to represent France independently. At the same time, they challenged the king, still grieving over the death of the seven-year-old Dauphin, by agreeing to pay their taxes only as long as this National Assembly remained in session. This unheard-of defiance led an angry and ill-advised Louis XVI to close the Parliament House to the deputies of the Third Estate and declare a Royal Session. When on June 20 the deputies, barred by soldiers from entering the hall, convened as a separate body on the tennis court at Versailles all hope that the States General would indeed rejuvenate the realm faded and the course of bloody civil destruction that France was to pursue for the next five years became inevitable.

But for Danielle, this was an idyllic summer. Linton wisely made no attempt to change the personality that had developed during her unconventional upbringing, and indeed had no wish to do so. He was firm in his insistence that she adhere to a proper conduct when in company. Any lapses in either behavior or language were received with a stony silence and a withdrawal of his company that Danielle found infinitely more unpleasant than his previous methods of showing disapproval. As a result these lapses occurred less and less frequently. Since Justin was totally accepting of her need to alternate the rigors of self-control with the freedom to roam the countryside astride the dappled mare, they soon reached a happy compromise. They spent days hunting in the woods, fishing the streams, and sailing the little bay. Danielle was initially somewhat nervous about the latter activity, her experiences on the *Black Gull* having given her a certain dislike for the sea, but her enjoyment of physical activity of all kinds soon overcame her reluctance and she rapidly became competent at handling the small sailboat. Linton enjoyed teaching her—she was so proficient at most things that it made a pleasant change to instruct her in something other than the proper way to go on in Society.

His greatest surprise, however, occurred one afternoon when, on returning from a ride with March, he was informed that Lady Danielle would like him to join her in the Long

Gallery. He arrived to find her in shirt, britches, and stockinged feet examining the family portraits and gazing through the many long windows that made up the wall of the gallery facing the sea.

She turned eagerly at the sound of his entrance. "Ah, milord, there you are. I have been waiting for you this age. We shall fence together, *n'est-ce pas?*"

"Shall we indeed?" He raised a quizzical eyebrow, removing his jacket and placing it carefully over the back of the chaise longue under a window before examining the pair of foils resting on the seat. Their tips were carefully buttoned.

"You are full of surprises, brat," he observed, calmly pulling off his top boots before rolling up the ruffled sleeves of his shirt.

Danielle laughed delightedly as she picked up one of the foils, making a quick pass in the air that told him very clearly that this was no tyro. "The best of three hits, milord. We are agreed?"

He said nothing, merely picked up the other foil and faced her, its tip resting on the ground at his feet.

Her own flashed in salute and the next minute he found himself in combat with one of the best fencers he had ever been privileged to face. Her expression was now intense, all laughter gone, and the slight body moved on the polished floor with all the agility of a dancer. His swift thrust in prime was parried instantly and countered with a flanconnade to his left hand. He had not been expecting such a sophisticated maneuver and the tip of her blade grazed his side.

"One to me, milord," she said tranquilly, stepping back.

"On guard!" His foil flashed in a thrust in tierce but was instantly parried; for a moment their blades locked and she had bounced back, feinting to the right before parrying his swift lunge and sliding under his suddenly opened guard.

Linton dropped his point and held out a hand. "We will have a return match tomorrow, infant. And you will not, then, take me by surprise."

"Are you being ungenerous in defeat, sir?" she asked, taking the proffered hand.

"Not at all. But I did not know what to expect. Where did

you learn the art?"

"Marc, *mon oncle*," she replied briefly.

"That explains your skill." Marc de St. Varennes was a noted duelist who, if rumor were to be believed, fought only to the death, and since he had met his own at the hands of a peasant mob and not on the duelling ground his supremacy was without question.

It was a soft, rose-pink evening in early September when their summer idyll came to a close. Linton was to leave for London at dawn the following morning, Danielle and her grandparents to follow several days later.

"I wish I could travel with you, milord," she murmured wistfully as they walked toward the cliff top. "It will take forever, boxed up in that stuffy old coach."

"You may ride some of the way—I am sure that March will have no objection," he replied absently. "A week will see you in Bedford Place."

"I shall ride all the way," she stated firmly. "Can you imagine how tedious it would be to listen to Grandmama and Hannah rabbiting on for hours at a time about the latest fashions and whether Monsieur Artur is still the best hairdresser in town?"

"'Rabbiting,' brat, is not a word you will use, please."

"Oh, is it very vulgar?" Her eyes twinkled.

"Very," he said firmly.

"Do you think I shall set the town by the ears, sir?" She frowned toward the horizon and the red ball of the setting sun slipping into the dark sea.

"Only in the nicest possible way, Danny." He turned her toward him, one hand taking her chin. "I predict that you will take the town by storm, my love. You will behave impeccably at all times—well, most times," he amended with a soft laugh. "And not gallop in Hyde Park or take your carriage down St. James's or tell people that they are idiotish—even when they are. And you will be the most beautiful woman in London and I the most envied husband." His lips came down slowly and the soft petal of her mouth opened in eager, willing invitation. She was no longer afraid of her reactions and to his secret delight had begun to make demands of her own. As his hands felt for

149

the satiny skin of her breasts she moaned softly, moving against him, slipping her arms around his neck, holding his head captive against her face as her own tongue pushed between his lips on its own voyage of exploration.

Justin tipped her backward over one supporting arm as his hand pushed down the neck of her gown, lifting the soft breasts out of their concealment. Danielle gasped slightly as the cool evening air stroked the bared flesh and long fingers caught the erect nipples, rolling them between manicured tips. A deep tension was growing in the pit of her belly and she became aware of a strange dampness in the secret part of her body. His mouth found one breast, licking, nuzzling, nibbling, drawing from her a deep involuntary groan, half protest, half wanting. Something was sliding up the silken length of her leg, pushing aside the skirts and petticoats, reaching the ruffled cuff of her pantalettes.

"No!" She tried to push away his hand as it continued its journey over her cambric-clothed thighs, sliding suddenly between them to discover the moist center of her desire. Embarrassment engulfed her in great hot agonized waves.

Justin raised his head from her breast, but left his hand where it was, scorching through the thin protection of her drawers. "You have such passion in you, my sweet," he murmured huskily. "You must not deny it." His eyes, heavy and languorous, burned their message of reassurance and deep sensuality into her own anxious ones. He frowned suddenly, wondering if he had believed her too readily when she had said she knew about the physical side of marriage. Leaning against the low wall he drew her between his knees, holding her lightly by the waist. "You understand what happens between a man and a woman, do you not?"

"Oh yes," she announced cheerfully and then the pert little nose wrinkled slightly. "Only, I am not quite certain of exactly . . . well . . . exactly where things are. I understand the principle, you see, but not the practice," she finished in a rush.

"Well, I am glad that you do not. His eyes glinted. "The marriage bed, my love, is the only fit place for such understanding."

150

"But that is not true of everyone," she began seriously. "You have had many mistresses, have you not? They have not learned their practice in a marriage bed."

"Quite true, but that is not your destiny, my child. You will be rid of your virginity this day, three weeks, and after that will be both wife and mistress."

Danielle sucked in her bottom lip as that deep frown wrinkled her brow. "I suppose, milord, that I must be satisfied with that for now."

"You must indeed," he declared firmly and then his lips curved slightly. "One thing I have been meaning to mention for quite some time. I have a name, Danielle. Do you think you could use it?"

"I should call you Justin, or Linton?"

"Either will do, but I think I prefer the former." He smiled.

"We will strike a bargain then." Her dimples peeped mischievously. "If you will refrain from calling me 'brat,' or 'infant,' or 'wretch,' or 'vagabond,' or 'my child,' in that toplofty way, I will call you Justin."

"We have a bargain—but you must behave like Danielle to earn the name."

"La, sir! And how else should the future Countess of Linton behave?" She swept him a graceful curtsy totally at odds with the impish gleam in the big brown eyes.

Shaking his head in mock reproof he tucked her hand under his arm and began to walk back across the wide sweep of lawn toward the house.

such foolishness, she had no desire to annoy her husband at
this juncture.

Chapter 8

Linton was at his breakfast in Grosvenor Square about ten days later when his cousin was announced. Lord Julian, following hard on the heels of the footman, was resplendent in a blue satin coat opened over an embroidered waistcoat, pale yellow britches, and silken stockings embellished with large silver clocks.

"Linton, you're a dog! Indeed you are, 'pon my soul," he declared as greeting.

"Now what have I done to deserve this, Julian?" the earl asked mildly, putting up his glass to survey his cousin with a degree of polite interest.

"Why this marriage of yours, of course, to the de St. Varennes. Who is the chit, m'boy? Where did she come from? It is the outside of enough, y'know, to announce your engagement out of the blue like that, and then disappear incommunicado for the rest of the summer!"

"I am very sorry to have inconvenienced you, cousin," His Lordship responded softly. "Will you join me?" He gestured to the laden breakfast table.

The soft tones had the same effect on Lord Julian as they had on Danielle and he instantly recollected himself. It was hardly polite to storm into a man's breakfast parlor before noon, demanding information that could quite reasonably be considered very personal.

"I'll take a tankard of ale with you, coz," he said, seating himself at the table. "No, really, Justin, it is typical in you to hand the town the best *on dit* of the year and then leave everyone talking."

"If it is so typical, I cannot imagine why you should sound so surprised," His Lordship observed thoughtfully, sliding into his beef.

"But when we last met you had no thoughts of marriage, I'll lay odds."

"You would lose, Julian," my lord responded calmly.

That effectively silenced his interlocuter who began to have an uneasy suspicion that his cousin was going to reveal nothing of this extraordinary circumstance. He tried a different approach.

"You would not believe what the gossips have been makin' of it, Linton." He laughed. "I dare swear Bath this summer was steamier and more sulfurous than ever! No one has even seen the girl and it's rumored she has everything from a wall eye to a crooked back and is to be kept in seclusion at Danesbury whilst she provides you with heirs."

"Oh, I do not think that plan would suit Danielle," His Lordship said consideringly. "She was not educated to accept the role of brood mare, you see."

"What!" Lord Julian's mouth dropped open and remained that way for some considerable time whilst his cousin tranquilly continued with his breakfast.

"Do shut your mouth, dear fellow. It is most distracting," he requested mildly when it seemed that the other was likely to remain in this condition indefinitely.

"Beg pardon, but, well . . . Gad, Justin! What manner of girl is she?"

"You will find out in good time, Julian. She is to be presented at Court this evening and the gossips will, I am confident, have plenty to feed upon. Now, tell me, if you please . . ."

But Lord Julian was not to discover what his cousin wished to know. The sound of voices in the passage reached them and Linton, a frown in his eyes, laid down his fork as the door opened and Bedford, face and voice expressionless, announced: "Lady Danielle de St. Varennes, my lord."

Danielle, in a swish and flurry of velvet skirts, entered the room and began speaking almost before the butler had completed his dignified announcement.

"Milord, you have to do something about this, *immediatement*! If you do not speak to *Grandmère* straight away we shall all be in the basket!"

Both men had risen at her entrance, Lord Julian much more hastily than Linton, who did not immediately respond to this impetuous speech, merely lifted his glass and examined the small figure of his affianced bride in steady silence. She was looking utterly enchanting in a severely cut dark green velvet riding habit, heavily adorned with silver lace and little frogged buttons down the front. The skirt was caught up over one gloved arm and a tricorn hat of the same material perched rakishly on top of her head, a long, green feather curling to her shoulder.

Her voice faltered and her eyes dropped as the silence lengthened and he continued to look at her. "I suppose, milord, that you are going to tell me that I should not be here?"

"I make it a habit never to tell people things that I feel sure they already know," he responded levelly.

Lord Julian felt a twinge of fraternal sympathy for this entrancing creature. He knew from experience exactly how she must be feeling and gave a slight cough, hoping to divert his cousin.

"Ah, Julian, it seems you are to have your wish sooner than anticipated," Linton said smoothly. "Danielle, may I present Lord Julian Carlton?"

She curtsied gracefully and as Julian received the small hand in his, raising it to his lips as she swam upward, his gaze fell upon an enchanting heart-shaped face, enormous liquid brown eyes, and a pair of full lips opened in a warm smile over even, pearly white teeth. He was lost, instantly and forever, and no longer in any doubt as to why his cousin was about to forsake his long bachelor career.

"My lady, I am honoured. You are utterly *ravissante*," he murmured reverently. "Linton is indeed a fortunate man."

Her response devastated him. A light musical laugh, another curtsy as she said, "Indeed, sir, how kind in you to say such a thing to restore my dignity after such a set down! I am

155

delighted to make your acquaintance for we are, after all, to be in some way cousins, are we not?"

"And friends, I trust. I just wish I had seen you before Linton." He smiled and was rewarded by the appearance of a pair of deep, utterly mischievous dimples.

"Sir, I am sure that that is most improper of you, but Milord warned me that you are a rake."

"Oh brat!" Linton sighed as Lord Julian looked utterly taken aback by this candor.

"Indeed, ma'am, I must protest." He laughed, making a quick recover. "My reputation is much exaggerated."

"Oh, how very disappointing, sir," she murmured, lowering her lashes.

"Danielle, do not, I beg of you, further compound your indiscretion," Justin broke in swiftly, torn between amusement and annoyance. "Who accompanied you here?"

"Oh, I did not come alone, sir. You need have no fears on that score," she reassured him brightly.

"I am indeed a fortunate man," he responded sardonically. "Do you care for some coffee?"

"Oh yes, please, and a slice of that ham, if I may. I left in such a hurry, there was no time for breakfast." With swift movements she stripped off her gloves, removed her hat, and tossed them carelessly onto a chair before seating herself opposite and giving him what she hoped was a winning smile.

"You are a sad romp, my child," he said severely, slicing the ham thinly. "If this matter is so urgent, why did you not send me a message so that I could come to you?"

"Well, I did think of it," she confessed, pouring coffee from the heavy silver pot, "But the house is in such an uproar and I was afraid *Grandmaman* would get to you first." Her eyes sparkled. "Even poor Grandfather has gone to his club, and he hates to leave the house before noon."

"I think you had better tell me the whole, without further ado." Linton resumed his seat, crossing one elegant leg over the other, twiddling absently with his glass on its long riband.

"Well, you see, *Grandmère* wishes to disguise me as a bird's nest and I will have none of it. Can you imagine anything more idiotish, milord? A sort of cage with real birds and feathers—at least they are to be stuffed birds, I think. Real birds could be something of a problem as they have most uninhibited habits."

She grinned at him over a forkful of ham and Lord Julian began to have the strangest sensation of déjà vu. Sometime, somewhere, he had met this captivating bundle of mischief before.

"I do not think we need concern ourselves with the less pleasant habits of birds," Linton said repressively. "You will be pleased to confine yourself to the facts. So far I am quite unenlightened."

"You are also being most disagreeable," she retorted, shooting him a defiant look that Lord Julian, in the act of swallowing a mouthful of ale, intercepted.

"Good God!" he ejaculated, as the look and the taste on his tongue transported him to a sunny stableyard on the road to Dover.

They both turned toward him in surprise and then Linton sighed at the expression of astounded recognition on his cousin's face.

"Yes, Julian," he said resignedly, "just so."

Danielle looked between them frowning, and then comprehension dawned. "I see you recognize me, my lord. It is a very long and involved story but you will . . . you will say nothing of it to anyone, will you?"

"Good God, no! Of course not! Wouldn't dream of such a thing!" Lord Julian expostulated, still in a state of shock. "But, Gad, Justin! You boxed her ears, I saw you!"

"Yes, was it not infamous of him?" Danielle declared warmly. "I was not even drinking the horrid stuff!"

"Children, children, when you have quite finished shredding my character for an action which I have already admitted to have been overhasty, although thoroughly provoked, could we return to this matter of birds' nests?" Justin sighed wearily, beginning to feel uncomfortably like an unpopular schoolmaster in charge of a schoolroom of rowdy pupils.

"Well, it is a matter of total simplicity," Danielle stated, returning to her ham and helping herself to a piece of bread and butter. "I will not wear anything so absurd and *Grandmère* continues to insist that I should and if she goes on in this way I shall lose my temper and very likely say something that will cause her to fall into strong convulsions and most probably become ill, since she is quite old, you understand, and then I shall not be able to go to Court tonight and I daresay we shall be unable to be married."

"Dear me, the matter is more serious than I thought," Justin murmured, with a supreme effort controlling his quivering lip. "We must avoid such a consequence at all costs."

"You find this *amusant*, milord?" She glared at him, a dangerous glint in her eye.

"If you scowl at me like that, brat, I shall be tempted to forget Julian's presence," he replied gently, flicking open his snuff box to take a pinch between thumb and forefinger.

Danielle prudently altered her expression before inquiring politely, "Well, what is to be done, milord?"

"What do you think Julian? You are considered something of an expert in these matters, after all." My Lord turned to his cousin, still sitting in abstracted silence, staring into his tankard as if all the answers were contained therein.

"Oh, what?" He looked up hastily. "What d'you say, dear boy?"

"I asked your opinion on the question of birds' nests," His Lordship replied calmly.

"Birds' nests, yes, yes, quite so . . . quite so."

Danielle gave an inadvertent gurgle of laughter. "Poor Lord Julian! We have quite destroyed your peace, have we not? Do not trouble yourself with the question, I beg you."

"No, no, no trouble at all, ma'am, happy to be of service," he reassured her hastily. "Can't for the life of me see why M'Lady March wishes to disguise you as a bird's nest. Not at all the thing. Is she feeing quite well, d'you know, m'dear?"

This was too much for Danny and she went off into a peal of laughter so infectious that even Linton's rather grim countenance lightened somewhat.

"Julian, Danielle is, I think, referring to her coiffure for her presentation this evening," he explained patiently.

"Oh, well why didn't she say so. All this talk of birds' nests—it's enough to confuse anyone."

"But I did say so," Danielle protested indignantly, then added thoughtfully, "At least I think I did. Anyway it is a monstrous affair, all lacquer and powder and stuck with dead birds and feathers and twice as tall as I and I will not wear it."

Fortunately for her audience, their knowledge of prevailing fashion was sufficiently deep to enable them to adapt this horrendous image to more realisic proportions.

"Who's to dress your hair?" Lord Julian asked after a short period of cogitation.

"Monsieur Artur, and he is quite the most idiotish person, always waving his hands about and speaking in an accent that he considers to be French, but it most assuredly is not."

"But he is the best in London, m'dear." Lord Julian was scandalized at this slanderous dismissal of such a noted artiste.

"Then it is no wonder everyone goes around looking so ludicrous," she declared roundly. "But I do not intend to be in their company, and if you, milord, are going to insist, I should inform you that we are not yet married and you do not have the right of command."

"Do not challenge me, Danny, please," His Lordship begged mildly. "It will make things most uncomfortable for us both. I do not, as it happens, think that what you have described will look well on you at all. You are far too small."

"*Exactement!*" she declared with satisfaction. "I shall look positively top-heavy."

This inelegant expression earned her a raised eyebrow from Milord and a hastily suppressed chuckle from Julian.

"The powder and feathers are *de rigueur* at Court, but I think we can find a satisfactory compromise," Linton stated. "The lacquer and the birds we can do without."

"And you will tell *Grandmère* so?"

"You may regale Julian with the salient facts of your story, brat, avoiding unnecessary detail, if you please, whilst I find my coat. I will accompany you to Bedford Place. Is your groom with your horse?"

"No, I sent him home and had your servants stable the mare. I thought we might be some considerable time, you see, and as I knew you would ride home with me it seemed wasteful to keep Harry kicking his heels." She gave him her ravishing smile and

159

the earl, with an almost defeated headshake, left the room to exchange his embroidered dressing gown for more suitable attire.

Justin, Earl of Linton, married Danielle de St. Varennes on a green and gold day of Indian summer, the last Saturday in September. It was indeed a quiet wedding, attended only by family and very close friends of the groom and the bride's grandparents, with the notable inclusion of the Prince of Wales, without Princess Caroline, from whom he had been scandalously and openly separated for four years, and William Pitt, who watched the proceedings with a most remarked air of satisfaction. However small the guest list, the occasion was of an elegance bordering on the magnificent. St. George's in Hanover Square was bedecked with hothouse flowers of a delicacy and simplicity that matched the bride's fresh youthfulness, and the music, selected with great firmness by the bride, resounded through the nave on the soaring tongues of the choir.

The Earl of Linton, in midnight blue satin, Dresden lace foaming at his neck, and the most magnificent sapphires at throat and fingers, his hair powdered and curled in a manner that Danielle for one found rather intimidating, stood before the altar attended by his cousin, watching his bride's measured progress down the aisle on the arm of the Earl of March.

She wore a gown of white velvet opened over a white satin underdress thickly encrusted with seed pearls. Her mother's flawless pearl set was clasped around wrist and throat and the exquisite tiara held her long flowing veil in place, to fall down her back over the velvet train. She carried white roses to complete a veritable picture of maidenhood on its last voyage. The earl's lips quivered slightly as he remembered the pithy comment she had delivered on this very subject during the ceremony rehearsal the previous afternoon.

She stood beside him now, her head demurely bent to the bouquet between her gloved hands. They were quite steady, he noticed. When the moment came, the Earl of March took her hand and gave it into the possession of the Earl of Linton before quietly stepping back. Lady Lavinia buried herself in her handkerchief; her tears were of joy for her granddaughter and grief for her daughter who had most truly been sacrificed on the altar of matrimony. It needed all her resolution to remind herself that Louise's had been a self-sacrifice. She had been as headstrong as her daughter but Lucien, Vicomte de St. Varennes, had been, alas, no Earl of Linton who would most assuredly cherish his wife as he was now firmly promising to do.

Danielle's own responses were firm and clear. Only the slight tremor of the fingers between his as she promised her obedience gave any indication of inner turmoil.

The earl bent his head to the small ear revealed by the upward sweep of her curls caught under the veil to whisper, "Do not worry, my brat. I will make it very easy for you to fullfil your vows, I promise." Her fingers gripped his tightly and a soft choke that he was convinced was laughter came from beneath the veil. The heavy gold band slipped over her left finger and the earl himself raised the frothy veil to look into a pair of very grave brown eyes before he bent to brush her lips with his own.

The remainder of the afternoon passed in a curious dream for Danielle, now Countess of Linton. She stood for what seemed hours beside her husband in the ballroom of March house, receiving their guests. The congratulations from this group at least were sincerely uttered, though doubts still fluttered in the concerned breasts of Linton's family and friends—with the exception of Lord Julian who, after the formalities of the receiving line, bore her off to meet the younger members of the vast Carlton clan with as much proud possession as if he himself were the groom. Linton watched with an amused tolerance as he devoted his own attentions to the older generation and the Marches. His mother and sisters were fortunately well acquainted with Lady Lavinia and were soon settled for a comfortable coze. The Countess of March graciously received the many compliments on her granddaughter's beauty and deftly fielded the many probes as to her circumstances.

Danielle, surrounded by an admiring circle of Julian's

cronies and feeling as if she had never before enjoyed herself so much at a party, absently took a glass from the tray offered at her elbow by a liveried flunky. Before she could raise it to her lips, however, it had left her hand. Startled and not a little put out, she looked up at her husband now standing at her shoulder.

"You will prefer the champagne, my love," he said placidly.

"But how can I know that until I taste this?" she demanded, frowning deeply.

"Try it, by all means, but curb your reactions." He held the glass to her lips and watched with great amusement as an expression of astounded horror crossed the intent face.

"*Mais, c'est abominable!* Whatever is it, Justin?"

"Ratafia, my dear, and now you know you will be able to avoid it in the future."

"It is fit only for . . ."

"Madam Wife," he interrupted her swiftly, "will you allow me to escort you to the dining room?"

The wedding had taken place at noon and was followed by a reception that included what Lady Lavinia had erroneously described as, "A simple nuncheon, for you know, my dear, people will have dinner engagements and will not wish to be quite overeaten by the evening."

"This is *Grandmère*'s idea of a simple buffet?" Danny choked as they reached the long, first-floor dining room. The tables groaned under the weight of soufflés and syllabubs, stuffed quail, dishes of deviled eggs, capons and pigeons in a delicate wine sauce, dishes of artichokes, buttered cauliflower, and mushrooms, interspersed with lobsters, buttered crab, and several Scotch salmons.

"You know," she said suddenly, "when one has been truly hungry, painfully hungry, this seems a little . . . a little too much. You understand, milord?"

"Perfectly," he said quietly. "Do you prefer not to eat now?"

"That would look a little churlish." She smiled. "Perhaps a morsel of the crab and some salmon."

"Come and sit with my mother whilst I procure you a plate and a glass of wine."

162

At three o'clock, Lady Lavinia, prompted by a quiet word from the groom, hastened to send her granddaughter upstairs to change her wedding gown. "Linton wishes to leave within the hour, my love," she explained. "If you are to reach Danesbury by dusk you must get ready now."

In Danielle's bedchamber, Lady Lavinia began with great hesitation on a mother's duty to a bride on her wedding day. "I do not know how much your mama may have told you, my love, about the duties of a wife . . ." She began hesitantly, but was instantly interrupted.

"Dear ma'am, pray do not. I understand much more than perhaps is seemly and what I do not, Milord had promised to teach me."

"Dear God!" the Lady Lavinia was betrayed into uttering. "You have talked of such things with Linton?"

"Indeed, ma'am," Danielle said coolly, resisting the mischievous urge to declare that more than talk had taken place between them.

"Well, he is, of course, a great deal older than you," her ladyship muttered uneasily, "And he has much experience of the world." That thought gave rise to another, much more difficult to explain to this eager creature who seemed to repose such utter trust in her husband. But it was a necessary, though unpleasant, task.

"Danielle, gentlemen frequently find that a wife is not always sufficient for certain . . . uh . . . certain needs . . ."

"*Grandmère.*" Danielle whirled from the mirror. "I have not the intention of being a complacent wife. If Linton sets up a mistress I shall most likely cut his throat in the night!" She crossed the room hastily to take her shattered relative in her arms. "Now I have shocked you, and I am truly sorry for it, but you must understand that I am rather different. I can promise you, Linton will have no need of a mistress whilst I am his wife."

"Oh Danielle, whatever is to become of you if you speak like that in Society?" Lady Lavinia moaned, more shocked than she had ever been.

"Why nothing at all, ma'am, because I shall not," her outrageous granddaughter reassured cheerfully. "Can you

163

imagine Justin's reaction if I did?" Her lips curved in an impish smile. "Come, *Grandmère*, let us not discuss this further. It is embarrassing for you and quite unnecessary, I do assure you."

With that Lady Lavinia was obliged to be satisfied. Reflecting that Linton certainly appeared to have the measure of his bride whose sophistication, while certainly shocking in one so young, perhaps boded well for a good understanding between husband and wife, she turned her attention thankfully to Danielle's toilette.

Radiant in a crimson traveling dress of her favorite velvet, Danielle descended the wide, shallow staircase to be received on the arm of her husband. "That hat, my love, is going to have to come off very soon," he whispered.

"Do you not care for it, my lord?" she questioned innocently. "I thought it monstrous pretty, myself."

"It is very fetching, but those ridiculous feathers will tickle my nose," he replied solemnly. "I do not find sneezing compatible with the activity I intend to pursue once we are away from this bear garden."

"Oh, infamous, Justin!" she whispered, laughing up at him. "How can you refer to this so elegant gathering in such a fashion?"

"Goodness me!" the Dowager Countess of Linton exclaimed in a low voice to her daughter. "I do believe Justin has made a love match. Do you not see the way he looks at the child?"

"And the way she looks at him, ma'am," Lady Beatrice replied, an uncomfortable stab of envy piercing her ample breast. Ten years of marriage and six children had, she thought, cured her of the romantic leanings of her youth—not so, it appeared.

The light traveling coach bearing the Linton arms stood at the door. Justin handed his bride into its upholstered interior after a slightly tearful farewell from her grandparents before entering himself and closing the door firmly.

"Now, my love," he said with satisfaction, seating himself beside her. "Let us rid ourselves of that hat."

"But, Justin, we have not yet left the square." She made half-laughing protest.

"True," he concurred and pulled the blinds over the

windows. "Now we are free of prying eyes, so I will have no more excuses, if you please." The hat left her head to be tossed carelessly onto the opposite seat and the Countess of Linton found herself ruthlessly crushed against a broad chest as imperative fingers lifted her face to receive a kiss, at first gentle and exploratory, then increasing in demand and possession as the earl, for the first time, truly gave rein to his passion.

When finally he released her lips she remained in the circle of his arm, sobbing for breath and composure as the pulsing heat in her body slowly receded. "You . . . you have kissed me many times before, milord, but never quite like that," she stammered in wonder.

"Before, my little love, I had to keep myself in check." He smiled gently, running a long finger over the bridge of her tip-tilted nose. "Today, I may anticipate a little."

Danielle absorbed this slowly. There was so much that she still did not understand about this business of lovemaking, particularly its effects on her mate.

"How soon before we reach Danesbury?" she asked carefully. It seemed a natural enough question in the circumstances.

"We are not going to Danesbury today" came the totally unexpected reply.

"But why is that?" Danielle pushed her hands against his chest in a quite unsuccessful attempt to right herself.

"I do not wish to spend unnecessary hours of my wedding day boxed up in a chaise," he replied placidly. "And neither do I wish you to become tired, my love. Not yet, at least."

"But . . . but you told the other chaise with my abigail and all the luggage to go straight to Danesbury. I heard you."

"I have dressed and undressed you before, Danielle. Will you not allow me to do so again? Surely, I was not so very unskilled," he teased, running soft fingers through the lightly powdered curls resting against his shoulders.

"You were most skilled, milord," she murmured mischievously. "I seem to remember remarking on how very experienced you were."

"But you will be a little more discreet today, my brat?"

165

She laughed softly and possessed herself of his hand, examining the long beringed fingers with frowning concentration. "But I have no clothes, Justin, no toilet articles. Is it to be as it was that first evening in Paris?"

"Not quite. I have everything you will need for one night, which, I take leave to inform you, madam, will be very little! Now try to sleep a while, I wish you rested when we arrive at our destination."

Their destination turned out to be a pretty, whitewashed inn on the banks of the River Thames about fifteen miles from London. An apple-cheeked woman enveloped in a voluminous white apron came to the door to greet them, wreathed in smiles as she bobbed a curtsy.

"My lord, you made good time, indeed. My felicitations, sir, and to you, my lady. Welcome to the Swallow's Nest. As you instructed, my lord, you and her ladyship are the only guests and everything is prepared exactly."

"My love, may I introduce Mrs. MacGregor? To me she has always been Biddy." Linton smiled.

"And to you too, I hope, my lady. I've known His Lordship since before he was in leading strings."

Danielle gave the woman her smile. "Then, Biddy, you shall tell me some stories of that time. I have a great desire to know what manner of child My Lord was."

"A real imp, m'lady." Biddy laughed, totally won by this frank, open manner. "Now many's the time I've . . ."

"Biddy, not now, please," His Lordship interrupted, anxious to forestall a long catalog of reminiscences which would probably not reflect too favorably on his boyhood character.

"Goodness me, what can I have been thinking of?" Biddy recollected herself briskly. "You must be tired, my lady, after your journey and such an exciting day. I'll show you to your apartments and you need have no fear you'll be disturbed. There's a cold supper waiting for you and Jed's best burgundy." She bustled ahead of them into the inn, up a flight of oak stairs, and along a passageway to open a door at the end. Danielle walked into a long, sunny room running the length of the inn. It was both bedchamber and parlor with a bright fire in the grate, an oak piecrust table set for dinner, flanked by two carved wooden chairs, tapestry-covered armchairs, and an enormous canopied bed, fluffy with feather pillows and a patchwork comforter. A worked screen stood to one side of the fire and a pink-cheeked girl emerged from behind at their entrance.

"Your bath's all ready, m'lady." She curtsied. "If you'd like me to help you . . . ?"

Danielle glanced up at Linton and his lips curved. "I think, Maggie, that My Lady would appreciate your assistance," he said calmly. "Ah, here is the luggage. You will find everything you need in the portmanteau, my love. I shall go and talk to Jed for a while—it's been many months since we met. I shall join you in about half an hour." He pinched her cheek lightly, smiling reassuringly into her suddenly anxious eyes and left her.

With Maggie's help she got out of the crimson traveling dress, the wide hoop, petticoats, stockings, corset, chemise, and pantalettes and stepped behind the screen into the sloping-backed tub of hot water. It had been typical of Justin that he had sensed she would feel more comfortable this first time preparing herself alone and Maggie did not intrude on her thoughts, merely busied herself tidying the discarded clothing and unpacking the portmanteau.

"I have laid everything ready on the bed, m'lady," she called softly from the other side of the screen. "Will there be anything else?"

"No thank you, Maggie. You have been most helpful." The door clicked shut and she was truly alone.

The gown on the bed took her breath away. It was of ivory silk, caught under the bosom to fall in a straight line to her feet. The low, wide neckline was threaded through with a dull gold ribbon to be drawn and tied above the cleft of her breasts. She slipped it over her warmed nakedness and the soft material rustled against her skin, and clung most immodestly to the curves of her body. It was the sort of garment to cause raised eyebrows and gasps of shock from the likes of Lady Lavinia, but her husband clearly knew what pleased him when it came to the bedchamber. She sat at the dresser to brush the powder out of her curls, allowing the ringlets to fall as they pleased around her face and on the nape of her neck. She decided that she was, on the whole, pleased with what she saw. Her eyes carried an unusual brightness which, if anything, made them seem even bigger, and her skin glowed with an inner light that she knew reflected the trepidation and anticipation surging somewhere in the pit of her belly.

The door opened and she whirled from the mirror, unable to restrain the slight, startled gasp as Linton came in. He said nothing at first, merely removed his coat and shoes before crossing toward her.

"You must not be nervous, Danielle," he whispered, sweeping the hair from the back of her neck and bending to kiss the soft, vulnerable skin.

A slight shudder ran through her as his lips burned against her bent neck and his tongue stroked smoothly upward into the indentation of her skull.

"Come, my love. It is time for me to show you just how enjoyable this matter of loving can be." His hands cupped her elbows, lifting her off the dresser stool, drawing her toward the long pier glass where he positioned himself behind her as she faced her image.

"First you must understand the beauty of your body and see something of the effects desire will have." His hands reached in front of her, cupping the soft breasts, the heel of his palm lifting the nipples under the thin silk, before he untied the ribbon at the neck of the gown and slowly bared her shoulders and breasts, catching them in his hand as they fell free.

Danielle looked at them in the glass, their whiteness startlingly blue-veined, their tips suddenly small and hard under his caressing fingers. "Do you think I am perhaps a little inadequate, milord?" she asked hesitantly.

Laughter sprang in the depths of those black eyes as they met hers in the mirror. "Were you any better endowed, my sweet, you would be, to use your own inelegant expression, positively top-heavy! See how comfortably they fit in my hands?" But those hands were now pushing the gown further, sliding it to her waist. She gasped in soft protest as one long finger played in the small, tight bloom of her navel, but her

168

protest went unheeded as, with a deft movement, Justin slipped the fine silk over her slender hips to fall in a whisper around her ankles.

She stood, long-legged, clean-limbed before her reflection and the tall figure behind her allowed a whisper of contentment to escape his lips as he began to stroke over her belly, her hips, and down her thighs.

"Ah, but you are perfection, Danielle. Do you see how straight and slim your legs are, how flat your belly, and how sweetly round your little bottom?" He turned her sideways slightly, running his hand down the long length of her back, meandering lazily over the curve of her hips and down the backs of her thighs.

Danielle swallowed. Under the soft caress of his fingers, the honeyed warmth of his voice, a deep tension was building, sending fluttery shivers across her skin and the blood pounding through her veins. He drew her against him, one arm circling her waist and a curious hardness stirred against her buttocks. She stiffened suddenly and then moaned involuntarily as his hand curled itself in the springy triangle of fair hair at the base of her belly. She moved her own hand, pushing him away, but he shook his head slightly and continued to finger the mound beneath. His breath whispered across her neck and the fingers reached further.

"You must not," she pleaded softly, unable to withstand the moist weakness filling her secret places.

"Oh, but I must," he insisted gently. She clenched her thighs and buttocks against the invasion, but he pushed with firm determination between them, parting the silky, swollen petals to bring tears of shame and delight to her eyes as her entire body shivered and shook beneath an onslaught of heat and icy cold that misted her skin with a fine sheen of sweat.

"See how heavy your eyes are, my love?" he whispered. "How your breath comes fast when I touch you like this. See how your breasts swell and stand out? Don't resist your desire. It will bring only exquisite pleasure, I promise you."

"Is there pleasure for you?" she whispered.

"Can you not feel it, my love?" He pressed her against him again and the hard bulge of his awakened manhood burned against her flesh.

"Come, Danielle. I will show you the extent of my pleasure." Lifting her easily, he carried her to the bed, laying her down tenderly.

Slipping out of his britches, undergarments, and stockings, he reached for Danielle's hand and drew her to her feet. Her eyes were wide as saucers as she gazed at his nakedness, unable to look away from the slender trail of black hair curling from his navel down to the evidence of his passion. The thought of allowing him inside a body that she still thought of as belonging only to herself sent a thrill of fear down her spine.

"Touch me, Danielle," he commanded quietly. "If you learn the shape and the feel of me, you will not be frightened."

Tentatively she stretched her hand to enclose him. He was hard, yet soft, the blood pulsing strongly against her fingers. Her other hand ran hesitantly over his muscled chest, touching the hard buttons of his nipples. Justin exhaled on a soft groan and looking up she saw his eyes were closed, the handsome head thrown back. It occurred to her, then, that in some way she was giving back the pleasure she had received from him and that that pleasure was not something to be hidden or denied.

"Lie on the bed now, Danielle." The soft command was enforced by his hands pushing her gently backward. She obeyed in watchful, waiting, trusting silence as he stretched himself, long and lean, beside her. His head bent to her breasts, drawing the nipples between his lips as his hands stroked languorously over her body creating a dreamy lethargy that was hardly disturbed as he again began to explore her vulnerability.

"Keep still, my love." A hand pressed firmly into her belly and the next instant she felt fingers sliding inside her, moving gently. Her hips bucked in protest, arced against the firm pressure on her stomach, and then began to move of their own accord in rhythm with the alien exploration within.

"I will be as gentle as I can," the soft voice stated evenly. His own passion was well in check now as, with quiet deliberation, Justin began to bring her to the brink of ecstasy. The tension within Danielle now built to an unbearable peak as those

170

skillful fingers unerringly played on the sensitive center of her passion, until, with a small cry, she took her release in the only way possible, the muscles in thigh and belly tightening convulsively as the searing sweetness flooded and spilled over, leaving her gasping, heavy with involuntary relaxation. He swung himself over her supine frame guiding his manhood within the still pulsating entrance to her body. For a second, the brown eyes beneath him opened in shock, but in the aftermath of her climax she had neither the strength nor the will to tighten her body against him. The soft barrier of her innocence opposed his path and with swift resolution he drew back slightly before driving deeply.

Danielle cried out at the abrupt shaft of pain, but her body was still relaxed and the moment passed as swiftly as it had come.

"All over, my sweet." He spoke softly, pushing the sweat-dampened curls away from her face, bending his lips to hers in a kiss of overpowering sweetness. "Now we shall both take our pleasure."

His eyes never leaving hers, he began to move smoothly, rhythmically, adjusting his speed and position as reactions flitted across the mobile face beneath him. He was taken as much by surprise as Danielle when her half-closed eyes suddenly shot open on an expression of astonished wonder. Her back arched as her legs curled around his buttocks, pulling him hard against the cleft of her opened body. The demanding movement destroyed all control and his passion gushed hot and fast within her. Danielle cried out again, holding his throbbing manhood inside until he fell, spent, crushing her breasts beneath his exhausted weight.

It was a long time before Justin shifted sideways, disengaging himself as he drew her into the curve of his arm.

"Dear God, Madame Wife, will you never cease to surprise me?" he muttered weakly.

"Was that not the right thing to happen?" Danielle pushed herself onto one elbow, examining his face intently.

"Absolutely the right thing, my love, just a little unusual. Virgins do not, in general, achieve such delight without some practice."

171

"Perhaps, in general, they do not have such skillful or experienced tutors," she murmured, lowering her lashes over an impish gleam.

"I am glad that the loss of your innocence has not meant the loss of your wit, my brat." He laughed.

"Now, little love, we must eat some of Biddy's supper. I dare not risk hurting her feelings, and, besides, we need to keep up our strength, we have a long night ahead of us."

Danielle smiled with anticipation at his words as she took the outstretched hand and rose languidly to her feet, crossing with long strides to the discarded gown in its rumpled heap before the mirror.

"I think, milord," she stated definitely, as her head emerged from the silken folds, "that this is not the kind of garment normally worn by wives."

He laughed appreciatively, coming to smooth the material over her hips. "No, it is a gown for a mistress, Danny. And, unless I much mistake the matter, I have acquired a mistress to gladden the most exacting heart."

Danielle smiled, her eyes meeting his in the mirror. "Can one love a mistress, Justin, as one can love a wife?"

"If they are one and the same, my sweet, there can be only inexplicable joy. For you, too, since you have both husband and lover."

"Yes," she whispered, turning within his embrace to face him. "For me, also, only inexplicable joy."

Part 2 : Out of the Chrysalis

Chapter 9

"I fear, Peter, that I must return to town in the morning." The Earl of Linton did not look up from the close-written sheet in his hand.

Peter Haversham had recognized the bold black script immediately. The Countess of Linton was an inveterate note writer and in the six months since she had transformed the stately pace of life at Linton House he had received any number of these hastily written communications containing information, prettily worded requests, and, on occasion, terse instructions.

"Nothing wrong, I trust, my lord?"

"Not yet," Linton replied with the grin that still fascinated his secretary by its novelty. Justin leaned over to fill his glass from the decanter of port resting at his elbow on the smooth mahogany table in the dining room at Danesbury. A ray of late afternoon sun caught the crystal glass, turning the drops into translucent amethysts. "Her Ladyship informs me that if I do not return in time to escort her to Rutland House on the morrow, she will substitute a dancing bear for my presence." He passed the decanter to his secretary, who was striving with remarkable lack of success to keep a straight face.

"Do you really think she would, sir?"

"Do you really think she would not, Peter?" His Lordship questioned gently, his own eyes glinting with laughter.

"I should rather imagine," Peter said thoughtfully, "that Lady Danny will, as usual, set a new fashion. It will become all the rage for ladies to go about attended by dancing bears."

"Quite so, m'boy." The earl swung a dusty, top-booted leg from its casual perch across the carved arm of his chair. "It is to avoid such a catastrophe that I must return—my social duty, do you not agree?"

"Indubitably, Lord Linton. Little of urgency remains here. I will speak with the steward in the morning and expect to be in town myself tomorrow night."

As his employer made to leave the dining room a sudden thought struck Peter. "Ah, my lord? You don't think that perhaps Lady Danny has already acquired a dancing bear?"

"Sweet heavens!" The earl paused, his hand on the porcelain doorknob. "A mangy, flea-bitten, starved, much abused animal in need of rescue, no doubt!"

"Well, after the monkeys, sir," Peter murmured diffidently, "it seems possible."

"Probable, rather," His Lordship observed. "What the devil are we to do with it, Peter?"

"I am certain Lady Danny will have some plan in mind, sir," the other offered consolingly. "She did with the monkeys, if you recall?"

"Will I ever forget?" Justin said feelingly.

Both men looked at each other, each remembering clearly that afternoon . . . Justin, with a group of friends in search of a quiet glass of claret and some conversation, had walked into his usually orderly hall to find a scene of anarchy strongly resembling Dante's Inferno. His entire household, it seemed, from the lowliest kitchen maid and bootboy to the austere Bedford were gathered in squawking, gasping wonder. Peter Haversham, in a state of white-faced shock, stood by the open library door, clutching its knob as if it provided the only escape route from a veritable madhouse.

Justin, initially, had eyes only for his wife, perched precariously and quite immodestly astride the topmost banister rail at the head of the curving stairs. Her skirts and petticoats were hitched carelessly around her, revealing a most indecorous length of silk-stockinged leg, dainty ankles, and kid-slippered feet. She appeared to be holding a bunch of

176

bananas, he thought incredulously, offering them at great risk to life and limb toward something chattering and swinging from the immense chandelier in the hall.

"Danielle! Get off there!" His voice cut through the startled throng who fell instantly silent.

Not so Danielle, who said reproachfully, "Did you have to shout like that, Justin? Now you have scared them again and I nearly had them."

"Get down this instant, brat!" the earl thundered, forgetful in the urgency of the moment of the impropriety of thus addressing his wife in front of the servants. It was a voice very few of his audience had heard before, but it brought Danny, in a flurry and swish of silk and lace, to the safety of the landing.

Linton turned, quizzing glass raised, toward his butler. "I find it extraordinary, Bedford, that my entire household can find no better employment in the middle of the afternoon?" It was said very gently, very politely, but brought a dull red tinge to that gentleman's normally somber countenance. Bedford bowed, turned to the group behind him—a swift movement of his hand and only the earl, his startled friends, Peter, and Danielle remained. The latter came down the stairs to join them.

"It's just a pair of monkeys, milord," she explained hastily. "Some organ grinder was treating them most dreadfully and they are so thin and starved and I am sure he has beaten them and they have sores around their necks . . ." She fell silent as her husband raised an imperative palm.

"Give me that damn fruit," he instructed sternly, making for the stairs. "You may explain later why you have seen fit to turn the household into a menagerie."

"Oh do not be absurd, Justin." Danny choked back her laughter, running behind him as he strode up the stairs. "I am not turning anything into a menagerie. If Peter hadn't behaved in such an idiotish fashion none of this would have happened."

"What the devil has Peter to do with this?" Linton paused, halfway up the stairs.

"Well, he screamed," Danny said scornfully, shooting the accused a baleful look.

177

"They attacked me," Peter protested furiously, "and I did not scream."

"They did not attack you! They were just trying to make friends. What possible harm could a pair of scrawny little monkeys do you?"

"I think I have heard enough," Linton said repressively, anxious to prevent the development of a full-scale argument between his wife and his secretary. His sympathies were very much with the latter whose wounded sensibilities would quite clearly require considerable soothing later, but the earl was having difficulty controlling the deep surge of merriment that had become so much a part of his life since he had brought his wife to London to take her rightful place as Countess of Linton.

Reaching the head of the stairs, he swung an immaculate leg across the banister, bracing himself with one hand against a carved pillar.

"Justin, you'll fall," Danielle yelped, seeing for the first time exactly how precarious the position was.

"I am less likely to do so than you, hampered by those petticoats," he stated.

"Well, I *was* going to put on my britches . . ." she murmured mischievously.

"Remind me to beat you one of these days, Danny," Linton said conversationally, stretching toward the gibbering creatures, swinging just out of his reach.

Danielle gurgled, well aware that her husband was only feigning annoyance, and watched with admiration as, with soft-spoken commands and the enticement of the bananas, he received first one of the frightened creatures and then its companion, handing them to her with the brisk injunction to keep them away from Peter and not let them loose again if she valued her skin . . .

"Let us hope, Peter, that she has already disposed of the unfortunate creature," the earl said, returning to the reality of the dining room at Danesbury as he shook these memories aside. "Otherwise, I feel sure we shall be obliged to house it here, in the stableyard."

Peter chuckled softly. "I rather think, sir, that even Lady

Danny will fail to achieve John's consent to such an arrangement."

"Never underestimate my wife, dear boy. It's a lesson I learned many months ago. She has already contrived to change most of the time-honored practices in the stables with John's positively eager consent."

"And Bedford's cellars, also," Peter added with a smile.

"Just so. However, I do draw the line at dancing bears so, if you will excuse me, dear fellow, I shall make my arrangements for an early departure."

Linton left his secretary musing quietly that however cataclysmic had been the changes wrought by the Countess of Linton in the last six months, they had all, without exception, improved the general tone and quality of life. Both Linton House and Danesbury had lost their somewhat somber air and even such austere individuals as Petersham and Bedford had capitulated, after only the shortest period of dignified reserve, under the bright charm and unquestioned competence of their employer's young bride. Peter's own work load had been lightened considerably by Danielle's insistence on taking over the accounts of both establishments. She accomplished the task with a degree of stern consistency that had swiftly earned her the respect and grudging admiration of those hitherto responsible for the housekeeping and management of Lord Linton's households.

The greatest change of all, however, had been in the Earl of Linton himself whose countenance these days was rarely impassive. True, on occasion, it assumed the black glower of an impending hurricane, sending all but Lady Danny scurrying out of sight. True that the household was at times shaken by tempestuous scenes quite unsuited to a nobleman's establishment. But it was also true, although everyone forebore to discuss the fact, that these scenes ended in the bedchamber whence the earl and his countess would eventually emerge, wreathed in smiles and quite at peace with one another.

Linton had found a se'ennight away from his wife quite long enough and was more than willing to respond to her importunate summons. The demand had been bolstered by some remarkably frank and uninhibited statements that brought a smile of anticipation to his lips as he contemplated their reunion. Petersham merely bowed when informed of their premature departure and drew his own conclusions from His Lordship's expression.

It was later than he intended when Linton left Danesbury the following morning and owing to one of his chestnuts throwing a shoe just outside the little village of Chiswick, it was after ten o'clock that evening when the racing curricle drew up in Grosvenor Square.

Bedford greeted His Lordship with a low bow and the information that Her Ladyship had said he was expected.

"Lady Linton has left for Rutland House?" the earl inquired, stripping of his gloves.

"Yes, my lord, about an hour since."

"Who escorted her?" Linton shrugged out of his dust-covered driving cape, resisting the urge to substitute "what" for "who."

"Lord Julian, sir." Bedford refrained discreetly from mentioning that Julian had been but one of half a dozen gallants who had assisted at Her Ladyship's toilette before escorting her sedan chair with much laughter to Rutland House. "Have you dined, my lord?"

"Indifferently, Bedford, but it will suffice." Linton shuddered slightly. The only inn in a position to provide dinner at Chiswick had been patently unused to the delicate palates of the Quality. "Did Her Ladyship use the chaise?"

"No, my lord, the chair."

"In that case, have the chaise brought round. I shall leave within the hour." Linton mounted the stairs to change his traveling clothes for those more suited to the Duchess of Rutland's ball. He was tempted to bathe and await the return of his wife, but knowing her indefatigable ability to dance the night and morning hours away decided that he would be better advised to fetch her himself.

Thus it was that on the stroke of eleven, just as she was preparing to leave her post at the head of the great staircase, the Duchess of Rutland was gratified to see the unmistakable figure of Justin, Earl of Linton, mounting at a leisurely pace toward her.

"Linton, how delightful!" she exclaimed, extending a plump hand. "We understood you were in the country, although your entrancing little wife did say there was a possibility you might honor us with your company."

Justin bowed low over the hand, brushing his lips across the heavily ringed fingers. "I find I completed my business rather earlier than expected, your grace."

"How fortunate for us all, Justin." Her grace gave him a shrewd smile. "I rather suspect, though, that even had you not done so, you would not have remained out of town overlong."

Justin laughed softly. "How right you are, Amelia. Where is my lady wife?"

"I am not certain, but if you look for the men you will assuredly find her."

A frown passed over His Lordship's previously smiling countenance and the duchess made haste to explain herself. "I implied no criticism, Justin. But you must know that Danielle is like the proverbial honeypot. She has only to walk into a room to draw every eligible—and not so eligible—buck to her side. But she is always the soul of propriety."

"I think 'always' might be a slight exaggeration," Justin corrected, taking snuff with delicate insouciance. The frown, however, had left his face and the duchess breathed an imperceptible sigh of relief. It was not wise to arouse the earl's ire at the best of times and he would tolerate no breath of criticism of his wife.

"That wife of yours, Justin, for all her youth is well up to snuff," she declared firmly. "I suspect that she does nothing unintentionally and even her occasional . . . uh . . . misdemeanours, are carefully calculated. She enjoys surprising people, Linton, but rarely goes beyond the line of what is acceptable."

Justin nodded. He had noticed the same thing himself, but had also noticed that Danielle escaped Society's censure for acts that would put others, at least temporarily, beyond the pale. It had something to do with a certain flair she possessed, combined with her irresistibly charming manner and her most extraordinary beauty. In six months she had earned an undisputed place as one of the leaders of the ton—an extraordinary feat for a new bride, particularly one so young.

"Well, if you will excuse me, Amelia, I shall go in search of my bride."

Amelia laughed. "By all means, and if you remove her shortly I guarantee that you will be the hero of the hour for every young woman present."

Danielle, at this moment, was standing on the wide terrace outside the first-floor ballroom, a glass of champagne in hand, surrounded by her admiring court. She teased, flirted lightly, laughed at acceptable sallies, and treated those unacceptable with an icy indifference, but her mind was elsewhere. She knew that Justin would arrive this evening as surely as if he had promised, and she waited only for the soft footfall, the light amused tone, the caress of his fingers on her bare shoulders. Her body, well versed now in the arts and joys of love, ached for the feel of him, resented the vast loneliness of her empty bed as she fell into slumber and awoke to the same emptiness. Even in sleep she missed the warm possessive relaxation of his hand on her stomach, her buttocks, breasts, as she curled tightly against him. His insistence that she remain in town while he dealt with urgent matters at Danesbury had led to a monumental argument. She had capitulated eventually only because he was right—it would have been unthinkably discourteous for both of them to have been out of town for her grandparents' ball which had taken place three days previously and which, contrary to expectation, she had enjoyed enormously, except for the empty bed at its end. They had parted friends and lovers, but she was anxious to dispel any lingering reserve at what she now recognized to have been a display of childish obstinacy.

Justin paused in the open door to the terrace, stealing a second to view his wife unobserved. The urchin of his memory was gone as totally as if she had never existed. Her eighteenth birthday had passed last month—at her insistence with total lack of remark. The date would always carry for her the memory of the massacre of her family and was one she saw as a day of mourning rather than celebration.

Her face, now lifted in laughter to some comment of Julian's, stunned him anew, its beauty that of a mature, experienced woman who knew the pain of loss as well as the joy of love. Her hair was unpowdered, drawn into a soft knot at the nape of her neck with artfully arranged ringlets circling her ears and caressing the wide alabaster brow with feathery tendrils. Her refusal to wear powder had at first amused him and then aroused his admiration as he realized how exactly right she was to defy convention. That wheat-colored hair with its strawberry tinge stood out in its simplicity amongst the ornate confections of her peers. Monsieur Artur had been relegated with the utmost disgust to the fiery depths of Hades. She had somewhere found a young French émigré who had seized on her unconventional ideas with the utmost enthusiasm and was beginning, as a result, to become much in demand amongst those far-seeing mamas who wished their daughters to emulate the success of the young Countess of Linton.

She was wearing a gown of bronze satin looped up over enormous side panniers to reveal an underdress of ivory, threaded with gold ribbon—simplicity itself, almost plain to a fault if you discounted the superb cut and did not allow your eyes to move upward to a neckline that barely covered her nipples. Her breasts rose in a soft rounded swell, lifted by the hidden stays, their creamy whiteness accentuated by the bronze of the gown. Justin felt an unreasonable shaft of irritation as one young buck leant overly close to her, ogling the gorgeous bosom.

"You appear to be amusing yourself, milady." He stepped forward into the circle of flickering light provided by the many-branched candelabra on the low parapet. If he had been in any doubt as to his wife's feelings for him, they would have been dispelled instantly as she whirled to face him, her eyes a smoldering glow of love and anticipation.

Danielle fought the urge to run into his arms. Public displays of marital affection were not considered at all the thing in society. While she did not herself give a button for such foolishness, she had no desire to annoy her husband at this juncture.

"Why, my lord, what a pleasant surprise. I was not expecting you for another week." She moved out of the circle, hand extended in greeting.

"Oh, infamous madam," he murmured, raising her hand to his lips. "You must have known that I dared not risk the consequences of disobeying your summons."

"Dared not, sir? La, but I must protest! I had no idea I was such a stern mistress." Her eyes sparkled with laughter as she gazed at him in naked admiration. In his black velvet coat, black knee britches with diamond buckles, plain white silk stockings, and profusion of Dresden lace, he stood out from the richly dressed, heavily jeweled throng—the epitome of elegance amongst popinjays.

"You are about to suffer the consequences of your importunity, ma'am. I am come merely to take you home." The noise and laughter around her faded to a distant buzz as Danielle read the deep sensual message in the black eyes holding hers. They both seemed to exist in a bewitched private circle of mutual adoration and passion until someone behind them shifted, coughing slightly, bringing the scene into sharp focus again.

"Dear me, sir," Danny protested with a light laugh, "I have but just arrived. I cannot possibly leave now. Why, my card is completely filled." She indicated the dance card hanging by a thin ribband from her wrist.

"Nevertheless, Madam Wife, you will make your excuses." There was an unmistakable note of authority in the calm voice that told her clearly that the time for games was not now.

"As my lord commands." She swept a low curtsy, head bowed in meek submission and Linton's lips twitched. A less submissive wife than his would indeed be hard to find.

"Linton, you are a tyrant. I swear it." An artificial laugh accompanied the slightly peevish tone and Justin turned with raised eyebrows to view the speaker; a willowy gentleman in an impossibly wasp-waisted coat, powdered hair piled high over an enormous ladder-toupet, and so many fobs and seals adorning his garments that hardly a stitch of material was left untouched.

"Do you really think so, Layton?" Justin inquired softly, lifting his quizzing glass and subjecting the macaroni to a minute, disdainful scrutiny that brought a dull flush to the pallid complexion.

"He is most certainly *not* a tyrant, and it is most discourteous in you to say such a thing." Danny rushed quite unnecessarily to her husband's defense. "Maybe, if you did not lace yourself so tightly, sir, your humor would be . . . Oh!" She fell silent as Lord Julian with brutal lack of ceremony squeezed her upper arm. Danielle, far from resenting the brotherly interference, gave him a warm grateful smile and made haste to retrieve the situation.

"Gentlemen, I must bid you good night. My Lord is but newly returned from Danesbury and I am certain is fatigued after his journey." She shot him an impish grin. "Is it not so, Linton?"

"Absolutely, my love," her husband replied smoothly as he took her hand and tucked it firmly under his arm. "If you are quite ready . . ."

Danielle sank into an elegant curtsy as she smiled around the group and allowed herself to be led away toward the French doors into the ballroom.

"You wretch, Danny," Linton said when they were out of earshot. "I would much prefer the sobriquet of tyrant to that of milksop who is exhausted after a day's travel!"

Danielle chuckled. "Well, I had to say something, milord."

"You had already said quite enough. How could you have referred to Layton's corset in that fashion?"

Danielle reassured herself with a quick underlash glance that he was, in fact, amused. "You must admit he looks quite ridiculous, Justin."

"I do admit it and was in the process of indicating that fact when you flew into battle."

"Do not pretend to be cross, for I know quite well that you are not," she declared stoutly. "Now, how am I to leave here discreetly whilst abandoning all my promised dance partners."

"I am certain the room is full of damsels who will be overjoyed to take your place. I must confess, milady, that when I married you I did not expect to have to remove you bodily from such a vast circle of admirers." The smile that accompanied this was so full of pride and love that she could not resist a small skip of pleasure, an action that brought a deep chuckle from her companion. "Come, we must make our excuses to the duchess. More than that will not be necessary. Your intended partners will discover your absence soon enough."

They progressed through the ballroom, objects of considerable envy for both sexes and all ages. The Earl of Linton had been causing female hearts to flutter since his sixteenth year. Until Danielle de St. Varennes had appeared in a Parisian back alley, hope had continued to spring eternal in the bosoms of young ladies and their mamas. That hope had been dashed by a schoolroom miss. Tongues had wagged with malicious pleasure until it had become apparent that however unconventional the chit, she had the patronage of the bear leaders and hardly a male member of the ton would listen to a word of criticism. Young ladies interested in keeping their beaux learned to mention the Countess of Linton only with praise and to keep their envy to themselves.

The Duchess of Rutland was in the large drawing room above stairs enjoying the company of her cronies who preferred conversation and the card tables to the youthful pleasures of the ballroom. "Ah, Linton has found his wife," she said to the Dowager Countess of Linton, seated beside her on the sofa. "Do they not make an entrancing couple?" The dowager's response was not encouraging.

"There is your *maman*." Danielle stopped in the doorway. "I would like a glass of champagne and I suddenly find myself *very* hungry. May we not go to the buffet before we leave?"

"By all means, my love." Justin escorted her to the supper room. "If you will tell me exactly how hungry you are, my dear, I will bring you supper." The solicitous smile was belied by the question in his eyes. Whatever had struck Danielle so suddenly, it was definitely not appetite.

"I am not at all hungry." Danielle confirmed his suspicion. "I just do not wish to meet your mama."

"Enlighten me, pray." He took snuff, the tender amusement quite gone from the blue black eyes.

"She took it upon herself to give me a thundering scold just the other day and to tell me, if you please, that in your absence it was her duty to inform me how to go on in Society. I . . ." Danielle bit her lower lip. "I am afraid that I told her I did not accept her authority. She . . . she . . . may have thought me a little impolite."

"And were you?" her husband asked. "Just a little impolite?"

Danny shook her head. "No, *very* impolite."

"Well, since I have no desire to spoil our reunion tonight, you shall tell me the whole some other time. For now, you will greet your *belle-mère* with due decorum and we will make our farewells. I grow impatient, wife."

"I, also, husband," Danielle murmured, meeting his gaze with such candid sensuality that Justin inhaled sharply. Whatever she had done to offend his mother was of no importance—this glorious, uninhibited creature who brought him such pleasure would inevitably offend, on occasion, such a high stickler as the dowager countess, but Justin was in no wise prepared to curb a nature so freely loving, not if it would mean, as it surely would, the loss of his beloved wild mistress.

He steered her back to the drawing room and watched with quivering lip Danielle's meek obeisance to her mama-in-law and that lady's stiff response. His mother greeted him with the request that he wait upon her on the morrow. "I am at your service, ma'am." Justin bowed and turned to the duchess. "Your grace, I regret that we must take our leave."

"I am sure that you do," Amelia said with a tranquil smile. "Danielle, my dear, you must call upon me. I understand that you no longer patronize Lutèce, and I insist upon being the first to follow in your footsteps. There is something most distinctive about that gown, do you not agree, Matilda?"

Matilda had never been able to fault her daughter-in-law's attire and acceded with a small sniff.

187

"I was unaware, my love, that you had ceased to patronize Lutèce," Justin remarked, handing his wife into the light chaise. "How long ago was this?"

Danielle shrugged. "Some weeks, my lord. I do not recall exactly."

"Another émigré, Danielle?" He sat beside her on the blue squabbed seat.

Since last October and the attack on Versailles when the king and his family had been forced by the people to take up residence in the old Parisian palace of the Tuileries and the National Assembly had followed, Parisian life had become a hotbed of excitable politicking and rough justice. Merchants had been leaving the city in droves, taking with them only what they could secrete about their persons, abandoning their houses and businesses and leaving their employees and domestic servants to roam the streets. Many of them had come to London, where they found themselves frequently in financial circumstances so reduced that they were hard pressed to put bread in their mouths. But they were skilled at many trades and Danielle had kept her ears open. Her hairdresser was a case in point and now, apparently, her dressmaker—a lady who, no doubt, had once presided over a sizable Parisian establishment but now had only her own skills to sell.

"Do you object, Justin?"

"Not a whit." He smiled. "But I am inclined to play outraged husband when my wife's décolletage leaves so little to the imagination." Stretching a lazy finger he removed one breast from the bare concealment of her neckline. "A little higher, in future, my love—if you please."

Danielle made no response except for a small sigh as his long fingers moved over the exposed nipple. The chaise drew to a halt and Justin swiftly tucked the smooth globe back into her gown. "You may be a married lady, Danny, but I do not care for the ease with which that exposure was accomplished. You will instruct your new dressmaker so, will you not?"

"*Bien sûr*, milord," she murmured, shooting him an underlash look of pure mischief before alighting from the chaise on the footman's waiting arm. It seemed an aeon ago that the urchin Danny had first seen Linton House and had clung for an instant to her protector's shadow. She was now undisputed mistress of this huge establishment and most definitely the undisputed mistress of its master.

Danielle skipped up the steps to the opened door where Bedford stood bowing in the light flooding from the hall. "Thank you, Bedford. Is it not wonderful that My Lord was able to conclude his business so rapidly?" She stripped off her elbow-length satin gloves.

"Just so, my lady." Bedford looked over her head to direct a withering look at the new footman who was not accustomed to the candid way matters were conducted these days in the house of Linton. The footman's smile died in embryo.

"You had a pleasant evening, my lord?" Bedford bowed again as Linton stepped into the hall behind his wife.

"Thank you, yes. You may send the household to bed now, Bedford."

"Yes, my lord. There is a message for you, in your bookroom." The butler lowered his voice and Justin looked at him sharply before inclining his head in brief acknowledgment.

Danielle registered both the lowered voice and the sharp look. She walked down the corridor toward the bookroom. "We should take a glass of port, Linton, before we retire."

Justin followed her swiftly. Danielle cast only the briefest glance at the missive resting on the silver salver on the desk before going over to the decanter. "Will you take a glass, sir?"

Linton recognized the handwriting instantly and chose to ignore the letter. He went to his wife, removing the decanter from her hand. "You will oblige me, Danielle, by going to your bedchamber and telling Molly that she may go to bed." His lips nuzzled her neck. "I wish to unwrap you myself, this night."

"Will you not read your message, milord?" She leaned backward as his hands slipped again to her bosom. "There must be some urgency; n'est-ce pas? The messenger arrived so late."

Justin sighed. Danielle's sharp eyes rarely missed things. "Open it and read it for yourself, Danielle, if you are so

189

anxious to know its contents." He released her, picked up the letter, and handed it to her, together with the silver paper knife. His conscience was quite clear on the subject of Margaret Mainwairing, and Danielle had never evinced anything but a sophisticated acceptance of his premarital existence.

However, she shook her head. "I have no desire to read your personal correspondence, Justin. We shall exchange confidences in the morning. I shall tell you how dreadfully I upset your *maman* and you shall tell me all about the lady who sends you mysterious messages late at night when you are supposed to be out of town for another week. Is it agreed?"

"Agreed, wife. Will you now dismiss your maid?"

"Shall I also dismiss Petersham for you?" Her eyes danced wickedly as she moved to the door. "I might also enjoy unwrapping *my* present."

Odd's blood, but she was beautiful—half Danny, half Danielle; urchin eyes under the elegant coiffure, the eager, wanting body beneath the formal gown. Justin, Earl of Linton, wanted his wife as he had wanted no other woman. "Go on," he instructed. "I shall join you in five minutes."

Danielle slipped from the room with a soft laugh and a rustle of her satin skirts, satisfied that the lady who penned notes to *her* husband in violet ink on scented paper was no threat to the Countess of Linton.

"You may go to bed, Molly." She whisked into her chamber, closing the door behind her. She was in the old "blue room." Justin's suggestion that she take over the countess's traditional suite of rooms in the west wing had been received with backstreet indignation—her husband was suggesting that they sleep at opposite ends of the house? Justin, with secret delight, had cut short her profanities and agreed to their adjoining bedchambers and Danielle's private sitting room in the west wing. The blue room was now white and gold with a small powder closet built into one corner. Danielle generally ignored her own sitting room in favor of her husband's private parlor where she was frequently to be found with a book or asleep on the sofa in the late afternoon.

Petersham had become quite accustomed to Her Ladyship's presence as he laid out my lord's evening clothes, and was even resigned to the ever-open connecting door and Lady Danny's unconventional appearances when the earl was involved in the sacrosanct activity of tying his cravat.

Molly had been dozing in a brocade armchair beside the dying fire and leapt to her feet, blinking rapidly. "M'lady, I didn't expect you so soon."

"No, and you may go to bed, *immediatement!*" Danielle kicked off her bronze kid pumps. "My Lord is home."

"So I understand, m'lady." Molly picked up the shoes and hid her smile. "Shall I help you with your dress?"

"Yes, perhaps you had better," Danielle agreed thoughtfully. The gown was delicate and, while Justin was never clumsy . . . "And the hoop also, if you please."

If she pleased! Molly busied herself with the tiny fastenings. Her abrupt elevation from below-stairs maid-of-all-work to personal maid to the Countess of Linton still produced nightmares of disbelief.

Danielle had surveyed the ranks of impeccably qualified ladies' maids marched by her at Peter Haversham's direction with a curling inside. She would never be able to deal with any one of these stiff women with their disdainful noses and unmovable opinions as to what was right and proper. She would have Molly, the housekeeper's granddaughter, and no other. Justin had agreed instantly, recognizing his wife's need for companionship of her own age. There had been tempestuous rumblings belowstairs at this unforeseen advancement of one of the lowliest members of the hierarchy. Molly's tears at the unkindness had led to a confrontation between Danielle and Bedford, who had found himself requested by an icy aristocrat to keep his house in order. His dignified complaint to the earl had resulted in the simple statement that if Bedford wished for a recommendation to work elsewhere, the Earl of Linton would be happy to furnish it. End of confrontation and Molly reigned supreme in the countess's bedchamber and Bedford's staff held their tongues.

Now Molly hung up the bronze satin gown in the wardrobe

and surveyed her mistress clad in petticoats and chemise. "Will that be all, m'lady?"

"That will be all, thank you, Molly." The earl's voice came from the connecting doorway as he appeared, still dressed in his evening clothes.

"Yes, m'lord." Molly bobbed a curtsy and disappeared. It was a familiar scene.

"Now, milady." The earl crossed to his wife. "We were talking about unwrapping, as I recall."

It was dawn when Linton awoke. He lay relishing the sensation of the soft body beside him—one week away from her was definitely too long. As if echoing his thought, Danielle rolled onto her back and murmured sleepily, "I have missed you, sir. In future, I shall not permit you to leave me behind when you go about your so tedious business."

The earl smiled and flipped her onto her stomach. Since he had no plans in the foreseeable future for leaving her, any full-scale arguments could safely be postponed. He said only, "I do not accept ultimatums, madam," and began to nuzzle his way down the long narrow back.

Danielle stretched and purred, whimpering with pleasure when he took her little pink toes into his mouth. Then she murmured, "Tell me, milord, about the lady who knows you so well that she writes pretty messages in the middle of the night."

Justin groaned. "Not now, Danny, please."

"Now is a good time," she insisted. "While you are doing these so nice things to me, I shall not feel jealous of the lady. And then I will do some so nice things to you while I tell you what your *maman* is waiting to tell you when you call upon her this morning." Her tone indicated that she considered such a course of action perfectly logical and reasonable and she was probably right, Justin reflected, running his tongue along the high arches of her feet. Danielle squirmed deliciously.

"Very well," he murmured, slipping his hands between her thighs. "The message was from Lady Mainwairing. Once my mistress . . ."

"But no longer?" she interrupted, her body tensing beneath the stroking fingers.

"No longer," Justin reassured. "Even had I the inclination, brat, I would not have the stamina to keep more than you satisfied in the bedchamber."

Danielle seemed content with the statement. "But what then does the lady want of you?"

"She wishes me to call on her urgently. In friendship only, and we are still friends, Danny."

"Was she greatly upset when you became married?" Danielle tried to turn over, but a hand in the small of her back kept her in place, and since the other hand was exquisitely busy elsewhere she gave up the attempt.

"A little," Justin said judiciously. Margaret had, in fact, been greatly upset—not by the prospect of his marriage, but by his statement that he intended to be a faithful husband. But she was a wise woman, accustomed to accepting the inevitable, and rather than risk losing his friendship had capitulated with a shrug and the cynical statement that a thirty-seven-year-old widow could hardly compete with the charms of a seventeen-year-old.

"But why does she send you the so urgent message?"

"I do not know exactly." Justin turned her over, taking her face between his hands. "She asks for the advice of a friend in a troublesome matter. Do I have your leave to offer it, Madam Wife?"

Danielle, looking up into the blue black eyes, realized with a surge of joy that the question was asked in all seriousness. "But of course you must. One must always stand by one's friends."

"Danny." Justin shook his head in wonder. "You are the most amazing creature." He kissed her tenderly, but she responded with such fierceness that he realized tenderness was not what she required at the moment and gave her what she wanted, plundering her mouth with a rapacious tongue. She met thrust for thrust, her body lifting against his, her legs curling around his buttocks, drawing him against the cleft of her body.

Afterward she lay, her head cradled against his shoulder, one hand stroking dreamily over his belly. "If you are in a good mood, I should perhaps make my own confession." Her teeth nibbled his sweat-damp, salt-tasting skin. Justin sighed, running his hands through the curls on his breast. "Was it so very dreadful, infant?"

"It should not have been," Danielle asserted. "It was very early in the morning, you understand. Well before seven and there should not have been anyone around." A faintly aggrieved note had crept into her voice.

"Astride, in britches, no groom and galloping *ventre à terre* in Hyde Park?" Justin sighed again. He received no answer and took the silence correctly for an affirmative. "Who saw you?"

"I do not know." The aggrieved note was no longer faint. "Your *maman* would not tell me. But I cannot abide tattletales and if ever I find out I shall tell them so."

Justin grinned, imagining the scene. However, he controlled his inner merriment and said severely, "I thought we had agreed that while you may do as you please at Danesbury, in town you will abide by the rules."

"But you would not allow me to go to Danesbury," Danielle replied in accents of sweet reason. "It would be wise in you, I think, to permit me to accompany you in the future." She was out of his arms before he could react and danced across the room, the brown eyes gleaming in mischievous invitation.

The challenge was quite irresistible. Justin sprang from the bed and lunged for her. Danielle, with a laugh, leaped sideways and dodged behind a chair. The chase took them around the room, over the chairs and the tumbled bed and into My Lord's connecting suite. Here there was more scope and Justin gave up the fleeting thought of the absurdity of a thirty-five-year-old leader of Society playing tag, stark naked, with the equally naked minx who, for better or worse, was his wife. She was too quick for him, though, and, changing his tactics, he stood still. Danielle stopped also, her face flushed, eyes bright, bosom heaving under her swift breath.

"Come here," Justin demanded. She shook her head, the tip of her tongue running over her lips. "Come here." He held out his arms and smiled.

Danielle examined him thoughtfully. "You are very beautiful, my husband." She walked into his arms.

"Wretch! Whatever did I do to deserve you?" Justin murmured as the soft pliant body reached against him.

"I expect you were very good when you were young," she informed him complacently.

Chapter 10

"It seems to me, Peter, that the farrier has overestimated his expenses." Danielle looked up from her study of the ledgers piled on the desk in Linton's bookroom. It was later that same morning but there was no trace of the provocative sensual mistress of My Lord's bedchamber in this calm matter-of-fact lady of the house. She wore a simple morning gown of sprigged muslin over a very small hoop. Her unpowdered hair hung in soft, unconfined curls to her shoulders, and she was frowning.

It was a frown Peter Haversham was well accustomed to and one that boded ill for a comfortable morning. "I could find no fault with them myself, Lady Danny."

"Ah, but you do not understand these matters, Peter." She tapped an item in the ledger with an imperative forefinger. "Maximilian was shod two months ago. John and I agreed that he should be put to pasture for three months because of a strained tendon. It is not possible that he should then have required four new shoes a month ago. *C'est une bêtise!* We will not pay this Monsieur Harker. He is a stupid man to think he can play such a trick."

A very stupid man, Peter reflected. But then there were few farriers working for the vast estates of the aristocracy who expected their bills to be subjected to the minute, informed scrutiny of a shrewd eighteen-year-old countess.

"I have also a small problem here, Peter." She skimmed through the pages of the ledger. "This shipment of '73 claret was returned to the wine merchant—there was one musty bottle, you understand, so it was necessary to return the whole. We could not lay down a hundred bottles when the one Bedford and I sampled was contaminated."

"No, indeed not, Lady Danny," Peter concurred, wondering, nevertheless, how many other households returned an entire shipment on the basis of one bad bottle.

"But the wine merchant has billed us for carriage charges. We will pay half. *Ça c'est reasonable, n'est-ce pas?* If he has a further problem, we take our account elsewhere."

"Are you making my poor Peter miserable, Danielle?" Linton closed the door behind him as he stepped into the room.

"Indeed not, milord," Danny protested. "At least, I do hope not. Am I making you miserable, Peter?"

"No, no, certainly not," Haversham made haste to disclaim. "Not as miserable, at least, as the farrier and the wine merchant will be."

Linton chuckled. He had had a most unpleasant meeting with his mother during which he had gently informed the lady that he or, in exceptional cases, the Earl and Countess of March were the only people who had the right to take his wife to task. Looking at Danny now, he was reassured that the confrontation had been correct. The urchin side of her was his and only his and it was a side of his wife that Justin cherished. Just as he cherished the puckered brow, the firm lips, and the sharp uncompromising eyes as she unraveled the intricacies of his household accounts.

On more than one occasion in the last six months he'd listened to Peter's admiring explanations of how much wasteful expenditure had been cut, and then how the money saved had been designated to improve the tenant farms and the lot of various individuals who, through ill health or misfortune, found themselves in difficulties. Danielle, in the two months of their honeymoon, had ridden the acres of Danesbury, more often than not in britches, and had learned in those few weeks more than Justin had ever deemed it necessary to know. That knowledge she had proceeded to turn to good use and should one of the earl's factotums be so misguided as to disagree with her, he found that the tomboy countess could play many parts.

198

"We are hardly in financial straits, my love," Linton now said, examining the ledgers. "These are no great sums."

"No," she agreed. "But the principle is great. If you allow yourself to be robbed in small ways, my lord, then you give tacit permission for greater losses."

Justin remembered that he had married a de St. Varennes—a strong streak of economy ran in the blue veins of that branch of the French aristocracy. His wife had also known the extremes of poverty and near starvation. Waste of any kind was intolerable, but then neither was she miserly, as anyone who had cause to request her generosity was well aware. He pinched her cheek. "You will do as you think fit, my love."

Peter discreetly averted his eyes from the smiling exchange. They behaved sometimes as if he were not in the room, but strangely he felt enormously complimented by this easy acceptance.

An alerting knock on the paneled door and Bedford appeared. He carried a heavily embossed silver tray on which reposed a visiting card. "My lady." He bowed and presented the tray to Danielle.

She took the card, read it, and replaced it. "Would you tell the chevalier that I will join him directly?"

"In the drawing room, my lady?"

"Yes, thank you, Bedford." Danielle smiled and the butler's thin lips twitched in involuntary response before he left the room with ponderous tread.

"You have a visitor?" Justin poured two glasses of sherry, handing one to Peter. Danielle rarely took wine before noon.

"The Chevalier d'Evron," Danielle replied. "You have met, I think, Linton."

"I do not recall, but I daresay you are right." Justin actually remembered clearly his introduction to the chevalier—a sharp-nosed, thin-faced Frenchman, his body taut with a tension that had immediately communicated itself to Danielle. Justin had found this most disturbing, but without knowing why. He had dismissed the encounter in the fond hope that it would disappear from reality as easily as it did from memory and as far as he knew Danielle's acquaintance with the chevalier was slight. But slight acquaintances rarely paid morning calls without an ulterior motive. However, he had no justifiable cause for concern so he bowed to his wife and returned to his sherry and Peter.

Danielle's frown deepened as she mounted the stairs to the drawing room. She and D'Evron communicated briefly when they met at social functions, and when necessary sent terse notes. Only a matter of considerable importance would have brought him to her doorstep.

"*Bonjour, chevalier.*" She greeted her visitor, closing the door firmly behind her.

D'Evron turned from one of the long windows overlooking the street. "*Bonjour, comtesse.*"

"*Voulez-vous prendre un verre?*" Danielle laid a hand on the knotted bellpull.

"*Non, merci.*" The chevalier waved a hand in quick denial of the offer of hospitality.

"*D'accord. Asseyez-vous, s'il vous plaît.*" Danielle sat herself on a brocade wing chair and indicated that her guest should take its fellow. "*Qu'est-ce qui se passe, mon ami?*"

The direct question brought the direct answer. "I need your help, *comtesse*, in a desperate case; a situation in which your position and power as the Countess of Linton may make all the difference. You are an English lady and my own position as a mere Frenchman is not sufficiently powerful."

Danielle nodded. Bourgeois prejudice against the French was considerable, and the chevalier would be tarred with the same brush as his more unfortunate compatriots. "It is more than money this time, then?"

So far her contribution to the refugee cause had been purely financial. She had provided money and custom. Money to alleviate immediate difficulties, and her business and that of others of the *haut ton* to those who had the wherewithal and the courage to set up business again in a foreign land. Hairdressers, modistes, and jewelers, once under the patronage of the Countess of Linton, were beginning to make a living. But there were many others with problems that could not be solved in this way and she knew that the chevalier worked tirelessly to intercede for his countrymen whenever he could.

"There is a family in Steeplegate, *comtesse*. They live in great poverty. Monsieur found work with a shoemaker and madame has been taking in laundry. However, she is . . ." The chevalier colored slightly. "In a delicate situation and can no longer manage the heavy work. Monsieur injured his hand severely and was dismissed by the shoemaker. There are several young children in the family and the landlord intends to evict them this afternoon because they are behind with the rent."

"Then we must pay the rent," Danielle said simply. She received no allowance from Justin, merely carte blanche to draw on his bankers for whatever sums she required. It was an extraordinary arrangement and one that, if it became known, would cause many eyebrows raised in horror—the Earl of Linton maintaining no financial control over a bride barely out of the schoolroom! However, Linton had seen the absurdity of giving his wife pin money when she held the reins of his various households with such obvious competence. He never questioned her expenditures and Danielle had never thought to ask his permission to spend what were on occasion sizable sums to relieve the difficulties of her countrymen.

"I fear that will not suffice, *comtesse*," D'Evron said with a heavy sigh. "The landlord wishes to be rid of them. He finds the children troublesome and can extort the same rent from one tenant as he can from this family of five, soon to be six. Even had they the money, they face much difficulty in finding new lodgings with such a large family."

"*Cochon!*" Danny spat, rising to her feet. She paced the room giving vent to her outrage at this example of inhumanity in language that stunned the chevalier who knew nothing of her history. "Ah!" She stopped suddenly. "*Mon Dieu*, but what have I been saying? *Je m'excuse, chevalier.*" She glanced anxiously at the door, half expecting to see her irate husband.

D'Evron couldn't help smiling. His friend and accomplice was no longer the sophisticated countess but rather resembled a guilty child caught in her naughtiness. "Please, milady." He made haste to reassure her. "There is no need for apology. I quite understand."

"But I do not think Milord would," Danny murmured. "At least, he would understand my feelings but not that manner of expressing them."

D'Evron said nothing since an appropriate response failed to come to mind.

"*Eh bien.*" Danielle shook herself out of her uncomfortable reverie. "We shall visit this *bête* together. I feel sure we can . . . persuade . . . him to change his tune. At least until after madame is confined. Then, perhaps, if they care to live in the country, I shall contrive to settle them at Danesbury."

"But your husband, *comtesse?*" D'Evron demurred. But Danielle dismissed the half-spoken objection with an airy wave. Justin would make no protest at a needy French family settling on his estates.

"*Allons-y, chevalier.* You have your carriage?"

"I am most grateful for your assistance, *comtesse,*" D'Evron said hastily, "but should you not change your dress?"

Danielle's peal of laughter reached Justin as he mounted the stairs. The chevalier was clearly a more amusing companion than he had thought. He decided against joining them and continued on to his own apartments to change the morning dress necessary for waiting upon his mother for the buckskin britches and top boots of the horseman. He would ride with his wife in Hyde Park this afternoon in an attempt to quieten the gossips' tongues should her early morning adventures be as generally known as his mother feared.

"I will change immediately," Danielle declared. "You will wait a few minutes, *mon ami?*"

"*Avec plaisir.*" The chevalier bowed, resigned to a considerable wait. A lady's idea of a few minutes spent on changing her attire was rarely consonant with reality.

However, it was but ten minutes later when Danielle emerged from her bedchamber and ran headlong into her lord.

"Where to in such a hurry, infant?" Linton laughed, taking in her driving dress of olive green velvet, a lace jabot at the high neck its only adornment. She wore one of her favorite tricorn hats, leather driving gloves, and a serviceable pair of riding boots instead of the kid or jean half boots that would normally be considered sufficient protection for a drive through the city streets.

"I am going for a drive with the chevalier, milord," Danielle informed him.

The earl put up his glass and surveyed her feet. "In riding boots, Danny?"

"Ah well, my others have a loose heel, *tu comprends*," she improvised glibly. "And these are, after all, *très comfortable*."

Now what the devil was she up to? But Justin said merely, "I was hoping you would ride with me this afternoon, ma'am."

"*Ventre à terre*, milord?" Her eyes danced wickedly.

"No, most definitely not," he declared. "With sober decorum. I am hoping that the sight of you correctly dressed and escorted will dispel all memories of a hoyden galloping through the park at dawn."

"That does not sound at all *amusant*, sir."

"And driving with the Chevalier D'Evron *is* amusing?" he inquired.

Danielle frowned, but her lips curved. "I do not yet know, milord. But I shall find out, shall I not?"

Justin swung his riding crop at her departing rear and Danielle skipped with an indignant ouch. She stuck her tongue out at him over her shoulder before gathering up her skirts and taking prudent flight in the direction of the drawing room.

Linton shook his head with a rueful smile. There could be no possible objection to her driving with D'Evron. He was perfectly respectable and received in all the best houses. He was known to be quiet and sober to a fault and not overly enamored of the Season's round of gaiety—a sensible man in short. So why then did Justin feel this sense of unease? But as he had agreed long ago with Pitt, Danielle required the lightest hand on the strongest curb—a hand so light that she would be unaware of the curb. He would draw back on the reins only when it was evident that he had no choice, and in a year or so she would be sufficiently established, matured by motherhood perhaps, to have her own hands on her own reins. Linton frowned at the last thought. He was in no hurry for his brat to grow up too quickly—her childhood had lacked the usual elements of play and security and she was entitled to some playtime now. But, nevertheless, it was a little strange that she had not yet conceived. However, she was barely eighteen and if her body was not ready he could afford to wait awhile before setting up his nursery.

203

Since Danielle was otherwise occupied, Justin decided to pay his visit to Margaret Mainwairing. The ride to Half Moon Street was a pleasant one on this crisp March afternoon and the earl was conscious of a degree of pleasure in the prospect of his ex-mistress's company. Margaret was a sensible woman and, while her companionship could never be as stimulating as that of his wife's, she could be restful. She had not Danielle's ready wit and sense of fun, but, in spite of her self-imposed seclusion from Society's larger gatherings, kept herself well informed as to the latest *on dits* and had considerable perspicacity. Justin was intensely curious as to what had led her to such an indiscretion as last night's urgent message—something of moment, undoubtedly. Margaret was always the soul of discretion.

A lad ran to hold his horse as he dismounted outside the small pretty house on this quiet unfashionable street. It was a street for indigent widows, young married couples, and young sprigs making their first forays into society without sufficient means. Margaret was far from indigent but had no wish for grandeur. She also had no wish for the genteel seclusion of Kensington—who would visit her in Kensington? Half Moon Street was both well placed and respectable, entirely suitable for the retiring widow of a gentleman of respectable lineage and moderate fortune.

"Good day, Liza." His Lordship smiled at the maidservant who took his hat with a bobbed curtsy. "Is your mistress at home?"

"Abovestairs, my lord." Liza tried to hide her surprise at this unexpected appearance. My Lord had not visited Half Moon Street in over a year and the reason for his absence was no secret to Lady Mainwairing's household. Had he already tired of his bride?

"Will you not ask Her Ladyship if she will receive me?" Linton put up his glass and examined the maid with a raised eyebrow, his voice gentle.

Liza blushed and made haste to her mistress's boudoir. Justin looked idly around the small, well-remembered hall. Everything appeared in order: visiting cards on the silver tray on the piecrust table, the smell of beeswax and lavender that he always associated with Margaret's house.

"My Lord Linton. How delightful in you to call." Lady Mainwairing almost ran down the straight staircase, hands outstretched in greeting.

Justin raised them both to his lips as he bowed. "Your servant, ma'am."

"Pray come into the parlor. Liza, you will bring the claret for His Lordship." She moved swiftly to the left of the stairs, Justin following, and whisked into the bow-windowed parlor overlooking the street. "My friend, I am truly grateful. I have been at my wits end, or I would never have written to you in such a fashion."

Justin closed the door behind him. She looked drawn and tired and every day of her thirty-seven years, her pale complexion unrelieved by the lavender silk gown. He felt only friendship and a deep regard for her. "Tell me how I may help you, Margaret."

Margaret, if she had cherished any hopes of a lingering passion in her erstwhile lover's bosom, now relinquished them. This was not the cynical, world-weary lover of their past. He looked ten years younger now that the full lips had lost their cynical twist and the blue black eyes carried no boredom, only interest and more than a hint of humor.

"She is good for you, the little de St. Varennes," Margaret said involuntarily. In earlier days, Justin would have responded to such a personal comment with an instant stiffness and a sardonic set down. Now he simply smiled and Margaret gasped at the transformation. Before she could say anything further, however, Liza appeared with decanter and glasses.

Justin took an appreciative sip, reflecting that Danielle would also approve. It was a reflection, though, that had no place at the moment. "How can I help you, Margaret?" he repeated.

"It is Edward."

"Edward?" Margaret's son, Justin knew. "Is he not at Oxford still?"

"He has been sent down." Margaret paced the room, plucking at her sleeve, her face averted.

205

"That is no great sin," Justin said, puzzled. "I was sent down myself for a term . . . a cockfight, as I recall, in my rooms," he mused with a reminiscent grin.

"This is no prank, Justin. Edward has gambling debts that he cannot pay." Margaret looked at him directly, her face haggard as she confessed Society's one unforgivable sin.

"Can you not pay them for him?"

"I have done so, but it does not alter the fact that he is disgraced. He played beyond his means and had to admit that fact. I settled his IOUs but by then the damage had been done."

Justin nodded. Society would tolerate any peccadillo except one involving honor. But Edward was young, young enough to live this down. "He is but a babe, Margaret, and memories are short. If he remains out of town for the Season I dare swear that by next season all will be forgotten if he conducts himself well."

"But he is not prepared to do so." Her voice was low. "I cannot control him, Justin. His father would perhaps have been able to but Edward is beyond my management. I . . . I am greatly afraid that gambling is in his blood. He will have a respectable fortune when he comes of age, but not sufficient for . . . for this." She looked at him, the blue eyes wide with appeal and glazed with unshed tears.

"There is no fortune sufficient for the true gambler," Justin observed with a frown. Too many families had been ruined by that unfortunate predeliction. "Is your son in town?"

Margaret nodded. "I do not know exactly what is happening but I fear the worst. He is a friend of Shelby's . . ."

"If he is running with that crowd, then you may as well consign him to the devil," Justin interrupted harshly.

"Please . . ." she whispered.

"What is it you wish of me, my dear?" Justin strode to her and took the cold hands between his own. "You have only to ask."

"Will you . . . will you talk to him?" At the look of horror in Linton's eyes she went on hastily. "You have much experience with the young, Justin. You seem to know just how to teach them to go on in the right way . . ."

"You refer to my guardianship of Julian?" Justin frowned.

"My cousin had his share of youthful high spirits, I grant you, but rarely went beyond the line of what is pleasing." He did not add that Lord Julian Carlton's youthful indiscretions would be more readily forgiven by society than those of Edward Mainwairing. Julian's fortune and lineage far exceeded the respectable.

"I was thinking also of your present circumstance," Lady Mainwairing went on, dropping her eyes. "Your wife is not always the soul of propriety but she is very young and you manage to control . . ."

Justin released her hands abruptly and took snuff from an exquisite enameled box. His eyes were bored, face expressionless.

Margaret made haste to retrieve her mistake. "Pray forgive me, Justin. I spoke without thought. I meant no criticism . . . I was thinking only that your position and your experience of guiding the young might help Edward."

"I suggest you buy him a pair of colors, Margaret, and see what a little military discipline will do for him. It would certainly remove him from the company of Shelby and his like."

Margaret stiffened her shoulders. "I do beg your pardon for intruding, Linton. I am most grateful for your kindness in sparing the time to listen to my woes." She managed a brittle little laugh.

Justin sighed and accepted his fate. Why was it that ever since that afternoon when he'd yielded to a ridiculous impulse to rescue a grubby brat from a baker's belt, he found himself unable to resist an appeal for help. He was now to take some wastrel stripling under his patronage. It would have to be done discreetly, of course. Open patronage of his ex-mistress's son would give the gossips food for their crying tongues and then he would have Danny's reactions to contend with. He shuddered slightly at the prospect.

"I will do what I can, Margaret. I may, at least, discover the extent of his gaming and how deep his involvement with Shelby. When I have done so, we will talk further."

"I shall be forever in your debt, Justin." Her smile was watery but so full of genuine gratitude that the earl felt ashamed of his earlier sharpness. It was a small enough task to undertake for an old friend.

He left her then and turned his horse toward St. James's and his club. It was as good a place as any for discreet inquiry and with any luck he would find his cousin. Jules was close in age to Shelby and would be more cognizant of that rake's circles than Justin. Had Lord Linton been aware of his wife's whereabouts and activities on that March afternoon, he would have lost whatever scant interest he had in the affairs of Edward Mainwairing.

Danielle and the chevalier, after a halt at Hoare's bank where Danielle had drawn a substantial sum, left the relatively clean, well ordered streets of central London for the backslums of the East End. The streets narrowed and their progress was slow as the chevalier's curricle drew uncomfortable attention from the area's inhabitants.

D'Evron glanced sideways to his companion and was amazed at her apparent calm. She carried some hundred guineas in her reticule but what the chevalier did not know was that she also carried a small, silver-mounted pistol. The filth, poverty, and hostile curiosity seemed not to trouble her in the least but, again, D'Evron was not to know that the Countess of Linton had once survived in circumstances as bad, if not worse, than those evident around them. The chevalier, in spite of frequent forays into this wasteland of squalor, was still ill at ease and could only marvel at the gently bred aristocrat sitting beside him, expressionless except for her large brown eyes that seemed to take in every minute detail of the scene.

They turned into a reeking alley, barely wide enough for the curricle. The grays stepped delicately over the uneven cobbles where every kind of filth had found a home. Children played in the running kennels, dodged beneath the horses' bellies; sad-eyed women with mewling babes at their shrunken breasts looked at them with the blankness of accepted despair; their menfolk, almost as scrawny, spat obscenities.

Danielle stepped down from the curricle, hoisting her velvet skirts to her knees, revealing the well chosen, sturdy riding boots. She splashed through the stinking soil of the kennel saying not a word to the chevalier as she beckoned an emaciated scrap of tattered humanity. "You will hold the horses, *mon petit*." She handed him a shilling and the bright gleam drew a sharp breath from the watchers in the street. A group of men advanced as one body. Danielle did not stop to think whether they were threatening herself or the child. The group found themselves facing a silent controlled figure holding a pistol. They backed away and the chevalier decided that he need have no guilt about embroiling the Countess of Linton in these affairs. Aristocrat she might be, gently bred she was most certainly not. Was the so impassive earl aware of this side of his child bride?

D'Evron dismissed the interesting question. The chevalier was a pragmatist with a job to do and he used what tools were available. If they proved to be sharper than he had expected, so much the better.

He rapped on the half open door with the silver knob of his cane. Receiving no answer, he stood aside to allow Danielle admittance. The narrow dark passage stank of boiled cabbage and fish heads. The stench of poverty and Danny's nose wrinkled with remembered distaste as she returned her pistol to her reticule.

The man who emerged from a door at the end of the passageway looked well enough fed; brawny shoulders—their muscles turning to flab and the broken nose of the ex-heavyweight. Little piggy eyes, Danielle thought. But the eyes widened as they took in the sight of this lady. She was still holding her skirts high to avoid soiling them on her boots and her expression of distaste had Mr. Barkis rubbing his hands obsequiously as he asked how he could serve my lady.

"You may take me to your tenants," he was informed. "After I have spoken with them, I will speak with you."

The little eyes narrowed speculatively. Mr. Barkis had recognized the chevalier, but he was of no account, just another émigré frog eater of no power or influence. The lady, on the other hand, was icily English. If she had an interest in that pathetic group upstairs then perhaps there was something to be gained.

"Of course, my lady." He bowed low. "If you will be pleased to follow me." He opened a door without knocking and

Danielle walked past him without acknowledgement. D'Evron followed, closing the door firmly in Mr. Barkis's face.

It was a small room; a minute fire of sticks and lumps of charcoal tried unsuccessfully to throw off some heat. There was no furniture, except for three thin pallets on the floor. But some effort had been made to sweep and dust.

A woman with pinched cheeks and a hugely swollen belly held a baby of about a year, three others tottered, crawled, and sniveled around her. Danielle bent to pick up one infant who was showing an unhealthy interest in her unsanitary boots. She wiped his nose on her cambric handkerchief and smiled at the child's mother.

"*Bonjour, madame. Je suis Danielle de St. Varennes.*" It seemed simpler to introduce herself thus in the circumstances. When she accosted Mr. Barkis she would be the Countess of Linton.

Madame Duclos knew the name, what Parisian did not? Amazement flashed in the weary eyes but it died under the smiling regard of this young girl who was now sitting on the floor with the little Gérard in her velvet lap.

"The chevalier has told me something of your circumstances, madame. I am here to help you if you will permit . . . *non, petit chou*, you may not have that." Laughing Danielle removed the painfully thin baby fingers from her bracelet. "*Votre mari, il n'est pas ici, maintenant?*"

"My husband is looking for work, milady." Madame Duclos looked nervously at the chevalier who smiled his encouragement. Haltingly she told the pathetic story of panic and flight, the long days of waiting for the passports, the sums expended in bribery, the need to leave everything behind except what cash and material goods they could carry easily. All their assets had been tied up in the small but growing shoemakers in St. Michel. The Ducloses had been solid, comfortable members of the bourgoisie, no great aspirations for wealth but contented with their lot. Jean Duclos had seen the danger clouds on the horizon and had thought only of his young family. They were neither aristocracy nor peasants, could identify with neither rich nor poor and, as a result, could well be amongst the first victims of the tide of insurrection that was still an ill-conceived bubble—a mountain spring waiting to trickle down the steep slope to become a part of the wildly rushing river. He had thought he was doing the right thing by removing his family from potential danger, only to find that a hostile land had no succor to offer.

Danielle listened to the story, controlled her growing rage at the treatment they had received since reaching London, and asked a very few pertinent questions.

"When do you expect to be confined, madame?" It was her last question.

"In one week," Madame Duclos answered.

Danielle looked around the room and imagined giving birth. Children underfoot, petrified witnesses to their mother's pain and labor; water that could not be brought to the boil on the tiny fire; dust, dirt, blood, and agony. But for every Madame Duclos there were a hundred others. She could not rescue them all with her wealth and privilege and it was better to settle for what she could do. She could pay for the midwife, for heat, food, and a roof. There was no time to remove the family to Danesbury before the baby arrived and she certainly could not people Linton's estates with French refugees. After madame was confined then she could find room for *this* family, but if the rest were to be helped, she must accept the limitations of what she could offer.

D'Evron watched her face as she thought. The change was quite startling, as startling as the appearance of the pistol. She looked older, much older than her eighteen years, a wealth of experience, knowledge, and acceptance showing on the small face of the pampered aristocrat. "*What* was she? He knew *who* she was, but all preconceptions now vanished into the mist. It was a question that would be asked many times by many people in the next several years.

"Madame, I will arrange matters so that you may remain here until after your confinement." Danielle set the baby on his knees and stood up. "If your husband is willing to pursue some trade other than the one he knows, then I can perhaps arrange for you to move to my husband's estate in Hampshire. The air will be good for the children and you will have a little land." She smiled hesitantly, recognizing the paucity of her

211

offer in the light of their previous existence in Paris and the other woman's hesitation at accepting what was, in the final analysis, charity.

But Madame Duclos had lost her pride many months ago. "We shall be most grateful, milady."

"Then I will talk to the *bête*, Barkis." Danielle was all brisk business as she turned to the chevalier. "*Mon ami*, you will accompany me." She counted out bills into Madame Duclos's lap. "This should suffice for your present needs, madame. Should you need me, you may send a message to this address." She wrote rapidly on a visiting card. "The chevalier will keep me informed of your progress and I will make the necessary arrangements for your removal to Danesbury."

Tears filled the other woman's eyes and Danielle averted her gaze and turned swiftly to the door. "You will be troubled no longer, madame."

Mr. Barkis, after three minutes in the company of the Countess of Linton, was happy to receive the past due rent and the following month's together with a substantial sum for his trouble. He promised to find a reliable midwife when madame's time came and decided that the presence of wailing tots upstairs was infinitely preferable to another encounter with this lady of Quality with the snapping eyes, the frigid tones, and the most clearly defined threats.

"We must make haste, chevalier." Danielle glanced up at the sky. It was now late afternoon and she wished to be home before Linton who would be bound to remark on the dust and mud splashes on her dress and the malodorous filth on her boots.

"Do you still have your shilling, *petit*?" she asked the tattered child who now relinquished the reins to the chevalier. When the boy shook his head, she slipped another coin into the grubby palm, discreetly this time so that his watching elders would not again relieve him of his earnings.

"I am most grateful for your assistance, *comtesse*," D'Evron said slowly as they picked their way across the cobbles. "I hope it will not be necessary to trouble you in this way again."

"On the contrary, chevalier, you will trouble me whenever you wish. There is much to be done and I will play my part most willingly."

"Your husband, milady . . . ?"

"Linton must know nothing of this," she said firmly. "I rely on your discretion." Danielle was in no doubt that Justin would forbid further excursions of the kind she had just made, and if he did so she would be forced to defy him. He had fulfilled his whispered promise on their wedding day and made it easy for her to keep her vow of obedience, but in this instance he would demand it of her and the consequences for their relationship of open defiance were not to be contemplated.

D'Evron said nothing and kept his own unpleasant reflections to himself. The earl was a noted swordsman and an even more noted shot, but the chevalier rather suspected that he might resort to a horsewhip on this occasion and no one would blame him.

It was almost six when they drew up outside Linton House. The young countess was now distinctly anxious. They were to dine at seven and go to the play afterward, a treat that Linton, knowing his wife's love of the theater, took care to provide regularly.

"We must contrive a little better next time," Danielle said as the chevalier handed her down from the curricle. "We will conduct our business before noon."

"*D'accord, comtesse.*" He raised her hand to his lips and then watched as she ran up the well-honed steps to be received by an impassive Bedford. If the butler noticed anything untoward in his mistress's appearance or in her impetuous haste as she disappeared up the curving staircase, it did not show on his face.

Danielle exploded into her bedchamber. "We must make haste, Molly. Help me with these boots, if you please. No! Do not touch them with your hands." Molly knelt and took the boots in a towel and pulled, wrinkling her nose at the rank odor.

"Help me with my gown, Molly, and then take the boots away. They will stink out the room." Danny turned impatiently and the girl, quite accustomed to her mistress's inelegant expressions, unbuttoned the velvet driving dress

213

with due speed. "*Merci*," Danielle said swiftly. "I can manage now. Make haste with the boots."

The Earl of Linton, mounting the staircase, narrowly missed being returned in an undignified manner to the foot as his wife's maid, clutching a pair of boots at arm's length, slipped against him. Molly's apologies were so profuse, her speech so scattered that he forebore to question her and continued on his way with a shrug. Danielle's unconventional ways had communicated themselves to the maid and it seemed unjust to take the servant to task for something that was not her responsibility.

Petersham was waiting for him, carefully brushing invisible motes from a cream brocade evening coat. Abandoning his task, he helped my lord out of top boots and deep blue superfine coat, easing it reverently over the powerful shoulders. A muttered expletive came from next door, and Justin with a smile went through in shirt and stockinged feet to find his wife struggling fiercely with her laces.

"Ah, milord, you are home," she said, showing him a face pink with her exertions. "These so stupid strings have made themselves into a knot and I cannot undo them."

"How very inconsiderate of them," Justin murmured soothingly, coming up behind her. "But where is Molly?" He wrestled with the recalcitrant knot.

"Oh, she will return directly," Danielle said airily. "I asked her to bring me some tea. Ah, thank you." She breathed a sigh of relief as the stays were finally released. Molly, unfortunately, chose that moment to reappear.

Justin's eyebrows shot up at the conspicuous absence of a tea tray.

"Molly, you have forgotten my tea," Danielle declared, shooting the girl a look pregnant with warning. "But never mind, we have no time. I shall take a glass of sherry instead. You will bring me one, sir?"

Justin bowed his acquiescence and went through to his own apartments where decanters of sherry, Madeira, port and cognac were kept filled in his parlor. He poured sherry for Danielle and returned to her bedchamber. She was sitting at her dresser in a soft silk wrapper while Molly dressed her hair.

"Ah, thank you, sir." She gave him a radiant smile that somehow did little to dispel his unease. His brat, Justin strongly suspected, was hip deep in mischief. In the presence of Petersham and Molly he could hardly probe, but he would have her under his eye all evening, so investigation could safely be postponed.

As it happened, he lost all interest in her activities of the afternoon. Her conversation over the dinner table was too swift and witty to allow him the time for reflection, only for response; her pleasure in the play entranced him. One of his greatest joys these days was to provide her with the pleasures that she had missed during those long years in Languedoc and he sat through the farce, his gaze riveted on the small face, alive with laughter beside him. She was amused by every feeble sally, every vulgar piece of slapstick, her gloved hands clasped in her lap. During the tragedy her expression registered every emotion as vividly as that of the actors—a child experiencing the magical world of fantasy for the first time.

Margaret Mainwairing sat in her box, also ignoring the stage, watching instead the man whose mistress she had been for five years and she felt only envy for them both, an envy untouched by malice.

"Justin," Danielle whispered in the interval, "who is the lady in the gown with the tobine stripes? She seems monstrously interested in us."

"Where?" He raised his glass and examined the inhabitants of the neighboring boxes.

"In the third tier." Danielle lifted a finger to point, but her husband caught her hand in time.

"Unladylike brat," he chided. "One does not point in Polite Circles."

Danielle merely chuckled. "Do you see her. Her hair is à la capricieuse, I think."

Justin did see her and sighed. "The lady is Margaret Mainwairing, infant."

"Ah," Danny frowned. "Then you will introduce me, n'est-ce pas?"

"No, I will not," Justin stated.

"But why not?" Her smile was all sweet innocence that quite

215

failed to deceive her husband. "Is she not perfectly respectable?"

"She is perfectly respectable, but it would not be appropriate to introduce my wife to my ex-mistress," she was bluntly informed.

"People will talk?" Her eyes sparkled.

"A great deal." He turned with some relief to greet the arrival of a group of Danielle's admirers. He had little hope that she would allow the matter to rest there and his forebodings were proved lamentably correct when, at the end of the play, in the press of crowds in the foyer, she disappeared from his side. When he found her, she was engaged in an animated conversation with Lady Braham with whom she was but slightly acquainted. Margaret Mainwairing, however, was a member of Lady Braham's party.

He arrived at Danielle's side just in time to hear her say, "I am so pleased to make your acquaintance, Lady Mainwairing. I understand you have been a friend of Linton's this age."

"Yes, indeed," Margaret murmured, an appreciative smile in her eyes as she saw Justin's expression. "May I offer you my felicitations, Lady Linton." She then extended her hand to the earl. "Good evening, Linton."

"Ma'am." He bowed low over the hand before turning politely to greet the rest of the group whose well-bred faces barely concealed their shocked astonishment. "You will excuse us," he said with a smile. "Our party awaits . . . Danielle?" He gave her his arm and she laid her hand on the cream brocade sleeve, two irrepressible dimples dancing in her cheeks.

Once out of earshot, she said, "You cannot be cross, Justin. You did not introduce me, yourself, so it was all quite proper. But I thought Lady Braham was like to swoon when she was obliged to introduce me." She chuckled delightedly but her husband maintained a severe silence as he handed her into the chaise which bore them to the Piazza where he had arranged a small supper party for his wife's entertainment. The temptation to take her straight home at this point was considerable, but he could not disappoint his guests.

His cousin, Sir Anthony Fanshawe, Lord Philip Courtland,

and the young Viscount Westmore were waiting for them as the earl, still in stony silence, escorted Danielle to the table.

"Justin is most annoyed with me," Danielle announced, sitting down with a swish of skirts. "I contrived an introduction to Lady Mainwairing—she was his mistress before he was married as I'm sure you are aware." She smiled around the stunned circle of faces. "It seemed to me necessary that society should be aware that I know of these things and I have only friendly feelings for Lady Mainwairing. Now all is *convenable, n'est-ce pas?*"

"Odd's blood," Lord Julian said in shaking accents. It was a sentiment echoed by his companions. "What will you think to do next, Danny?"

"'Twas not at all the thing, Danny," Sir Anthony agreed. "A man's wife is not acquainted with his mistress,"

"But Lady Mainwairing is no longer Justin's mistress," Danielle said tranquilly, sipping her champagne. "Have I not just demonstrated that fact? It was my object, you understand. You are not being at all wise." She dismissed their stupidity with an airy wave. "If Lady Mainwairing were still Justin's mistress, then of course I would not know her. Since I do, she cannot be."

"Logical." Lord Philip nodded, most struck with this reasonable statement. "She has a point, y'know."

A short reflective silence fell around the table and Justin, who to his surprise was now enjoying himself hugely, sat back twirling his quizzing glass on the narrow silk riband. Danielle, in her usual fashion, had cut through the hypocritical layers of society's conventions and had most effectively put the kiss of death to any malicious scandal-mongering. Who would whisper to her about her husband's erstwhile mistress when she had so clearly demonstrated that there was nothing they could tell her?

"Let us put aside Danielle's regrettable want of conduct and address ourselves to our supper," he said. "I do not think that the Piazza is a suitable forum for such a discussion."

"No, no indeed not, 'pon my soul," Viscount Westmore agreed heartily. "Not a subject for the ladies either."

Danielle went into a peal of laughter. "But I raised the

217

subject, Westmore."

"We were talking about ladies," Julian said severely.

"Oh, infamous, Jules! Justin, will you not defend me from such rudeness?"

"On the contrary, brat," her husband drawled. "I will endorse it. Eat your supper."

It was a riotous party and Justin resigned himself to the now familiar role of schoolmaster presiding over a rowdy schoolroom. In Danielle's company the four young men who fancied themselves as sophisticated, blasé members of the *haut ton* lost their world-weary airs, treating Danny as they would a favorite sister, but with the added spice of light flirtation with a beautiful woman securely married to the Earl of Linton who himself regarded the proceedings with patent amusement.

And that night, Linton had in his bed both wife and mistress—a wild creature in the mood for play who moved over him with eager hands and mouth, made love to him with uninhibited joy in his body, and then gave him her own to do with as he wished.

Chapter 11

"Your face, Justin, was a picture." Margaret Mainwairing laughed reminiscently as she handed him a glass of port late one evening several days after the excursion to the theater. "But not as funny as Sally Braham's."

"Who was like to swoon, I am reliably informed," said Justin dryly.

"The child is quite delightful, but are you certain you can handle her?"

"I have little need to do so." He sat in a deep wing chair, crossing one black-velvet-clad leg over the other. "Danielle's mischief is rarely without purpose. Your son's, on the other hand . . ." He sipped his port, one eyebrow lifted.

Margaret accepted his tacit refusal to discuss his wife with a respect tinged with regret. Danielle had intrigued her and the marriage even more so now that she had observed husband and wife together. But she said only, "It is as bad as I feared?"

"I do not make it a habit to frequent gaming hells," Justin said carefully. "However, last evening I paid a visit to the Blue Angel." He frowned. "Edward is still a minor, Margaret, but those establishments will turn a blind eye to such detail in the interests of plucking a fat pigeon. Were they aware of the true nature of your son's financial circumstances, they would bar him. But as he runs with Shelby's crowd . . ." He shrugged.

"What am I to do, Justin?" Margaret looked at him, desperation in the sloe eyes.

"If he will not listen to reason, then you have no choice but to let matters run their course. He will find himself at *point non plus* soon enough and the doors will be closed to him."

"But by then we shall both be ruined," Margaret whispered. "Can you do nothing?"

"I can make his true circumstances known, if that is what you wish. It will be acutely humiliating both for him and for you."

"Will you speak with him first? Tell him what you mean to do? Mayhap he will listen."

"I have no authority over your son, Margaret." Justin stood up. "I am sorry, m'dear. I will drop a word in his ear, but no more than that. If that does not suffice, then, with your permission, I will disseminate a little information. After which, I imagine, he will be glad to accept a pair of colors. I cannot promise a top regiment, but will do what I can."

"I thank you, my friend." Margaret accompanied him to the door. "You will visit me again soon? Tell me what has transpired?"

"Assuredly. Good night, Margaret." He took her hands, bending to kiss her cheek before stepping out into the quiet nighttime street. A closed carriage passed him as he turned toward the Strand, but Justin was blithely unaware of the interest his presence afforded the occupants.

Danielle had not yet returned from Almack's Assembly rooms when he arrived home and he went into his bookroom to write a terse note to Edward Mainwairing. A missive, addressed to Danielle in bold black script, lay on the desk. Justin examined it idly. The writing was most definitely masculine but notes written according to the rules of dalliance should appear with Danielle's hot chocolate of a morning, not arrive late at night. Justin found that his reaction to the message was somewhat similar to his wife's when faced with Margaret's urgent summons. He was more than ordinarily curious. But Danielle would doubtless apprise him of the contents with her usual directness.

He heard her voice some fifteen minutes later bidding a cheerful good night to the porter and Justin went into the hall to greet her.

"Milord, you are before me." She moved toward him, all

smiles. "I have had a famous evening. You would not believe the latest *on dit* about Lady Massey. She is apparently enceinte and she must be all of thirty-three, but her husband is a very old man—sixty if he is a day. However, her lover is *un jeune homme* and it is said . . ."

"I can well imagine what is said." Justin, mindful of the night porter, eased her ungently into the bookroom. She wore a gown of dull gold over an oyster satin underdress. The de St. Varennes diamonds caught the light from the branched candelabra. But in spite of their many-faceted brilliance, they paled beside the vibrant sparkle of her eyes, the soft radiance of her skin.

"You have an admirer, my love." Justin indicated the note, watching through narrowed eyes as she examined it. Did he imagine the slight stiffening of those slender shoulders as she read the contents?

"It is only the Chevalier D'Evron. He wishes me to drive with him tomorrow." Danielle ripped the note into small pieces and tossed them onto the tray.

"And will you do so?"

"*Mais, d'accord.*" Her lower lip disappeared between small pearly teeth. "We speak French together, Justin, and talk of France and the past. It is good to be with a compatriot, *tu comprends?*"

"*Oui, Danielle, je comprends.*" It seemed a reasonable statement and he was quite prepared to let it go at that until she spoke again, hesitantly.

"There is something I think I should tell you, Justin."

The hairs on the nape of his neck prickled, but he merely inclined his head in invitation.

"I have been drawing some considerable sums to assist the émigrés from Paris who find themselves in difficulties." Danielle perched on the arm of a chair and began to twist the diamond ring on her finger. "I should perhaps have mentioned this earlier, milord, but for some unaccountable reason it did not occur to me to do so." She looked up with a rueful smile.

"And why does it occur to you to tell me now, my love?" Justin was conscious only of the strangest sense of relief.

"I think it is probably because I shall be needing to spend

rather more," she said candidly.

"I see." The earl took snuff. "Tell me, Danny, are you asking my permission or merely apprising me of the facts?"

"The latter, I think, sir." Her face was grave. "I could not refuse to help. Their situations in many cases are quite dreadful. Most of what they had, they have been forced to leave behind and it is hard for them to find work and . . . the children, Justin. They are hungry."

There was nothing of the mischievous sprite about her now. Not for the first time Justin reflected that his wife's personality was as many-faceted as the brilliant prisms encircling her throat.

"D'Evron is also involved?"

She nodded. "The chevalier discovers the need and does what he can to alleviate matters. There are others beside myself who provide money and also work. D'Evron is attempting to set up a network of assistance. One person alone can do little and your entire fortune, Justin, would be a mere drop in the ocean."

"I do trust, Danny, that you will refrain from dropping my entire fortune into that ocean." Justin regarded her quizzically and she gave a low laugh.

"I will sell my diamonds first, milord."

"And I will oblige us both by assuming that remark was made in jest. But I should warn you that I did not find it in the least amusing."

"No, my lord," Danielle murmured meekly, dropping her eyes.

"Impossible brat," Justin said without rancor. "You will, of course, do as you think fit whilst maintaining some control over your philanthropy. Is it agreed?"

"Agreed." Danielle gave him a radiant smile. "I keep very careful records, Justin. Do you care to see them?" She moved to the rolltop desk and opened a small drawer, reaching into the back for a sheet of paper covered in immaculate calculations. Justin examined the figures, fascinated. She was incredibly meticulous and while the final sum was certainly sizable it was no more than many a giddy wife lost in an evening over the pharaoh tables.

"You trust D'Evron to act for you in these matters?" he asked bluntly, handing back the document.

Danielle flushed with annoyance. "I am not quite such a numbskull as you appear to think, sir. If I did not trust him, I would hardly give him carte blanche with your money."

"No, no of course not. Forgive me, Danielle. I meant no aspersions on the chevalier's character or on your perspicacity." Linton made haste to retrieve himself. "Come, let us consider the matter closed for the moment. I should be glad if you will keep me informed as you think necessary."

"Well, there is just one other matter," Danielle said, seizing the opportunity. "There is a family by name of Duclos that the chevalier has mentioned to me. I should perhaps explain how I would like to help them . . ."

Danielle lay awake through most of the night, miserable in her guilt. She had lied to Justin for the first time and she could not quieten her conscience by saying that it was a lie of omission rather than commission. She had deliberately given him a half truth that would provide her with an excuse to be in D'Evron's company and would ease any suspicions as to her other activities.

Justin slept in tranquil peace beside his wife, his hand on her hip moving unconsciously to keep pace with her tossings and turnings. When he awoke at dawn she was deeply asleep, in her first deep sleep of the night. He slid from the bed, drawing the covers over the creamy shoulders, examining the small face with a frown. Even in sleep there was a tension, a small crease between the straight eyebrows. She looked much as she had done in those fugitive days in Paris. Justin wondered if the plight of her countrymen was causing her to relive her own privations—if so, his efforts to distance those memories for her were as naught. But there was only so much one could do to heal another, and Danielle was most definitely in control of her own destiny, for all that she was a brat and a vagabond with a mercurial temper and a wicked tongue.

*   *   *

It was some two weeks later when Danielle stepped out of the hired sedan chair onto yet another filthy lane just off Fleet Market. "You will wait for me," she said tersely to the bearers who, since they were clearly not to be paid at this point, had little option.

Danielle had now made several of these excursions without the protection of the chevalier and there was no hesitation in her step as she walked into the narrow hallway where layers of grease formed a shiny patina on the walls. Muted voices came from a room on her left and she turned the doorknob with the tips of her gloved fingers. The small room was bitterly cold; little daylight came through the exiguous grimed window and what light there was flickered uncertainly from tallow candles. The girls working at the long table were little more than children, their arms mere sticks poking through ragged sleeves. Not one of them raised their eyes from their stitching at Danielle's entrance. The reason for their lack of interest rose heavily from a chair in the far corner. The woman's arms were like tree trunks splotched with large brown freckles; her gown—if it deserved such a name—was a dirty gray, hair, of similar color, wisped beneath a filthy ragged cap.

"You be needin' somethin'?" she wheezed. Danielle took a step back from the gin-sodden breath.

"How can you expect these children to work without light?" Danny demanded. "They'll ruin their sight."

Mrs. Bumbry was taken aback. Her mouth hung slack and the yellow-stained eyeballs stared. She was not accustomed to being taken to task for her working conditions and certainly not by young ladies of Quality, and, unless she was headed for Bedlam, she was being confronted by Quality. Her girls provided the undergarments that went on the backs of stolid bourgeois matrons and Mrs. Bumbry had contact only with the agent who commissioned her, provided the materials, and haggled over the price.

A choked giggle came from the table. Mrs. Bumbry's arm swung and the giggler fell off her stool to collapse in tears amidst a heap of discarded material, scraps of thread, and much dust.

Danielle restrained herself. To jump to the child's defense

would only bring down further retribution on her head once her defender had left. "You have an Estelle Lançon indentured to you, I think."

"What's that to you?" Mrs. Bumbry grunted.

"I wish to break her indenture. I think, if you want your girls to continue with their work, we should talk elsewhere." Danielle walked to the door, the skirt of her riding habit caught over one arm. She had decided some time ago that riding habits were the easiest form of dress for these forays into London's underbelly. Mrs. Bumbry followed the slim figure, not because she wished to but because quite unaccountably she seemed to have no choice. "Do you perhaps have a parlor?" Danielle inquired sweetly. "Or somewhere where we may be private? Please do not concern yourself about the dirt. It does not worry me in the least."

Mrs. Bumbry, who had never concerned herself about dirt except on her girls' fingers when it might be transferred to the materials, looked around the small hallway with new eyes. She had conceived considerable dislike for this young woman who stood tapping an elegant booted foot on the grimy floor, her cold brown eyes quite at variance with the polite smile.

Mrs. Bumbry opened a door onto a small parlor of overstuffed chairs and dust-laden tables.

"Thank you." Danielle walked past her, whacked an armchair with her riding crop, stepped back as the dust rose, and decided to remain on her feet. "You have the indenture papers, madame?"

"Estelle's indentured to me for three years." Estelle also happened to have the neatest fingers when it came to placing delicate stitches.

"Nevertheless, Mrs. Bumbry, I am come to break the indenture. We will agree on a price."

The other woman's eyes shifted. Maybe she could afford to lose Estelle for the right price. There were hundreds of others dying for want of work, maybe not so neat, but they could be trained. "'Ow much?"

"One hundred guineas." Danielle knew that it was much more than Mrs. Bumbry had paid for her slave girl and she knew also that it was only the beginning of the bargaining.

"I couldn't let 'er go fer that," Mrs. Bumbry whined. "One of my best workers, Estelle is. An' I spent months trainin' 'er."

On a starvation diet supplemented by a heavy hand, Danielle reflected. "I would like to see her papers," she said. "You will understand that I cannot negotiate without seeing what I am negotiating for?" Her tone was benign, her manner reasonable, and Mrs. Bumbry decided that the game was worth playing.

"Hundred and sixty," she said, laying Estelle's papers on the desk. "Not a penny less. I worked with that girl for months and she don't even speak the lingo."

"May I see?" Danielle moved round the desk and the next minute the papers were in her hand. "One hundred guineas, Mrs. Bumbry. It is a great deal more than you deserve."

"You give those back, you hear?" the woman shrieked. The door burst open and a man twice the size of Mrs. Bumbry appeared.

"What's goin' on 'ere?"

"Nothing at all," Danielle said calmly. "Is this . . . uh . . . lady, your wife? Because if so, I think you might be well advised to fetch the smelling salts. She is a little distrait, you understand."

While they gobbled, one in fury, the other in total incomprehension, she tore the indenture papers into shreds and laid one hundred guineas on the desk. "You may count them if you wish. But I think you will find that the sum is correct." With that she swept from the room, crossed the hall, and opened the door onto the sweatshop. "Estelle?" Her voice was soft. "*Viens avec moi, petite.*"

The girl was perhaps ten, her eyes sunken in the pale face, and she held her body as if prepared for a blow. "What do you want of me, milady?" she whispered.

"*Rien du tout, ma petite.* I am come to take you home. Your *maman* has need of you." Estelle hesitated, her gaze darting fearfully toward the door. A yellowing bruise stood out on her cheek.

"*Allons-y*, Estelle." Danielle took the girl's hand, conscious that every moment of hesitation lessened her advantage of surprise. When the two in the parlor recovered there was no knowing who they would summon to their assistance, and not even D'Evron knew that the Countess of Linton was in Sheep's Alley this afternoon. She had her pistol, of course, but it was a threat best kept for emergencies. She hustled the girl out of the house where the sedan-bearers still stood, picking their teeth and kicking the cobblestones.

When he saw the two of them, the leader spat into the kennel. "Cost yer double."

The scrawny Estelle and the far from ample Danielle weighed considerably less than a tall, well-muscled man. But Danielle was in no mood for argument. "Ça va," she said shortly and pushed Estelle ahead of her. It didn't seem to matter that she had spoken French, her meaning was quite clear to the chair-bearers who trotted off rapidly, away from this unsalubrious neighborhood.

Danielle had accepted that respect for her rank deteriorated in direct ratio to the distance she went from Grosvenor Square. An unaccompanied woman, however well dressed and haughty her bearing, was accorded scant respect. Her money was all that mattered and the indefinable aura of authority that was created simply by the presence of the pistol in the deep pocket of her habit.

She pushed aside the greasy leather curtain to give directions to the bearers and then scrunched up on the narrow seat beside Estelle, taking the child half onto her lap. She explained that Estelle's father had found work in the kitchens of a hostelry on the outskirts of town. Her mother and the children would be lodged above the stables and Estelle was needed either to help in the hostelry or to watch the little ones while her mother worked. It was hardly an ideal situation for a family who had once commanded three domestic servants and a successful, if modest, *épicerie* in Corbeille Esson. But it was the best that D'Evron could do for them and unimaginably better than the hovel in Eastgate and Estelle's servitude in Mr. Bumbry's sweatshop.

Danielle remained in the chair while Estelle ran into her mother's arms, then gave the bearers instructions to return her to Grosvenor Square. They were lean, fit young men, but their journey this afternoon had been long and arduous. Danielle would have paid them off except that she had no certainty of finding others to take their place in the squalid slums where chair-bearers never penetrated. Besides, they would be paid handsomely for their exertions and probably would not take kindly to losing their customer to rivals, anyway.

Just before they reached Grosvenor Square, Danielle rapped sharply on the wooden frame and the chair halted. "I will alight here. I thank you for your trouble." The sovereign she handed the leader drew a small gasp and four tugged forelocks. Danny responded with a nod and set off on foot to traverse the few hundred yards to Linton House. She was in no physical danger at this point but much in danger of social censure should her unaccompanied walk fall under an unfriendly eye.

"Danny, what in Hades are you doing?"

"Jules!" She greeted him with a smile of relief. "You will give me your arm, will you not?"

"I should rather think so! What are you about, coz? Going about town in a common sedan? Justin will be . . ."

"In quite a taking," Danny finished for him serenely. "But since he will not know of it, we need have no fear."

Lord Julian, knowing his cousin, was not at all sure of that fact. "Danny, you have been up to something, and I insist on knowing what."

"Insist, Jules?" Her eyebrows arched as they reached Linton House, Danielle in the perfectly respectable company of her husband's cousin.

"Yes, damn it, insist." Julian stopped at the bottom step. "If you do not tell me what you have been doing, I shall tell Justin exactly what I saw."

"Jules, you would not! You could not be such a tattletale."

"You would be surprised, ma'am," he returned, grimly he hoped.

Danielle had a great need to unburden herself and Julian, while he might hem and haw in an elder brotherly way, would as like as not enter into her story with considerable enthusiasm. She did not believe for one minute that he would be capable of bearing tales to her husband and told him so roundly, before saying that she had need of a confidant but he

228

might regret finding himself in that position.

Julian was quite certain of that fact but felt curiously responsible. His memories of the defiant urchin on the Dover road had not been completely extinguished and he had a lively sense of what his cousin's wife was capable in the right circumstances. If she was unable to tell Linton, then it was best that she tell him—at least that way one member of the family would know what she was up to.

Danielle told him the whole in the seclusion of her own sitting room and Julian listened in horror. His animadversions on the character of a man of honor who would involve a lady in such activities were met first with anger and then with laughter. "Jules, *mon ami*, the chevalier has in no wise importuned my services. I do what I wish to do and it is quite safe, I assure you." The small pistol appeared from nowhere.

Julian took a step back. "Danny, please. Give it to me, your finger might slip."

"*My* finger!" Danielle went into a peal of laughter. "Idiot! If you doubt my ability to handle a firearm, you must ask Justin. He will vouch for my skill, I assure you."

"Maybe so." Jules gestured uneasily. "I would feel more comfortable, though, if you were to put it away."

"*D'accord.*" Danny shrugged and returned the small weapon to her pocket. "Now you know my story, Jules, and you will breathe not a word, on your honor?"

"I will not pledge my honor, Danny." Julian was suddenly serious. "If you should disappear when you are on one of these ridiculous journeys, you could not expect me to say nothing."

"No, of course not, but such an event is most unlikely. But I cannot tell Justin because he will forbid it and then I shall refuse to do his bidding and we shall really be in the basket, *n'est-ce pas?*"

"Without doubt." Julian nodded gloomily. However indulgent his cousin was of Danielle's peculiarities, there was a line he would draw eventually. So far these two had continued to avoid a major battle with a delicate dance of compromise, but Justin would never accept Danielle's present activities—not necessarily because they were indecorous, although they were

229

certainly that, but because they were dangerous.

"I have made you my confidant and as such have made you miserable." Danielle was suddenly all smiles as she took his hands. "You will not concern yourself about this, *tu comprends*, Jules?"

"I will try," he said, unable to resist the infectious chuckle. "But if you are in difficulty, you will call upon me. You give me your word."

"You have it, *mon ami*. Now, I must dress. We are to go to the opera tonight and I think we have dinner guests. In fact, I am sure that we do." Danielle pulled a face. "Justin's mama and several of her friends. The women are all cats and the men fuddy-duddies, but I must appear demure and correct. So you will excuse me."

Julian made his way back to his lodgings on Albermale Street, his mind much exercised by Danielle's revelation. He had the most uncomfortable feeling that he was duty bound to attempt to call a halt to her wanderings, but how to do that without involving Justin? And he could not break a confidence. Perhaps he should talk to D'Evron, put it to him that he could not in honor involve the Countess of Linton in these dangerous waters . . . Yes, Julian decided, that was the correct if not the *only* course of action available to him.

He ran D'Evron to earth later that evening at White's. The chevalier was playing piquet with the elderly Lord Maulfrey. There was no sign of Linton, fortunately, but he would be escorting his party to the opera and safely out of the way for some hours.

Julian strolled over to the piquet table, greeting the two men with a disarming smile. "A word with you, D'Evron, when you are finished playing?"

If the chevalier was surprised at this request from a bare acquaintance, there was no indication on the thin face. "At your service, Lord Julian."

Julian joined the macao table where Sir Anthony Fanshawe held the bank. "Do you care to take my place, Jules?" A young buck tossed a pile of guineas on the table and arose with a world-weary sigh. "The cards have the devil in 'em tonight."

"I thank you, Markham, but the luck's not running well for me, either. I'll watch the play."

Sir Anthony shot his friend a quick look. Jules enjoyed play as a rule, although he never lost his head, but he was looking unwonted serious this evening.

When D'Evron rose from the piquet table he found Julian Carlton waiting to catch his eye. He nodded imperceptibly and the two men walked together out of the salon. "You have business with me?" the chevalier asked in a low voice.

"D'ye care to accompany me to my lodgings? I've an excellent brandy."

They walked through the streets in silence, each deep in his own thoughts but both aware of nighttime dangers. They carried swordsticks and walked in the center of the narrow lanes, eyes alert for footpads.

"Cognac, D'Evron?" Julian's lodgings were comfortable, bespeaking the affluence of a young bachelor who had never had to concern himself with income. D'Evron accepted with a gracious bow and looked around the well-appointed sitting room. They had been greeted by an elderly manservant who had accepted his dismissal with the dour injunction that His Lordship not dip too deep into the cognac. Julian had merely laughed and explained, as the chevalier had already guessed, that Graves had been with him since he was in short coats. They were a lucky breed, these English aristos, the chevalier reflected.

"You wish to talk to me of Danny, Lord Julian?" The chevalier was some fifteen years older than his host and judged it were time to initiate matters.

"Of Lady Linton, yes," Julian stated in dignified accents.

The chevalier showed no signs of discomfiture at this frozen reprimand and Jules sighed. "She has told me the whole, D'Evron, and it will not do. She went to the Eastgate alone this afternoon in a common chair . . . If Linton were to hear of it." Julian shuddered. "It is dangerous, chevalier, and you must cease to involve her."

"It is, indeed, dangerous." D'Evron sipped his cognac. "However, my lord, Danny is more than capable of handling

231

such dangers. I have seen her do so."

Julian thought of the pistol. "That may be so, but prowling around the backslums rescuing indentured servants is no suitable activity for the Countess of Linton."

"Perhaps the countess should be allowed to decide that for herself," the chevalier said quietly.

"If you did not involve her, that would not be necessary."

"On the contrary, sir. Danny is now so deeply involved of her own accord that there is little I could do to prevent her. I freely admit my initial guilt, but she now works alone. We communicate, certainly, but her name is now well known to those we serve and she may be called upon without my knowledge. She does what she considers best."

"And Linton?"

"The earl's feelings are not my concern." D'Evron spoke firmly. "Danny and I are equal partners in this venture and she takes her own risks. She would not have it otherwise and her presence is needed far too much for me to play careful courtier even if she were to allow me to do so. Maybe, you do not know her too well, my lord. *I* would not dare to attempt to impose limits on her activities."

"Linton would. And that is what concerns me." Julian refilled his glass. "It is also what concerns Danny. Do I make any sense, D'Evron?"

"You do, but Danny will make her own choices. She knows what she is doing and has chosen to deceive her husband. She is no naive chit, Julian."

"No, but she is young." Julian persevered, although he knew the battle was lost.

"Young in years, perhaps, but not in experience." The chevalier placed his glass on the table. "I sympathize, but there is nothing I can do. Danny has confided in you and what you decide to do with the confidence is your decision."

"What the deuce *can* I do with it?" Jules exclaimed. "I'm not about to bear tales to Linton, although he'll have my hide if he ever finds out."

D'Evron smiled. "And mine also, I fear, my lord."

"Yes, by God." Julian refilled their glasses gloomily. "Let us drink to concealment, D'Evron."

It was a most dissatisfied Lord Carlton who retired to bed somewhat under the hatches in the early hours of the morning. If Danny could be persuaded to accept his protection on her missions of mercy then maybe all was not lost, but his powers of persuasion seemed lamentably lacking these days and his cousin-in-law was a damnably stubborn creature.

Chapter 12

"I do not quite understand you, Beatrice." Danielle looked at her sister-in-law directly, her eyes hard and cold.

Lady Beatrice dropped her own gaze into her satin lap. But she was here at the instigation of Mama and must do her duty by her brother's wife however unpleasant that duty. "Danielle, my dear, I wish merely to put you on your guard. It is best that you hear these things from a member of your family than from a gossip's tongue. Mama feels that if you are aware of what is being said about Linton then you will be better able to ignore it. It is not unusual, my love, and the wise wife turns a blind eye. If you react in public, it will be considered disgraceful want of conduct."

"You mean, I take it, that should someone be so kind as to inform me that my husband has taken up with his former mistress, I might scratch the cat's eyes out. You would be right, my sister." Danielle smiled sweetly—a shark's smile that caused Lady Beatrice to fear for her own eyes. But incautiously she persevered, mindful of her mother's instructions.

"Danielle, you must not take it hard. Justin is a great deal older than you; it is not to be expected that he will live forever in your pocket. A man has needs that a wife cannot satisfy, particularly a mere child. Why, even my own Bedlington has his little adventures." She laughed airily. "They do not worry me."

"If I were to be bedded with Lord Bedlington, they would not worry me, either. I should be glad of the respite," Danny said brutally.

Her sister-in-law's color changed, became puce, then deathly white and puce again. "How dare you!" Her voice shook.

"Well, how dare *you*?" Danielle snapped back. "I am, as it happens, well aware that my husband holds Lady Mainwaring in *friendship*. She has asked his advice on a delicate family matter and he has been good enough to assist her. Now, I suggest you leave because I should warn you that I am about to lose my temper. You may tell your mama that I am suitably grateful for her solicitude but should be more grateful if she would allow me to mind my own affairs." She stood up and hauled on the bellpull. "Lady Bedlington is leaving," she informed Bedford curtly.

Beatrice left without another word, her back stiff, mouth set. Never had she been so humiliated and by an ill-mannered babe to boot. What had happened to her urbane brother that he should take to wife such a wild creature, with no sense of propriety? How could she have said such an unpardonable thing? The fact that Danielle had hit the nail on the head with her caustic animadversions on the sexual attractions of Lord Bedlington only added fuel to the lady's ire.

Justin became painfully aware of the estrangement existing between his wife and his family when, in response to an urgent summons from his mother, he appeared in South Street to be coldly informed by the dowager countess that, while she would not, of course, cut Danielle in public, private social intercourse between them must now cease. His wife had been unpardonably rude to Beatrice and by extension to herself. She refused to tell him the issue and his sister, when questioned, had a fit of hysterics that required smelling salts and a mountain of cambric handkerchiefs to stem the flood. Justin, resisting with difficulty the urge to slap his sister back to her senses, bowed curtly and left. His brother-in-law, when accosted, could throw no light on the situation and managed to convey to Justin with much hemming, hawing, and humphing that his peace was quite cut up. The house was in an uproar and Beatrice burst into tears whenever she saw him. What was a man to do with a household of hysterical women, for God's sake, except go to his club?

Justin had scant sympathy for his brother-in-law at the best of times and none at all at this moment. He said coldly that if Bedlington chose to have his life made a misery by a pair of nagging women that was his affair. Linton did not.

Danielle, however, had some explaining to do and he strode back to Linton House in search of those explanations. He was not mollified by finding his wife closeted in the library with the Chevalier d'Evron. There was a strained look to her eyes that reminded him forcibly of those early days and did nothing for his temper.

D'Evron took his leave instantly with a courteous bow to Justin and a most elegant leg for Danielle, whose responding curtsy was impeccably formal.

"That man is always here," Justin stated with unusual irritability, pouring himself a glass of Madeira.

Danielle looked at him in surprise. "Do you object, Justin?"

"Do I have cause to?" he snapped.

"Oh, do not be absurd. What has put you out of temper?"

"I have just spent an unpleasant hour being informed by my mother and sister that they wish to have no further contact with you outside the inevitable social meetings. Why?" He turned to face her and drew a sharp breath at what he saw. She was rigid with fury, her lips a thin line.

"I suggest you ask them, my lord."

"I have done so. Since they will not tell me, you will. I am not prepared to find myself in the midst of hysterical feuding women. What did you do?"

"I did *nothing*." Danielle could not believe that Justin was accusing her of initiating things. He always took her part and in this instance should be doing so even more. "Your interfering sister, at the instigation of your mother, took it upon herself to give me some advice and information that was quite uncalled-for and prompted only by mischief. I encouraged her to leave the house." Since Justin had neglected to pour her a glass, she took up the decanter of Madeira, but her hands were shaking so much that she put it down again.

"I do beg your pardon." Justin filled her glass. "Danny, will you tell me what was said?"

237

"No," she stated flatly, taking a steadying sip of the tawny wine. "If you wish to know, you must find out from your sister. *I* am no talebearer. Does it not occur to you that her reluctance to tell you herself might be to do with your possible reactions? She holds you in some considerable awe. I have no desire to be private with either your mother or your sister so the arrangement suits me very well. You have my assurance that I will show all due respect in public. Now, if you will excuse me, I am having luncheon with Lady Graham and I must change my dress." She was gone in a swirl of muslin before Justin could recover his wits sufficiently to prevent her.

He stood nonplussed for a few moments as he accepted with a slow, rueful grin that he had lost that encounter, and he had lost it because he had attempted to deal with a child and been met with the dignified anger of a woman. Danielle's code of honor was absolute, as well he knew from experience. If she was not going to tell him then he'd best accept that fact. There was no question as to whose side he was on, even without the facts, so he must simply resign himself to the cold war until it petered out. It would do so eventually.

Danielle maintained a rigorous silence as Molly helped her to change. Molly knew the signs of Milady's anger well enough by now, just as she knew it was not directed at her. She kept her own tongue still, therefore, serenely going about her tasks, ignoring the snapping eyes and the impatience when Molly's fingers slipped on a tiny cloth-covered button. She was rewarded with a smile and a quick kiss as Danielle prepared to leave. "Bless you, Molly. I don't know how you put up with me."

The statement made no sense at all to the servant who set about tidying the room in the knowledge that no one could have a better position than hers. The countess was generous to a fault, never unjust and, on occasion, treated Molly as she would a best friend.

But Danielle was miserable. However much she tried to deny it, Beatrice's words had sown the seeds of doubt in a trusting soul. Justin had told her about Edward Mainwairing and it had not occurred to her to question the truth of his explanation. It did not do so now, but like a bee sting embedded in her flesh, the thought throbbed—if he is spending so much time with the woman who had been his lover for five long years, how could he resist the temptation? Society would regard the infidelity with a benign eye. Danielle's intolerance, on the other hand, would be heavily censured. She was a wife only—the property of her husband with no rights, either legal or personal. And she should be grateful that she was not abused, not required to account for every penny spent, not treated with the indifference her lord might accord a chair or a piece of china. Danielle, growing up in the male-oriented house of de St. Varennes, knew the pain and indignity callously inflicted on her sex without retribution or concern. And this London society was no better; more hypocritical, if anything, since such cruelties occurred in private, were privately condoned under the blind eye of a woman's lot.

Danielle saw pitying glances now wherever she went, eyes hastily averted as she came into a room, voices suddenly lowered or raised in bright small talk at her approach. She tried to ignore them, tried to persuade herself that they were a product of her overactive imagination, but the poison seeped into her pores. She had been too full of joy and love in the very early days of her marriage to recognize the barely concealed signs of envy, and was now unable to recognize the pleasurable malice as Society saw a minute crack in the fabric of the Linton's marriage and proceeded to take hammer and chisel to create a yawning crevice.

The Earl of Linton was seen going in and out of the house on Half Moon Street at all hours of the day and night and the little de St. Varennes could lose her complacence and join the ranks. How could an eighteen-year-old chit expect to hold the interest of a thirty-five-year-old who had been on the town for seventeen years? The sooner she gave Linton an heir and settled down in resignation, the happier she would be. A nursery full of brats would keep her occupied and take her mind off such frivolous nonsense as a love match.

Danielle struggled in grim silence. She was as bright and cheerful as ever, publicly as happy in her husband's company as always. Only in private did Justin notice the withdrawal which was almost always followed by a passionate hunger that for a while slaked his growing unease. His brat was growing up, he told himself firmly whenever she had a reason for not participating in a treat he had planned, or preferred to take tea with a group of matrons rather than ride with him. It was right that she should do so, cease to be the giddy exuberant girl; his outrageous brat of the sharp tongue and quick impulses. But in the constant presence of Danielle, Justin missed Danny.

It was a beautiful April night when the last nail hammered into the coffin and Danielle gave up the pretense. She had retreated, overly full of lemonade, to the retiring room at Almack's where she was in the process of wrestling with her skirts and the commode behind a worked screen, when two elderly dowagers entered the room to collapse on a sofa before the open window and fan themselves and, incidentally, the smoldering fires of Danielle's confusion.

"'Pon my soul, Almera, but I was like to swoon when I heard news of that marriage." The dowager duchess of Avonley tried to adjust her stays, which were pinching like the devil. "Just fancy! Linton takes the mother as mistress and the daughter to wife. I wonder whether it was the Rockford or the de St. Varennes that appealed." She wheezed with laughter and Danielle froze behind the screen.

"Louise was beautiful." Lady Almera sighed in fond reminiscence. "She had not an easy time of it with the de St. Varennes. No one could blame her for taking pleasure when it came."

"Nor young Linton." The dowager fanned herself vigorously. "D'ye think the child knows, Almera?"

"Linton's a man of sense," her companion answered as if such a question were ridiculous. "What's it to the chit, anyway?"

"Why nothing, of course. She cannot expect a man seventeen years older than herself to be without a past . . . but her own mother! 'Tis monstrous amusing, Almera, d'ye not think?"

Clearly Lady Almera did, judging by the cackle of laughter that reached Danielle, rigid behind the screen. She straightened her skirts and with head held high moved into the room. "Good evening, your grace, Lady Almera." She paused for a moment to check her coiffure in the mirror, threw them both a tiny smile, and returned to the ballroom.

"Jules, I do not feel quite the thing. Will you escort me home?" The request was whispered but none the less urgent and Lord Julian looked at his cousin-in-law with concern.

"Immediately. Do you have the headache?"

"A little." She smiled wanly. "It is too hot, Jules."

"Devilish hot," he agreed. Since when had Danny found a ballroom to be too hot? "I will procure your carriage."

When he set her down outside Linton House she refused his escort inside, pleading the headache that she must instantly take to bed and Julian, perforce, was obliged to agree. It was but eleven and Linton would not return for some time. He had said he was dining with friends but Danielle, in a world turned topsy-turvey, no longer knew what to believe. It was rumored that her husband was again the lover of Margaret Mainwaring and she had just heard from people who had no knowledge of her presence that he had been her mother's lover. There had been ample opportunity for him to tell her that and he had not done so. How could she then trust?

Danielle found that she had no difficulty accepting the fact that her husband and her mother had once been lovers. She lay in her darkened chamber and thought. It was a peculiar circumstance, certainly, but no more than that. Justin must have been barely a man at that time and she herself a nothing in eternity—unconceived and unthought of. But he had not told her and if he could not tell her such a fundamental fact how much more would he keep secret?

When Justin came home he found his wife apparently asleep, her breathing even in the dark room. She had been looking fatigued just recently and was in sore need of an undisturbed night. He tiptoed from the room to seek a lonely bed next door. As the door closed, Danielle buried her face in the pillows, muffling the sound of her sobs.

She awoke the next morning after a few broken hours of sleep, quietly determined. If Justin chose to play Society's game then would she also. She would be his wife, his hostess, would manage his households, but she would be no willing playmate. She would not refuse him her body when he

241

required it, but neither would she offer it. He could take his pleasure from Margaret Mainwairing.

Danielle sipped her hot chocolate, propped up against a fluffy mountain of pillows and read the *billets doux* scattered over the satin spread. Ordinarily, the effusive notes would have amused her and she would have shared their contents with Justin, calling through the connecting door as he attended to his morning toilette. This morning she pushed them aside with a desultory hand and concentrated instead on her plans for the day. There was work to be done with a family lodged near St. Paul's and she was in fair mood to wage battle.

"I will get up," she announced to Molly, throwing aside the bedcovers. "A riding habit, I care not which one."

When Justin appeared, expecting to find his wife pink and pearly beneath the covers ready to exchange accounts of their separate evenings, he found only a brisk lady in riding dress who proffered her cheek for his morning salute, laughed brightly, and said she was already late for her appointment. He bowed her from the room and returned to his own chamber to exchange the brocade dressing gown for morning dress, a deep frown creasing his brow.

Things went from bad to worse. Danielle suffered from an inordinate number of headaches that necessitated her early retirement of an evening and Justin, faced with the pale face, smudged eyes, and clearly effortful smile, could not doubt her excuse. After the second week he probed gently and received only a listless response. There was nothing the matter with her, only she would be glad when the Season was over. But when he suggested they go to Danesbury for a se'enight she was full of protestations. How could they miss the Duchess of Richmond's ridotto? And besides she had a host of other engagements . . .

He had capitulated with apparent serenity and attempted to court his wife, arranging elaborate surprises, on one occasion waking her at five o'clock in the morning to tell her to don her britches because they were riding to Richmond where they could gallop without fear of prying eyes and sharp tongues. She had complied, but with such lack of enthusiasm that Justin felt as if he had received a glove in his face. After that, he left her

242

alone. She was always polite, never turned him from her bed, but he found he had no stomach for the passive body beneath him, obedient to her conjugal duty. Reassuring himself that Danielle was going through a period of adjustment that had been inevitable—her past experiences bore no relation to her present and she must at some point reconcile the two—Justin made the biggest mistake of his life and countenanced her withdrawal.

They became polite strangers, meeting by accident on the staircase, exchanging small talk over the dinner table. Justin returned to his bachelor existence and his wife played her part, surrounded by admirers, the very soul of gaiety, except that she was becoming thin and the brown eyes huge in the small face. She was also seen much in the company of D'Evron.

More often than not, though, she ventured alone into the backslums to deal, with an icy tongue and a handful of guineas, with the exploiters. The Countess of Linton was now well known and urgent notes reached her daily, scribbled in hasty French on scraps of paper with the blunted end of a quill pen. Danielle responded to them all and by so doing managed to push her marital problems into the background. She had a job to do and a purpose to fulfill and the triviality of London's Season rapidly lost all appeal. Nevertheless, she took her part in the round of balls and assemblies, ever gay, ever flirtatious, never a crack showing in the public facade.

Justin endured in stolid silence, certain that he was doing the right thing. The child and the woman would come together eventually, and he must stand aside. He ached with loneliness but kept the ache well concealed.

Early one rainy afternoon, returning from his club with a piece of scurrilous gossip that he hoped might amuse Danielle, he was informed that My Lady had not left her bedchamber today. Much puzzled he mounted the stairs and entered his wife's room without ceremony. At first it appeared empty as well as cold and dismal. There was no fire in the grate, no lighted candles, and the rain beat desolately against the windows.

"Go away," a voice muttered peevishly from the bed. Danielle was visible only as a small curled mound, just the tip of her wheat-gold head appearing above the coverlet.

"What is it, Danny? Are you ill?" He crossed anxiously to the bed.

"No. Go away. I just want to be alone," the same voice grumbled crossly.

Justin pulled the cover away from her face and laid a hand on her brow. She seemed quite cool. "Do you have the headache again?" he asked gently.

"No."

"Well, if you will not tell me what is the matter, I must send for the doctor."

"I don't need the doctor." Danielle thumped onto her side facing away from him. "I just have the bellyache. It's quite normal and will go away if you'll leave me in peace." She twitched the covers overhead again.

"Oh, I see." Justin frowned. It had been nearly four weeks then since he had last shared her bed. He was usually so attuned to her body that her monthly cycles were as well known to him as they were to Danielle. His lack of awareness on this occasion served only to emphasize the lonely estrangement of their lives. Well, he was not going to accept his dismissal this time. "Come," he said briskly. "You may have the bellyache but that is no reason to suffer in misery. Why do you have no fire and no light? It is a wretched day and this room is as cold and dark as a tomb."

"I like it like that," Danny said petulantly. "I feel miserable and it suits my mood."

Justin smiled slightly. This Danny he could deal with. "Well, it does not suit mine, child." He tugged on the bellpull and when Molly appeared a minute or two later she saw His Lordship kneeling by the grate, setting a taper to the kindling.

"My lord, please," she gasped in horror. "I will do it."

"It's done," he said tranquilly, rising to his feet. "I suggest you light the candles and draw the curtains."

"I . . . I am sorry, my lord," Molly stammered, twisting her hands. "I would have done so before but my lady said . . ."

"I understand completely, Molly," Justin reassured. "I know exactly how stubborn Her Ladyship can be."

A muttered expletive came from the bed where Danny now

ay on her back, the covers pulled down to her nose as she regarded them balefully.

"You will feel a great deal better, my love, when you have washed your face and brushed your hair," Justin told her, pulling the heavy gold drapes across the long window, shutting out the dark, rain-sodden afternoon. The room had undergone a complete transformation; the fire blazed cheerfully and the soft candlelight illuminated the gold, cream, and white of the furnishings. Only Danielle remained untransformed.

"Now, Molly, you will be pleased to fetch your mistress some broth."

"I do not wish for any broth," Danny wailed.

"Would you prefer gruel, then?" her husband asked cheerfully.

"I loathe gruel!"

"Then it had best be broth. See to it, Molly."

"Yes, my lord." Molly bobbed a curtsy and made haste from the room.

The water in the ewer was cold, but Justin decided that the chill might have a salutory effect and wrung out a washcloth.

"What are you doing with that?" Danielle demanded warily.

"I intend to wash your face, brat. You are looking rather grubby and disheveled. I am persuaded you will feel more the thing when you are tidy."

Danny's arms flailed in protest, but her husband just laughed and caught both her wrists in one large hand. "You will not succeed in preventing me, Danny, so I suggest you submit with a good grace."

Danielle snuffled and snorted under the vigorous application of the washcloth, but with her eyes unglued and her cheeks tingling, she did feel a little less cross.

Justin brushed her hair until the bright curls shone again, but his movements were tender and caressing and Danny found herself leaning back against his shoulder automatically, with all the old trust and comfort. Justin felt it, too, and his heart leaped. He toyed with the idea of taking advantage of the moment and attempting again to discover what had been troubling her in recent weeks, and then he dismissed the idea. If she withdrew from him, he would lose this moment and it

245

was too precious. There would be other opportunities and all the more so if he played a casual game, rebuilding their love brick by brick, unobtrusively.

"There, that is a great improvement," he announced, plumping up the pillows and settling her against them. "Now, you shall take a glass of port for your ache and eat some broth and I shall tell you a very funny story that will quite chase away the megrims."

Danielle chuckled. "You are skilled at nursing, milord. Even more so than my old nurse. She used to weep when I was ill, you see, and that did not help matters at all."

Justin touched the tip of her nose with a light forefinger and went to his own parlor for the port. If only he could have her defenseless and in need of comfort for more than the hour or so afforded by this monthly inconvenience, he could get to the bottom of whatever it was.

Danielle required little encouragement to eat the steaming bowl of broth, rich from the ever bubbling stockpot belowstairs. She found Justin's story hilarious and choked violently on a toast crumb which led the earl to observe, as he patted her back and mopped up the slurped soup, that she was still as much of an urchin as ever. The remark was intended in jest, but it brought so many painful memories of those early good times when he'd cared for her, scolded her, and loved her and she had accepted it all in youthful trust and naiveté, that Danielle stiffened in sadness and the impudent retort that rose so naturally to her lips was swallowed.

"What is it, Danny?" Linton asked involuntarily.

"Why nothing at all, Justin." She laughed, that brittle laugh that he had come to dread. "I think I will sleep for a little while and then I shall be quite restored."

"I will leave you then." He rose from the bed and took the tray, placing it on the dresser. "Do you care to stay home tonight, my love? We haven't played chess together this age."

How easy it would be to say yes, to eat dinner together in his parlor as they had used to do, play chess and talk companionably and then to bed, to sleep in the circle of his arm. But the image of her mother and then of Margaret Mainwairing, eagerly awaiting Linton's footfall, was engraved on the retina of her mind's eye. "Have you forgotten, my lord, that we are promised to the Wesleys' this evening? There is to be a recital—a harpist as I recall."

"I had forgotten, I must confess. You could, perhaps, plead your sickbed as excuse." It was a last, desperate attempt, but he saw in her eyes, now strangely blank, that it would not do.

"There is nothing the matter with me that an hour's rest and a bath will not cure, Linton," she said briskly. "And it will be a most interesting soirée, I dare swear."

"Indeed, my love," he concurred dryly. "If my absence will not disturb you, I should prefer to spend the evening at Watier's."

"But of course, my lord. We do not need to live in each other's pockets, after all."

Linton bowed his acquiescence and left her chamber, desolation twisting like serpents in his belly. He had married a loving child—a child grateful to him for his help, a child who, from the depths of her inexperience, had perhaps mistaken gratitude for love. For a few months they had lived an idyll until Danielle had lost her naiveté as she took her place in the world of sham and pleasure. If she no longer loved him, then they faced a bleak future. He could have married any number of eager eligible young damsels who would have born his children, acted as his hostess, run his households competently if not with Danielle's devastating efficiency, but Justin in his foolishness had waited for something else, and he had found it in the mercurial Danielle. He could not now imagine his life without her, but he was beginning to imagine his life without her love. While she did not say the words he dreaded, he could still hope, still plan a campaign whereby he would woo the woman as he had never needed to woo the child.

The following morning he appeared in her bedchamber, resplendent in a frogged silk dressing gown, his hair in a neat queue at the nape of his neck. "You are feeling more the thing, I trust, love?" He bent to kiss her—a simple morning salute.

"Indeed yes, I thank you, sir," she responded politely. "Did you pass an enjoyable evening?" She was looking quite entrancing with her curls tumbled about her shoulders, her skin fresh from sleep, and a profusion of lace and ruffles

247

adorning her negligée.

"I have urgent business at Danesbury." Justin smiled and rifled carelessly through the scattered notes on her coverlet. "Your admirers are always faithful, my dear." But Danielle merely shrugged lightly. "Will you accompany me?" He returned to the original subject with apparent ease. "Apart from the pleasure *I* shall take in your company, there are matters of the estate that you might wish to concern yourself with."

"If you require my presence, sir, then of course I shall be pleased to accompany you."

It was said in the way she had given him her body until he had found himself unable to take in that way—a dull "as you command, my lord."

"I do not *require* your presence, Danielle. I merely wished for your company. However, since I am sure you have more exciting things to do in town, I shall see you on my return." He refrained, with the greatest difficulty, from slamming the connecting door. Had he looked back to see the stricken expression on his wife's face, subsequent events might have taken a different turn.

During her husband's absence, Danielle threw caution to the winds and intensified her activities with D'Evron. No longer concerned that Justin might remark on her erratic comings and goings in riding dress when she had taken no horse from the stables, or that he might look askance at the frequent visits from the chevalier, she was out at all hours, frequently returning late at night, heedless of the concern this was causing Bedford who controlled the backstairs whispers with Molly's more than ample support, but awaited the return of His Lordship with more than usual eagerness.

On one particularly tricky expedition, just a few days after Linton's departure, Danielle called upon Julian's help.

"I must go at night, Jules, and the chevalier is unable to accompany me," she explained calmly. "You need not involve yourself, but you will drive me and wait outside, then all will be *comme il faut.*"

"What the deuce do you mean, *comme il faut?*" His Lordship exclaimed. "You cannot go to Billingsgate at any time, and

248

certainly not in the middle of the night."

"Not alone, no," she agreed. "But with you, I will have no fear. It is the only time I can speak with Monsieur Farmé and he is not being at all kind to his wife, you understand. He works at the fishmarket from dawn till dusk and then drinks his earnings. *C'est abominable!* Madame does not even understand how to do the marketing in this country and he will not help her in the slightest. The baby has the croup and monsieur complains constantly about the crying at night but he will not give money for medicine. It is necessary to persuade him to see reason."

"Danny, you cannot mean to interfere in the private affairs of man and wife?" Julian looked at her in horror. "It is no business of yours."

"It most certainly is," Danielle declared. "Am I to stand by and watch this happen? Do not be absurd, Jules. If you do not choose to accompany me, then I will go alone."

Thus it was that the young Lord Julian found himself in a bare, grimy apartment smelling strongly of fish, surrounded by wailing tots and coughing babies, watching his cousin's wife confront a mountainous man much the worse for liquor. Julian could not follow the exchange. It bore no relation to the upper class French he had learned, but the effect of a diminutive aristocrat speaking the language of the gutter was quite apparent on Monsieur Farmé's face.

Madame was an emaciated figure in a ragged gown, her eyes, red with weeping, sunken into the pale face. Her hands fluttered and twisted as Danielle's angry words flew through the room and Julian found himself obliged to calm and soothe the woman while his cousin-in-law fought the man. It was a most disconcerting role reversal, but seemed only appropriate since Danielle was clearly more capable than he of dealing with Monsieur Farmé.

"*Eh bien, monsieur, nous sommes en accord, n'est-ce pas?*" Danielle, in the twinkling of an eye, was the Countess of Linton speaking the language of a de St. Varennes. "You will provide your wife with monies on which she may conduct your household and I will find someone who will assist her in making her way about the market. I will also send *un médecin* to look to the babe. His bill will be small, and you will pay it without delay, I think." She gave him her shark's smile. It was one Julian had never seen before and would rather not see again, he decided. Danielle had issued no threats, no blustering accusations, but it would take a stronger man than Monsieur Farmé to resist the implied consequences of continuing along his present course.

Danielle took Madame Farmé to one side and spoke a few words. As she took her hand in a gesture of farewell, madame felt the crispness of a roll of bank notes slipped into her palm that instantly clenched into a fist. "I will visit you again, madame, in a day or so, just to see how you are going on." Danielle turned all smiles to the recalcitrant husband. "Monsieur Farmé, I look forward to meeting you again."

Farmé didn't appear as if he reciprocated the courtesy and Julian felt an absurd urge to laugh at the man's discomfiture. He restrained himself, however, and encouraged Danielle back to the waiting curricle that was guarded by his own tiger who, after a few bewildered moments, had reverted to his origins and was exchanging slang with an interested group of spectators.

Julian handed her into the curricle, took the reins, and instructed the tiger to stand away from their heads. The boy did so, springing up behind with an agile twist of a wiry body.

"It is the outside of enough, Danny," Julian said eventually, once he had negotiated the narrow streets. "You cannot continue in this way. I am convinced the place was flea-ridden—I begin to itch already."

"Nonsense." Danny waved her hand in careless dismissal. "If there are fleas you can see them. There were none there. Bedbugs, mayhap, but since you are not obliged to sleep in the beds, you need have no fear."

"Have you no sense of propriety?" Julian demanded, knowing the answer full well.

"None whatsoever, Jules," she said cheerfully. "But I am truly grateful for your assistance. I hope it will not be necessary to ask for it again."

"You damn well will ask for it," Julian stated fiercely. "I begin to think I must lay the whole before Linton. I had no idea of the conditions in which you were acting."

"Jules, you cannot!" Danny exclaimed. "You promised."

"More fool I," he said glumly. "But I do not know what's to be done."

"*Mon ami*, you must cease worrying. It is not necessary, I assure you."

Lord Julian remained unconvinced by this assurance and more than ever certain that in all honor he could no longer be Danielle's accomplice in deceiving her husband. But in all honor how could he do otherwise?

As it happened, Julian need not have concerned himself. The balloon was to go up very shortly and not at his instigation.

Chapter 13

Linton returned from Danesbury after a two-week absence that he had deliberately prolonged in the vague hope that Danielle would miss him and be in a more receptive mood on his return. He was also resolved that they would not follow the crowd to Bath for the summer season. He would take Danielle back to Mervanwey and in the quiet haven where they had passed such an idyllic summer last year, he would attempt to recapture his loving bride. It was quite possible, of course, that Danielle would object to the plan but, for once, Linton was prepared to exercise the husband's right of command and brook no argument. If he was again reduced to dragging her through the countryside on the end of a leading rein, then so be it.

He found Danielle in the bookroom, dealing with correspondence. Her eyes lit up as she saw him and for a second he hoped, but then the warmth was extinguished almost as if it had never been. "Why, Linton," she said, offering her cheek for his salute. "I did not expect you so soon."

"I had hoped you might have missed me," he replied with a smile as dry as fallen leaves. "But I am sure you have been well amused."

"Tolerably so." She shrugged her slim shoulders. "I have been looking at the leases of two houses in Bath. It is almost the end of the Season and we must make a decision before they are all taken. You must tell me which one you prefer and I will instruct Peter to deal with the arrangements."

"We do not go to Bath," he said, deciding that confrontation at this point could hardly worsen matters.

"And why not, pray?" Her eyes snapped and her mouth took on that mutinous pout that always spelled trouble.

"Because I do not wish it," Justin told her flatly. "We will go, instead, to Mervanwey."

"And if I do not choose to do so?"

"I regret to inform you, Madam Wife, that this is not a matter in which you have any choice." Her jaw dropped and she stared at him, speechless with indignation, her body stiff with rebellion. "You are looking sadly pulled, my dear," Justin went on. "A few months of sea air will restore you, I am convinced."

"Well, I will *not* go," she declared.

Justin raised his glass and subjected her to that unnerving scrutiny. "No?" he inquired gently. "I beg leave to inform you that you are mistaken."

Danielle proceeded to inform *him* in a very few well-chosen epithets exactly what she thought of this autocratic statement.

Her husband remained unmoved throughout the tirade, looked merely bored, in fact. When she fell into a frustrated silence, he pinched her cheek carelessly and said he hoped she had sufficiently relieved her feelings.

Danielle made a sound like an infuriated kitten and flounced out of the room. It had been months since Justin had treated her like that and Danielle knew full well that if he had made up his mind on the matter, to Mervanwey they would go. She toyed momentarily with the idea of settling on one of the Bath houses herself and presenting him with a fait accompli, but in her heart of hearts knew that such childish defiance would not work. It was interesting, though, that he was prepared to spend the summer away from the charms of Margaret Mainwairing, or perhaps he intended to leave his wife safely out of the way in Cornwall while he took his own pleasure elsewhere. Well, if that was his plan he would find himself obliged to revise it.

Justin took himself to White's, deciding that fighting with his wife was infinitely more satisfying than the cool polite distance of recent weeks. At least she was forced to respond to him in a familiar way he could handle.

254

The Earl of March had been waiting for three days for his grandson-in-law to return to town. No one seemed to know when to expect him, not even Danielle, and Charles had stationed himself at White's where he knew Linton would come within hours of his arrival in Grosvenor Square. Accordingly, he was much relieved when his patience was rewarded by the sight of the powerful figure in dove gray britches and a superbly cut coat of blue cloth with silver buttons. A diamond pin nestled in the immaculate folds of his cravat and his hair was but lightly powdered.

Linton greeted friends and acquaintances with casual ease but a slight frown showed in the blue black eyes as he recognized the unmistakable signs of constraint in the returned courtesies. He could almost feel the speculative eyes on his back as he made his way to the Earl of March, who had been betrayed into an urgent gesticulation when he had caught his eye.

"What's to do, March?" he asked bluntly. "I have the distinct impression that my appearance has caused a degree of embarrassment."

"No doubt." March sighed heavily. "You had best talk to Lavinia without delay, Justin. She has been in such a taking, I have been at my wits end to know what to do for the best."

"So Danielle has set the town by the ears in my absence," Justin observed, his lips tightening.

"You must talk to Lavinia, dear boy. She is better able than I to explain."

"Then I will do so at once. I'm obliged to you, March." Justin bowed and turned on his heel. Whatever the little wretch had done this time, it was clearly more serious than one of her usual pranks.

Lady Lavinia was not the calm matron Justin was accustomed to. She greeted him with a mixture of reproach and relief that he wisely allowed to run its course before saying, "You had best tell me the whole, ma'am."

"It is such a scandal, Justin." Lavinia paced the drawing room. "I cannot think what you were about to leave her alone for such a time. And your mother has been here every day, insisting I do something because Danielle will not mind her.

255

But what can *I* do? The child will not mind me either."

"Ma'am, I am quite in the dark as yet," Justin prompted, beginning to despair of ever hearing this horrifying story.

"Justin, she has been seen entering and leaving D'Evron's lodgings any number of times in these last two weeks, at all hours of the day and night, and quite unaccompanied," Lady Lavinia moaned tragically. "Not that it would be much better if she had been. She is also always to be seen driving in his company, but they do not drive in the park or anywhere respectable, they are always heading out of town." Lady Lavinia's geographical knowledge of London was confined exclusively to the few square miles inhabited by the ton, any area outside that was a foreign land.

"Am I to understand, Lavinia, that Danielle is considered to be D'Evron's mistress?" Justin took snuff with an insouciance that amazed the countess.

"That is what is said," she replied with a defeated sigh. "I have no idea whether or not it is true, but she is so indiscreet and . . ." She hesitated before continuing bravely. "You will forgive me for saying this, Justin, I cannot but have helped noticing that there has been some estrangement between you recently. If you have angered her in some way . . . she is so impulsive." Her voice faded.

"So, you are suggesting that she has taken a lover in revenge? I think not, ma'am. My wife, as you so rightly say, is both indiscreet and impulsive, but she is not vindictive. She has business with D'Evron concerning her compatriots who find themselves in difficult circumstances. This business has my approval and it would be wise to let that be known widely and without delay. However, I do not approve of her manner of conducting that business in my absence, but you may safely leave that matter in my hands. The scandal can be easily scotched if D'Evron is seen also in my company and their work together with the émigrés is made open knowledge."

"I will do as you say." Lavinia nodded thoughtfully. "I think I will arrange a dinner party with D'Evron as guest, you and Danielle, of course, and several others of importance. Yes, that will serve very well. But you will put a stop to her jauntering?"

256

"You may rest assured that I shall do so," Justin said, a grim note in his voice that quite reassured Lady Lavinia.

Linton went next in search of his cousin. In truth, he was not as sanguinely convinced of Danielle's fidelity as he had led Lady March to believe. He thought it unlikely but not as impossible as he would have considered it two months previously. Danielle had changed out of all recognition and he was no longer sure of her, no longer sure that he knew her well enough to predict her emotions and actions. He strongly suspected that his young cousin would know the truth; he and Danielle were like brother and sister and even if she had not taken Julian completely into her confidence, he was no fool and would probably have judged the situation accurately.

He ran Julian to earth in Albermale Street and was, for once, thoroughly taken aback by his greeting.

"Odd's blood, Justin, where have you been? I have been out of my head with worry. It is the outside of enough to disappear for two weeks and leave me to . . ."

"I was not aware I had entrusted you with any charge, Julian," Justin interrupted curtly. "You may offer me a glass of claret and come out of the boughs, if you please."

The cold tones had their usual effect and a flustered Lord Julian begged pardon and poured the claret.

"Now," Justin said, reclining lazily in a large chair with ear pieces. "You will tell me the true nature of Danielle's relationship with D'Evron."

"You must ask her yourself. Gad, Justin, I cannot understand why you have not done so before." Lord Julian ruffled his powdered chestnut locks with uncharacteristic carelessness. "I have done what I can to make light of the rumors; I have tried to persuade her that she cannot go on in this way, but she will not listen to me."

"She is, then, D'Evron's mistress?" Justin asked, his quiet tones hiding the cold nausea rising in his gorge.

"Oh, do not be absurd, coz!" Jules exclaimed. "Of course she is not. She has eyes only for you and you must be a blind man not to see it."

"Danielle has made it a little difficult for me to do so," Justin said slowly. "But I have been something of a fool, I

257

fear." He smiled ruefully. "I am a great deal older than she, Jules, and thought to let her grow up in her own fashion."

"By abandoning her," Julian declared brutally. "She has more bottom than sense, or at least than sense of self-preservation," he amended. "She actually has a deal of sense where others are concerned. I just wish she would not go off on these flights of . . ."

"Flights of what?" Justin prompted when his cousin's impassioned speech seemed to peter out.

"You must ask her yourself," Julian repeated. "But the sooner I am freed of this burden of secrecy the happier I shall be, however angry you may be at my part. If you've a grain of sense, coz, you'll stand for no prevarication this time."

"I can safely assure you that I will not be angry." The earl smiled. "I know how persuasive Danny can be. But I thank you for your advice, Jules." Linton stood up. "And for the claret. A '67, was it not? One of Danny's favorites."

"She insisted I buy it." Julian was somewhat thrown by this seemingly casual non sequitur. "She has taken my cellar in hand and buys for me as she does for you. So far I have not been able to fault her judgment."

"And I'll lay odds you never will." The earl laughed. "She has much experience in these matters and quite the purest palate." He took his leave of a greatly relieved Julian who now felt much as Lady Lavinia did—that all would be put to rights with due speed.

Linton was forced to bide his time, however, when he arrived in Grosvenor Square to be informed that My Lady had joined a party to Hampton Court and was not expected home until after dinner. At midnight, he informed the night porter that he would wait up for Her Ladyship himself, and sent both Petersham and Molly to their beds. In his present mood the fewer members of the household awake when Danielle eventually decided to return the better.

He stood at the library window overlooking the square, watching for the carriage. It appeared at last bearing the Westmore Arms and the young viscount escorted Danielle to the door. They were both laughing, a fact which exacerbated

My Lord's anger even further, although he supposed he should be happy she had been engaged in such an irreproachable entertainment as a young people's excursion.

The door swung open before Danielle could hammer on the brass knob in the shape of a gryphon's head. "You have had a pleasant evening, I trust," her husband said, his tone level but his eyes on fire. "Good evening to you, Westmore." The greeting was so clearly a dismissal that the viscount bowed, stammered a hasty good night to Danielle, and retreated to his carriage.

Danielle, feeling distinctly uneasy, sailed past her husband with a rustle of pomona green satin and made for the stairs.

"Danielle, I wish to talk to you." Linton closed the heavy door. "Will you come into the library for a few minutes?"

Danielle had a foot on the bottom stair and now yawned deeply. "It is very late, Linton, and I am monstrous fatigued. We can talk in the morning if you wish it."

"If you put me to the trouble of fetching you, you will regret it," he said pleasantly, holding open the library door.

Danielle hesitated for barely a moment before sweeping into the library, two flags of color flying on her high cheekbones. "What is it you wish to say to me, my lord, that cannot wait until the morning?"

"A very great deal as it happens. I do not care to return to town after a mere two weeks absence to find my wife the butt of every scandalmongering tongue. I do not care to walk into my club to be met with embarrassed whispers and sympathetic eyes. What can you have been thinking of, Danny, to be so free in D'Evron's company? I'll not have it bruited abroad that I wear a cuckold's horns."

"Oh, I see." Danielle's voice shook. "It is the Linton pride. While Caesar may do as he pleases, Caesar's wife must be above suspicion. Well, I will tell you, my lord, that I do not hold with such hypocrisy and I will not live my life by those rules."

"What the devil do you mean?" Justin stared in stupefaction.

Danielle cursed her unruly tongue. She had no intention of confronting Linton with her knowledge of his infidelity. Her position was humiliating enough as it was, but some shreds of pride remained to her.

"I meant only that I find Society's double standards intolerable," she muttered, turning away from him. "If I *were* to be having an affair with D'Evron and conducting it discreetly, there would be no overt censure. I am not, but an innocent friendship is considered incomprehensible. Some sordid construction must be put upon it and I will not tolerate it."

"And I will not tolerate your continuing in this manner," Justin said tautly. "You may find the rules hypocritical but, so help me, you will learn to live by them. You will now tell me exactly what you have been doing with D'Evron that has thrown Julian into such fits and has caused you to behave with such disgraceful impropriety."

Danielle walked to the window, pulling aside the curtains to look out at the slumbering square. She would have to tell him now. Perhaps, unconsciously, she had hoped by her outrageous carelessness to force this confrontation. Her duplicity nagged at her constantly, like an aching tooth, and if Julian had been obliged to admit to Justin that he knew the truth, then she was in honor bound to release him also from his burden of secrecy.

"Very well. But you will be much displeased, I fear."

"Doubtless I shall," he responded equably, his tension receding as he recognized that the battle had been won with no more than a slight skirmish. "It would be difficult to be more so than I am already, however, so you can have little to lose by the truth."

"I have not told you before, you understand, simply because I was afraid you would be out of reason cross and forbid me to continue. Then I would be obliged to refuse you and matters might become *un peu difficile.*" Her free hand waved expressively.

"Cut line, Danny," her husband advised.

He heard her out in incredulous silence. Danny was scrupulously truthful, leaving none of her adventures out of the recitation and explaining Julian's unwilling part.

260

"You must not blame Jules," she said anxiously. "He had no choice but to keep my confidence."

"I have no intention of holding Julian responsible. He will stand forever in my debt. The chevalier, however, is a different case."

"Not so very different," Danielle told him. "I have had no gun to my head, Justin. I have done simply what I needed to do and D'Evron has had no say in the matter. He has done his best to protect me from annoyance but realized early on, I think, that I needed no such protection. I have my pistol with me at all times, you understand." She offered this last with a kindly smile of reassurance that brought a gleam of amusement to His Lordship's eye, an amusement not unmixed with admiration. He had thought she had changed, the indomitable urchin become Society Lady—not so, it seemed. Was it this dichotomy that had caused the tension and withdrawal? She would not have enjoyed deceiving him, of that Justin was convinced, and the strain of keeping her activities a secret must have been immeasurable. No wonder she had been avoiding his company like the plague, obviously petrified that she might inadvertently give herself away. She was naturally indiscreet, after all. It must have been torment for her to have been forced to rein in such an open, high-spirited nature. She had been quite correct in her assumption that had she asked his permission at the outset he would have refused it out of hand. But Justin was wiser now, and he wanted back the blithe loving spirit of his wife.

"I shall ask only two things of you, Danny," he said after this considering silence.

"Milord?" She looked at him in surprise. She had expected anger, hurt at her own deliberate deception, a flat injunction that she cease her activities forthwith, but Linton showed no signs of annoyance and appeared strangely at ease.

"First, you stop your wanderings in and out of D'Evron's lodgings unless you have *my* escort. No other will do, you understand? Not even Julian."

Danielle nodded. "I did not truly intend to set the town about the ear."

261

"Fibber," he accused sternly. "You knew quite well what you were about so you need not play the naive baby with me. The damage is not irreparable and we shall come about nicely if you do exactly as you are bid."

Danielle subjected her satin slippers to a sedulous scrutiny and remained silent.

"Second." The earl resumed. "You will make no more of these excursions unaccompanied. I do not care what escorts you choose and I will accompany you myself when I may, but you will not again go alone. Is it understood, infant?"

"I think I may call upon Jules, Westmore, Tony, and Philip," she said reflectively. "I am sure they would be more than willing. Yes, milord." She gave him a radiant smile. "I see no difficulty in complying with your wishes."

"I am indeed a fortunate man," Linton murmured. "I should warn you, though, that I have not changed my mind about Mervanwey. Your people must manage without you throughout the summer."

"It will be hard for the chevalier, but I daresay he will manage," she responded with an easy smile as relief at the unburdening and his reaction flooded her. This point she could concede and maybe, just maybe, she could win her husband back from the arms of his mistress. It occurred to Danielle then, in the blinding illumination of truth, that for once in her life she had not fought. She had given up her husband with barely a whimper. In this most vital matter, she had bowed to society's rules and accepted the conventional charade in the disguise of pride. Well, she would do so no longer. She would compete with Margaret Mainwairing and the mistress would find a worthy opponent in the wife.

"Just what is going through that pretty but excessively devious little head now?" Justin demanded, watching the series of emotions play over her mobile features.

"Is that so very hard to guess?" Danielle responded, her eyes narrowing seductively. "I had not thought you obtuse, husband." She shrugged nonchalently and walked to the door.

Justin lunged for her, swinging her round to examine her upturned face. "You have given me little reason to be otherwise just recently, Madam Wife."

"No," she agreed simply.

"I'll not allow it to happen again, Danielle," he promised softly. "I'll have the truth from you from now on . . . Is it understood?"

Danielle dropped her eyes lest he read the lie in them. It was a lie of his own making after all. She slipped her arms around him. "Take me to bed, love."

Chapter 14

"I am unconvinced by Desmoulin's words, Linton." William Pitt, Earl of Chatham, paced the Turkey carpet in his study, a deep frown creasing his brow. "It is too simple to say that it is finished."

"The king is in the Louvre, the National Assembly at the Tuileries, the channels of circulation are being cleared, the market is crammed with sacks of grain, the Treasury is filling up, the cornmills are turning, the traitors are in full flight, the priests are underfoot, the aristocrats are at their last gasp, the patriots have triumphed."

"Bravo, Justin." Pitt applauded. "You have a formidable memory."

"It is Danielle who has the memory." Justin laughed. "I have heard her quote Desmoulins with such scorn on so many occasions that the words are engraved on my mind."

"She does not believe it either, then?"

"No, and she hears much from those in flight who are in a position to know," Linton replied soberly. "There are frequent lootings and lynchings of the so-called enemies of the people. Since Orléans left Paris for London, the Palais Royale has been turned over to the populace. Orléan's gracious palace is now a place of gambling houses, cafés, taverns, and prostitutes and the police are constantly busy there. But it is also the center of popular political life in the city. How can anything sensible come out of discussions conducted in such wild and uncontrolled surroundings?"

"There are too many factions," Pitt said. "The Jacobins and the Cordeliers are perhaps the strongest, but new ones appear every day and each has a newspaper to inflame and incite an excitable audience." He walked the floor in ponderous silence and Justin waited in a shaft of early May sun pouring through the open window. His prime minister was taking his time to reach the point, but Justin was under no illusion that he had been summoned simply for a chat about the political situation pertaining in Paris in the summer of 1790.

"I need some firsthand information, Justin. Will you take a glass of claret?"

"Thank you. And you wish me to furnish it?"

"Yes, I have not asked you before . . ." Pitt smiled slightly. "I thought it only reasonable to allow you time to settle the business of marriage."

"That was indeed generous of you." Linton sipped his claret. "I do not know, in all truth, how I would have answered you had you made your request earlier."

"I had surmised as much, which is why I chose to put neither of us in such an awkward situation, my friend. However, this need not be an extended trip—two, maybe three weeks at most." Pitt scratched at a gravy stain on his cravat. "You would not, I suppose, consider taking Danny with you?"

"No, I would not." It was a flat, soft-spoken negative.

"I was afraid not." Pitt sighed. "It is just that the information she gleans from the émigrés here and her own deductions are immensely valuable. And her past experiences have equipped her . . ."

"I do not wish Danielle to roam the streets of Paris again in a pair of tattered britches. She has done enough of that. While I countenance her activities in London, I do so only with the greatest reluctance. But she is *not* to be in France at this time. God knows what effect it would have upon her."

William Pitt was well accustomed to weighing the opposition, and accomplished at concession when it was clear no other course was available, so he merely bowed and asked Linton how soon he would be able to leave, since it was rumored that the royal family would move to St. Cloud in June and not return to Paris until October.

Justin pondered the question. He and Danielle were planning to leave for Mervanwey at the beginning of June. Should he suggest she go now with her grandparents while he made the journey? Such an arrangement would certainly set his mind at rest, but Danielle would be bound to rebel. There was still something about her that puzzled him, but he could not put his finger on it—an expression he caught when she didn't know he was looking at her, an occasional brittle quality to her joy in their renewed loving. But then she carried the burdens of many these days and he could only relieve her of a few. He would not add to them by taking her to Paris, but the sooner he got her away from London the happier he would be. However, there would be bloody enough battle with his wife, anyway. She would feel less left out if she could continue her work in London than if she were packed off to the wilds of Cornwall. He would just have to hope she got into no trouble in his absence.

"Within three days," he informed the prime minister, "you wish me to observe the working of the National Assembly, to hear the voices in the clubs, and, perhaps, to penetrate the Tuileries and mingle with the court?"

"If you can accomplish that much without aid, Justin, I shall be more than satisfied," Pitt responded. "I expect not so much, but whatever you can tell me . . ."

"I am, as always, at your service, sir." Linton made an elegant leg. "If you will excuse me now, I shall make my preparations."

Chatham's lips twitched. He could well imagine the most arduous part of those preparations, having enjoyed an increasingly friendly and informative relationship with the young Countess of Linton in the months since her marriage. Chatham thought it most unlikely that Danielle would view her husband's plans with equanimity.

Had Linton been aware of the greater shock in store for him that evening, he would have viewed the upcoming confrontation as a mere bagatelle. He had agreed to take Danielle to Vauxhall Gardens that evening, an excursion that required considerable sacrifice on his part since he found the place tedious and the crowds quite abominable. But he had found it impossible to resist Danny's coaxing and the flattering declaration that she could not enjoy herself half so much without his presence. It was to be hoped that gratitude at his sacrifice and a thoroughly enjoyable evening would ameliorate the inevitable tantrum.

When he entered his wife's bedchamber before dinner he found a lively scene. Danielle was sitting before her dresser mirror in an underdress of palest pink satin, a wide lace panel threaded with seed pearls running down its center. Jean-Louis, her émigré hairdresser, was arranging the curls in a daringly simple knot on top of her head that left her neck and ears bare and drew instant attention to the outrageous décolletage. Half a dozen young bucks lounged around the chamber in ardent discussion, which broke off at the earl's appearance.

"Ah, milord." Danielle turned instantly to him, ignoring the pained mutter of Jean-Louis, whose delicate endeavors to insert pearl-headed pins in the knot were thus interrupted. "You are just in time to settle an argument."

"Indeed." Linton surveyed the assembled company with polite interest. "I should be happy to do so, my dear."

"I have decided to wear a patch tonight," she told him, "and no one can decide where it should be placed."

Linton's eyes skimmed over her bosom. He had long given up his husbandly strictures on her neckline; Danielle knew perfectly well what she was about when it came to her clothes. "I cannot imagine why there should be any question," he murmured, taking one of the black silk patches from the tiny box on the dresser and placing it carefully on her right cheekbone.

"The sorceress." Danielle gurgled with laughter. "What think you of My Lord's choice, gentlemen?"

"It is your husband's choice, Lady Danny." Viscount Lancing expressed the collective view with a bow to Linton. "The matter is decided."

Justin watched with well-concealed amusement as the young gallants melted from the room. The art of dalliance was one he had enjoyed himself many years ago and he bore these youngsters no ill will for their fascinated admiration of his wife.

"Well," Danielle announced. "Since you have sent my advisers away, you must take on the task single-handed. What perfume shall I wear, milord?"

She used only the most delicate fragrances, never a hint of musk or gardenia. Smiling, Linton took her wrist and applied the scent of freesias before pressing his lips to the pulse point which quickened in the most gratifying fashion. He would have liked to have kissed the wide full mouth curved in a smile of absolute tenderness, but in the presence of Molly and Jean-Louis such a display was unthinkable. Instead, he sat in a brocade armchair and waited until her toilette was completed and Molly carefully slipped a rose pink ballgown over Jean-Louis's simple-appearing creation. The gown had sleeves to the elbow, where lace studded with seed pearls frothed in perfect harmony with the lace panel of the underdress.

"*Tu est ravissante, mon amour,*" Justin whispered as she pirouetted before him. Whatever had happened to his brat? It was most bewildering—one minute she was there and the next she wasn't. But the unpredictability was never less than exciting.

Danielle was entranced by Vauxhall Gardens. For the first half hour she could not help looking anxiously at Justin to see if he was enjoying himself, but her husband, resplendent in sapphire velvet and lace, appeared not at all bored although, on occasion, she surprised a preoccupied frown between the black eyebrows. But it disappeared the instant her eyes met his and she dismissed it for the moment. He had been with the prime minister that afternoon and no doubt had heard some disquieting news. She would discover what in the privacy of the large bed later.

In the pavilion, the earl trod a measure with his wife before losing her to the flock of eager courtiers anxious for her hand. Danielle, however, made her excuses soon enough and returned to his side.

"Do you care to listen to the recital in the concert hall, Justin?"

"I care to do only what you care to do, my love," he responded, replacing a dangerously loose pin in her coiffure.

"Then let us go to the Grecian temple at the end of the Long

Walk." Danielle took his hand. "We shall pretend that we are clandestine lovers and you are about to elope with me."

"Could I persuade you to do so, ma'am?"

"Could I persuade *you* to do so, sir?" she returned mischievously.

"Do you doubt it?" He raised her hand to his lips and kissed the soft palm.

"Then let us do so, immediately. You shall carry me off to your bed and make a dishonest woman of me."

"We have not yet had supper," Justin objected.

"Oh, pah!" Danielle dismissed such mundane considerations. "My appetites run in directions other than green goose and burgundy, sir."

"I beg leave to inform you, Madam Wife, that you are a most immodest woman," her husband said severely. "We will stroll to the temple and then take supper. The box is bespoken and our guests will be discommoded to find themselves hostless."

"Oh, you are so prim, husband." Danielle sighed. "But I dare swear, anticipation will make the pleasure greater." A slight sadness crept into her eyes. The pleasure would indeed be great, but not as it had been before making love with her husband had acquired such a desperate intent.

Linton, from his own standpoint, found that the anticipation of privacy with his wife this evening merely increased his unease. But he played his part masterfully and enjoyed Danielle's pleasure in the vivacious scene. Colored lamps lit the walks along which strolled every manner of person, respectable or otherwise, and Danny's sharp tongue was busily employed in witty observations on the company. She continued to hold his hand, scorning the offer of his arm and Justin shrugged—what did it matter that she made her pleasure in his company so obvious? His fingers twined around the small gloved ones which squeezed back warmly.

At supper, Danny, contrary to her earlier statement, displayed a hearty appetite and kept their party much amused with her comments on the scene. In addition to Julian and his usual cronies, the Earl and Countess of March joined them, together with D'Evron and several young ladies of Danielle's

270

age whose mamas considered the chaperonage of Linton and Lady March to be unimpeachable. The young ladies, for their part, enjoyed the flattering attentions of Jules and his friends, blushed prettily when addressed by the formidable Earl of Linton, and gazed enviously at his countess who treated her husband with no apparent deference and whose gown made them long for the time when they too could lose their maidenly decorum.

It was well into the early hours of the morning when Justin and Danielle finally regained Linton House where a sleepy night porter let them in. "You must maid me tonight, milord," Danielle said softly as they ascended the wide staircase. "I told Molly not to wait up."

"It will be my pleasure, my love. However, since I fear I was not so considerate with Petersham you will wait for me, I trust."

"I fail to see how I may do otherwise," Danielle responded. "This hoop is so enormous, I cannot imagine how I may rid myself of it alone."

"I will not keep you waiting long." Justin disappeared into his own chamber, unable to hide his grin from the dozing valet who sprang to his feet at My Lord's entrance. The grin died as Linton submitted to Petersham's ministrations and prepared himself mentally for the disclosure he must make.

"Thank you, Petersham." He adjusted the folds of the long velvet robe. "I shall not require you further this night."

"Good night, my lord." Petersham bowed himself out of the chamber and Linton went through the connecting door.

"I have been waiting this age," Danny said indignantly. "Did you have a comfortable coze with Petersham?" She had contrived to rid herself of the overgown and to loosen her hair which now tumbled over her shoulders. The patch had gone, also, but the scent of freesias filled the room and Justin smiled at this evidence that his wife had been freely applying his favorite perfume.

"Now do not be cross, Danny," he said, unbuttoning her. "I was not enjoying a comfortable coze with Petersham, merely preparing myself for the night."

271

At that she laughed. "Help me out of this ridiculous hoop, love. I wish to hold you and cannot when this wire puts such a distance between us."

He did so swiftly and then took her hands. "Danielle, I have something to tell you. It is best told now."

"Milord Chatham?" Danielle looked at him seriously, all play vanished from her eyes.

"How did you know?"

The slim shoulders in the white camisole shrugged. "You have looked a little distrait this evening. Is the news bad then?"

"No, not exactly." Justin turned her and began to unlace her stays. "Pitt wishes me to visit Paris."

"Oh, I should like that of all things." Danielle spun around as the last lace was released. "I have been homesick for France for many months and there is much to be learned that one cannot learn simply by listening to . . ." Her voice died away as she read his expression. "I am not to come with you?"

He shook his head. "No. My love, I don't wish to expose you to danger."

"Such nonsense!" she exclaimed. "There will be no danger and I am well able to protect . . ."

"No, Danny," he repeated quietly.

"Why not?" She reached behind her to unfasten the pearl necklace, her voice soft as she prepared herself for battle. She would achieve nothing by throwing a tantrum, only by sweet reason. Justin clearly had some misguided opinions on chivalry and she would put him to rights carefully and unobjectionably.

"I would never know where you were," her husband told her directly. "Or in what guise. I'll not having you roaming the Paris slums in britches again, Danny."

"And if I promise not to do so?"

"The answer is still no. Listen to me for a moment." He reached again for her hands but she twitched them away impatiently. "Danny, you have work enough to do here. I will be gone but two weeks and when I return we shall go together to Mervanwey. It is too soon for you to return to Paris—the

272

memories are too strong . . ."

"Am I not to be the judge of that, milord?" Danielle held herself in check. "I think it is the right time for me to return to those scenes. I am quite at peace with the memories and recollection will only serve to lay the ghosts to rest."

"Danielle, I must travel incognito and swiftly." Justin tried again, desperate to find a reason that she would accept and that would prevent his having to rely on the unquestionable veto that was the husband's right. "I cannot do that in your company unless we travel as we once did, and that I will not countenance under any circumstances."

Danielle thought rapidly. The idea of traveling again with her husband as master and servant, sharing bedchambers — although this journey they would also share beds—playing the urchin role in the kitchens made her toes tap with glee. Sadly she relinquished that plan. While it would be most amusing, it would not do except in dire emergency. But there had to be some way she could convince Justin that she would be useful and in no way an impediment.

"Justin, we do not have to travel in that manner. Neither must we travel as the Earl and Countess of Linton. We will be two members of the bourgeoisie, if you prefer. I can carry that role without difficulty. I will pad my skirts to give a matronly impression and speak as the shoemaker's wife . . ."

"I am not prepared to play the part of shoemaker," Justin expostulated, horrified at the vivid picture Danielle was painting. "I will go alone, unremarked, with my ears open. I do not deny, my love, your ability to act any part you choose, or your ability to collect information, but this is no expedition for the Countess of Linton. The last time you sailed on the *Black Gull* you were hideously seasick and there is every reason to suspect that you will be so again. Supposing you should be pregnant?"

"*Je ne suis pas enceinte*," Danielle heard herself say before she had time for reflection.

"How can you know that?" her husband asked dismissively. "You are as likely to be as not, and a voyage on possibly rough seas followed by a jolting carriage ride and the deuce knows

273

what other adventures . . . Danielle, you are a married lady and you may not go adventuring."

Danielle turned away, placing her pearls carefully on the dresser. She had kept this one secret so far, but her husband was not as other men, not the sort of husband her *maman* had warned her about, the sort of husband from whom one would need to protect oneself as Louise had done and as Danielle had been doing. But she had not been protecting herself from Linton, merely from consequences that she felt she was not yet ready to face. She had assumed that when she felt ready she would simply cease her precautions and no one would be any the wiser. But maybe it was right that he should know. It would, at the very least, disabuse him of ideas that she might need to take care of a prospective heir should she join him in his adventure.

"I know that I am not pregnant." Instinctively she sought the shelter of the deep armchair, tucking her feet beneath her, but meeting his eye. "I will tell you how I know, if you wish it. But I think, milord, that if you chose to divorce me you would find every court in the land sympathetic to your case."

Linton was capable only of a blank stare. His wife in camisole and pantalettes was a mere scrap of a figure curled in the big chair, but her personality filled the room and he had not the remotest idea of what she spoke.

Danielle read the confusion in his eyes and drawing a deep breath, took charge. "You will hear me out, Justin. It is a complicated story and 'twill be best if you don't interrupt." At his slight nod, she plaited her fingers, frowning deeply.

"*Ma mère a eu les difficultés . . . Pardon.*" She excused herself. "I will tell it in English."

"It matters not. Use whichever language is most comfortable."

"I will speak yours, Justin. You will perhaps understand the nuances better."

Justin, knowing that Danielle's idiomatic fluency in English exceeded his in French, bowed to her superior judgment.

"My mother had some considerable difficulty in bearing children. There were several stillborn babies before my birth."

274

Justin nodded and waited, still unsure what he was about to hear.

"After my birth, *Maman* was told that further pregnancies would endanger her life. *Mon père* was also told this most forcibly, but he felt that *Maman* was young, and with sufficient rest of six months or so should be able to conceive again and produce the male heir." Danielle looked directly at her husband. "My free speech does not shock you?"

"It hasn't done so for quite some time," he replied dryly. "Pray continue."

"After a 'sufficient time' my father forced his attentions on *Maman*. I think rape would be the correct word, although such a concept is not legally accepted between man and wife." Her eyes were large, her words carefully measured, but Justin heard the unspoken challenge and had no desire to pick up the glove.

"It became necessary for *Maman* to ensure that she did not again conceive, since she was unable to bar her husband from her bed. She had done so once before, at knife point . . . It was before I was born, but once I was born it was impossible for her to use such a threat, you understand? When she had only her own life to consider . . ."

"I understand."

"Old Nurse had spent her early years as maidservant in a convent. Nuns are very skillful apothecaries, milord, and not nearly as innocent of the world as the world would like to think." Danielle's smile had a cynical twist. "They make their own . . . mistakes . . . and if they are unable to prevent them, then they know how to conceal them."

Justin wondered if he was actually hearing any of this. He knew Danielle had had no conventional upbringing, knew that she had knowledge and experience well beyond her years, but what she was telling him now took him into a new realm.

"I have silenced you, I think."

"Almost. But I wish to hear the rest. You have not yet reached the point."

"No. I was explaining the background in the hopes that the point would be blunted."

"Let me hear it without more ado."

"Very well. The nuns also used their skill and knowledge to aid the peasant women who had neither the strength nor the financial resources to produce a child every nine months. They were able to abort a pregnancy and also to prevent. Belledame taught my mother how to prevent and my mother taught me. Please . . ." she said as Justin stood suddenly, his face gray. "Let me finish."

He sat down again. "I have not told you before because, as I was taught it, it is a woman's knowledge. I was sixteen when *Maman* and Belledame explained the principle to me and explained that I had no need to be at the mercy of my body when my husband took possession. They were not talking, milord, of husbands such as yourself." She offered a tentative smile that was not returned.

Against the odds, Danielle persevered. "I have not and do not yet feel ready to be a mother. Belledame assured me that the precautions will in no wise affect my fertility . . ."

"Enough!" Justin sprang to his feet, the blue black eyes hard and cold as quartz chips. "I do not wish to hear any more!" He strode to the connecting door. "I go alone to Paris and that is my last word on the subject."

The door closed behind him with a decisive click. The devil take the woman! He tore off his robe and thumped into bed. For nine months she had been playing her own game without a word to him. If she had no desire for motherhood so soon then he would not have quarreled with her. But the idea that she had taken such matters entirely into her own hands drove the Earl of Linton into a teeth-grinding impotent fury, and the utter determination that now more than ever would he compel her obedience in the matter of the journey to Paris.

Danny finished undressing and crept into bed. The secret had been told and she could consider herself lucky that her husband had not exacted the penalty with fist and crop. She lay in the dark in the wide lonely bed and decided that the matter of Paris must be postponed. For the moment she must think of some way of restoring her husband's badly damaged pride. If only she had thought to discuss the matter with him, but the knowledge had been given her like the passing down of a secret female rite—something that a man must never know, and Louise had impressed upon her daughter the need for absolute secrecy. Her possession of a knowledge held normally only by the inhabitants of harems and brothels would be considered disgusting.

But she had made a grave error of judgment in not telling Linton; or perhaps the error had been in telling him. If he was now disgusted with her . . . supposing he could no longer desire her, knowing what she had done. Danielle tossed and turned, for some reason icy cold although it was a warm night. It would not be surprising if he found her body distasteful and the idea that she could enter the act of loving simply for pleasure, hideously immodest. But he had taught her how to take that pleasure freely and joyfully. The nightmare picture of a loveless marriage where the conjugal union was simply undertaken for reproductive purposes tormented her thoughts. At some point she must give her husband an heir and maybe from now on he would only take her for that purpose. It would be an appallingly appropriate punishment. She would have no weapons then with which to fight Margaret Mainwairing, or any of the others who would fill Justin's empty arms. She shivered and flung herself onto her face, hugging a thick feather pillow hoping for warmth and comfort. None was forthcoming from the inanimate object and Danielle knew that she had no choice. Torturing herself with fruitless speculation would achieve nothing. She must find out the extent of Justin's wrath and what he intended to do. Maybe he would, indeed, divorce her. No, that was impossible, the House of Linton would tolerate no scandal of such magnitude, but he could do as the Prince of Wales had done with poor Princess Caroline and force a separation by locking her away in miserable exile in the country . . .

This was ridiculous! Danielle flung aside the covers and sprang determinedly out of bed. Typically, she didn't think to cover her nakedness as she gently turned the knob on the door to her husband's room and slipped into the moon-washed chamber. She could hear only his deep, rhythmic breathing

277

and stood immobile for a moment. Somehow she had expected him to be wide awake, tossing and turning miserably as she had been, and the idea that he had fallen so quickly asleep, Danielle found callous, disconcerting, and perversely annoying.

In fact, Justin was not asleep but at the sound of the turning knob had instinctively deepened his breathing and now watched the still figure in the moonlight through half-closed eyes. She was so damnably beautiful with those proud, perfect breasts, the narrow waist and flat belly and that impudent, entrancing little rear. Just what was she intending to do? he wondered—knowing Danielle, nothing predictable.

She stole on tiptoe across the room and round to the far side of the bed. Justin closed his eyes completely and waited with interest. Danielle shivered and with sudden resolve gently pulled back the covers and insinuated herself carefully beneath them. She lay very still, scarcely breathing until she was sure her movements had not disturbed her slumbering husband; but his breathing continued unchanged except for a small snore. Danielle tried to relax, but she was still freezing. She inched experimentally toward the figure at the far side of the bed, and when nothing changed edged closer still until some of the heat radiating from his body lapped her skin. Danielle turned softly onto her side, facing away from him, the only position she ever found comfortable for sleep, but it still wasn't right—she needed his skin. He was so deeply asleep he wouldn't even notice, she decided crossly, and traversed the final few inches.

"Danielle! Your bottom's like a block of ice!" Justin yelped, shocked out of his pretended slumber.

"You weren't ever asleep," Danny accused indignantly. "I was trying so hard not to wake you and you were awake all the time."

"I was," he agreed. "But I had a lively desire to discover what you were about. Why are you so cold, child?"

"Because I'm unhappy," she wailed. "Are you not?"

"Not particularly. I was too angry to be unhappy."

"Was?" she asked with a tremor of hope.

There was a long silence before Justin replied. "For some

278

extraordinary reason I find it impossible to remain angry with you for more than a few moments. I never know what you will do or say next and I don't imagine I ever shall. I have to remind myself constantly of your strange upbringing. I just wish I had thought a little more of the consequences of that upbringing before . . ."

"Before you married me," Danielle finished for him as cold fingers of desolation crept across her skin.

"Certainly," he agreed. "It would not have changed my plans in the least, but I would have been better prepared for disclosures of the kind you were considerate enough to make this night."

"I should not have told you then. *Maman* said that no husband could understand or accept a wife's need for control over . . ." She fell silent as Justin seized her chin between fingers that gripped like pincers and glowered down at her.

"You should have told me *at once*," he declared with careful emphasis. "I do not know what reason I may have given you for casting me in the role of some brutish lout who would keep you forever with a child in your belly. Had you made your feelings clear, there were certain precautions I could have taken myself and would have done so willingly."

"I did not think of that." Danielle frowned, diverted by the idea. "I am sure, since you have presumably fathered no bastards, that you are accustomed to such things . . . with Lady Mainwairing, no doubt?"

"We will leave Lady Mainwairing out of this, if you please, and anyone else that you think to drag into this discussion," he said, a razor's edge to his voice. "Why did you not trust me?"

Her unruly tongue again! Why had she mentioned Margaret? Now she had both to evade the question and retrieve the situation. Danielle thought rapidly.

"It was not a matter of trust, Justin. It was just that so many things are so very new to me and I am used to managing alone and . . . and . . . I daresay I make the wrong decision at times. But I did not mistrust you."

Not in that way, at least, and the truth shone clear in the wide brown eyes beneath him and Justin sighed in resignation.

It was pointless to play outraged husband, however legitimately, in the face of this extraordinary innocence that marched hand in hand with a powerful sense of self-determination and a knowledge of the world's vicissitudes that far exceeded her years. He'd married Danielle de St. Varennes for all those reasons and there was no going back, even had he wished to do so. And he most definitely did not.

"I would like you to think very carefully if there is anything else I should know . . . anything at all," he stated. "I had thought we were done with secrets after the previous affair, but clearly this one escaped your notice. Are there any others?" Danny shook her head. "Be sure of yourself, Danielle," he warned. "If anything comes to light after this, you will not find me so tolerant again."

"There is nothing." His affairs with Louise Rockford and Margaret Mainwairing were no secret to Justin, after all, and there was nothing she was doing that he did not know about. Danielle quietened the voice of conscience that mocked the spurious nature of such an argument. She touched his face with gentle fingers, smoothing the frown lines between the straight eyebrows. "I cannot promise never to do things that I will not tell you about, but they will be small things of no importance."

"Like what?" he asked cautiously.

"Like going to a public ridotto at Ranelagh when you had said it would be a vulgar masquerade and I would not enjoy it in the least."

"And did you enjoy it?" His eyes gleamed.

"No, you were quite correct. I thought it pretty at first, but it became tedious and Tony was very happy to escort me home at an early hour. But I wished to see it for myself, you understand."

"Of course," he agreed smoothly. "Why should you accept the second-hand opinion of your husband, after all?"

"You did not exactly forbid it," she reminded him, moving her hands to the well-muscled shoulders.

"I was not aware, Wife, that I was in the habit of forbidding anything. I know better than to throw down the glove where you're concerned." His head went back as Danielle's hands moved over his chest, pushing him down onto the bed beside her, flicking her tongue across his belly. And Paris? The question died on her lips. Time enough tomorrow to deal with that question. Her head moved downwards and Justin groaned softly as she pleasured him with mouth and fingers and took her own joy from the giving.

Chapter 15

It was nearly midmorning before the earl and his countess awoke and the life of the household continued in quiet deference to the sleeping master and mistress. Petersham and Molly waited in the kitchen as they had been doing since seven o'clock, neither of them commenting on whatever extraordinary circumstance had turned the normally early risers abovestairs into slugabeds this morning.

Peter, who had been waiting since eight-thirty to discuss with my lord his travel plans and itinerary, paced restlessly around his room, mentally running through the arrangements. A message had been sent to Forster to ready the *Black Gull* for voyage. He would need a day or so to retrieve the crew from their shore leave and most probably to sober them up. Since the yacht was to remain in Calais to await the earl's return from Paris, they would need adequate provisions as the English sailors treated French food with the utmost disdain—red meat and plentiful supplies of ale would be needed.

Justin awoke first. As he stirred, the small figure beside him muttered in protest and snuggled closer. Smiling, he turned on his back, relinquishing his spoon-shaped hold on her body. There was another protesting murmur and she wriggled backward against him. He patted her hip. "Danny, wake up. It's past ten o'clock."

"It cannot be!" Danielle's eyes shot open and she struggled up against the pillows. "How have we slept so long?"

"It was near morning when we went to sleep—or have you

forgotten?" he teased.

Danielle had not forgotten and her dimples peeped.

Justin laughed. "Come, brat. You must return to your own bed and summon Molly, and I must get up. I have much to do today."

The latter statement brought a small pout to the full lips as she remembered the Paris journey, but to Justin's relief she made no comment and slipped from the bed to stretch luxuriously in the morning sunlight. His loins stirred at the sight of that warm supple body that a few hours ago had flown with him to the heights of ecstasy. "Please, Danielle," he begged huskily, "do that where I may not see you. I become uncomfortable."

"Then I shall make you comfortable." Danielle leaped onto the bed with a chuckle and pulled off the covers. "Why, my lord," she declared in feigned awe. "You must indeed be uncomfortable. Let me just . . ."

"No!" he exclaimed as her hands reached for him. He wrestled her backward and then himself sprang from the bed. "Out!" He strode to the door to her chamber and opened it.

Danielle linked her hands behind her head and moved her body seductively on the bed, her tongue running over her lips as she regarded him through eyes narrowed with desire and challenge.

"Well, don't say you were not warned." Grinning broadly, Justin crossed back to the bed. Danny squealed as he hauled her upright, put one broad shoulder against her stomach, and tossed her over effortlessly.

"Brute! This is no way to treat a wife." She pounded his back with her fists and the broad shoulder beneath her quivered with merriment.

"That rather depends on the wife," he declared, striding with her into the other room. "This one deserves little respect." She was dumped in an unceremonious heap into the middle of her own bed and lay laughing up at him, her hair fanned out over the coverlet.

"Kiss me good morning, Husband."

"When you are dressed," he told her firmly. "I have not sufficient willpower to do so, now."

"Then I shall claim it anon," she responded.

"I await the moment most eagerly, ma'am." He bowed punctiliously and Danielle went into a peal of laughter at the ludicrous combination of his nakedness and the elegance of the movement.

Justin beat a hasty retreat and she pulled the bell for Molly, arranging herself decorously in the cold unslept-in bed. She had some careful thinking to do. When Molly appeared with the tray of hot chocolate and sweet biscuits, she found her mistress somewhat abstracted.

Danielle had no intention whatsoever of being left behind when Justin went to Paris. Such a shared adventure would suit her plans to perfection. They would be partners in an endeavor that would exclude all others, and Justin would know that only his wife could partner him on such an expedition. Her presence would only be useful and his scruples about exposing her to danger were quite ridiculous when one considered her past and what she was presently doing amongst her countrymen. How best to persuade him of this was the puzzle. He had been alarmingly definite last night, but then matters had become somewhat confused and since the confusion now appeared to be sorted out quite satisfactorily, Danielle could see no reason why he should persist in his obstinacy.

"Molly, I shall take a bath," she announced. "You will put out the new morning gown—the gold cambric, if you please."

Molly assented with a bob. Within the hour Danielle was examining her appearance with considerable satisfaction. The gold of her gown did very nice things to her eyes, and her hair, freshly washed and curled at Molly's expert hands, feathered around her face in an artfully ingenuous style. Milord should find the picture irresistible, Danny decided, dismissing the tiny stab of doubt with a nonchalant shrug.

She descended the broad staircase with a light step, greeted Bedford with a radiant smile and asked where My Lord was to be found.

"In Mr. Haversham's room, my lady."

"Thank you, Bedford." She tripped down the corridor in her silk-shod feet, knocked perfunctorily on the door to Peter's small sanctum and entered immediately.

"Good morning, Peter," she said cheerfully.

"Good morning, Lady Danny." Peter put down his papers hastily and bowed, but not before Danielle had seen the appreciative flash in his eyes.

"My lord, I am come to claim a promise."

The earl's lips twitched as he put up his glass and examined her appearance. "That is a most fetching gown, my love."

"Is it not?" She twirled with a satisfying swish. "You are not, I hope, milord, going to renege on your debt."

"How could you ever think such a thing?" he chided, holding the door for her to pass out. "Shall we go into the library?"

"As you wish, sir." The look she cast her husband pricked Peter Haversham with envy. Dolly Grant would make him a good wife when he was in a position to offer for her, but he began to wonder whether he wished for a "good" wife, modest and well aware of her place, stolidly willing to help his career, run his household, and bear his children. It had been the perfect dream that one day he would turn into reality, until the Countess of Linton had indicated what a marriage *could* be like.

While Peter cogitated in his solitary room, the Earl of Linton was making good his promise to his wife in the library. The good-morning kiss was remarkably thorough and it was a somewhat disheveled Danielle who eventually drew back with kiss-reddened lips and tousled hair.

She had little of the true coquette in her makeup and came straight to the point without considering whether a little further flirtation might ease her path. "About Paris, Justin."

Linton sighed and wondered why he had thought the matter closed. "No, Danielle. I said that was my last word and so it remains."

"But you have not considered," she said firmly. Justin waited in patient resignation. "I will not be a hindrance to you, quite the contrary. I will be in no danger, or at least," she amended with scrupulous honesty, "no more than I am accustomed to. I am not enceinte and I *am* able to gather information that Milord Chatham will find useful. We will travel in whatever guise you choose, and you should know that

I can keep up with you on horseback, even riding sidesaddle and . . ."

"Danielle, I do not doubt your riding skill or your ability to respond effectively to potential danger. I have not stood in the way of your work in London, but I will *not* take you with me to Paris. I am prepared to spy for Pitt myself, but I will *not* involve you. The matter is at an end."

Danielle heard the decisive note, the implacable ring in the level voice. "Spying is a harsh word, sir," she said quietly.

"It is, nevertheless, the correct one. I shall be in search of information and I do not wish those who furnish me with that information to be aware of my purpose. There is, therefore, double jeopardy. There is turbulence in the streets and should my purpose become known the personal danger will be doubled. I cannot keep my wits about me when I must worry about your safety."

"I am able to take a care for myself," Danny reiterated.

Justin gave up the attempt to reason with her. "You are my wife, ma'am, although you appear to forget that fact. Your safety and your welfare are my responsibility and mine alone. I choose not to jeopardize either. If you refer to the subject again, I shall postpone my departure for as long as it will take to see you safely to Danesbury where you will remain, under watchful eyes, until my return. Do we understand each other?"

We do indeed, Danielle thought grimly—on one level at least. "Very well," she said with a dismissive shrug. "I wish to drive your chestnuts. Will you accompany me?"

"Since you may not drive them without me, I appear to have no option." With a conciliatory smile, Justin tilted her chin and kissed the corner of her mouth, happy to settle the issue in such a relatively peaceable fashion. "Do you wish to do so immediately?"

"As soon as I have changed my dress."

"In half an hour then?"

"Twenty minutes, milord." She swept from the room, kissing her fingers with an impish smile that put all Justin's fears to rest. A little early, as he would have realized had he

287

been able to see inside his wife's head at this moment.

Danielle changed into her driving dress, her mind whirling as various plans came and were as quickly discarded. Justin was quite wrong and since he could not be persuaded by words and reason then she must take matters into her own hands. He would most probably be very angry, but she could weather the storm. It would be no worse than many she had encountered at the hands of her father and uncles and would carry no bitter crust of mistrust between husband and wife. It would be a simple matter of defiance, too late for Justin to do anything about. He might storm and rage but in the end would perforce accept the loving reason that insisted they share whatever danger came their way. France was, after all, the country of her birth and she had a right to participate in its trouble, just as she had both right and obligation to give her adopted country whatever help she could.

The devil take Society's prohibitions, Danielle thought indelicately, as she returned downstairs. She would deceive her husband on this occasion, simply by apparent compliance. He would be disabused soon enough and he had created the situation himself, after all. Conscience thus quieted, Danielle rejoined Linton.

In the next twelve hours she made her secret arrangements with a calm efficiency. Peter Haversham answered her innocent-seeming questions as to My Lord's travel plans and the preparations of the *Black Gull* with blind openness and it never occurred to him to mention Danielle's eager interest to Justin. Her curiosity was natural enough given the closeness of their relationship.

Danielle paid a visit to a young French matron who had contrived to bring into exile an adequate wardrobe suited to the social position of an affluent burgher's wife and left the house with a substantial parcel. Molly would need to put in some tucks and take up the hem. It would be a simple enough task, but when Molly heard what else would be expected of her, she gazed at her mistress aghast.

"B . . . but my lady, it will be quite impossible."

"Oh stuff!" Danielle declared. "We have only to ensure that we are hidden aboard the *Black Gull* before she sails and once she is well under way I will reveal myself to my lord. You will be in no danger and it will be a famous adventure, I promise. You would like to see Paris, would you not?"

Molly said that she did not think she would at all, particularly not in disobedience to My Lord's direct orders. But Danielle told her she was a poor spirited creature and the earl's wrath would not fall upon her head. "It is more like to fall upon my back," she said with a cheerful insouciance that stunned her maid. "I need you, Molly, and your presence will only please My Lord, I assure you. We can travel with the utmost gentility as respectable members of the bourgeosie, man, wife, and the wife's maid. In the Tuileries, where I shall appear as the Countess of Linton, formerly a de St. Varennes, it would be considered strange if I were unaccompanied by my personal maid. All will be convenable, you will see."

Molly merely shivered and nearly rebelled when Danielle handed her a pair of britches and a shirt with the brisk injunction to try them on immediately. Since they were tailored for Danielle's slender frame, it was something of a struggle and Danny frowned crossly at the result. "You look even more like a girl than ever! But if you move the buttons on the shirt and fasten the britches with a belt, it should suffice. But you must wear a cloak to hide the round bits. Now I must seek Julian's aid. 'Twould be better to enlist the chevalier but since I have promised not to go to his lodging without milord's escort, I cannot do so."

Molly was at a loss to understand why, when her mistress was about to disobey her husband so flagrantly and outrageously, another minor infraction should matter. But then she did not understand Danielle's code of honor—a promise was a promise.

Jules proved harder to persuade, and in fact remained steadfast in his refusal until Danny hit upon the happy notion of informing him that in that case she would take her horse and ride the eighty miles to Dover alone and at night. Julian decided that he could not take the risk of calling her bluff and began to wish heartily that his cousin had chosen a conventional bride who would not embroil her innocent relatives in her madcap schemes. "Y're a spoiled brat, d'ye know that?" he declared with a resigned sigh.

"I most certainly am not," Danielle denied, a flash of anger in the brown eyes. "It is simply that in this instance I know better than Justin and he is being quite idiotishly stubborn."

"And you will, of course, succeed in persuading him of that fact," Jules said sarcastically. "I wish I could be there to see it."

Danielle, too well aware of how much she needed his cooperation, bit back the retort and said mildly, "We will come to you at five this afternoon, then? If we leave after dinner, we should reach Dover by early tomorrow morning, well before Justin. He intends to catch the tide that rises around six tomorrow evening. Molly and I will mingle with the lads carrying provisions on board and hide ourselves until the *Gull* is well under way."

"How the deuce do you mean to do that?" In spite of himself Lord Julian was intrigued.

"There is a small cabin next to the master cabin," Danny explained. "It is used only by Petersham when he travels with Linton. I think it unlikely that we shall be discovered there."

"Unlikely, but not impossible," Julian stated.

"Certainly," she agreed. "But there is no such thing as a flawless plan, Jules. One must simply have one's wits about one. I shall contrive, never fear."

She would, too, Jules thought moodily as he saw her back into the phaeton with its matched bays that had been her husband's birthday gift once he was satisfied of her driving competence.

Danielle returned to Grosvenor Square and accosted her husband in the library where he was reading the *Gazette*. "Justin, I have decided that since you are to leave very early in the morning and I do not wish to quarrel with you, and I will because I shall be cross, I will spend this night with *Grandmère*. You have no objections, I trust."

Justin regarded her thoughtfully. This was the first mention of his journey since the last confrontation and there were distinct thunderclouds lowering in her eyes. However, if this was the method by which she chose to deal with the situation what right had he to complain?

290

"You will not dine with me, love?" he asked with a quizzical smile.

"No," she said gruffly, swinging her hat by its ribband. "I am to dine at the Mayburys' and then go to the ball at Almack's. After which I shall return to March House."

"Then we must make our farewells now?"

"Yes, if you please. I shall leave within the hour as I intend to dress at March House."

"I consider it cruel punishment to deprive me of your company, my love."

"You are depriving me of yours," she snapped with credible annoyance. "It is not the other way around."

"Clearly your plan is the best one," he said dryly. "I have no wish to part with you in anger, so . . ." He took her in his arms. For a moment her body was stiffly resistant, but gradually and inevitably she relaxed, her mouth opening eagerly beneath his and for a fleeting instant Justin almost changed his mind. Why deprive them both of this when even Pitt acknowledged her ability to hunt and gather the necessary information? And Danny was as streetwise as he was himself—more so. But no. She was his wife now, the Countess of Linton, and no urchin waif. He could accept her work in London because she used her position to achieve her goals, but he would not make a spy of his wife. Drawing back, he brushed a stray curl from her forehead. "I will be gone no more than three weeks, Danny."

"Unless there is a storm or a dead calm to prevent the *Gull*'s sailing home." She shrugged. "Or unless you fall foul of footpads in a back alley, or are discovered in one of the clubs when tempers run high and a spying stranger in their midst is not to be borne . . . I wish you godspeed, Linton." With that she disappeared, leaving her husband disconsolate and not a whit suspicious, while her own spirits danced at how easily that had been accomplished. There would be a penalty to pay, no doubt, but she would pay it with good grace. Once Linton understood her motives then they would act in this business together.

Danielle and Molly left Linton House without unnecessary fuss, Danielle in a simple afternoon gown, Molly in her usual habit of correct maidservant. They were obliged to take the

Linton town chaise to avoid remark, but Danielle, once in situ, gave the coachman orders to deliver them to Lord Julian's lodgings, saying that His Lordship would convey them to March House after an expedition to the Botanical Gardens. It was not the coachman's place to question his orders or Her Ladyship's arrangements and he did neither. Since it didn't occur to Linton to check up on his wife, the deception escaped notice.

Julian put his bedchamber at Danielle's disposal while his manservant prepared dinner. Jules was quite accustomed to the sight of his cousin-in-law in britches, but his eyebrows shot up when he saw Molly.

"It will do very well, Jules," Danielle reassured. "Molly will wear a cloak to disguise herself. We are exceeding sharp set. You will not object if Molly dines with us?"

"Not in the least." Jules smiled warmly at the girl whose face betrayed her terror at this extraordinary circumstance. He pulled out a chair for her and seated the servant, allowing the countess to perform the office for herself. Danielle did so without the flicker of an eyelash and addressed herself to her dinner, encouraging Molly to do likewise with all the warm concern of a close friend.

At eight o'clock that evening, Lord Julian Carlton found himself driving his racing curricle to Dover in the company of two women from vastly different stations in life, both wearing boys' dress. One of them fell asleep almost immediately, while the other, a peaked cap hiding a mass of wheat-gold hair pulled down over her face, gave him a running commentary on his driving skills. When they changed horses and he became weary, she took over from him until the next stage and then relinquished the reins and fell asleep herself, sitting upright, barely losing consciousness but quite clearly taking her rest— much in the manner of an old campaigner, Julian reflected.

They encountered almost no traffic during the long night hours, but as dawn broke, turning the sky to a glorious rose-shot pink, the post road became lively with farm carts and other commercial traffic. It was still too early for the Quality to

292

be out on the roads. Danielle suggested that they stop and break their fast before the sight of three people picnicking by the roadside should draw too much attention.

It was impossible for them to patronize an inn in their present guise, a fact of which Danielle, with her usual foresight, had reminded her cousin the previous evening. Graves had therefore been instructed to put up a picnic basket and the three travelers made a hearty meal of bread, cheese, and ham.

"We should save some food for later," Danielle said efficiently. "I am unwilling to attract notice by buying provisions in the town. We shall hide in the fields until afternoon and then go on board before My Lord arrives, which will not be before five o'clock, I understand from Peter."

"Is there anything you have forgotten, Danny?" Jules asked in considerable admiration.

"It is to be hoped not," she replied with a grin. "You will wait at the Pelican until the *Gull* sails, it is agreed? Should anything go awry, I will find you there, and you may escort the Countess of Linton and her maid back to London in suitable costume and irreproachable decorum."

Julian laughed. It was impossible to do otherwise with this wicked sprite who had laid her plans with such intelligent care, foreseeing and planning for any eventuality. He was by now convinced that Linton had been mistaken in his nevertheless understandable edict. Danielle would be no hindrance to his work, only a valuable asset.

They reached the outskirts of Dover at nine o'clock and Julian left his charges in a meadow where a small stream, well shaded by willows, provided a sylvan waiting room.

"I will wait at the Pelican and it is to be hoped I do not encounter Linton." He deposited the portmanteau under the trees. "Are you sure you will be able to carry this, Danny?"

"Indeed," she replied. "It is but half a mile to the quay and when we go on board it must look as if we are struggling with some considerable weight that requires two people to manage."

Julian nodded and left with some trepidation but buoyed up with the thought of sirloin and ale, hot water and a comfortable bed.

Danielle passed the morning in thought. In spite of her near sleepless night she was too keyed up to follow Molly's example. The servant was snoring rhythmically in the shade. They were well hidden from the road, but the sound of horses and carriages came clearly through sun-soaked summer air, and Danny kept half an eye out for possible intruders while she thought about visiting Paris.

From all accounts, it would be quite a different city from the one she had known—a seething hotbed of political turmoil as the deputies to the National Assembly fought to hammer out a new constitution based on a democratic system of government in a country which had known only the absolute rule of an inherited monarchy. The Assembly held itself to be the representative of the sovereign people and all therefore had the right of free speech and unreserved criticism. There was no question that the government might resign if a bill dear to its heart was rejected, or that the opposition would produce alternative legislation—there was no government party and no opposition party. It was a system riddled with anarchical possibilities; so unlike this calm well-ordered British method of government, and yet Danielle felt all of the excitement of her countrymen as they melted down the lead of the past and recast the image of the present and the future. But those who were doing this were new to the task and must learn by their mistakes, if indeed they were able to do so as powers of oratory and rhetoric became the marks of the prominent. Danielle de St. Varennes lay on her back beside a quiet country stream in a peaceful English meadow and chewed a succulent stem of grass as excitement curled her toes. She would soon see all this for herself.

She awoke Molly when the sun shone directly overhead through the filigree of the willows and they shared the remains of the picnic. "You will be hot, I fear, Molly, in the cloak," Danielle said with concern as she shrugged into her own stuff jacket. "But there is little we can do about it. 'Twill not be for long."

Molly found that she did not particularly care about physical discomfort, her heart was beating too wildly and she appeared to have lost all sense of personal control in the last twenty-four hours. She merely did as she was told and endured stolidly, drawing what comfort she could from the warm kindness and friendship of her extraordinary mistress, who never ceased to reassure her that Molly would come to no harm from this adventure. That seemed most unlikely to the young girl who had never before left London. But who was she to question the assurances of a mistress for whom she felt only the most dogged devotion and loyalty? And from whom she had received only kindness.

The two figures, shouldering the portmanteau, set off down the white dusty road shimmering in the sun's afternoon glare. They drew no remark. Such a sight was not uncommon in a sea port and the village was a hive of activity as the yachts crowding the quayside made their preparations for catching the evening tide. Lads from the various inns scurried and jostled, exchanging competitive insults as they hauled crates of ale, sides of salt pork, and baskets of bread aboard the various vessels. Profanities filled the air as seamen wrestled with sheets, swabbed decks, and polished brass in readiness for the arrival of the yachts' owners who must find only a sober crew and everything in shipshape readiness for departure.

The *Black Gull* was unmistakable, her gangway down, her paintwork and trim pristine. Danielle stopped on the quay and told Molly to rest their burden. The girl did so with a heavy sigh and Danny, wiping her damp brow with her sleeve, felt a pang of guilt for the maid swathed in the thick cloak. Her own head itched beneath the cap but she dared not take it off and scratch the sweat-soaked curls. Her shirt was sticking to her back and the worsted britches clung hot and damp to her thighs. Poor Molly's clothes were uncomfortably tight and constricting at the best of times. She must be abominably uncomfortable.

"*Courage, mon amie,*" Danielle whispered and was rewarded by a tremulous smile on the pink face. "We will wait until someone heads for the *Gull* and then we follow."

It didn't take long and the cover was better than Danny had hoped for. An entire procession of laden-bearers appeared from the Pelican and made for the gangway of Linton's yacht. "Come, Molly. You will be comfortable very soon." Danielle heaved the portmanteau onto her shoulder, Molly took the other end, and with one final effort they trotted across the quay to mingle with the procession.

"Oy! You there!" A seaman accosted them as they gained the head of the ramp.

"Watcha want?" Danny demanded, breathing heavily. "This 'ere weighs a ton, mate."

"Watcha got?" he inquired, stepping closer.

"Books." Danny spat disgustedly over the side of the ramp. "Can't think wat 'e wants wiv 'em."

"Nah!" the sailor agreed contemptuously and spat longer and further than Danny. Having made his point, he appeared to lose interest in the two struggling bantams and returned to oiling the thick coils of rope that must be made to run smoothly through their cleats.

Danny headed unhesitatingly for the companionway. No one took any notice of them at all. Had she seemed uncertain of her direction they would have found themselves in difficulties, but she remembered the way all too well. There were few people below decks and those they met were far too busy to ask questions or offer advice to a pair of lads who seemed to know what they were doing.

Danielle closed the door to "Petersham's" cabin and leant against it with an exultant laugh. "Journey's end, Molly. Now all we must do is remain undiscovered until we are well into the Channel. It will take perhaps two hours from the time we weigh anchor, depending on the wind and tide, before the yacht cannot safely be turned to beat back against the tides." She looked around the small cabin with a slight shudder of memory.

"For the moment we will stow the portmanteau beneath the bunk. There will be room enough there for me also, should anyone chance to enter. You may hide in the wardrobe." She pulled open the door to a narrow space set in the cabin wall. "It will be a squeeze, but I think you will manage."

"Yes, my lady," Molly murmured, throwing off the heavy cloak and helping Danielle to shove both cloak and portmanteau beneath the narrow bunk.

"It is a great nuisance that there is no key to this door," Danny grumbled. "But I will listen and if I hear footsteps we must hide instantly. It is unlikely, since I cannot imagine why anyone should wish to come in here, but we must be on our guard."

Lord Julian had bespoken a room at the front of the Pelican overlooking the busy scene on the quay. He chose not to visit the taproom or stroll around the town once he had recovered from the rigors of his night's drive, having a lively dread of coming upon Linton who would undoubtedly evince interest in his young cousin's presence in Dover.

At two-thirty, he positioned himself at the window and watched. To his eyes, the two small figures were unmistakable and he whistled in unheard congratulation as he saw Danielle and Molly blend with the group entering the *Black Gull.* His heart paused as he witnessed the exchange between the sailor and Danielle. Of what was said, he remained in ignorance, but the results were clear. The two figures did not reappear as he maintained his lonely watch, aided by Mine Host's excellent burgundy, and late afternoon saw Linton appear in his racing curricle. To Julian's relief, his cousin strode instantly on board without availing himself of the Pelican's hospitality.

At six o'clock the *Black Gull* weighed anchor. Julian, with a heartfelt sigh of relief, consigned Danny and her bewildered maid to Justin's care and went below to seek out the landlord and consult about his dinner.

Justin visited his cabin briefly on his arrival in order to change out of his driving dress and into the britches and shirt that would stand him in better service on deck. He was blissfully unaware of the two figures next door, cowering in wardrobe and beneath bunk at the sounds of his arrival. Once comfortable, he returned to the deck to eat dinner with Forster in the wheelhouse where they discussed necessary matters pertaining to the yacht's seaworthiness and exchanged amiable conversation of a nautical kind.

It was a beautiful night. Justin stood his turn at the wheel with peaceful pleasure as the guiding stars came to light, bright against their velvet background. It was a time he would have liked to have shared with Danielle, he reflected. Even her sensitive stomach would have been unaffected by this milk calm sea, and her pleasure in the pure elemental quality of stars, sea, and gentle wind would have enhanced his own. Their progress would be slow this night and he had constantly to catch a fading breeze, turning the wheel until the sails bellied, far from full but sufficient to maintain way.

Once they had weighed anchor, Danielle relaxed her guard on the door. No one would have need to disturb them now. But the yacht moved slowly and she waited in punctilious patience for three hours, an hour over her original estimate, before leaving Molly and slipping into the next door cabin. They were both hungry, but Danny was convinced Justin would regain his cabin within the hour and once the explosion had passed, supper would be forthcoming. She stripped off her clothes, dropping them carelessly on the Turkey carpet, and, finding water in the ewer, sponged the dust and sweat from her body. She yawned as a wave of irresistible fatigue smothered her, quite extinguishing the demands of her grumbling stomach. The wide bed with feather mattress and linen sheets tempted like the devil on the mountain and she lay down, drawing the covers to her chin. Just for a moment . . . only a doze that would give her added strength to deal with discovery. . . .

"Will you be sleeping below, m'lord? It's a fine night." Forster indicated the black water sighing gently beneath the prow, the studded sky, and the soft breeze. They had some company on the crossing, judging by the flashing lanterns across the water.

"I think not." Linton placed his hands on the deck railing and breathed deeply. "I will fetch my cloak and sleep beneath the stars. When think you we should reach Calais, Forster? Not by dawn, I'll lay odds."

"No, my lord." Forster sniffed the wind. "I don't think it'll die on us, but it'll not pick up this night. Midmorning, I'd say."

Justin nodded his agreement. "I'll be on the road by noon, then. Eight hours hard riding will bring me close to the gates of Paris. The delay will be of no great moment. I'll enter the city tomorrow morning as I had intended." He went below in search of his boat cloak.

The instant Justin turned the knob on his cabin door he had the sense that something was amiss. He stood just outside the

298

door, trying to identify the indefinable something that lifted the hairs on the nape of his neck. In the same instant he realized it was the sound of breathing, his eye fell on the discarded pile of clothing, a dark shape on the carpet in the moon's glow. Stepping into the cabin, he closed the door softly and wondered why he had not guessed. It was always possible, of course, that outguessing Danny was a chimeric hope and it was time he accepted that. His bed was occupied by a lump and he trod stealthily toward it. As usual, the covers came over her nose leaving only the closed eyes and the crown of her head visible. If he pulled back the sheet, he would find her body curled in a perfect position to invite his itching palm. He resisted the temptation with some difficulty. How the devil had she managed to get here?

Justin turned away from the bed and scooped up the heap of clothing as the retaliatory plan took shape. With a grim smile, he picked up his own portmanteau—Danny should have no opportunity to rifle his possessions in the absence of her own. He collected his boat cloak and left the cabin as quietly as he had entered it, removing the key from the inside and locking the door on his sleeping wife before pocketing the key.

He opened the door to the neighboring cabin, intending to dispose of his burdens, and gazed in disbelief at the petrified maidservant who had leaped from the bunk and now stood, wide-eyed and mesmerized like a rabbit faced with a fox.

"What the devil are you doing here, girl?" Linton's horrified eyes took in her attire, the shirt and britches stretched to begging point over the ample curves of bosom and hip. He thought of his sailors and slammed the door at his back.

"P . . . p . . . please, my lord," Molly stammered. "My lady . . ."

"It's all right, child. I'm sure you are not here of your own choosing." Justin tossed Danielle's clothes onto the bunk and dropped his portmanteau to the floor. "How long have you been on board?"

"Since midafternoon, my lord." Molly recognized Danielle's clothes and her pulse slowed. She had nothing to fear from the Earl of Linton, who clearly already knew the worst.

299

"Have you supped?"

Molly's stomach was emptier than she could ever remember it being and the prosaic question brought a dimension of reality to this dreamlike situation. "No, my lord. We finished our picnic at noon, but it was necessary to remain concealed until . . ."

"Quite," he interrupted, in no need of explanation on that point. "I shall be gone about ten minutes. Do you have any clothes other than those you are wearing?"

"Oh, yes, my lord," Molly said, eagerly latching onto something that must please him. "My own clothes and her ladyship's are in the portmanteau."

Linton glanced around the tiny cabin. "And where may that be?"

"Under the bunk, my lord."

"I see. Well, in my absence you will dress yourself properly. I am quite unable to vouch for your safety attired as you are."

"I wore a cloak, my lord," Molly offered. "Her Ladyship thought it would be best."

The earl turned away to hide a quivering lip. "Ten minutes," he said and left the cabin.

When he returned with a tray of bread, cold meat, fruit, and a tankard of port, he found Molly in gown, apron, and cap looking immeasurably more at ease. "Eat, child," he said, placing the tray on the table. "And while you do so, you may tell me the whole."

Molly had gone through too many novel experiences in the last day and a half to find sitting down to eat in the company of her employer more than a little strange. Linton leaned against the door, twiddling his glass as the girl recounted the tale. He made no attempt to interrupt, except for the occasional question, but at story's end he had the complete amazing picture.

"Rest now, Molly," he said. "I am sure you have need of it after your adventures and you must prepare yourself for some hard traveling in the next two days. You need have no fear that you will be disturbed before morning and then only by those I send to you."

"Thank you, my lord," Molly whispered in a wash of relief.

"But My Lady . . ?"

"You may safely leave Her Ladyship to me," Justin assured, in a rather unreassuring tone.

Back on deck, he wrapped the heavy cloak around him and lay down, resting his head on a coil of rope. He had been outguessed, outplayed and outmaneuvered and there was nothing to be gained by complaint. Danielle's planning had been superb and her insistence on Molly's presence a stroke of genius. They might have to travel a little more slowly but since they would be together that mattered not one iota. Pitt had requested her input and he would now have his wish. If Justin played his cards right, he could keep both Danielle and Molly safely lodged in the Tuileries where Danny could gather her own information, whilst he roamed the streets and clubs with one less task to accomplish. His wife was his partner and since she had no intention of being anything else the Earl of Linton had best accept that fact with a good grace. He would, however, exact a small penalty just to make a point. He fell asleep under the stars, a tiny smile curving the well-sculpted mouth on his last waking thought. How would the spitfire below decks react to that penalty?

Danielle slept the sleep of the dead, blissfully unaware of the events of the evening. She slept for eleven hours and awoke bemused. Light flooded the cabin from the round porthole and the yacht moved gently beneath her. Memory returned. Where was Justin? Had he not visited his cabin last night? Clearly not. She swung her legs over the edge of the bed and looked around her. Her clothes were missing. Justin's portmanteau was missing. With prescient foreboding, she tried the door. It was locked. Justin *had* visited the cabin. Danielle knelt on the padded seat beneath the porthole. She could see nothing but sea, so they had not yet reached Calais. The chronometer on the table told her it was eight o'clock and her stomach told her that it needed food urgently. A carafe of water stood on the table, but it was in lonely isolation—not even an apple to bear it company. And she had no clothes.

Footsteps in the passage outside had her diving for the bed, but there was no sound at her door. She heard, instead, Molly's voice and another, the sound of a door closing and retreating

301

footsteps. Danielle ran to the wall. "Molly?"

"Yes, my lady." The voice was muffled but recognizable.

"Is all well?"

"Oh yes, my lady. The cabin boy has just brought me my breakfast." Danielle's belly tightened in protest at the thought. "My Lord brought me supper last night," Molly rattled on, unaware of the pangs on the other side of the wall. "He was all consideration, my lady." There was a pause. "But I was obliged to tell him the whole."

"Yes, I'm sure you were," Danny said with a fair assumption of cheerfulness. "I told you you would have no need to worry. Enjoy your breakfast and I will talk to you again soon."

Danielle found that she had no desire to tell her maid of her own imprisonment or of her hunger. She returned disconsolately to bed, but the young fit body had no further need for rest, only for food, clothes, and action to use up the surge of energy. Damn the man! He was entitled to his revenge but this was going above and beyond the line. It was clever, though, Danny mused, leaving the bed to pace the cabin and, considering the way they had first met, it was also remarkably appropriate. She had been prepared for his fury, but this . . ? Looking again through the porthole, Danny saw the pink ramparts of Calais castle standing guard to the harbor. Justin would come soon then, unless he was intending to leave her like this for the duration of his trip to Paris. Unlikely, Danielle decided, scanning the pile of books on the table. They were all on navigation and she found what appeared to be the primer and curled on the window seat, allowing the warm sun to stroke her naked body.

It was thus that Justin found her an hour later when the *Gull* docked and he unlocked the master cabin. "Good morning, Danielle."

"Good morning." She hardly glanced up from the book. "This business of navigation is most interesting, sir. But I do not quite understand the quadrants although I am well versed in geometry. You will explain them to me, *n'est-ce pas*?"

"There will be time enough at Mervanwey, during the summer," he responded, the cool tone belying the admiring

302

amusement. He had wondered how she would greet him, and now he knew. "It would be best if you would return to bed," he continued, still impassive. "There will be some comings and goings in the next minutes."

"But of course. As you wish, my lord." Danielle fervently hoping that one of these comings and goings would involve food, dived under the covers. She watched surreptitiously as a burly seaman appeared with her portmanteau and Justin's, Molly following hard on his heels. A large tin tub was the next arrival, together with a succession of steaming jugs whose contents splashed into the tub. To Danielle's great disappointment, there were no further comings and her lips tightened on the stubborn determination that she would not give her husband the satisfaction of hearing her ask for food.

"Take your bath now, brat," Justin said carelessly. "There is no knowing when next you will have the opportunity. The Tuileries is a warren of a place and hot water in short supply, I would imagine."

So she *was* to go with him and her carefully thought-out arguments of persuasion unnecessary. Danny's heart skipped in triumph as she got into the tub. Justin read her expression correctly and had a flash of regret for his restraint of the previous evening. But he said simply, "Lay out Her Ladyship's riding habit, Molly. We shall travel on horseback this afternoon."

"Yes, my lord," Molly murmured obediently, but her expression was distinctly unhappy.

"What is it, girl?" he asked, puzzled.

"It . . . it is just that I do not ride very well, sir," Molly told him miserably. In fact, she did not ride at all and regarded horses as monstrous dangerous beasts.

"There appears to be a flaw in your plans." Justin turned to his wife, splashing happily in the tub.

"No, not at all, milord," she returned with a bland smile. "I had always intended to take Molly up behind me. We will make better speed in that manner, anyhow."

At this news, Molly's expression lightened considerably and Justin turned to find a clean shirt in his portmanteau, hiding the amusement in his eyes. As he stripped off his shirt, Molly made a strange little mewling sound and he swore under his breath. The girl, of course, would be horrified at the prospect of her lord's bare chest. "Would you return to your cabin, Molly," he said calmly, keeping his back to her. "You will find a nuncheon there and I suggest you eat heartily. We shall not dine until late this evening. Afterward, if you wish you may go on deck. You will not be molested."

Molly bobbed to My Lord's back and fled in relief, while Danielle pouted crossly. By dinnertime *she* would have been without food since the noon of the previous day—a fact that her heartless husband seemed not to consider.

"Do you not care to bathe, also, milord?"

"I have done so already, on deck," he replied.

"In the open air?" Danny forgot her hunger for the moment at this diverting prospect. "I wish I could do so."

"I do not think, brat, that you would enjoy having buckets of cold water thrown over you by a group of seamen."

"No, I daresay you are right," she agreed, stepping from the tub. "Have you sent someone to find horses?"

"I have." He turned to look at her and Danielle deliberately let the towel fall.

"Do I please you, sir?" Her eyes twinkled.

"On the contrary," he said in a blighting tone. "At the moment, you displease me enormously."

"Oh." Crestfallen, Danny made haste with her dressing, thankful that the riding habit was a relatively simple garment and she had no need to ask for help. She was beginning to develop the unpleasant suspicion that this eagerly awaited journey was not going to be as amusing as she had anticipated—not with an empty belly and in the company of Linton in his present mood.

"You will wait here," Justin told her, once he had pulled on his top boots and shrugged into his coat. "Will it be necessary for me to turn the key on you?"

Danny shook her head and returned to her perch on the window seat where she picked up her book again, biting her lip hard. Justin almost relented but her earlier look of triumph still rankled and he decided he was not yet ready to give up his little game.

He left the cabin and went in search of Forster and information about the horses. When he returned it was in the company of the cabin boy staggering under the weight of a laden tray that Danielle regarded with naked relief. But she kept her seat until the boy had left and pretended to read with feigned indifference to the unmistakable French smells of fresh-baked bread, garlicky sausage, and ripe cheese.

"You may cease your pretense, infant. I know full well that you are ravenous. Come to the table; we have little time to waste." He filled a glass with milk from a copper pitcher and handed it to her.

Danielle drank deeply and then caught Linton's pained frown. "Oh, do I have . . . ?"

"Yes, you do," he interrupted. She wiped the milky mustache from her lips with a checkered napkin and decided to take the bull by the horn.

"My lord, may I please ask a question?"

Linton propped his elbows on the table and rested his chin in a cupped palm as he looked at her quizzically. "Now, I wonder why you are asking my permission," he mused. "What possible difference would it make if I said no? Since that little word appears not to exist in your otherwise extensive vocabulary."

"Oh, pray do not be odious," she begged. "I may deserve it, but it is most unpleasant. Could you not instead just be furious as I thought you would be and then it would be all over?"

"Make no mistake, Danielle, I *am* furious," the earl said grimly, "and I expect to remain so indefinitely. If you do not care for the consequences of your actions, you should have thought a little more clearly before."

It was pointless, then. If he would not respond to her in any way except for this frigid near-indifference, she would have done better to have stayed at home. If he saw her only as a troublesome responsibility, then there was no hope for the partnership that would have made all right.

"I will not accompany you to Paris," she said, fighting back the tears.

"You most certainly will! You do not suppose that I would trust you out of my sight after this?"

"You need have no fear." Cold anger came to her aid. "I understand full well what you want of your marriage. I'll not interfere with your pleasures again, my lord."

"And what is that supposed to mean?" Justin pushed back his chair, completely nonplussed by this attack that seemed to come from nowhere.

Danielle shrugged. There was nothing left to lose. "I had thought, since I do not appear to be sufficient satisfaction in the bedchamber, that maybe we could at least share danger together. I am perhaps too young and unsophisticated for you in some areas, sir, but I have much experience of this present business. Since you do not acknowledge that, we will settle for the sham marriage of convenience. I will be perfectly discreet, I assure you."

Justin had allowed this dignified speech to run its course only because he was quite dumbfounded. He had intended to punish her with his simulated annoyance for just a few more minutes before bringing the charade to an end, and now she was talking apparent nonsense. Except that she wasn't, because Danielle never talked nonsense.

"You have been keeping something from me, have you not?" He rose from his chair and came to stand, towering over her. "I warned you the last time that I would not be so tolerant again."

"I have kept nothing from you that you do not yourself know . . ." The fire died from her voice. "Perhaps you were not aware that I knew, but . . ."

"Knew what?" Justin pulled her to her feet and Danny's knees began to quake.

"Let me go!" She yanked herself from his grip and fled across the state room. "If you did not wish me to know of your . . . your . . . renewed . . . relationship with Lady Mainwairing, you should have told your mother and sister to keep still tongues in their heads."

Justin's jaw dropped. "My *what*?"

"Well, it is common knowledge that you have taken up with your previous mistress." Danielle sought cover behind the bed, even as she fired her arrows.

Justin found a thread he could grasp. "My mother told you this?"

306

"Your sister," Danny returned. "At your mama's instigation. She was afraid that if I heard from someone outside the family, I would react in an indecorous manner."

Sarcasm dripped as she mimicked Beatrice, and Justin, who knew his mother and sister only too well, finally understood. This had been behind the estrangement between Danielle and his family, and Danielle had been harboring this viperous secret all these months, before, through, and after their own reconciliation that had followed the revelation of her activities with D'Evron.

"Come here," he instructed, his calm voice belying the hurt that fuelled his fury.

Danielle decided that that was the least safe option she had. She moistened her dry lips with the tip of her tongue and stood her ground.

"It will be the worse for you if you do not," he said quietly, reversing her decision.

Danny stomped across the cabin toward him. Justin did not touch her. "Why did you not tell me of this before? You knew the true nature of my relations with Margaret."

"I thought I did, but since everyone else put a different construction on them, I realized I was wrong." Somehow, the hoped-for note of dignified outrage wasn't ringing true.

"You thought I would deceive you? You *still* think I have deceived you?"

Danielle looked at him, her eyes wide. Could she have been wrong? "If . . . if it is not true, then I beg your pardon," she stammered inadequately.

"I do not understand," Justin said deliberately, twisting the knife, "exactly what I could have done to deserve your mistrust."

"You might have trusted *me* enough to tell me that you had been *Maman*'s lover," she flashed, unable to bear alone the guilt of this tangle.

"Sweet heaven!" Justin felt the ground of his righteous wrath slip from beneath his feet. "Who told you that?"

"No one *told* me." Danielle stiffened her knees and her resolve. "I happened to be behind the screen in the retiring room at Almack's when the Dowager Duchess of Avonley and Lady Almera Drelincourt happened to be discussing, with considerable amusement, the idea that you had taken the mother to mistress and the daughter to wife. They appeared to find it monstrous funny, my lord. I did not."

Justin winced, imagining the horror of that revelation on this direct creature. "I should have told you, my love, but I did not think to do so. It happened long before you were born and I was little more than a child myself. Had I thought anyone would still remember I would, of course, have spared you that. To tell the truth, I did not realize anyone knew of it."

"That is no excuse," Danielle said fiercely. "It was a fundamental fact that you should have told me long ago. I do not find the concept hard to accept, but . . . but you might have told me a little of her when she was happy. It was an unpardonable deceit to have kept that from me. I do not care how many mistresses you may have had, but I should have liked to have heard from you that one of them was my mother. After everything that has happened between us . . . my circumstances . . . the way we met, that you should keep that from me! How could I help but lose trust?"

"I do not know how to ask your forgiveness," the earl said, feeling desperately for the right words in what was probably the most major crisis he had yet faced. "The only occasion on which I thought of that interlude was in the Inn of the Rooster when you were telling me of your escape from Languedoc. It seemed inappropriate at that time to mention it, and afterwards . . ." He paused. "You have kept me so busy, my love, that I have not thought of it. It was an unpardonable thoughtlessness, and I know not how to make amends."

Danielle felt as if Atlas's burden had been lifted from her shoulders. He should have thought to tell her, but he had not deliberately deceived her. If she had confronted him, instead of losing all faith in a man whom she should have known would never knowingly have given her cause to do so, the issue would have been dealt with long ago. It was all the fault of this damnable society where living a lie was quite natural. Until she had become a part of that society it would not have occurred to her not to face her husband with the rumors.

"It is over," she said quietly. "I have been foolish and you have been thoughtless. We are even, *n'est-ce pas?*"

308

Justin felt a surge of relief as he reached for her and she came willingly into his arms, her body soft and trusting. "We will begin anew, my love. Only truth between us from now on—however unpalatable."

"Only truth," she concurred, meeting his gaze.

"Your word, Danny."

"Word of a Varennes."

"Then I am satisfied. Let us take horse, Madam wife, and begin our enterprise."

Chapter 16

"What think you of the little de St. Varennes, Madame Verigny?" Marie Antoinette passed a desultory needle through the tapestry of her embroidery frame as she posed the question to one of her ladies.

Madame Verigny looked across the queen's crowded salon in the Tuileries Palace to where Danielle sat on a low chair apparently engaged in animated conversation with a clearly admiring group of courtiers. *"Elle est très jeune et très belle."* Madame's laugh was brittle. "And not unaware of her charms, I think. Her husband should have a care—when midsummer weds with spring there is always danger."

"Tu as raison," Marie Antoinette agreed. "But I think that is a marriage made in heaven. They have eyes only for each other. *La petite* is a coquette, *bien sûr*, but do you notice the way her eyes light up when the earl is near? It is almost indecorous." She laughed, a rare sound these days. "I find her a refreshing addition to our exile and we are in sore need of some warmth and sunlight in this gloomy place."

Madame Verigny agreed. The Tuileries was a damp dank contrast to the glittering airiness of the many-windowed Versailles. The perimeter walls were high, the gardens overgrown with trees, and the steep scarp of the Seine prevented any approach from the south. The Swiss Guard were in constant attendance, an ever-present reminder of the royal family's need for protection, although since the mob attack on Versailles last October there had been little overt hostility. But the court remained immured inside the walls of the Louvre and the Tuileries and avoided exposure to the world of the city. As a result, their only amusements were gossip and backbiting, and an addition to the coterie was indeed welcome.

Danielle, after four days, was heartily sick of the place. It stank of unwashed bodies and chamber pots hidden behind tapestry screens. Both men and women spent an inordinate amount of time scratching as the lice dropped from their elaborate coiffures to feast greedily on the tender flesh of backs and bosoms. Danielle, perforce, wore her hair lightly powdered because to appear otherwise would be seen as a gross insult to the queen, but she scrubbed herself in cold water both night and morning and spent the larger part of every night in pursuit of bed bugs who had a more than comfortable home in the feather mattress and appeared to find Danielle's blood considerably sweeter than they found Justin's. Justin, in desperation after the first night, had scoured the apothecaries for a lotion that faithfully promised to repel all boarders and had bought coarse linen sheets to lay on the mattress as an added barrier. But his wife still leaped from the bed with a stream of profanities at least half a dozen times a night to hold a candle above the mattress in fruitless search of the beasties who vanished into the feathers the minute there was light.

She was waiting now for Justin's return from the Assembly which, since the removal from Versailles, had its home on the north side of the Tuileries Gardens in what had once been a riding school built for the young Louis XV. The building was close to both the Tuileries and the Palais Royal where, in the former, the royalists debated with a passion equal to that of their rival faction in the latter. Covered passages now ran between the clubs and *hôtels* of the Place Vendôme, where administrative offices were set up, and members of the Assembly could travel easily between the new parliament house and their offices, regardless of the weather.

Justin had promised to escort Danielle to the Assembly in the late afternoon, once she had performed her duty as guest of the queen's court and could slip away without undue remark. Faithful to his promise he strode into the salon at around four o'clock, making his obeisance to Marie Antoinette before acknowledging his wife.

"I was just saying to Madame Verigny how pleasant it is to have company from the outside, my lord." The queen smiled at the tall, sober-suited figure. "But you are no courtier, sir. You are rarely with us." She tapped his wrist with her ivory fan.

"I beg pardon, Madame, if I appear neglectful," Linton murmured. "Danielle and I are most grateful for your hospitality, but there are matters of her estate that I must settle."

"It was most fortuitous that she was in England at the time of the *jacquerie*," 'Toinette said with a shudder. "Such a terrible story. The poor child must have been devastated."

"She was," Linton concurred truthfully. "But I feel sure that your kindness in receiving her has done much to restore her spirits."

"She does not appear to lack for spirit," Madame Verigny said tartly, and found herself on the receiving end of a frigid stare. Color crept into her cheeks and she returned to her embroidery as my lord made a deep leg to Her Majesty and went to his wife.

"That was unwise of you," the queen said to her companion. "I do not think My Lord Linton takes kindly to criticism of his wife, implied or otherwise, and indeed I do not myself think she has deserved it." Crushed, Madame Verigny made no response.

Danielle greeted her husband with impeccable lack of enthusiasm before excusing herself from the attentive group. "Dear God, but I am like to *die* of boredom, Justin," she declared as soon as they reached the corridor. "*Maman* always said Louis's court was a dead bore but I did not realize how much truth she spoke. You must allow me some freedom soon or I shall do something dreadful, I feel certain."

"Tomorrow," he soothed, "you shall don the gown of the burgher's wife and visit the shops, with Molly in attendance."

"But poor Molly has the most dreadful *mal d'estomac*. She insists it is the food and I daresay, if you are unused, it might have an adverse effect, but I think it was perhaps unkind in me to have brought her. Do you think so?" She looked up at him anxiously.

"I think, my love, that Molly will regale her children and her grandchildren with this tale of adventure and there will be no mention of her discomforts," Justin reassured with confidence.

"Well, I hope that you are right. Perhaps she is feeling more the thing already. I will visit her before we leave."

Danielle found Molly in the slip of a room adjoining the chamber occupied by the earl and his countess. She was still wan-faced and laid upon her bed, but the worst purging was now over. She managed a small smile as Danielle bathed her forehead with lavender water and matter-of-factly emptied the chamber pot out of the window. "I will procure you some bouillon when I return," Danielle promised, quite unsure how she was to manage such a thing in this rabbit warren of corridors peopled by faceless individuals, but she was determined nevertheless and Justin would help her.

"Tomorrow, we shall take the air if you feel able to leave your bed. I feel sure it will do you the world of good, Molly. The air in this place is quite fetid and must be most unhealthy. I shall send my lord for vinegar and scent to dispel the atmosphere. In fact, I cannot imagine why I did not think to do so before." So saying, she left Molly's chamber to give her husband the requisite orders which he received with a nod of comprehension and wondered why he had not thought to take such an elementary precaution himself.

They arrived at the parliament house in the middle of a vociferous debate. The long low narrow building was poorly lit and far too small to handle the haranguing tongues. Justin and Danielle squeezed into the public gallery that could accommodate a bare three hundred souls and Danielle gazed in fascination at the scene before her. She had visited both the House of Lords and the House of Commons in London under the auspices of Pitt and Linton. Nothing in this disorderly tumult remotely resembled that well-regulated process of debate, except for the seating where members sat across from one another separated by a gangway. There were three members on their feet simultaneously and the president, who held the position for but two weeks at a time, was quite unable to maintain order. As the voices rose in a floodtide of rhetoric, not one of them could be heard clearly.

"It is a madhouse," Danielle whispered.

"Yes, but do not say so aloud," her husband warned. "It is not always thus and some worthwhile legislation is coming out of this."

Danielle accepted the rebuke and lapsed into willing silence, concentrating on what was being said and forming her own impressions until she began to make sense out of the tumult. Her ears pricked at the comments of her fellow spectators, and she concentrated on those around her. It was what she did best, this picking up of unconsidered trifles, gauging the mood of groups and drawing her own deductions. It was what Pitt would want of her and why Justin, who could not do this himself, had accepted her companionship, once it had become a *fait accompli*, with only simulated annoyance.

Once back in their chamber he listened to her and shared his own impressions before they joined the court at dinner, Danielle having first procured a cup of bouillon for Molly by dint of shameless and lavish bribery.

Dinner was a long and tedious affair, the food ill-prepared in the poorly equipped kitchens that had not been required to feed the court since Louis XIV had built Versailles. It arrived at the table cold having been brought vast distances through draughty corridors, and the conversation for the most part was insipid. Justin fared better than Danielle in this last, since he was at least able to talk politics with those courtiers sensible enough to have an opinion. Danielle, on the other hand, was obliged to listen to the malicious gossip of bored women and their complaints at the discomforts of the Tuileries. There were few who evinced an intelligent interest in the state of their nation; they had never been encouraged to do so, after all, in the pleasure-oriented world of Marie Antoinette's court.

It was toward the end of the meal that she became aware of the interested scrutiny of a pair of pale eyes. Their owner was a stranger to her, but that was not surprising since the composition of the court was constantly in a state of flux. As her eyes met the stranger's, he smiled, the expression lightening the long, aristocratic face. Danielle smiled back and the man murmured something to his neighbor.

"Who is the gentleman in the blue velvet?" Danielle asked Madame Cloury beside her. "He wears his hair in pigeon's wings. I have not seen him before."

Madame Cloury glanced across the table casually. "Oh, that is the Comte de St. Estèphe. He rarely honors us with his presence." The plump white shoulders lifted, the movement causing one full breast to pop free of a neckline so low it barely qualified as such. Quite unconcerned, madame tucked the errant flesh away again. "He is a dour creature, St. Estèphe," she continued. "His wife died in childbed some years ago. She was a poor little dab of a thing and petrified of her husband. It was said that he used her dreadfully and he is always so dark looking I am sure it was true." She shuddered deliciously and dropped her voice. "Two years ago, his mistress cut her wrists and died. It caused such a scandal but no one could implicate St. Estèphe, you understand. But since then he has spent little time at court and takes his mistresses from the demimonde and they, *naturellement*, must take their chance."

Danielle, in spite of her distaste for the game of character assassination, was intrigued. The man looked innocent enough, although his eyes were cold and reminded her of those of a gaffed fish. But the smile had appeared warm and friendly enough. He could hardly be held responsible for the thin lips and fishy eyes that had accompanied him into the world. He was perhaps a year or so older than Linton, she decided. His dress was simple to a fault amongst this glittering throng. His only jewelry was an enormous sapphire on his index finger and his hair, while correctly powdered and curled, was a far cry from the massive creations around him. All of which put Danielle quite in charity with the man. She was wondering how best to contrive an introduction when the queen rose from her place in the center of the long table on the dais, signaling the withdrawal of the ladies. Danielle resigned herself to the inevitable hour or so of simpering chat and indifferent performances on the spinet before the gentlemen, flushed with port and cognac, would decide to join them.

Roland, Comte de St. Estèphe watched her leave, a tiny smile curling his lips. He stroked his angular chin thoughtfully and glanced up the table to where Justin, Earl of Linton, sat, twirling his port glass absently as he leaned back in his chair—perfectly at ease, it seemed, except for those shrewd blue black eyes that were everywhere. They had also watched the departure of the young countess and the look they carried interested St. Estèphe mightily.

The news that the Lintons were visiting the French court had brought him hotfoot from his estate in Dijon to meet his enemy for the first time. He had been waiting many years for the appropriate opportunity. Now, he moved his seat to a vacant one opposite the earl. "Milord Linton, I believe."

"Yes, indeed." Justin's eyebrows lifted in inquiry.

"St. Estèphe, at your service, sir." The *comte* bowed his head, examining the earl's expression intently for an unguarded flicker of recognition, but there was none. Either the man was a consummate actor or he did not know the story. "My father spoke often of yours," he said musingly. "They were good friends at one time, I believe."

Justin's face was a blank. "Forgive me, *comte*. My father died some eighteen years ago and I have a lamentable memory."

Not with those intelligent eyes, St. Estèphe thought. But Linton looked genuinely apologetic so the *comte* shrugged and smiled. "Ah, well, it was many years ago that they were friends. Before my own birth, I believe, so it is hardly surprising. But I am most happy to make your acquaintance, my lord."

"And I yours," Linton replied automatically, wondering why he disliked the man after a mere ten minutes in his company. It wasn't just that he had been put at an embarrassing disadvantage—the *comte* had rescued him from his predicament with impeccable courtesy after all. Perhaps it had something to do with that calculating gleam in those eyes so pale as to appear almost opaque.

St. Estèphe, well satisfied, excused himself and went off to greet other acquaintances in the peripatetic fashion that was considered quite *comme il faut* at this stage of the dining ritual. He was one of the first to join the ladies in the long salon which remained dark and gloomy in defiance of the early summer evening. He made his obeisance to his queen who lightly chided him for being so long absent from court. The *comte* replied with the acceptable mixture of regret and flattery

317

before turning the conversation adroitly to the Countess of Linton.

"Yes, she is a taking little thing," Marie Antoinette agreed. "Quite charming and refreshingly naive. We are enjoying her visit. They are here to settle matters of her estate after her family was massacred . . . Well, we will not talk of such gloomy subjects; they do little to lighten the atmosphere in this dreary place. Do you care for an introduction?"

"Of all things, Madame."

"You should be warned, though." The queen smiled. "If you pay her too close attention, you will have Linton to reckon with. He regards her with an unfashionably jealous eye. She is very young, you realize."

"I shall take great care," St. Estèphe promised, but his heart sang at this piece of information. The challenge would be greater and the revenge all the sweeter in those circumstances.

When the liveried flunky bowed beside the Countess of Linton with the message that Her Majesty wished to speak with her, Danielle rose from the sofa with alacrity. She had been covertly watching the exchange between the *comte* and 'Toinette and her ears were burning unmistakably.

"Madame." She curtsied deeply.

"I wish to present the Comte de St. Estèphe, Danielle. He is most eager to make your acquaintance."

"You do me too much honor, sir." She curtsied again and swam upward, giving him her hand.

"The honor is all mine, my lady." He was in the act of pressing his lips to the small hand in a manner rather more ardent than the ritual demanded when Linton walked into the salon.

Justin frowned. What the deuce was the man doing slobbering all over Danny's fingers? And Danielle herself seemed to be enjoying it, judging by the delicate flush on her cheeks and the musical peal of her unmistakable laughter. That his wife was a natural flirt did not ordinarily disturb Linton in the least. It was harmless enough and she knew well how to freeze the gallant who stepped beyond the line of dalliance. But the *comte* made him as uneasy as the Chevalier D'Evron had once done—the sense that he was not just what he seemed.

318

Justin most definitely did not want his wife embroiled in undercover adventuring with yet another of her aristocratic countrymen, however innocent and worthy the cause. But he could not remove her from the queen's side until she had been dismissed and Marie Antoinette appeared to be enjoying herself.

Danielle had chosen to play the part of ingenue during this visit to the French court. It was one that provided a perfect mask for what she was really about and people talked freely in front of the little de St. Varennes, who was such a sweet child with her innocent questions and naive observations. The queen found her delightful and was now much amused as the world-weary sophisticate played gently with the innocent who tossed her head coquettishly and blushed prettily. The *comte* was equally delighted—the child was making it so easy for him. He would turn her head tonight, be cool and distant tomorrow, and repeat the process until she knew nothing but a piqued confusion. The rest should be simple . . .

"Madame." It was Linton's deep voice.

"Ah, Linton. Are you acquainted with the Comte de St. Estèphe? He has been amusing your wife quite wickedly."

"I am indeed grateful to you, St. Estèphe," Justin said smoothly. Danielle's hand slipped into his and he smiled down at her. The look that the *comte* intercepted threw that gentleman back on his heels. It was not, then, as he had thought. This was no marriage of convenience between a man of middle years reluctantly accepting the family duty, and an eligible young aristocrat with many childbearing years ahead of her—a giddy young woman who could be persuaded of the dullness of her loveless marriage and her entitlement to one brief fling.

The *comte* decided that he must avoid jumping to conclusions in future. The game would take rather longer to play, and he must have a care to his hand—something a little more devious than his original plan which had, after all, been rather crude. No, on the whole, he decided that he was pleased with this turn of events. The St. Estèphes had waited close on forty years for their revenge on the house of Linton—a little longer would make no difference.

"I wish for some music," Marie Antoinette declared, suddenly bored now that the appearance of the chit's husband had put an end to St. Estèphe's flirtation. "Danielle, you will play for us."

"I play indifferent well, Madame," Danielle demurred, and a deep frown of displeasure darkened Her Majesty's countenance.

"I should like to be the judge of that myself," she said coldly.

"As you command, Madame." Danielle curtsied and made haste to obey the royal edict.

"Now you may regret your misspent youth and wish you had practiced a little more," Justin teased in a low whisper as he escorted her to the spinet.

"That is unkind, milord." But she could not help a chuckle. "Anyway, it is 'Toinette who will suffer." She took her seat on the embroidered bench. "Do not stand beside me, Justin. It will only make me nervous."

"I was intending to turn the music for you," he said with a fair assumption of hurt.

"Then you will have idle hands, for I shall use no music."

Justin barely controlled his grin as he wondered what she was about. This conventional gathering would not take kindly to Danielle's extensive repertoire of earthy country songs, particularly if she chose to extemporize as she did at home, much to the somewhat shocked amusement of Jules and his friends. He left her and took a seat where he could see her face without his observation disturbing her concentration.

Danielle thought for a moment, her fingers running over the keyboard as she dug out the memory. Then, with a small satisfied nod, she began to play, singing softly at first and then with increasing power as the memory of long afternoons in Languedoc took over from this grim, stuffy room of as yet unacknowledged imprisonment. She played the songs her mother had played, Cornish folk songs and the songs of Languedoc—the songs of the people, sometimes haunting and plaintive, sometimes filled with the elemental joy of those who lived their lives by the elements.

What was she? St. Estèphe gazed in fascination. She played

and sang from memory the words of a culture that few in this room had ever acknowledged existed, let alone troubled to learn. And there was no mockery in her hands or voice. He glanced at the husband who sat smiling, eyes half closed, clearly quite at ease with this facet of his wife. Perhaps the child was not the simpleton she appeared. The *comte* looked around the room. In general, attempting to entertain this court was a thankless activity. Conversation scarcely paused and even 'Toinette lost interest after the first few bars. But the de St. Varennes was heard in silence. The applause when she had finished was muted, but when she looked to the queen for permission to leave the spinet she received an imperative beckoning finger.

"Where did you learn those pretty songs, Danielle?"

"From my mother, Madame," Danielle replied. "I am happy that they pleased you."

"They provided a most refreshing change," Marie Antoinette said. "A little light, of course, but that is no bad thing these days. You shall play for us again tomorrow."

Danielle accepted her dismissal with a deep curtsy and even deeper relief. She was now free to leave the salon and did so with a comprehensive look at Justin that told him to follow her with all decent haste.

He did so within the half hour and found her in a silk wrapper pacing the bedchamber like a jungle cat suddenly behind bars. "Justin, if you do not take me out of here for a few hours, *immediatement*, I shall go quite mad and I am sure you would not care for a wife in Bedlam."

"No, I do not think that would be at all the thing," he concurred gravely and was rewarded with an involuntary chuckle.

"Justin, I am quite in earnest," Danny persisted. "I cannot continue in this way without relief."

"Forgive me, my love, but I was under the impression that this was what you wanted. You went to considerable trouble to achieve this end, as I recall." It was quite irresistible, but Justin regretted the teasing remark instantly as a veritable tempest of shoes, books, and pillows was launched at his head with Danielle's usual accuracy, accompanied by a torrent of

321

invective that seemed even richer than usual.

"Danny, do stop," he begged, dodging a flying hairbrush that crashed into the wall, narrowly missing the mirror.

"How you can say such a thing after everything I have been through," she stormed. "All those women, chatter, chatter all the time, and the place is so dirty and it stinks! But you go where you please, talk to whomever you please, amuse yourself . . ."

"Danny, I do *not* amuse myself. I am merely executing my half of the task whilst you execute yours."

"Oh, yes. That is so easy to say, is it not? Tomorrow, you may stay here and I will put on my britches and visit the Palais Royal . . ."

"You will *not*." Her husband was betrayed into a shout of protest, knowing full well that Danny never made idle threats.

"And why not, pray? I should do every bit as well as you, I daresay; probably better since the language is my own."

"That may be so, but I will not permit it." Odd's breath! One of these days he would learn not to say that! But before he could soften the statement Danny had dived beneath the bed to emerge in the wink of an eyelid with the heavy porcelain chamber pot which she brandished menacingly over her head.

Justin tried not to laugh as she advanced on him, a slender, scantily clad figure rigid with a determination that he knew he must diffuse. "Danny, if you try anything with that damned pot, I shall use your hairbrush in a manner for which it was not intended." He backed away, watching her warily, and saw with relief the sudden speculative gleam in the brown eyes.

"You would not." Danielle paused in her tracks.

"Throw it and see," he responded.

She lowered the prospective missile. "Now you have made me want to laugh," she reproached with a comical grimace. "That is most ungallant of you. I was enjoying my anger."

"Well, I have a better way for you to utilize your surplus energy. Put on your britches and we will go together to the Palais Royal."

"That was exactly what I wished to propose until you made that nasty remark."

"For which I beg a thousand pardons." He apologized

322

meekly and Danielle chuckled as she threw off the wrapper and donned her beloved britches, twisting her hair into a knot that disappeared beneath the cloth cap.

"Molly is sleeping well," she informed Justin. "I think she has quite recovered from her sickness, but tomorrow I will buy food that she may prepare for herself. It will be better so, do you not think?"

"I think so," he agreed, walking to the open window looking out over the garden. "I will meet you under the third tree. Come here and let me show you."

Danielle was instantly beside him and he slipped an arm around the narrow waist. "I will leave first since my comings and goings will not be questioned. Follow me in five minutes. If you are challenged by the guards, I feel sure you will find a way to persuade them of your credentials."

"*Mais, bien sûr*, milord. I am a mere servant lad in search of a *putain*."

"A part you will play to perfection," he said dryly. "In five minutes then."

While the Earl and Countess of Linton roamed the cafés and clubs of the Palais Royal, listening to the impassioned talk and maintaining a generally low profile except for the occasions when Danny entered the ring with all the enthusiasm of a backstreet worker and turned the conversation into an alley that provoked the interests of the information-gatherers, Roland, Comte de St. Estèphe, sat in his darkened chamber and thought of his father on his death bed.

The old man had been as vicious under the imminent sword of death as he had been all his life, the words spurting forth with a venom that exhausted his last strength. But he had exacted the promise from his son and heir that the insult would not go unavenged. His wife had paid dearly for her infidelity with the young English earl, but the earl himself, when challenged, had turned the tables and driven his point through the shoulder of the *comte*. He had refrained from delivering the coup de grace in tacit acknowledgment that he had been in the wrong—one did not seduce another man's wife with impunity, but unknowingly he had left alive an enmity that would span the next generation.

Roland, throughout his childhood, had become accustomed to the abuse inflicted upon his mother and had learned the lesson well. By the age of twelve he was sexually active and used the maidservants freely. They had little choice but to submit to the rape and those few who resisted bore the marks of their resistance as examples to their fellows.

The contempt for womankind engendered in the young Roland by his father's brutalization of his mother became crystallized when he heard the death-bed story. He stopped not to consider that his mother may have sought, like Louise de St. Varennes, a brief respite from the abuse that was her lot in life, thought only of the betrayal and, after his father's death, treated the widow with the same venomous cruelty that she had received in her husband's lifetime—and all women who fell into his path, vulnerable and eager for his attentions. Women deserved no other form of treatment and he would take his father's revenge on the house of Linton through the woman. It was entirely appropriate and when Linton, after the event, challenged him then he would face a finer swordsman than his father had faced and there would be no quarter this time from the "guilty" party.

But how to achieve the seduction of a bride who looked with such doe eyes at her husband? The fact that Linton appeared to love his wife merely added spice to St. Estèphe's plans, but if the wife could not be persuaded to play her husband false . . . He smiled in the darkness. There were many methods of persuasion and he had always preferred the less gentle ones, particularly with such a diminutive, fair-skinned piece of frailty.

Closing his eyes, the *comte* mused pleasurably on the prospect of having that frail body in his hands. She would not resist him for long and when he eventually returned her to her husband . . . The excitement brought about by these reflections sent the *comte* off in search of release and the young kitchen maid that he found was, as a result, unable to leave her bed for a week.

The next morning he positioned himself behind a tapestry screen in the corridor outside the Lintons' apartments. He thought it unlikely he would succeed in taking her from the palace, but his plans would be best laid after careful observation of her movements.

The earl left the chamber first and strode purposefully down the corridor, elegant yet unremarkable in a silver gray cloth jacket and knee britches. He looked as if he had business other than pleasure to attend to, St. Estèphe reflected, but the nature of that business was not what concerned him.

What did concern him emerged some ten minutes later and the *comte* stared in disbelief. The young countess was almost unrecognizable in a dull round gown of brown merino, stolid, serviceable, and horribly bourgeois. She wore a plain chip hat with a heavy veil, carried a wicker shopping basket of the kind carried by all French housewives, and was accompanied by a wan-faced maidservant, also with a basket.

"Let us make haste, Molly. I do not wish to be seen abovestairs in this guise. Once we are in the back corridors we will be unremarked."

The *comte* waited until they had rounded a corner and then followed stealthily as they made for the working part of the palace. The Tuileries and the Louvre housed over two thousand souls of every station in life and the presence of a respectable French matron clearly on her way to market would attract no attention. Danielle exchanged cheerful greetings with those they passed and the *comte* gasped in surprise. Gone was the delicate speech of the aristocrat, in its place a country twang. What the devil was she? he wondered for the second time.

He followed at a discreet distance as they walked briskly through the streets of a city that in these days was far from a quiet, restful place of residence. Street corners were covered with posters announcing the latest regulations of the commune, print shops abounded, and the sellers of newspapers cried their papers and pamphlets from every doorway.

His quarry appeared unaffected by the signs of tension, the beating of a drum, the sudden alerting peal of a church bell, the pounding of a patrol of militia down narrow alleyways. She went in and out of shops, haggling ferociously over the price of an ell of stuff and a yard of ribbon. In the open market on the rue St.-André des Arts she bought bread, wine, fruit, and cheese, selecting the produce with all the fastidious care evinced by her fellow shoppers with whom she blended as easily as a chameleon on a leaf. Not even one of the spies of the *comité des récherches*, mingling with the crowds, noting looks and recording remarks, would find anything unusual about her.

But why? St. Estèphe was quite at a loss as the conviction grew that there was much more to the Countess of Linton than met the eye—a master of disguise who sang the songs of the people! Quite clearly he was going to have to find out a great deal more about her before making his move; and London was the place to glean that information. But he couldn't leave Paris at the moment. Not until he saw which way the political wind would blow eventually; not while he had a foot in both camps.

St. Estèphe was a shrewd and cautious man, building contacts amongst the revolutionary factions as carefully as he played the committed aristocrat at court. When France decided which way it would jump, he intended to be on the right side, preserving his material wealth in the only way possible—by a position of undisputed power in the government that must at some point stabilize. For the moment he played a waiting game, sensing the potential danger in aligning himself too soon with any one faction—unlike that ambitious fool Mirabeau, whose domineering manners and open desire for power had alienated both sides. The king rejected his advice and the king's confidants would not listen to him and he was without credibility in the Assembly, for all that he was quite the most capable politician around at the moment.

St. Estèphe would play his cards close to his chest—he cared not whether the king or the people achieved the final sovereignty but he knew that it would not be found in a middle course of moderation and compromise, and he would play whatever part was necessary when the time came. To do that, he must remain in Paris with his ear to the ground. The matter of Danielle and her husband must wait awhile longer. It would come to no harm for the keeping.

Four days later, as firmly convinced as St. Estèphe of the inevitability of a volcano of blood and horror that would tear the country apart, Justin and Danielle left Paris with a relief that was only surpassed by Molly's.

In the peace of the Cornish countryside, the married lovers passed an idyllic summer during which Danielle displayed an inordinate interest in making love in the strangest surroundings. Her powers of invention delighted her husband who, as Lady Lavinia remarked to the Earl of March, appeared to grow younger by the day.

Part 3: The Butterfly

Chapter 17

"I do not care for this at all, Justin."

Justin looked up from his solitary repast in the breakfast room at Danesbury the Christmas morning following their excursion to Paris and surveyed his wife. She was an entrancing sight as she came into the room—the white velvet wrapper as crisp as the snow-covered landscape beyond the French doors, her hair tumbling unconfined to her shoulders. Her feet were bare, he noticed, but at Danesbury Danielle rarely conformed and, as a result, their guests were always carefully selected. So far, not one of the small group had emerged from their bedchambers this holiday morning, but it was not yet ten o'clock. Linton, after failing to persuade an unusually drowsy Danielle to join him, had taken an early ride and was now addressing his breakfast with some enthusiasm.

"What business, my love?" he prompted when she seemed disinclined to expand her comment.

"This business of babies," she announced, lifting her bare toes to the crackling fire. "I was not aware that it would make one puke so distressingly, but it is the same every morning . . ."

"What did you say?" The earl choked on a mouthful of beef and had recourse to his tankard of ale.

"I beg your pardon," she apologized, warming her other foot. "It is a very vulgar word, but it is actually a very vulgar activity—this vomiting."

"I do not care what you call it," her husband spluttered.

331

"What is it that you are saying?"

"Why, that I do not care to be sick every morning." Her eyes widened innocently. "But *Grandmaman* says it is good because it means that the baby has taken firm hold . . ."

"What baby?" Linton exploded, wondering if he had taken leave of his senses.

"Yours, of course, milord." She turned from the fire and smiled.

"Danielle, I do not quite understand." Linton spoke carefully. "Are you saying that you have decided to conceive, or that you have already done so?"

"You are a slow top this morning, sir," she chided. "I would hardly complain in anticipation of discomfort; it is not my way."

"Come here." He pushed back his chair and patted his knee imperatively.

Danny deposited herself firmly on his lap and reached for a piece of bread and butter from the table. "It helps sometimes," she informed him, taking a healthy bite. "A little plain food seems to soothe the stomach. I cannot imagine, though, how I ever cared for coffee." She glared at the silver pot on the sideboard with the utmost distaste.

"Stop playing games now, Danielle." Linton turned her face toward him. "You have amused yourself at my expense quite sufficiently. When do you expect the child?"

"In June." She kissed his nose. "I did not mean to tease you so abominably, Justin, but . . ."

"You couldn't help yourself," he finished for her with a chuckle. "I wonder if you will ever be anything but an outrageous wretch, Danny."

"Do you wish me to be?" She scanned his face with a small frown.

"No." He shook his head. "And I can only hope that if you provide me with a daughter she will take after her mother."

"And if it is a son, he must take after his father," she said softly, placing her mouth firmly on his.

"Oh, beg pardon." Julian burst into this scene of conjugal harmony. "Didn't mean to be *de trop*."

"Oh, you are not, Jules," Danielle reassured, making no

332

attempt to move from her husband's knee. "You must break your fast. I was merely giving Justin one of his Christmas presents. I am with child, you should know."

"Sweet heaven," Julian muttered irreverently. "By Gad! I mean . . . well, my felicitations, Justin only . . . only do you think it is wise? Oh, that was not what I meant," he stammered, "but how is Danny to . . ."

"In the usual way, Jules." She went into a peal of laughter. "Oh, do not look so discommoded. Is it so very shocking?"

"No, of course it is not. It is only that I cannot imagine you as a mother," he replied candidly. "But you cannot go around blurting the news in that way, Danny." Julian helped himself to a dish of deviled kidneys. "If you are in a delicate situation you must be discreet. Must she not, Justin?"

"Oh, stuff," Danielle declared before her husband could respond to the appeal. "It is perfectly natural and quite to be expected . . . Oh, must you eat those, Jules? They make me want to p— To be sick," she amended hastily as Justin squeezed her waist.

"But they are quite delicious," Julian protested in puzzlement. "I have seen you eat them."

"That was before I became *enceinte*. I begin to wonder if I will ever have a taste for anything but bread and butter again."

"My love, I do not think a description of your symptoms is going to aid Julian's digestion," Justin put in mildly.

"Good morning, and a merry Christmas to one and all." Sir Anthony Fanshawe, in the company of Viscount Westmore, entered the breakfast parlor wreathed in smiles. They appeared not at all embarrassed by the position of their hosts and made directly for the chafing dishes on the sideboard.

"Jules has been saying that I may not tell people I am with child. Is that not absurd?" Danielle demanded.

Sir Anthony dropped a heavy silver spoon into the dish of scrambled eggs, and Westmore lost interest in the kedgeree. "You are?" they said with one voice. They were quite accustomed to accompanying Danielle on her forays into the backslums of London, had become used to the silver-mounted pistol and the terse instructions they received from a businesslike young woman who bore little resemblance either

333

to the social butterfly or to the mischievous imp who delighted in shocking them. But this simple news defeated their powers of imagination.

Justin was enormously amused as he read their minds and saw their startled recognition of the horrifying realms of discourtesy into which their astonishment had betrayed them. He accepted their stammered felicitations with a slight smile, still maintaining his hold on his wife, who showed no inclination to break it anyway.

Lady Lavinia bustled in opportunely. "Danielle, where are your shoes, child?" She chose this dereliction above the greater one—that of sitting upon her husband's knee in such a public fashion. But since scolding her granddaughter for that indecorous behavior would also implicate Justin, she found herself with little choice.

"Oh, my feet are quite warm, *Grandmaman*." Danielle smiled. "I have been telling my news."

Lady Lavinia paled and sat down hastily, her eyes on Justin.

"Just so, ma'am," he soothed. "There is a movement to persuade Danielle that she may not be so frank in other company."

"I should think so, indeed. Whatever can you be thinking of, Danielle? This is information for your husband alone."

"*Grandmère*, it was a Christmas present and as such should be shared with one's friends." Danielle left her husband's knee and went to kiss her grandmother. "We are amongst friends, are we not, *chère madame*?"

"Oh dear." Lady Lavinia sighed helplessly and embraced her granddaughter.

"Rest assured, ma'am, I shall be quiet as a church mouse on the subject to anyone else. But now I must dress for I have to ride to Seven Acre field this morning and pay a Christmas visit to the Ducloses."

"Danielle, you cannot ride in your condition," her grandmother expostulated.

"Now that, if you will pardon my saying so, ma'am, is a great piece of nonsense," Danielle declared firmly. "I will not be mollycoddled and have no intention of spending the next six months lying on the sofa with my smelling salts."

"Do you have any?" Jules was betrayed into uttering.

"No, of course I do not. It was merely a figure of speech," she returned impatiently. "I will ride until such time as I consider it unwise, and I will continue with my work in London until that time also. You have no objections, I trust, Linton?"

He shrugged. "None whatsoever, my dear. It would make very little difference if I had."

That brought a smile and the challenge in her eyes faded. "Will you visit the Ducloses with me?"

"I will ride with you, love, whenever you choose to do so yourself," he responded quietly.

Danielle nodded her comprehension. If her husband preferred only that she not ride alone, she could not quarrel with him and, indeed, had no desire to do so.

"Justin, you cannot permit her to racket about the countryside and the town in her usual outlandish fashion," Lavinia protested, once Danielle had left. "Supposing she should be thrown?"

"That is such a remote possibility, Lavinia, that I consider the risk an acceptable one. I do not think Danielle has been thrown from a horse since she was six years old," Justin said calmly. "She is no fool for all her teasing and will take no unacceptable chances."

"But, Justin, Danielle does not understand the meaning of an unacceptable chance," Lavinia lamented.

"I believe she does." Linton smiled. This pregnancy, as only he knew, was of Danielle's making, and she would not jeopardize it. Once set upon a course of action, she followed it through with single-minded purpose. She would never deliberately put herself in danger of miscarriage.

"But Louise had such difficulties and Danielle is so tiny." Lavinia, in her anxiety, quite forgot the impropriety of discussing such matters in front of three young bachelors. Fortunately, though, none of them appeared remotely put out; it was as if their mother were discussing a favorite sister.

"She is stronger than Louise, ma'am. But I take your point. I shall insist she visit Stuart as soon as we return to town and that she follow any specific recommendations he might make."

With that Lady Lavinia had to be satisfied. Stuart was the

335

court physician, considered the best *accoucheur* in Harley Street, and, for all Justin's easy tolerance of Danielle's unconventional ways, Lavinia did not doubt his ability to "insist" should he feel it was warranted.

The Ducloses who received the Earl and Countess of Linton later that morning were a quite different family from the one Danielle had first seen in the cold smelly room in London's East End. The children, plump and rosy, swarmed around Danielle as she distributed presents. Within a very few minutes she was involved in an energetic game of Hunt the Thimble around the stone cottage that bore all the signs of a well-managed orderly household. Monsieur and Madame Duclos regarded the scene benignly and appeared to stand on no ceremony with the young countess. They were more reserved with His Lordship until he accepted a tankard of monsieur's cider and a large slab of madame's heavy fruit cake with its thick crust of marzipan beneath the white icing. They relaxed completely when Danielle scooped up little Guillaume, now ten months, and deposited him on Linton's lap.

"My Lord must get used to babies, you see," she said with a twinkle. "Since he will have one of his own in June." The news was received with joyful exclamations of congratulation. Justin beamed delightedly, heedless of the baby's fingers busily engaged in pulling at his crisply starched stock. The kitchen was redolent with the aromas of boiling pudding and roasting goose and Danielle suddenly put her hand over her mouth and ran for the courtyard.

"Oh, la pauvre petite!" Madame Duclos exclaimed in instant female comprehension, and bustled after her.

"It was always so with madame," Duclos informed Justin placidly. "But it passes in a few weeks, you will see. And then she will want only the most impossible things. With Marie it was peaches, only peaches—in February, my lord!" He chuckled reminiscently. "I scoured the whole of Paris." Duclos sighed. "But that, of course, was in the old days."

"I shall make you a tisane." Madame Duclos reappeared, her arm around a pale Danielle. "It is just the thing."

"No, please, madame. It is not necessary." Danielle managed a wan smile. "I feel much better now and we must leave you to your dinner preparations."

"What nonsense! Sit by the fire; it will take but a moment." Madame set the kettle on the fire and began to select dried herbs from the long rack hanging from the ceiling. She placed the herbs in a stone mortar and began to pound them with a heavy pestle, clucking sympathetically all the while. Boiling water was poured over the mixture, creating an aromatic infusion that she then strained through muslin and poured into a cup.

"Drink this, child," she said briskly. Danielle's nose wrinkled at the pale green liquid but she sipped bravely and found that it was actually very soothing.

Justin noticed with relief that the color had returned to her cheeks by the time the cup was empty and decided that the sooner he got her home the better—home and ensconced by the drawing-room fire with her feet on a footstool and cushions at her back. Keeping her there would require considerable ingenuity but he'd have ample assistance.

Thus it was that Danielle found her guests curiously uninterested in outdoor pursuits. Piquet, backgammon, chess, and riotous games of charades seemed to be their preference. When she began to show distinct signs of cabin fever, Justin hit upon the notion of a fencing tournament in the long gallery and followed that success with an archery contest in the stableyard. Danny had not the skill with the bow that she had with the small sword and suffered what she considered an ignominious defeat at Julian's hands. She seized on Justin's suggestion that she work to perfect her technique and then challenge Julian to a return match. Her cousin-in-law played his part by scornfully maintaining that she could never defeat him. As a result, she received all the fresh air she craved a mere few paces from the house in an activity that required little physical exertion, all the while blissfully unaware of the elaborate machinations of her husband, grandparents, and friends.

"How long do you intend to keep this up, coz?" Julian asked softly one afternoon as the two men stood watching Danny at

337

her single-minded practice.

"For as long as possible," Linton replied. "This nausea concerns me, although I am assured by every female from Lady Lavinia to Molly that it is quite normal and, in fact, a good sign. But it taxes her strength although she will not admit it." He turned to smile at his cousin. "I am grateful for your help, Jules, and that of the others. But you must not feel obliged to remain here; it must grow tedious."

"Gad, Justin! How can you suggest such a thing? We'd all do anything for Danny, although," he added with a grin, "feigning fatigue at ten o'clock every evening has its absurd side. Not to mention creeping like guilty schoolboys downstairs again once we're sure she's in bed. I don't know what the servants must think."

"They know full well what's afoot, my friend, and are more than happy to assist in the deception." The earl chuckled, watching his wife bend the thin bow of pliant willow. "I strongly suspect, Julian, that you are about to meet your match. That is Danny's third bull's-eye in three straight shots."

"Did you see that, milord?" Danielle ran across the yard, her skirts tossed over one arm. "I think I now fully understand the science. We shall have our return match tomorrow, Jules. Will you make a wager on me, Justin?"

"Having just witnessed your performance, my love, I cannot fail to do so." He bowed and gave her his arm. "Will you not rest a while before dinner, though?"

"If it will make you comfortable." Her smile was soft.

"It will." He bent to kiss the corner of her mouth and Julian, quite accustomed to being ignored at such moments, left them to it and went back into the house.

It was the end of January before the earl and his countess returned to town. Danielle was now rarely nauseous and her complexion had regained its customary bloom. Apart from the tenderness of her swollen breasts, her body showed little signs of change, but with a common sense rarely evinced by her peers she wore her stays loosely laced even though her svelte body showed no need for such adaptation. With grim resignation she endured the examinations of the court's physician. With an equally grim determination she informed

338

her husband that she had no intention of lying upon her bed for the greater part of the day, and to the devil with Stuart's recommendations.

Justin stroked her belly with long delicate fingers. "My love, I ask only that you obey the dictates of your body, that you do not ride *ventre à terre*, and that when your condition becomes obvious that you withdraw from Polite Circles."

"*Mais, d'accord.*" She ran her foot down the bare calf beside her, curling her toes beneath the sheet. "You shall have your heir, husband, and if it is but a girl child this time, 'twill be a son next."

Justin propped himself onto one elbow to examine her expression in the light of the bedside candle. "It matters not, Danielle. The child alone is important."

"But you would prefer the son, surely?" Danielle thought of the old *duc* and his sons and the efforts she had made as a child to meet their expectations, all the while knowing in a deep subconscious valley of her awareness that at some point pretense would not be sufficient. She was a Danielle, not a Danny, and as such a shattering disappointment to the men of her family.

"I have no preference," Justin said softly. "Julian stands heir to the title if I have no sons and I am well satisfied with the arrangement. You may give me half a dozen daughters, Danny, and I shall be ruled by a monstrous regiment of women and be glad of it."

"I do not believe you will be glad of it at all," she retorted. "And I do not think it at all polite to talk of monstrous regiments." Sitting up with a sudden energetic movement, she swung one leg across his supine form and sat firmly on his stomach. "Now, my lord, since I have you at my mercy, I shall think how best to punish you."

Her eyes danced as she ran her hands slowly over his chest and then reached behind her, fingertips pitpatting down his thigh. Justin groaned as she enclosed him in one small hand, never taking her gaze from his face as she stroked him with delicate rhythm before lifting her body slightly and moving backward, guiding him within. Justin lay very still for a moment, watching her through half-closed eyes, savoring the sensation of the soft velvet walls imprisoning him. Her inner muscles tightened and he gasped with pleasure, but as she began to move, slowly at first and then with increasing speed as the tight coil of passion spiraled, he seized her hips urgently, holding her still.

"Not this way, my love; not at the moment."

"Why not?" Puzzlement showed in the passion-filled eyes and not a little indignation at this abrupt cessation.

"Because I know how energetic you can become in this position and you might hurt yourself. Over you go!" With a determined heave, he lifted her off and rolled her onto her back beside him. "For the next months, my love, you will play a rather more passive role in this business than you are accustomed. There will be no less pleasure, I promise."

Any protest she might have made failed to surface as Justin parted the long creamy thighs. His head lowered and her body arced with joy beneath a questing tongue that with all the delicacy of a butterfly on honeysuckle sipped the nectar of her passion. It was a long time of engulfing sweetness before he entered her, moving with the utmost gentleness, holding them both on the peak of the precipice until Danielle could bear it no longer and then discovered that she could, that she could bear this wonder for an eternity. But at last they fell together in a slow motion free-fall through pure ether.

"I think I shall be quite content to be passive," Danielle murmured against his shoulder.

Justin chuckled sleepily and patted her bottom. "You need not be totally without initiative, love."

"I do not intend to be so." It was supposed to sound like a dignified statement but a deep yawn detracted considerably from the desired impression and Danielle yielded willingly to the sleep of satisfied desire.

It was some two days later when she was going through the pile of invitation cards that poured daily into the house that she heard the sound of excitable voices in the hall. A footman's ponderous tone was denying Her Ladyship's presence in the house and the voices rose in voluble French.

340

Frowning, Danielle went to the library door, opening it just as Bedford appeared and in stony accents informed the owners of the voices that if they did not leave immediately they would be thrown out.

A woman's voice lifted in a sobbing wail and Danny went swiftly into the hall. Two men and a woman stood by the open front door, naked desperation on their faces. It was easy enough to see why the footman and Bedford were reacting as they were—the party bore all the signs of poverty in their bedraggled clothing and wooden-soled shoes; and they were none too clean, either. But Danielle knew well how dirt and misfortune were inextricable partners.

"*Qu'est-ce qui se passe, mes amis?*" She walked briskly toward them.

All three began to speak at once in an impossibly confused torrent and she held up her hand in an imperative gesture for silence.

"*Venez avec moi, s'il vous plaît.* Bedford, you will bring coffee and biscuits to the library, please." With an encouraging smile she ushered the group into the library and closed the door. "*Maintenant, vous voulez expliquer. Vous, monsieur?*" She indicated the man whose grizzled hair bespoke his seniority.

The story was preceded with elaborate, courteous apologies for the rude manner of their interruption, but speed was of the essence and they had been unable to afford the time to write to request milady to visit them. Danielle nodded. She had assumed something of the sort since her help had never before been requested in this way. The chevalier received the urgent visits since in his bachelor lodgings they would attract less notice than in Grosvenor Square. But D'Evron was in France at present gathering up-to-date information for Pitt, much as Danielle and Justin had done last summer.

A footman appeared with a tray of refreshments, his expression wooden as he placed it on a small rosewood table. "Thank you, I will pour the coffee myself." Danielle dismissed him with a courtesy that concealed her impatience. When they were again alone she turned to the elderly man. "*Continuez, monsieur.*"

She wished now she had asked Bedford to provide bread and

cheese rather than the dainty mouthfuls of petit fours that accompanied the coffee. She was reminded unpleasantly of Marie Antoinette, who had declared that if the people had no bread then they should eat cake. She would remedy her thoughtlessness later.

The old man told the story with a simple dignity that did little to prevent the cold chills creeping across Danielle's skin. His granddaughter, twelve years old, had been on her way to market that morning when the cry of "pickpocket" had rent the air from a man standing close to her. In the succeeding flurry, someone had bumped against her and a gold watch had fallen to the ground at her feet. The girl had been seized instantly, hauled before the magistrates, who, in the face of the evidence, spared no time to listen to her halting attempts to explain her innocence in a language she barely knew. As a result, *la petite* Brigitte was now incarcerated in Newgate Prison awaiting trial and the Robertses knew no one with sufficient facility in the language to plead her case.

At story's end, Danielle paced the library floor well aware that for once she had no idea what to do. The first priority was to effect the child's release from that hell upon earth. She could post bail if she knew how to do so, could even expend sovereigns in bribery, but to do that she must go to the jail herself, and there was no one to accompany her. The chevalier was in France, Jules and his friends were attending a prize fight out of town. Justin was her only hope and Danielle had no idea where he was, but every minute Brigitte spent in Newgate was a minute spent in danger of life and limb, not to mention the trauma of such an experience.

"You must allow me one hour." She made her decision with cold finality. If Justin could not be found in that time then she would go alone. It meant a broken promise, but the only alternative was to turn this stricken family from the door. He would understand that as he had understood everything else.

She left the Robertses in the library and instructed Bedford to send several men in search of His Lordship—they should try White's and Watier's and certain houses. She reeled off the names of Linton's closest friends and included the address on Half Moon Street. It was unlikely, since Edward Mainwairing had joined the Ninth Foot some six months ago, that Justin would have business there, but it was possible he might be visiting his old friend. She then requested that a substantial nuncheon be provided for her guests and went upstairs to don habit and boots, slipping a purse of sovereigns in the deep pocket together with her pistol. She threw a heavy cloak over her arm before descending to the bookroom where she scribbled a hasty note to Justin—a note of apology and explanation of her mission.

All efforts to find Justin failed and with a fair assumption of confidence she had the town chaise brought to the door and followed the distraught Roberts into its cushioned interior. There was no need for secrecy—in fact, Danielle decided, quite the opposite. She would need all the power and influence of her social position in this affair and she had made no secret of her destination in her note to Justin.

Fortunately, she was unable to see the coachman's face as he received his orders. But they were orders from the countess and Malcolm sprang his horses bearing the chaise with the Linton arms emblazoned on its panels in the direction of Newgate Jail.

She must first see the governor, Danielle decided, alighting from the chaise with a swish of skirts. The building was an intimidating mass of stone surrounded by high walls in which were set iron gates. The gates were manned by slovenly looking individuals who initially showed scant interest in the chaise and the presence of a small figure in a deep blue velvet riding habit adorned with silver lace. However, when that figure demanded to see the governor immediately and castigated them roundly on their inebriated state, they staggered involuntarily into a relatively upright position and much argument ensued as to who was to escort the lady.

Danielle stood tapping her foot during their deliberations and eventually said, "If you cannot make up your minds, only open the gates and I will find my own way. But the governor shall hear of your discourtesy forthwith."

The great doors clanged open and Malcolm watched his mistress disappear into the void of one of the most unspeakable places on earth, leaving him to mind an hysterical family of froggies who had been forbidden to follow the countess, and four high-steppers who showed a distinctly nervous apprehension at the excitable attention they received from the inhabitants of the alley outside the jail.

The Governor of Newgate was possibly as intoxicated as his employees, Danielle decided, when she was shown into his presence. His cravat was stained, britches and coat rumpled, and he struggled from his chair with some difficulty at the sight of a diminutive creature who, by dress and bearing, had no place in his realm.

"Pray be seated, sir," said Danielle. "I feel sure you will be more comfortable. I am come to post bail for one Brigitte Roberts. She was brought here this morning and is not yet tried. If you will tell me the sum set by the magistrates we shall be able to deal with this matter quickly."

The governor had not the slightest idea who Brigitte Roberts might be, knew only that there were some three hundred women in his jail and how they came and how they left was of little interest. The majority were destined for the hangman or transportation, and those who remained would probably die anyway. If they had money enough to purchase adequate food from their jailers, it would be taken from them by their stronger fellow inmates, and if they had not, then an inadequate diet, sickness, or violence would complete the task. He stared blankly at his visitor.

"If you do not recall the figure, sir, then we must contrive one." Danielle reached for the purse of sovereigns in her pocket. "You will have the child brought here and we will discuss the matter."

"I can't do that, my lady," the governor mumbled, his eyes fixed on the purse. "We'd never find her in there."

"Then I shall find her myself. You will come with me." It was an order, not a request, and three gold sovereigns fell on the table. As he reached for them, Danielle placed her hand over the shining coins. "There will be more," she said softly. "I'm sure that a suspected pickpocket will need a considerable bail. Let us find her and settle this business."

The coins went back into the purse and the governor licked his lips nervously. One less prisoner would go quite

344

unremarked in the maelstrom and he would not be forced to account for the loss. It was unlikely that this Brigitte Roberts would come to trial for months and a simple explanation that she had died of typhus would be easily accepted. But the thought of visiting the women's wards and cells filled him with dread. Did this unpleasantly determined young lady know what she was talking about with her blithe announcement that she would find the prisoner herself? If not, she would suffer considerable shock to her composure. The idea pleased the befuddled governor, who was accustomed to reigning supreme and in peace over his section of hell.

"You must find her yourself," he said slyly. "I will accompany you to the women's section, but the bail must be put up in advance." He made great play with a file of papers. "Ah, here it is. Brigitte . . .?"

"Roberts," Danielle supplied, prepared to play his game.

"Ah, yes," he muttered, scrutinizing a scrap of paper. "Bail is set for one hundred guineas."

Danielle counted out the sum without complaint. It was extortion but little enough to pay for a child's life and sanity. "No, Governor," she said as he made to pocket the coins. "The money remains here until I have the child. My chaise and coachman await me outside the gates and should any harm befall me . . ." She left the sentence unfinished, but drunk though he was the governor had no need of expansion. He led the way to the female side of the prison.

There were two wards and two cells inhabited by the women sent here for every gradation of crime; the untried mingled with those under sentence of death in a situation of unspeakable over-crowding. Danielle reeled as the stench hit her. Half-naked women crowded against the railing at their approach, begging and cursing, hands thin as birds' talons thrust between the bars. Children tumbled and wailed, trampled underfoot as their mothers surged toward the extraordinary sight of wealth outside their cage.

There was no bedding that Danielle could see on the filth-encrusted floor. In these surroundings the women cooked, washed, ate, and slept in the company of their children, many of whom had first seen daylight behind these bars and knew no other. Those who did achieve their release would find themselves back again soon enough, but on their own behalfs and not their mothers'.

Danielle thought of the rings on her fingers, the purse in her pocket, and knew that she could not go into the cage with them on her person. The governor was watching her reactions with a complacent smile.

"You!" Danielle turned imperatively to the turnkey. "You will go immediately outside the gate and bring my coachman to me."

The turnkey looked at the governor for confirmation of the order and receiving no sign either way obeyed. Danny tried to hide her hopelessness as she looked at the phalanx of women ranged against the bars. How was she to find a petrified twelve-year-old amongst this ferocious crowd? The smell of liquor was rank in the air—the women might be short of food and water for washing, but gin seemed in plentiful supply.

The jailer returned after what seemed to Danielle an eternity, but he was accompanied by Malcolm, whose broad shoulders and impressive livery reassured Danielle and had the hoped-for effect on the governor. "You will hold these for me," she said, stripping off her rings and handing them to Malcolm, together with her purse and her cloak. "Unlock the door."

"My lady, you can't go in there," the governor demurred, painfully affected by the reality of the stony-faced, liveried coachman and the sudden thought of what might happen to him should the Countess of Linton suffer injury.

"Well, it is clear that someone must," Danielle replied impatiently. "Send one of your men."

"I ain't goin' in among that lot." The turnkey backed away. "They'd 'ave me eyes out, soon as look at me."

"Oh, do not be absurd. You must be removing women from in there all the time."

The governor refrained from saying that it was a rare occurrence and when it did happen his men required the company of half a dozen others and the comforting presence of muskets. Since no such event had been anticipated on what had been a peaceful morning, he had neither the men nor the firearms available.

"Unlock the door," Danielle repeated, steeling herself for the inevitable when the uncomfortable silence looked as if it would go on forever.

Justin walked into Watier's to be informed that a member of his household had been in search of him but an hour since. As he received this message he was hailed by the Marquis of Louden.

"Justin, 'pon my soul. Your men appear to have been searching all over town for you. I received one myself not above half an hour ago."

"Indeed, George." Linton frowned. "Was there any message?"

"No. He wished to know if I knew your whereabouts. I suggested he might find you with the master." The master in question was the noted fencer, Armand Gaillard, who made a very satisfactory living matching his skill with that of the Quality.

"I was there, but must have left before the messenger arrived." Linton could not hide his anxiety from his friend. "If you will excuse me, George, I had best discover what so urgently requires my presence."

"Of course, dear boy," the marquis assured. "'Tis to be hoped it's nothing serious. Lady Danny is quite well, I trust?"

"She was when last I spoke with her. I daresay Peter has written one of his formidable speeches for me to deliver to the Lords and is anxious to ensure that I do not miss the debate." He made his tone light and the marquis laughed, gracefully accepting that Linton did not choose to share his obvious concern.

Tomas was walking my lord's chestnuts along St. James's when Linton reappeared on the steps of his club. Without a word, Justin took the reins and sprang into the curricle giving the tiger barely time to jump up behind as the horses leaped forward under the flick of the whip.

"What's amiss, Bedford?" Justin asked directly, pulling off his gloves as he strode into the hall.

"Her Ladyship left a message for you, my lord, before she left with the French persons." Bedford managed to convey, in spite of his impassive expression and calmly polite tone, exactly what he thought of the "French persons." He handed Linton the folded paper.

"Thank you." Justin went into the library before opening the message, his heart pounding uncomfortably. What he read sent him into a panic-stricken fury the like of which he had never before experienced. His wife, nearly five months pregnant, had dared to venture alone into that abyss of human misery and degradation that was Newgate. And she had broken her word—the one thing he had relied on without question. It mattered not that she had made no attempt to deceive him, had searched all over town for him, had gone on her errand with his coachman in attendance. His orders had been absolute and her promise made without condition.

White-faced, Justin yanked the bellpull and gave instructions for the curricle to be brought round again immediately. The horses were still in harness and Tomas, with a resigned shrug at this unusually unpredictable behavior of My Lord's, brought them out of the stables and back to the square.

"Where we goin', me lord," he gasped, hanging on for dear life as the horses, given their heads, raced through the streets causing all traffic in their path to cower against the curb.

"To Newgate," the earl spat out furiously and Tomas gawped in disbelief. It had to be Her Ladyship up to her tricks again, he thought. Nothing else could throw His Lordship into such a towering rage. But what the devil took her to Newgate?

The Linton chaise stood outside the gates of the prison. Of Malcolm there was no sign and the horses were being held by two men and a distraught woman, none of whom seemed capable of controlling the tossing heads and stamping hooves. A crowd of interested spectators shouted advice, much of it coarse and not at all to the point, and their yells merely served to exacerbate the highly bred beasts.

Linton sprang down and handed the reins to Tomas. "Do what you can," he instructed tersely. "I'll send Malcolm out directly."

"I'll 'elp, me lord." A scrawny urchin appeared suddenly at

348

Linton's feet. "Ah'm good wiv 'osses." Darting to the chaise he began to soothe the leaders with a series of clicking noises that unaccountably appeared to calm them.

"I'll manage, me lord," Tomas said. "The lad knows what he's about."

Justin strode to the gate. This time it opened instantly. Something extraordinary was going on this morning, and clearly anyone who had anything to do with the chaise and the lady had business inside the jail.

"You'll be wantin' the women's side," one of the guards offered as Justin stood for a moment irresolute, looking around the bewildering number of low buildings. "Leastways, that's where Bill took the coachman." He jerked a thumb to the left and laughed coarsely. "Jest follow your nose when you're inside. Can't miss it that way."

Justin tossed him a shilling and followed instructions.

"Unlock the door," Danielle said for the third time, controlling her shudder of horror. "I have not all day to waste on this tedious business."

Tedious! This fearsome little creature actually had the temerity to refer to the prospect of entering that hellhole as tedious! The governor gazed at her in awe and then gave the order to the turnkey.

Danielle walked into the cage, her hand deep in her coat pocket. The door clanged shut behind her and she was imprisoned in Newgate in the company of women who were more beast than human as they tugged at her clothes and begged piteously. For as long as she stayed in sight of the governor she was safe, but the women who surrounded her were the strongest, the leaders of the community who were able to achieve the front ranks. A twelve-year-old newcomer would not be found here.

"Let me pass," she commanded. "If you will find one Brigitte Roberts for me, you will be rewarded, I promise."

"What wiv, me lady?" someone whined, touching the lace at Danielle's throat. With a supreme effort Danielle pushed the hand aside.

"With guineas," she said shortly, averting her head from the foul breath. But the rankness was on all sides, a fetid miasma of disease-laden air. Something fluttered, the beat of a bird's wing deep in her belly, and Danielle paled—the life in her womb quickening for the first time in *this* place? She suddenly realized that in her efforts to save the life of a complete stranger she was endangering the life of her own child, of Linton's child.

"Get out of my way!" She pushed through the women who, for the moment surprised, fell back providing her with a path as narrow and unlikely as Moses' path across the Red Sea. Danielle marched through them and called Brigitte's name. But as she walked, the path closed behind her, shutting her off from the eyes of the three men outside the cage. She fought down the desperate fear, the knowledge that she was taking an unconscionable risk with so much more than her own safety. At the very end of the ward a group of semi-naked girls and women cowered in abject terror. She called the name again and a thin figure, her gown ripped from her back, face and hair thick with filth, looked up with dull eyes.

"You are Brigitte Roberts?" Danielle's voice was harsher than she'd intended, but her own fear was too raw now. What had happened to the child in such a short time to reduce her to this state? But there was no time for speculation. At the girl's nod she seized her wrist and pulled her to her feet, turning back to face what was now an impenetrable menacing wall.

"Wat's she got that we ain't?" a voice demanded. "Wat's a foine lady like you doin', takin' the likes of her outa 'ere?"

"Yeah, thas roight!" the voices rumbled, took up the cry. "Why 'er?"

"Because she's done nothing wrong," Danielle said brusquely as her heart hammered against her ribcage. "Let us through."

"Wat you goin' to do fer us, then, my foine loidy?" An Amazon of a woman stepped forward to stand chest to chest with Danielle. Brigitte screamed and the woman flicked Danielle's hat with a grimy finger. "This'll fetch a pretty penny," she said with an evil grin, showing a mouth of blackened stumps and huge gaps. The next instant, Danielle's

350

hat had left her head. "An' all this lace," the woman went on. "That's worth a few bottles of gin, eh, girls?" Her fingers caught the lace and there was a sudden ripping sound.

For an unreal moment, Danielle was again the urchin Danny fighting for survival in a Parisian backalley. She kicked out and her booted foot made contact with her tormentor's shin. It was a mistake, she realized hopelessly in the instant of action. Someone pushed her heavily from behind and she sprawled against the woman at her front. And then they were all on her, nails raking her face, fists punching into her arms, feet kicking wherever they could. The front of her habit tore under a pair of vicious talons that bit into the tender flesh of her breasts. In the first moments of terror Danielle had forgotten the pistol, but when the child, whose hand she still held somehow in a clutch as desperate as a dying man's, screamed again in hideous terror something clicked in her mind like the tumbrils of a safe and a cold wash of determination replaced the panic. For a second she fought with all the ferociousness of the women surrounding her until she got the hand that was not holding Brigitte free from a painful grip. The pistol was out of her pocket in an instant. She aimed high, but at this point cared not a jot whether the bullet found a human target. There was a shrill scream and her assailants fell back at the sight of the smoking weapon. Danielle, knowing she had but seconds before they realized the pistol was now useless until reloaded, hauled the whimpering figure beside her through the crowd that gave way in stunned silence.

Justin heard the shot as he entered the building and for a petrifying moment the vigorous pumping of his heart seemed to falter, then it picked up again as a rush of adrenaline drove him at a run in the direction of the sound. What he saw as he reached the group of men outside the railing emptied his soul of all but blind rage. His wife, torn, bedraggled, blood streaking her face and exposed bosom, hair a bird's nest of tangles, emerged from the sullen ranks of hard-eyed women, a pistol in one hand and quite the filthiest scrap of humanity in the other.

She appeared not to notice him until Malcolm stuttered, "My lord, I . . . I . . ."

"Give me those." Linton gestured to the purse, rings, and

351

cloak. "Go and help Tomas with the horses. He has eight to care for."

"Yes, my lord." Malcolm scurried away, convinced that he was to be turned off without a recommendation as a result of this day's work. But he had simply obeyed orders. Perhaps he should have gone into that hell himself . . . he shuddered at the thought. There was only so much an employer could expect of his servants and Her Ladyship had never once given him the opportunity to offer the sacrifice.

"Linton." Danielle looked at her husband with strangely blank eyes. "I have paid this *cochon*"—she pointed at the trembling governor—"one hundred guineas as bail for Brigitte. I do not think he deserves it. You will retrieve the monies, if you please." Her voice shook suddenly. "Do you see what they have done to the child, in no more than four hours? Give me my cloak." She pulled it out of his hands and made to wrap it around the shivering figure.

"You will wear this yourself, ma'am." Justin whisked it away. "If you could only see yourself." He threw the cloak around her, pulling the hood over her head. "The child will do well enough with a blanket. Fetch me one." He turned to the governor, who shrank from the blazing black eyes.

"I d . . . d . . . do not know where to find one, my lord," he stuttered.

"Then give me your coat, it will do as well."

Having the firm conviction that if he did not the jacket would be torn from his back, the governor pulled it off hastily.

"The money," Danielle said fiercely. "I will not leave here without it. It is in the room of this *bête*. He shall have not one penny and if he does not bring it I shall . . ."

"Be silent!" Linton clipped. "You will do only as you are bid."

Little Brigitte began to weep helplessly. "Now look what you have done," Danielle accused. "Come, *petite*. Put on the coat and I will take you to your *maman*. She is waiting for you outside with *ton père* and *grandpère*. You shall all come to my house where you may wash that filth from your hair and I will find you a gown to replace the one you have lost." She turned to her husband. "You will retrieve the money, please, and then

352

we shall be done with this unpleasantness."

"It is a long way from being done with, Danielle," he said with soft menace. "You may give what orders you please as to the care of the child and her family and I will deal with this ... person ..." He gestured disdainfully toward the cowering governor. "And then I shall deal with you." This last was said for her ears only and Danielle bit her lip as the walls of her determination began to crumble under the sure knowledge of her escape from one horror and the equal certainty that she was facing an icy rage, controlled now but barely so. Her eyes met Justin's in frightened appeal but there was no softening in the stony blue black gaze. She turned back to Brigitte.

"Come, let us leave this place." Taking the girl's hand again, she walked stiff backed down the corridor and out into the March sunlight.

Justin watched the rigid stance, thought of what she had been through, of the reckless impulse that had put herself and their child in acute danger, and for a moment his rage turned on himself. He had allowed her too much freedom, yielded too often to the self-determination that was *not* the right of any woman, any wife. He was her husband and husbands *must* be obeyed. He had been gullible for long enough, tolerant and easygoing for long enough. She had betrayed his trust and taken advantage of his understanding. He swung round to vent his pent-up fury on the governor and within minutes had the hundred guineas in his pocket and was striding across the courtyard, leaving hell upon earth at his back.

Had he been capable of the softer emotions at this point, he would have found the scene outside the jail affecting. The child was sobbing in the arms of her weeping family while Danielle, swathed in the cloak, stood to one side. The horses under the care of Malcolm, Tomas, and the urchin stood quietly in spite of the emotions of the spectators who yelled encouragement or wept tears of vicarious sympathy for the happy reunion.

But Justin, Earl of Linton, was filled only with a black glacier of rage and it would be much later before he recalled the scene and saw truly what his wife had achieved. He broke up the group like an avenging angel, sweeping his wife, in mid-sentence into the curricle, ordering Malcolm to follow them with the Robertses to Grosvenor Square. The urchin was told that if he wished for a job in the Linton stables he should go along with Malcolm, and the wiry figure scrambled onto the box of the chaise, a delighted beam on the grubby face.

"Let go their heads, Tomas." The tiger obeyed instantly, glad that he was not in Lady Danny's shoes at the moment. The anger radiating from my lord's powerful frame was an almost palpable force, although he spoke not a word throughout the entire journey.

Danielle sat beside him, shrouded in the cloak, the hood pulled well down over her scratched face. She began to shiver with aftermath and trepidation. Never had she seen her husband look as he did now, and never had she been so devoid of ideas as to how to placate him.

The curricle drew up outside Linton House and the chaise followed almost immediately. Justin alighted and lifted his wife from the seat. Ignoring her protestations he carried her into the house. "Send for Dr. Stuart, Bedford, and ask the housekeeper to see to the needs of the family. She will know what to do."

"Yes, my lord." Bedford bowed, discreetly ignoring the small figure in His Lordship's arms. What a to-do in a nobleman's household! But the butler was supreme at his job and with very few members of the staff any the wiser, had the Robertses ensconced in a back bedchamber, a footman dispatched to Harley Street, and everyone continuing about their business as if nothing untoward had occurred.

"Justin, I do not wish to see Stuart," Danielle declared unwisely as he set her on her feet in her bedchamber.

"I have no interest whatsoever in your wishes, madam," he informed her coldly. "Molly, you will fetch boiling water, towels, salve, and antiseptic immediately." Molly, completely at sea as to what catastrophe had transpired, bobbed a curtsy and fled the room, glad to be away from this suddenly awful presence of her master.

Justin unfastened the thick cloak and tossed it over a chair, still holding Danielle by a supporting arm. He examined her appearance with visible distaste. "You are a disgusting sight. Just look at yourself." His voice shook with suppressed fury as he pushed her in front of the pier glass.

Danielle averted her head, shrinking from the image of the bedraggled creature. In addition to the oozing scratches on face and breasts, large bruises were purpling on her cheek and arms and the ones on her legs and back throbbed beneath the ripped garments. She said nothing as Justin stripped away her clothes, throwing them into a heap on the floor.

"Get on the bed," he rasped, and she stumbled to obey, desperately thinking of something she could say that would return her husband to this stranger's body. But nothing came to mind and then Molly reappeared, staggering under the weight of a steaming jug and her other burdens. "Fill the ewer and bring it here," the unfamiliar harsh voice instructed. "Thank you. Take those clothes and burn them; then you may await Dr. Stuart belowstairs. Show him up as soon as he arrives."

Danielle heard the door close on the only friend she appeared to have at this moment and fought down the hot sparking tears of misery and fright.

"This will hurt." Justin shook antiseptic onto a towel, "but there is no knowing what filth those women carry beneath their nails." He washed the scratches thoroughly and she held herself rigidly still beneath the stinging pain of the antiseptic and his minute exploration of every inch of her skin for further open wounds. He washed her from head to toe with scalding water, lifting her limbs, turning her over with all the detachment he might have shown to a rag doll. And Danielle endured in silence. There was nothing rough about his movements as he anointed the bruises with cool salve, but there was little of tenderness, either. When he handed her a nightgown she put it on, her embryo protest at bed-in-the-afternoon dying in the face of that cold mask and thin lips.

Dr. Stuart bustled into the room with many apologies for the delay in responding to the summons. He'd been attending a birthing, but all had gone well, thanks be. Now what was amiss with My Lady Linton? His tone was jocular until he realized from the grim set of the earl's expression and the ashen face of the countess on the pillow that such an approach was inappropriate.

355

"Her Ladyship has suffered an accident—a fall from her horse," Linton informed him. "I am concerned about the child." There was the slightest emphasis on the "I" and Danielle's spirit curled in on itself in despair. How could he think that she was not also concerned? But then she had given him little evidence to believe so.

Stuart, tut-tutting in a suitably anxious tone, begged leave to examine Her Ladyship and Justin, without a word, pulled back the sheet and stood beside the bed as the doctor prodded Danielle's abdomen, asked if there was any pain, and then asked if she had yet felt the child quicken.

"This morning," Danielle said in a dull monotone, "for the first time."

"Was this before the fall, my lady?" Stuart asked, continuing to palpate her belly that still showed only the smallest curvature.

"Yes," she said unhappily, seeing Justin turn away with a muttered exclamation. How could she explain in front of the doctor that by the time she had felt the life stirring in her womb she had gone too far to withdraw. And would it have made any difference anyway? She had certainly forgot the fact of her pregnancy when she had taken up the cudgels for Brigitte Roberts, but even reminded of it she would not have done otherwise. It was quite inescapable and there were no apologies she was prepared to make. Something had happened that she could have done nothing to prevent. She would have gone into that cage to rescue Brigitte Roberts if the need had arisen four months hence as automatically as she had done so while her pregnancy was still invisible and unknown to all but the few.

"As there is no pain, my lord, and no bleeding we can hope that no damage has been done." Stuart pulled the sheet up. "It would be best if Her Ladyship remained in bed for three days and she should take an opiate now to still any restlessness. If her body is quiet then any disturbance to the child will be remedied."

"That will be done," Justin said. "How soon will it be safe for her to travel?"

"I would not advise a long journey, my lord."

356

"I am not suggesting one, just into Hampshire, by slow stages."

"In three days, then. If there are no adverse signs in the meantime."

Danielle listened to a conversation that was about her but took no account of her presence. She was powerless to interrupt, to demand what her husband had in mind, to protest the draught of laudanum that Stuart was pouring from a small vial—powerless until the physician left and she could face her husband in privacy.

She turned her head away, though, when the physician offered her the opiate and Justin said, "You may leave that with me."

"As you wish, my lord." The door closed behind Molly and Stuart.

"Drink this." Justin picked up the glass.

"No." Danielle sat up in fierce determination. "I have no need of it. I will rest, if that is what you wish, but I will not be drugged. Justin, please let us discuss what has happened. I do not think you understand . . ."

"I understand well enough," he interrupted harshly. "I understand that you are not to be trusted to take a care for yourself or for our child in your womb; that you are not to be trusted to keep your word and from this moment on I shall make a proper wife of you, madam. I accept full share of the blame but I will correct my faults as you will correct yours. Now, drink."

"No." But he moved behind her, catching her head in the crook of his arm, holding her with one arm as the other reached for the glass.

"You will," he hissed, tilting her head backward. Her mouth opened in protest and Justin tipped the contents of the glass down her throat, clamping her mouth shut until she swallowed with a choking gasp.

"How dare you!" Danny hurled herself at him as he released her from the vise of his arm. She had endured physical abuse this day for more hours than she could bear to remember and to receive such treatment from the one person who had always

357

viewed her body as a shrine, in whom she had reposed complete trust and confidence, shattered the last straws of her composure.

"Stop!" He seized her wrists. "I'll not have you causing any further damage to yourself or to the child." He pushed her facedown on the tumbled bed, clipping her wrists in the small of her back, and with a low defeated moan Danielle gave in, wondering as she did so whether she would ever be able to forgive her husband for this.

"*Lâches-moi*," she whispered and Justin released her instantly, a panicky shaft of compassion stabbing him as she turned on her side in a tight fetal curl. Gently he pulled the cover over her and went to sit on the chaise longue until her deep breathing told him that the sedative had taken effect.

Chapter 18

Danielle awoke some eight hours later, her throat dry and head fogged from the drug-induced sleep. But her body was languid with relaxation and she felt again the wondrous quiver in her belly that told her all was well with the babe. Her hands stroked comfortingly over her abdomen as her body whispered its message of loving reassurance to the life it contained.

"My lady?"

"What time is it, Molly?" Too lazy to sit up, Danielle turned her head on the pillow, smiling at the maid who now stood by the bed, her face anxious in the shadowy light of the single candle on the mantel.

"About ten o'clock, my lady. Can I bring you anything?"

"Some tea, please. I have a powerful thirst."

"I will bring it directly." Molly left and went speedily downstairs. She had been instructed to inform the earl the minute his wife woke, but with defiant bravery Molly decided to provide the tea first. A dreadful heaviness hung over the house and even the servants' quarters were affected. They all knew now much of what had happened, both Malcolm and Tomas being anxious to recount the story. Malcolm's tale in particular had fired the realm belowstairs with a fierce partisanship for Lady Danny—a partisanship that even Bedford had found himself sharing in spite of the shocking nature of Her Ladyship's actions. But when matters were going so badly abovestairs, those below could only keep the lowest profile imaginable and hope for a resolution between master and mistress.

Only Peter Haversham was unaware of the facts. His position did not allow him to question either the servants or his grim-faced employer. He knew only that something appalling had occurred and obeyed the terse instructions to arrange for the removal of the household to Danesbury for an extended period of time in discreet silence.

Molly brought tea to Danielle's bedside, brushed Her Ladyship's hair, and assisted her in washing away the sleep from her eyes before saying tentatively, "My Lord wished to know when you awoke, my lady. May I tell him?"

"Indeed you may, Molly." Danielle smiled reassuringly. "I thank you for your patience. You need have no fear that your delay will have unpleasant consequences."

"No, my lady." Molly smiled a smile of gratitude, comprehension, and friendship.

In her absence, Danielle sipped the tea, the hot fragrant liquid restoring some of her strength. She and Justin were about to have as monumental a fight as they had ever had and it must be the last on the issue of her independence. Their marriage would be made or broken on this rack of conflict and she knew only that it must be made.

Justin, having partaken of a solitary and seemingly tasteless dinner, was sitting in the library staring moodily into the fire when Molly tapped lightly at the door.

"Come in."

Molly shivered slightly at the bleak look on his face. "My Lady is awake, sir."

"Thank you." The girl left and Justin remained staring into the fire for a few minutes longer before getting heavily to his feet. He didn't think he had ever been more miserable as he trod up the stairs, and the main source of his misery was that he was about to make his wife very unhappy. But what possible choice did he have? If she was unable to take care of herself in an appropriate fashion, then he was going to have to assume that responsibility himself. She was still barely more than a child—just turned nineteen—in spite of her experiences, and she reacted to situations with all the willful impulsiveness of a child who had grown up with few external controls.

The sight of the small battered face on the pillow merely reaffirmed his determination. "How do you feel?" Taking her chin between long fingers he turned her face to the light, examining the scratch carefully. It looked clean enough, although still raw. "Unbutton your gown," he instructed quietly and she did so, revealing the claw marks on her breasts. When he expressed satisfaction with a curt nod, she buttoned the gown again and lay back against the pillow, waiting.

"You will remain in this room for the next two days," he began. "Apart from the fact that you need to rest, you are not a fit sight for anyone but myself and Molly."

Danielle winced at the cold statement, but she was in no position to argue with the truth so kept silent.

"On Friday we will remove to Daneshury where you will remain until just before your confinement. Then we shall return to London so that Stuart may attend you when the time comes. Since it is now clear that I cannot trust you to behave with any degree of circumspection any more than I can trust your word, I shall not let you out of my sight for the next four months."

"Justin, you must listen to me," Danielle said desperately. "I do not wish to go to . . ."

"You have a short memory, ma'am," he interrupted in glacial tones. "I have said once today that your wishes are no longer of the slightest interest to me. All that concerns me is your obedience and I give you fair warning that I shall compel it in whatever manner is necessary. You are reckless, foolhardy, stubborn, and abominably spoiled. I bear considerable blame for the latter, but it is not, I hope, too late to rectify my mistake."

"You cannot talk to me in that manner!" Danielle broke out, anger replacing her earlier despairing hopelessness. "I had no choice but to do what I did. Would you have had me leave the child in that hellhole? You saw what they had done to her in the space of a few hours. God alone knows what would have happened next. And as to my breaking my word, I did so only in the most precise sense. I did all I could to find you in the time available; I left you a message telling you exactly what I was doing; I was attended by *your* coachman. There was no secrecy

361

and no deception and I will not stand to hear you accuse me of behaving dishonorably."

Justin looked down at her, the pale cheeks flushed with outrage, the brown eyes huge with indignation. "There is logic in what you say, but the fact remains that I trusted you not to break a promise and you did. Whatever reasons you may have had for doing so, I do not consider them to be sufficient."

"Have you *no* compassion?" she threw at him. "How can you stand there talking self-righteously about promises when a child's life was at stake?"

"And did you once consider the life of *our* child when you rushed to the rescue?" he gritted, white now with the resurgence of his anger.

"It would have made no difference had I done so." Her voice was low. "It was a question of priorities and necessary risks. I am sorry if we do not agree on priorities and necessary risks but I shall continue to do what I consider right."

Justin wanted to shake her, shake her until those pearly teeth rattled and the defiance left her eyes, never to return. He took a step toward her, seizing her arms. Danielle winced as his fingers bit deep into a deep bruise, but she met his gaze without flinching and with a shuddering breath he released her. "You may thank your stars for your pregnancy, madam. It is the only thing restraining me at the moment." He gave her a mocking bow and left the room, desperate to get away from the maddening creature before he finally lost control.

Danielle did not sleep at all that night. Her bruises throbbed and her limbs ached, but the drugged sleep of the afternoon had done its work too well and she felt no fatigue. The scene with her husband went round and round in her fevered brain and she could pluck no straws of hope from anything that had been said. They were at total impasse and if she refused to yield Justin would force her to do so. If he did that, then there was no possibility of regaining their old footing. Danielle knew with absolute certainty that she could endure no relationship where she must be subservient, must obey the dictates of a master whether she considered them reasonable or not. But she loved her husband with every fiber of her being and knew that he loved her in the same way. So what was to be done?

At dawn she fell into a fitful sleep haunted by faces laughing in derision through blackened stumps; long talons that became the claws of a menacing flock of giant crows reached to tear her as she struggled to run on feet of cement. An enormous figure that she knew was Justin swept her up as she fell beneath her pursuers, but when she clung, sobbing with relief, she saw that he had no face.

The wracking sobs reached Justin next door as he lay staring into the early morning light, his thoughts, had he known it, identical to Danielle's. With a muttered exclamation he hurtled from the room and gazed in horror at the sweat-soaked figure writhing in the twisted sheets, tears coursing down her cheeks from beneath the closed eyes.

"Danny, wake up." He touched her shoulder urgently and her limbs flailed in unconscious panic catching him a glancing blow on the chin. "Danny!"

Her eyes shot open and she stared at him in total lack of recognition that he found more frightening than anything else. Swiftly, he disentangled her from the sheets and scooped her into his arms, sitting on the bed to rock her with soft nonsense words until the shudders ceased.

"You didn't have a face," she moaned. "It wasn't there. It was you but it wasn't—just a horrible white shapeless blank."

"Hush, now," he crooned, placing her hand on his cheek. "I have a face, my love. You can feel it and see it. It was just a nightmare."

She lay quietly in his arms then, as reality reasserted itself and the dream made sense and so lost its terror. "What are we to do, Justin? I understand that you were angry and . . . and frightened at what could have happened, and I did react without proper thought, although even if I had thought I would still have taken the same action. But I shall not be able to bear it if you make a prisoner of me and nothing will ever be right between us again."

"But how am I ever to have a moment's peace?" he asked, stroking the damp curls from her brow. "You will follow no course but your own and that is a course I can never predict. For the child's sake, Danny, I *must* remove you from temptation. There is no need for us to be miserable at

Danesbury and surely the prospect of my exclusive company is not *too* distasteful." He offered a teasing smile but Danielle did not respond.

"You do not understand what I am saying. You are right in saying that I will follow my own course, but that is because I *must*. I am not your possession, Justin; I belong only to myself. I love you with all my heart but you will not succeed in shaping me to your requirements. You may succeed in imprisoning my body and only *I* would question your right to do so, but there will be no gain for either of us, only the greatest loss."

Dear God! Justin looked down at the determined face in helpless frustration. "I am sorry, Danielle, but I must do what I must do," he said with quiet finality. "You must learn where your true priorities lie, and there is no one to teach you but myself. If you resist me, then we shall, indeed, be miserable, but in the interests of the greater good, that is a consequence I am prepared to accept." Quite gently, he put her back on the bed.

"My happiness means nothing to you, then?" Danielle turned her head to the wall.

"On the contrary, it means a great deal to me. But I believe you will be happier when you have learned to behave in a proper way, consonant with your position in society. You are still a child, Danielle, but you are soon to be a mother—the mother of *my* child. It is time to put your own childish willfulness behind you." He pulled the bell rope by the bed. "You must now get out of that soaked nightgown, take a hot bath, and return to bed with your chocolate. I will visit you later, and if I find you disobedient then, I shall be obliged to assume the role of jailer."

Justin left the room without another word, brushing past Molly who had appeared in the doorway in answer to the summons.

"What may I do for you, m'lady?" Molly approached the bed, looking in horror at her mistress's deathly pallor, the dry eyes huge and stricken.

"Nothing," Danielle said. She would not involve Molly in this that would bring the story of her marriage full circle. "I wish only to be left alone to sleep. Do not come again until noon."

Molly looked uncertain, but there was a grim determination in Her Ladyship's expression and voice that the servant knew not how to question. Bobbing a curtsy, she also left.

Danny met the first obstacle to her plan when she tried to fasten the britches that she had not worn for two months. It was quite impossible; so she would not be able to leave Justin's life exactly in the manner in which she had entered it. Shrugging, she dressed in her plainest riding habit, wincing at the renewed throb of her bruised legs as she walked around the chamber, gathering together the few possessions she would take. The de St. Varennes jewels were her own. How she would contrive to sell them, Danielle had as yet no idea, but there was no immediate urgency. She had money enough for a few months, and friends aplenty amongst her compatriots in London who were not known to Justin, and who would take her in willingly.

After the child was born, she would move to some country village where she would have more than enough money to set up as a young widowed recluse . . . What in the devil's name was she doing? Danielle stared at herself in the mirror. After the child was born . . .! She had no right to deprive Linton's child of its birthright. She had no right to deprive Linton of his child. She was no longer a free agent who could run away at will from *anything*. She had conceived this child with clear thought and she had been about to expose it to . . . Sweet heaven, but her husband had been right. She was everything he had said—reckless, foolhardy, stubborn, spoiled. The thicket of her self-made prison sprang up like the thorny hedge enclosing the Sleeping Beauty. Desolately, she sat on the bed cradling her abdomen. . . .

The earl was at his breakfast when he received a visit from the elder Monsieur Roberts. With quiet dignity the visitor refused all offers of refreshment and explained that he had come to inquire after My Lady's health and to express, however inadequately, their gratitude. There were no words, of course, when the sanity of a child had been saved. Brigitte had at last been persuaded to talk of her experiences and it was to be hoped that since that was the case the horror would eventually recede.

Justin had listened to the dignified elder's speech with but half an ear, lost as he was in his own desolation. He *was* doing the right thing, wasn't he? Danielle *did* have to accept her changed position, one that she had freely chosen despite the restrictions it would place on her freedom. If she didn't see those necessary restrictions herself, then he had the absolute obligation to open her eyes . . . didn't he? He became aware that his visitor had fallen silent. The words "sanity," "horror" still hung in the air.

"What happened to her, monsieur? I would like to know if you can bear to tell me." He heard in horrified silence as the old man described the near rape of his granddaughter, the way her clothes had been ripped from her and she'd been rolled in the ordure-stained hay on the cell floor, filth rubbed into her hair. Justin heard again Danielle's ringing accusation: "Have you no compassion?" He felt shrunken, a tiny, self-centered atom beside his wife's vast imagination, total empathy and utterly selfless humanity. She had not gone into that cage blind to the danger; she had a pistol in her pocket, had removed all of value on her person and since she had attempted to put up bail she had presumably gone in only as a last resort. He relived the terrifying scene and at last saw all the pieces that his fear-fueled rage had repressed.

Danielle was like no other woman and she never would be. He'd been ranting and raving like a conventional outraged husband and he might just as well have saved his breath to cool his porridge. His choice was quite simple. Either he enforced his will, as was his right, and lost his wife as surely as if he had never met her, or he accepted her on her own terms—for she was her own person and would be true only to herself. He'd always known it, of course. Why else had a man of his years and experience fallen hopelessly in love with a tyrannical, indomitable virago, seventeen years his junior, who turned his life upside down with the merest lift of her little finger? And except when she scared the living daylights out of him, as she had done yesterday, he relished every unpredictable moment.

"Danielle has come to no great harm," he reassured Monsieur Roberts gently. "But she must keep to her bed for the next day or so. I will give her your news of Brigitte. It will put her mind at rest."

The old man bowed, and Linton escorted his visitor to the door with an impeccable courtesy that told Bedford and his staff very clearly that anyone, however apparently disreputable, who came to the house seeking an interview with either the earl or his countess, should not be turned away unilaterally.

Justin took the stairs two at a time and burst, without ceremony, into his wife's chamber. On the threshold, he stopped dead, his eyes taking in the half-filled portmanteau, the pearls spilling from the opened jewel box, the figure of Danielle, fully dressed, sitting like an effigy on the bed.

She had been intending to leave him, to run from a tyranny, a bondage, that she could never accept. His heart raced and the clammy sweat of fear misted his brow.

"Danielle, you must not. Please, you must not." He crossed to the bed, kneeling to take her cold hands in his. She gave him a blank stare.

"No, I know I must not. I carry your child and, therefore, no longer belong only to myself. You have an obedient possession, sir. I have no need of further lessons."

"You are the most exasperating creature, Danny!" Justin released her hands and stood upright. "I come to you, full of apologies, anxious to make amends, only to find you sitting like some broken reed! Now, get back into bed this instant, because I have a great deal to say to you. I am prepared to accept that I was in the wrong in every area except the physical one. You will stay in bed for the next twenty-four hours, and on that score alone I will brook no argument."

The words, as he had hoped, punctured Danielle's listless resignation. "What is it that you are saying?"

"At this point, only that if you are not back between the sheets by the time I have set this room to rights, I shall summon up the energy to give you the trouble you have been asking for with such patience since first we met."

The blood that seemed to have coagulated in her veins began again to flow, warmed by the teasing note in his voice, the note that declared a return to normal. He was bullying her in the old way, the private loving way that conjured up the past and was not to be taken seriously.

Danielle threw off her clothes and slid into the tumbled bed, watching as Justin removed from other eyes all traces of her impending flight.

He turned to her and smiled, coming to sit on the bed beside her. "I have been very foolish," Justin said, taking her hands again. "The only excuse I can offer is that I was frightened out of my wits and they have only just returned to me."

"I also . . ." she began, but he laid a finger over her lips.

"No, you have not been foolish. You did what was right, and when you were about to do what was not right . . . to run from this . . . you found yourself unable to do so." He raised her hand to his lips, kissing her palm, before continuing with quiet resolution.

"My love, for the duration of your pregnancy will you agree to provide assistance only from this house? There must be others who can do some of what you do, not as well, I'm convinced, but they can be adequate replacements temporarily. There is no reason why you should not receive your people here, listen to the problems, and decide what is to be done. I accept that there will be emergencies and will ensure that you always know where I am to be found."

When she said nothing, only played intently with his fingers, he went on. "You must understand that this is simply a request—something that I am asking you to do for me. If you cannot agree to it, then I will manage as best I may. But I would like to feel that I and our child are as important to you as the rest of the world. We may not suffer so dramatically but you are all and everything to me, my love, and are certainly so to that babe and will be for many years to come."

A tear splashed hot on his hand. "*Tiens!* Now look what you have done." Danny sniffed vigorously. "You are so clever to turn the tables in that way. Now I feel miserably guilty instead of cross and determined to make you see things from my point of view."

"You have already done so, Danny. It is because you have that we are talking in this way. But you have not yet said whether you will accede to my request."

"You have left me no choice, milord, as well you know. I will resist your commands, but I am quite incapable of resisting such an appeal to my love for you and to my common sense. It will always be so. You may, on occasion, have to remind me of these things when I become involved in other matters, but you will have no need to play the bully again." She looked at him directly, without accusation or rancor but with firm assertion.

Justin sighed. "You needed the laudanum, Danielle, and I was too angry to reason with you. I cannot promise not to do the same again in similar circumstances."

Danny chuckled suddenly, and the sound brought Justin the most blessed relief. "This is a splendid conversation. We are dancing around each other, giving a little here and a little there. It is a true game of compromise, I think, but we understand each other now?"

"I understand that I am wedded to a lifetime of headaches and anxiety and that the woman in my bed will be the mother of my children only when she chooses and belongs only to herself and accepts no jurisdiction but her own. I am mad to accept it and even more so for liking it. I just beg that you will keep my hag-ridden existence a secret from Society."

"You are not hag-ridden!"

"Am I not?" His eyebrows shot up. "And by a nineteen-year-old-chit to add insult to injury."

Danny squirmed from beneath the sheets with an agile twist and flung herself against him, bearing him down onto the bed in helpless laughter. As they tumbled together, Justin, mindful of her bruises and delicate condition, found himself at a considerable disadvantage.

"Vagabond!" He managed to catch her hands eventually and yanked her arms above her head, scissoring her legs between his own. "Yield, you impossible wretch."

"I yield." Her body became soft beneath him; the brown

369

eyes glowed an invitation.

It was an invitation Justin ached to accept, and he shook his head with the greatest reluctance. "My love, you are not in a fit condition."

Danielle pulled a face, comical in its disgusted resignation. "No, I suppose I am not. You will not, however, expect me to restrain myself for more than one more day." Suddenly serious, she took his hand and pressed it to her belly. "Perhaps you cannot feel it yet, but our child is awake, my love. I think he is going to be in much mischief when he feels his feet."

"That would not surprise me in the least," Justin murmured, "since you will be guiding his steps."

She smiled and lay back on the bed. "It is a son, Justin."

"How can you know that?" Lying beside her he began to stroke her body in a long languid caress, carefully circumventing the bruises on her legs and arms.

"I know it." She smiled softly. "Women's witchcraft, husband."

On the night of June 21, 1791, Dr. Stuart was aroused from his bed by a sleepy manservant. His presence was required immediately in Grosvenor Square and the Linton chaise waited at the door. He dressed hastily but still careful of the folds of his cravat, the set of his coat. One did not assist at the *accouchement* of a countess in slovenly fashion, however inconvenient the hour; and babies were notoriously inconsiderate when it came to night and day. Hat correctly in place, bag of instruments in hand, the court physician entered the chaise with a calm disregard for the coachman's impatience. First babies were never in a hurry to enter the world.

Bedford stood in the open doorway, the lights of the hall throwing his figure into sharp relief as the carriage drew up. He was dressed as usual in dark cloth, not a fold or hair out of place, but there was both anxiety and excitement on his face. It was three o'clock in the morning and the entire household appeared to be up and about. Housemaids in dressing gowns popped up from behind pillars and in the corridors; Peter

Haversham in shirt and britches paced the hall; knots of footmen tried to look as if they had some work to attend to at this ungodly hour and Bedford, in his wisdom, made no attempt to send them about their business. A child would soon be born and while Lady Danny labored an anxious household kept watch and waited.

Stuart followed Bedford upstairs. No cries of agony reached him as he walked along the corridor to My Lady's bedchamber where the butler discreetly withdrew, leaving him to make his own entrance. As he did so a voice said distinctly, *"Mon Dieu! C'est abominable!* Give me your hand, Justin."

"You have it already, my love." The calm unmistakable voice of the Earl of Linton reached the doctor who stood blinking bemusedly at this unusually orderly scene.

"You do not mind that I hurt you . . . *Jésu!"* A gasp of pained protest drowned whatever else Danielle had been about to say as she used her husband's hand, disdaining the knotted bedsheet hanging ready from the bedpost to transfer some of the convulsive pain of this process of birthing.

"My lord, here is more lavender water." Molly handed Linton a fresh cloth and he nodded, ignoring the scrunching of his knuckles as he bathed the sweat-drenched brow on the pillow.

The physician looked around for a moment. The room was brightly lit, kettles of boiling water steamed beside the fire. His patient was attended by the Countess of March, brisk in an enormous white apron, the maidservant, and most extraordinarily by her husband. Husbands, in Stuart's extensive experience, *never* appeared in the birthing room.

"Ah, Doctor." Lady Lavinia turned to him. "The child appears to be in the birth canal, but there has been no progress for the last fifteen minutes."

Stuart scrubbed his hands vigorously in the bowl Molly held for him and nodded his comprehension. Women giving birth for the first time rarely knew what to do.

"I think that the next time I shall scream," Danielle said prosaically. "But you must not worry if I do." The physician exchanged an astonished look with Lady Lavinia but the

371

scream never came, only a stream of French that only Justin understood, fortunately for the delicate sensibilities of their companions.

Stuart made his own examination and his own decision. This woman was not one of his usual patients, out of her head with pain and embarrassment at her predicament. "My lady, you must push the child into the world now. It needs your help."

"Only tell me how," she gasped.

"Your body will tell you if you listen." It was the only answer he was able to give, never having gone through this himself. But having witnessed countless births he knew that some women were able to give spontaneous birth whilst others with no explainable physical difference were not. The more practice they had, of course, the better they became. This child was headfirst and its mother well in control and it would be a pity to have recourse to the shining instruments in his bag. They left marks on the child and tore the mother.

Danielle paused and let the pain have its way and then realized that this was not pain. What had happened before deserved no other name, but what she was experiencing now was a powerful physical demand, one that if she obeyed it produced no agony, only satisfaction. Her body, freed from the constraints of her mind, reacted automatically. As it contracted, she pushed, feeling the child make the long progress into life. There was a moment when Justin gasped—the moment when a sleek head appeared between her thighs and Stuart took over with smooth efficiency.

Nicholas, Viscount Beresford, catapulted into the world with a loud yell of protest, sound of wind and limb, to be held by his father while the cord was cut and tied and his great-grandmother wept freely and his mother demanded that her son be given to her this instant. Justin laid the blood-streaked scrap against her breast without attempting to control his own tears of joy, before taking the physician downstairs and informing the hovering household that his son and heir was healthy, Her Ladyship well, and anyone who wished to toast the baby's head should do so in the best champagne.

The lights blazed in Grosvenor Square that night and the champagne flowed. Danielle examined her son, counted his

372

fingers and toes, and gave him her breast. The child sucked greedily. When Linton eventually came back to the bedroom, intending to kiss his wife good night and disappear next door, she clung to him and said she was cold and needed him beside her. He put little Nicholas into the crib beside the bed and, ignoring all convention, climbed in to hold Danielle throughout the remainder of the night.

Chapter 19

On the night that the infant Viscount Beresford burst vociferously into the world, the seeds of tragedy were being watered in a small French town some ten miles from Verdun. The town bore the same name as the woman laboring in the peace of Grosvenor Square in a country where civil strife had been done with over a hundred years ago.

In the town of Varennes the tocsin pealed on the night of June 21, rousing the citizens and neighboring peasantry. They flocked in their thousands to bar the entrances to the town, to gape at and to secure the hapless family of Bourbons held in a room over an *épicerie* belonging to one Monsieur Sauce, the *procureur* of the commune who, in the absence of the mayor, had exercised his authority to halt the travelers in their four-horsed berline and to demand their passports.

The royal flight from the Tuileries had been planned with meticulous care over many months and only a chapter of accidents for which no one person was to blame resulted in its sorry conclusion.

During the winter and spring of Danielle's tempestuous pregnancy, the Comte de St. Estèphe became one of Marie Antoinette's closest confidants. After the return from their summer holiday in St. Cloud the previous October, the royal family had been made increasingly aware of the true nature of their imprisonment in the gloom of the Tuileries. The king reluctantly agreed to the secularization of the clergy but continued to practice his religion in the orthodox manner, refusing to acknowledge the bishops and parish curés who had taken the oath of allegiance to the constitution. In Louis's opinion they were mere minions of the state who had abjured papal authority and as such had no authority to hear the king's confession or to offer communion. The tide of public feeling ran high against a king who was not strong enough to refuse to accede to a measure he loathed and too stubborn to pretend that it had his personal approval.

Marie Antoinette, no longer the child who played shepherdess in the Petit Trianon while the people starved, finally accepted that the monarchy could never regain its popularity; they were prisoners of the people's whim and their only course was to break the chains. She busied herself with plans for flight—a flight that would take them under the protective umbrella of her family; a flight that would follow the path of so many aristocratic émigrés to Coblenz and the Austrian court. From there they would march on France, quell the revolution, and restore the Bourbons to an undisputed throne.

St. Estèphe listened to the elaborate plans, ran messages for his queen, heard her secrets while he planted the spies amongst the maidservants and flunkeys, and reported back faithfully to the revolutionary committee. And all the while he contemplated the abduction and eventual submission of the Countess of Linton. He learned much from the Chevalier D'Evron on his visits to Paris—information that made sense of that lady's extraordinary behavior during her stay at the Tuileries. An unsuspecting D'Evron, thankful only to find a self-styled friend of the Lintons who abhorred the possibility of blood and terror in his native land, spoke freely. St. Estèphe hugged his excitement; she would not be easy to break if all the chevalier said was true, but his pleasure would be all the greater.

On the day that Danielle fought for the life and sanity of Brigitte Roberts, the chevalier, in the company of St. Estèphe, witnessed Dagger Day. A mob, incited by a rumor that the royal family were intending to flee Paris by an underground corridor from the Tuileries to the prison at Vincennes, marched on the donjon at Vincennes. Nobles flocked to the Tuileries, armed to defend their king, and rumor was seen as confirmed. As far as the mob was concerned, their king had made an abortive attempt at flight and nothing could change that impression. He was no longer to be trusted as a supporter of the new regime and could be classified with the traitorous aristos who made up the émigré court at Coblenz—rich, dissipated, and riddled with plots to summon foreign powers to their side and put down the insurrection in their country.

From that moment the king's fate was sealed. Two months later, St. Estèphe stood in the inner court of the Tuileries palace watching as Louis XVI's attempt to take his family early for the traditional summer holiday at St. Cloud was aborted by a riotous crowd, yelling protest as they surrounded the coach, ignoring the harangues of the king's generals and advisers, ignoring the king himself as, for two hours, he attempted to persuade them that flight had been far from his mind. What had been on his mind was that in the seclusion of St. Cloud he would be able to celebrate Easter under the auspices of a non-juror priest and the public would be none the wiser. Instead, the people of Paris had seen only treachery. Eventually the royal family was forced to return to their rooms in the Tuileries.

St. Estèphe slipped from the courtyard. There was no longer any doubt but that the king and queen of France were prisoners; the last shreds of pretense had been torn away by the events of this day. Knowing Marie Antoinette as he now did, the *comte* was in no doubt that she would work to perfect her plans for escape, sure in the knowledge that there was no alternative.

The plan would fail, St. Estèphe decided, and he would do his part in ensuring that it did. And when it failed his own path would be clear. There would be no further need for duplicity—courting the queen, listening in patient attention to the complaints, the elaborate plans, reporting in secret to the committee. The reign of the Bourbons would be over and the sovereignty of the people absolute. At that point he would cast in his lot with the power-makers, consolidate his position, and find an official reason to visit London. He would offer his services to the chevalier and the Countess of Linton and by so doing achieve a double purpose—the trust of the young countess and valuable information for his government.

Nearly two months later the flight took place. St. Estèphe, to his fury, was left at the starting gate. He had thought he was in the queen's total confidence but realized that he had merely been used as a useful subject on the far outskirts of the coterie.

The fact that he had not known the details or the timing of the escape plan would not increase his status with the committee.

The plan was elaborate, circumventing the care of the Paris commune, alerted through St. Estèphe via one of the queen's maids that an attempt at escape was imminent. The mayor of Paris and the commandant of the palace guard were spending the night of June 20 in the Tuileries. Guards were posted throughout, but in the southeast corner of the palace there was one door left unwatched. It led directly by an unlighted passage to the royal apartments. The children, Madame Royale, and the dauphin, who was disguised as a girl, made their escape first. The king, dressed in gray coat and wig, impersonating a valet, followed some forty-five minutes later from the Petit Carousel at the north end of the Tuileries. At midnight, the queen appeared, dressed as a governess, and the journey began.

Twenty-four hours later it ended in ignominy at Varennes. The royal family were turned back and returned to Paris under escort, the third time in two years that Louis had been brought back as a prisoner to his capital.

The course of the revolution was finally set. Danielle, playing with her month-old baby on a rug beneath a spreading beach tree at Danesbury, heard D'Evron's account of the declaration of martial law—the massacre of the Champs de Mars when defenseless civilians were fired upon for no apparent reason by cavalry, artillery, and infantry, and the subsequent denunciations, arrests, and imprisonments in the name of public safety. Paris was now a panic-stricken city of hard faced, rebellious people who had lost all faith in their king and all trust in a National Assembly that could decree martial law and murder the people. The word "Republic" was on everyone's lips. The stage was set for the rule of the mob and the Reign of Terror.

"It is beginning then," Danielle said, absently tickling little Nicholas with a long stalk of grass. "The mob is a fearsome many-headed hydra when aroused. We shall have much work to do soon, chevalier." She frowned, biting her lower lip. "Our own kind will begin to flee in droves. There will be no safety for them when the people declare a republic."

"They have not done so yet, Danny," Linton reminded her.

There was something about that frown that made him distinctly uneasy.

"No, but they will," she said with quiet conviction. "It is only a matter of time. If it could be established without blood, a republic would be for the best, I think. The people have suffered too long under the *ancien régime*, but it will not happen peacefully and much as I despise many of my own kind, I cannot sit by and watch their slaughter."

Linton sighed. "You are not, I hope, proposing to visit Paris yourself and halt the progress of this horror with your little finger? Not that I don't think you could do it," he added with a grin. "The mere sight of you would turn Robespierre into a purring kitten."

The chevalier chuckled, but Danielle said somberly, "I do not consider it a laughing matter. You forget, perhaps, what I have seen."

The warm summer afternoon seemed to take on a chill and even the peaceful droning of the honey bees seemed to pause. The baby's face crumpled and he let out a loud wail. "*Ah, tu as faim, mon petit.*" Danielle lifted him up and rose to her feet. "I must feed him at once." She hurried across the lawn toward the mellow, timbered Elizabethan house, soothing the child's wails with promises of imminent satisfaction.

Justin watched her, smiling slightly. His son never had the opportunity to exercise his lungs since the smallest expression of need was instantly answered. As a result, the little viscount was plump and sunny tempered in his solipsistic world. But since he was rarely out of his mother's arms, Justin strongly suspected that they were in for trouble when they returned to London and Danielle found it impossible to be all and everything to the child for twenty-four hours a day.

"I do not think motherhood has changed her very much," the chevalier observed with the ease of friendship. "I would not put it past her to confront Robespierre and Danton."

"Neither would I, my friend. But if you can contrive to keep her sufficiently busy in London, we may perhaps avert my having to resist such a plan. We have been living in considerable harmony since the debacle at Newgate and I have no desire to disturb it."

The Lintons returned to London in October. The infant Nicholas, his nurse, nursery maid, and all the possessions considered necessary for his comfort were ensconced in a second chaise, while Molly occupied the first in solitary state, Danielle having chosen to ride in the company of her husband and Peter Haversham.

For a full day after their arrival, Linton House was turned upside down by a tempestuous countess who declared the traditional nursery apartments quite inadequate in their present condition for her son. They were too dark, shabby, and cramped; she did not care for the color scheme or the furnishings and something must be done immediately. When Linton observed mildly that they had been considered well enough for him, he had been roundly informed that there was no reason to visit *his* deprivations on the next generation.

The nursery party was housed temporarily in the west wing while an army of painters and decorators tore down the old curtains, covered the nursery walls with crisp white paint, the woodwork with glossy scarlet, and the floors with a deep blue carpet. Bright curtains fluttered at the windows and cheerful chintzes covered chairs and cushions before Danielle eventually pronounced herself satisfied and the household heaved a sigh of relief.

Not for long, however. Five days later, Justin walked into the hall after a leisurely ride in Hyde Park to be met by a hysterical nurse and a raging Danielle in driving dress, holding a bawling Nicholas.

"Out, woman, this instant!" Danielle pointed dramatically to the door.

"What the devil's going on?" His Lordship demanded.

"This . . . this . . . Oh, *c'est insupportable*! The only words that I can think of, I cannot use!" Danny stormed. "Hush now, *mon petit chou*, hush." The crimson-faced baby yelled louder and Justin took his son firmly out of his mother's arms.

"You are not going to calm Nicky unless you calm yourself," he said with good reason, patting the child's back. "Let us continue this unseemly scene in a little privacy." He strode to the library and the little viscount hiccupped and ceased his wailing as the steady hand on his back continued its comforting work and the strong familiar arms provided a safe haven from the chaos that had abruptly disrupted his orderly world.

Danielle followed, her skirts swirling under her impetuous stride. "I am sorry, but it is beyond bearing, Justin." Her voice was calmer now but the brown eyes blazed. "That . . . that . . . woman out there!" She gestured vigorously to the hall as she closed the door. "Nicky has been crying for hours while she has been sitting in the servants' hall gossiping! And she actually said that it was good for him not to have what he wanted sometimes if he was not to become spoiled! How dare she? I went out for two hours, just for a drive with Philip, and my child is *tortured* in my absence."

"That's a rather dramatic way of putting it," Justin murmured, sitting down in an armchair and giving Nicholas his seal to play with. It disappeared instantly into the small mouth and Justin wiped the residue of tears from the button nose and brown eyes. The child was the spitting image of his mother.

"It is not at all dramatic," Danielle maintained, but her eyes softened as she looked at them. "The woman must go. She's not fit to care for a child."

"Not for *your* child maybe," Justin said carefully. "By all means give her her papers, but she must have a month's wages in lieu of notice and a note of character. It would be unjust to do otherwise since her practices would be considered perfectly acceptable in any other household. Your standards are exacting, my love. *I* have no quarrel with them, but you should realize that they are somewhat unusual."

"But it is barbaric to leave a child to cry in that fashion. He is but four months old, how else can he express his needs?" she demanded, arched eyebrows meeting in a ferocious frown.

"An English nurse, my love, expects to reign supreme in her nursery. As far as she is concerned the child is in her sole charge. I remember my own." Justin laughed. "I held her in much more awe than I did my parents; she had a very hard hand and didn't scruple to use it."

"Well, I will not tolerate such a thing," Danielle declared. "If Nicky must be cared for by others than myself, then they

381

will do so according to *my* wishes. He is *not* to be made unhappy."

Justin thought of the years his son would spend at Eton, years which, if he did not conform, would be sheer misery. But Danielle was right—the child was as yet four months old and entitled to instant gratification of his needs. Time enough later to prepare him for the real world and to prepare Danielle for some facts pertaining to the upbringing of the heir to the Earl of Linton. He could not afford for his son to grow up at his mother's apron strings. At that moment Nicholas cooed at his father and smiled. Justin forgot all else but his overpowering love for this helpless trusting scrap. He buried his face in the soft fragrant roundness of the baby's cheek and Danielle, with a satisfied smile, left them and went to dispatch Nurse Barker in an orderly fashion.

Half an hour later she popped her head around the library door. "Justin, I am going to visit the Bouchers in Steeplegate. An aunt lives with them but they are desperately short of room. Tante Thérèse is well accustomed to babies and I am sure will be happy to take care of Nicky."

"I will come with you, in that case." Linton stood up carefully, the now sleeping child in his arms. "This may not be one of your usual excursions, but I still prefer that you not make it alone."

"*Comme tu veux.*" She shrugged easily. "I will put Nicky in his crib and Molly will look after him until we return."

Tante Thérèse was more than happy with the arrangement and the Linton household, perforce, became accustomed to the presence of an elderly voluble Frenchwoman who spoke little English but knew well how to make her requests and how to have them granted. Nicholas thrived, Danielle was content, and Justin even more so, now that his wife was no longer agitated at leaving the child and became once again the exclusive sharer of his bed.

The news from France grew ever more alarming as the king, having accepted the constitution then proceeded to use his veto in a manner that enraged the people. Hatred of the royalists seethed in the faubourgs and fanned the flames of fear of a royalist uprising. As Danielle had predicted, many of her own class began to leave their native land in spite of the constitution's decree that all émigrés would have their property sequestered and were to be considered traitors to the constitution and liable to the death penalty.

These were the people who knew now that they had done all they could for the royalist cause from within their country. To remain was to invite martyrdom. The trickle became a stream as they gathered support for the counter-revolutionary army that their idealistic eyes saw marching back into France with a blazing sword.

Linton House rapidly became a forum for discussions and plans, and new arrivals on English soil were directed there. Justin resigned himself to a house under occupation. At least while Danielle was playing mistress of ceremonies in her salon, she couldn't be roaming the backslums of London. Jules and his friends were almost always to be found participating in the debates, arranging contact with the other refugee centers in the Rhineland, offering financial support and their own swords with an enthusiasm that Justin regarded with benign amusement. It was only natural that these energetic young men should find espousing such a cause an exciting alternative to the social round of pleasure that had hitherto been their lot.

It was Danielle's attitude that surprised him, although he realized with hindsight that it should not have done.

"It is quite ridiculous, Pitt," she stated, striding in exasperation around the prime minister's bookroom one cold March afternoon. "It is all very well to have ideals, but not when they obscure the real issues. I listen to them rant and rave and plan a glorious revenge but they will not accept that it is too late for that!"

Pitt exchanged looks with Linton before saying, "Could you explain further, Danny?"

"Ah, surely you must know what I am saying?" was her impatient response. "*C'est une bêtise* and I had not thought you stupid, sir."

"Danielle! That is most unmannerly," her husband rebuked sharply, shocked by her rudeness out of his usual calm acceptance of his wife's directness.

Danielle flushed with mortification. "I beg pardon, sir. It is

383

just that I am angry and frustrated. I did not mean to be impolite."

William Pitt couldn't help his chuckle. The fiery young woman had been replaced by a contrite little girl trying to make amends after a scolding. "Pray don't mention it," he begged politely. "I do not mean to appear stupid, but I would like to hear you expand your thoughts."

"Well, it is perfectly simple . . . Oh, Justin, do not look at me in that manner. It makes my thoughts all tangled."

"You flatter me, ma'am," Linton murmured sardonically, but his lips twitched. "Continue in a more moderate tone, if you please."

Danielle sighed. "This emigration is exacerbating the outrage of the people. They are already saying that Paris is infiltrated with armed spies of the counterrevolution. They suspect secret agents of hiding in the cellars of the Tuileries, of disguising themselves as National Guardsmen and hatching plots to assassinate the patriot leaders. What the hotheads here do not understand is that the people will take their revenge on those members of their families that they have left behind. The depositions and arrests are happening every day; estates are being pillaged just as in the worst days of the *grande peur*' and these idiots talk rhetoric and do nothing practical."

"What should they be doing, Danny?" It was Linton who spoke, his earlier annoyance quite vanished.

"They should be trying to bring out of France those who are in danger," she told him succinctly. "There is still time and money and contacts enough to succeed. Those who wish to fight should join the Austrian army, the rest should be organizing a rescue mission. Instead they just talk and will not listen to D'Evron or to myself." She glared in disgust at a spot on the carpet as if it were in some way responsible. "Only Jules and the others seem to understand, but they can do nothing without inside help. How are *we* to know who to bring out, who to get messages to; we are not omniscient."

"Danielle." Justin gave voice to the horrible suspicion carefully. "You are not by any chance thinking of accomplishing this work yourself?"

"Well, someone is going to have to if these *imbéciles* cannot be persuaded to see sense."

"Oh dear," William Pitt muttered, filled with compassion for his friend.

"Well, let us hope that that is a bridge we will not have to cross," Linton said in a placid tone that earned him Pitt's instant admiration. "Come, my love, the prime minister expects a division bell within the hour and you and I will leave politics behind for the evening and spend some hours of dissipation at Almack's."

"Dissipation!" Danielle's laughter rang out. "On orgeat and lemonade, milord? And only the most decorous dances watched over by every cat in town."

"Oh, do hush, brat," Linton begged through his own laughter. "It is fortunate that Chatham knows you so well."

"*Mais, d'accord*," she declared with a lift of her eyebrow. "I would hardly speak so freely in front of him if he did not."

"Touché, I think, Linton." Pitt coughed to hide the bubble of merriment.

"Touché, indeed." Justin picked up his wife's cloak and placed it over her shoulders. "My sword arm is becoming somewhat weak these days."

"But not your sword?" Danielle whispered and Justin froze, wondering if he had heard her correctly but knowing that he had. That wicked whisper had been for his ears alone but it was still outrageous of her to make it in the prime minister's company. Pitt's attention was for a moment distracted by a paper on his desk and Justin smacked her bottom. Danielle danced away from his hand with a mischievous grin, her tongue peeping provocatively between her lips. Almack's could go to the devil, her husband decided. When Danielle was in the mood for play, there was nothing this town could offer in competition. His loins stirred at the thought.

"We will bid you farewell then, Pitt," he said, moving Danny in front of him and pushing her with a concealed hand toward the door.

"Yes, yes, indeed." Pitt was frowning over the paper. "You will pardon me if I do not see you out . . . there is something here . . ." His voice faded as the powerful mind switched tracks from the affairs of Paris to a domestic matter of some moment.

"*Au revoir*, Chatham," Danny threw over her shoulder, receiving mumbled thanks for her time and information.

"Wretch," Linton said with satisfaction, tossing her indecorously into the curricle. "No, you may not drive. I am in somewhat of a hurry and prefer the reins in my own hands."

"*Oui*, milord," Danielle murmured, the picture of docility as she handed over the reins. "Make all speed, I beg of you."

They arrived in Grosvenor Square in record time, Tomas clinging on with grim resignation.

"No, you don't," Justin hissed as Danny stepped sideways in the direction of the salon and the sound of raised voices.

"But I am sure that I hear the Comte de St. Estèphe," she protested. "What is he doing here?"

"I have not the slightest interest in St. Estèphe's movements, only in yours. And I know exactly how I wish you to move."

"La, Husband, but you are *so* importunate." Danielle fluttered her eyelashes and received a hooded look of clear intention in return. She scampered down the corridor to her own bedchamber where Linton followed, closing the door with a decisive click.

"You issued a challenge, madam," he declared. "Something to do with swords, as I recall."

"You have the sword," she said softly, "and I have its sheath."

"Exactly so." He tossed off his clothes, Danielle watching all the while, making no attempt to undress herself.

Naked, he strode toward her. "We will have these off, I think." Her outer garments were removed with swift but deft fingers and she stood in chemise and petticoats. "Brace yourself against the wall." The instruction was strengthened by his hands, pushing her until she stood as required. Her breath came swiftly now as her body prepared itself for what was to come. His hands slipped beneath the petticoats, found

386

the drawstring of her pantalettes, pulled, and the lace-edged garment rustled to her ankles. His fingers moved delicately but with the unerring skill and the knowledge born of three years of this shared glory. Playfully she resisted his deeper intrusion until he demanded with voice and hands that she part her thighs and be taken as the longing wanton that she was. Holding her petticoats high at her waist, he drove deep within her and Danielle maintained her balance with the wall at her back and her hands on his shoulders until the shuddering aftermath brought her to her knees.

Justin looked down at her and nodded contentedly. "That will teach you to make blatantly suggestive remarks in public." Catching her under the arms, he pulled her upright, sliding one hand beneath her petticoats again to grasp her buttocks, pressing her against him as his other hand held her chin and he kissed her with a hard soundness that indicated that what they had just had was merely a preliminary.

While the earl and his countess were taking their pleasure, Roland, Comte de St. Estèphe, sat in their salon making himself agreeable to the chevalier and the gathering of émigré nobles. Their conversation sickened him with its futile oratory as much as it did Danielle, but not a sign of this showed on the long, lean face or in the cold eyes any more than did his impatience as he waited for one or both of his hosts to appear. He had a clear brief from the Brissotin ministry, to become accepted as one of the émigrés at the British court, gather information as to their plots, learn the names of those still in Paris who would constitute a threat to the revolution, and foil what plans he could without jeopardizing his cover.

That cover was perfect for his own plans. What better way to win Danielle's confidence than by offering to help the cause? She was clearly a prime mover in this business and since her house appeared to be open to all involved, he could come and go as he pleased, become familiar with the routines of the household, and keep track of her movements. As yet the *comte* had developed no strategy and had deliberately refrained from forming one. The opportunity would present itself for an elegant revenge and he would wait in patience and preparation for that time.

None of the guests at Linton House that evening were vouchsafed even a glimpse of their hosts. They were kept well supplied with refreshments by Bedford and his staff who were resigned to the presence of what the butler privately referred to as "the club." The earl and his countess were served dinner in the private parlor, although the footman who laid out the dishes saw neither of them before he left discreetly. Justin had some difficulty concentrating on his dinner since Danielle was in the mood to play harlot and sat at the table in nothing but her skin, moving provocatively as she served them both, deposited herself on his lap to taste the food on his plate and the wine in his glass.

"Danny, please put on a wrapper," he pleaded through a mouthful of quail. "It isn't that I object to your sitting on my knee, but bits of you keep getting in the way."

Danielle merely smiled and diverted his fork into her own mouth. "You took me like a whore, milord, up against the wall with my skirts around my waist. I have a mind to continue the play."

"Oh, do you indeed." He pushed her off his knee with a sudden movement that took her quite by surprise, and twitched aside his robe. "Sit down again." His eyes burned their message and with a soft laugh of excitement Danielle lowered herself astride him.

It was the next morning when St. Estèphe saw her. She walked into the salon with a chubby laughing baby on her hip. The *comte* inhaled sharply: the chevalier had omitted to tell him that she had a child. He was not accustomed to seeing the aristocratic ladies of Versailles and now the Tuileries carrying their babies with all the natural ease of a country woman. In fact babies never appeared in Polite Circles—they remained with their wet nurse until ready to take solid food, and then in the nursery until old enough to make their bows or curtsies in respectful silence.

"*Comte*, I am delighted to see you." Danielle crossed the room, hand outstretched in welcome. "I am unable to curtsy, sir," she said with a laugh, "encumbered as I am. But we stand on no ceremony in this house. I bid you welcome."

He bowed low over her hand and murmured felicitations that judging by the child's size appeared to be about nine months overdue.

"This *petit méchant* is Nicholas, Viscount Beresford," she told him, tickling the child's chin. "It seems ridiculous that such a scrap should carry such a burdensome title, do you not think?"

Roland found himself at a loss for an appropriate response. When he had first seen this woman she had appeared a naive flirtatious child and he knew that the French court had considered her to be simply that—an ingenue bride. Then he had seen her move through the streets of revolutionary Paris disguised as a burgher's wife and she had not made one false move. Now he knew her to be the leader of a group of men who, judging by their conversation last night, held her in considerable respect. He could understand why. A quiet authority radiated from the slim figure, an authority that he suspected had little to do with the fact that she was on her own territory, a gracious hostess greeting her guests.

"A most handsome child, milady." He found his voice at last. Danielle smiled. He had clearly said the right thing.

"I think he takes after his father, but Linton will have none of it," she informed him cheerfully. The child wriggled imperatively in her arms. "Oh, very well then. You may get down and find your godpapa." She set him on his knees and Nicholas crawled rapidly in the direction of Lord Julian, who was inviting him with a crooked finger.

"So, *comte*, what brings you to London?" Danielle asked directly. "Let us move to the sofa. I am anxious to hear news of France."

I am certain you are, the *comte* thought, but he said, "The news is not good, milady, as I am sure you are aware. I am come to offer my services in whatever manner they can be used."

"You are not come then to wave the sword and spout rhetoric?"

Amazing woman! So, she was not taken in by any of this pointless scheming. She would be a worthy opponent indeed. "I think the time for such displays is past," he remarked carefully and received his reward.

"How good it is to hear such sense, *mon ami*. The chevalier and I are at our wits' end as to how to persuade our countrymen that they must think pragmatically and eschew

389

emotion. You will help us, I hope."

"In any way you command, milady."

"Oh, I do not command, *comte*, and you must call me Danny, everyone else does so." The smile was ravishing, not exactly flirtatious but full of warmth. St. Estèphe found himself responding as nearly in kind as he was capable.

"St. Estèphe. How delightful." Linton's cool voice brought the *comte* back to reality. The earl took snuff delicately as he greeted his guest, but his eyes carried none of the voiced message.

Danielle sensed the flash of hostility between the two men and frowned. Why should Justin have taken such a dislike to St. Estèphe and why was that dislike returned in full measure?

"Coz, this son of yours is a veritable plague," Jules complained, inadvertently diverting Danielle's thoughts as he attempted to prise his godson's fingers loose from an enameled snuff box lying on an occasional table. Nicholas wailed in loud protest as his prize disappeared.

"Nicky, no." Justin scooped him up. "You may not have that." Nicholas bellowed, an ear-splitting yell that made St. Estèphe shudder.

"If you cannot behave yourself, my son, you must return to the nursery," his father said firmly, pulling the bell rope.

"Oh, let me have him." Danielle moved swiftly but her husband shook his head.

"It's time he had a rest, Danielle. He cannot be allowed to tyrannize the drawing room." When the footman appeared in answer to the summons, he found himself in possession of a red-faced squawling infant. "Take him to Tante Thérèse, would you?" Justin requested pleasantly.

"Yes, my lord." The footman bore the child away quite cheerfully. It was not an unusual duty in the Linton household these days. The young viscount was quite accustomed to the brawny arms of footmen, coachmen, and even, on occasion, Bedford and the chef. His mother and Tante Thérèse spoke to him in French, everyone else in English and, except when he was thwarted, Nicky's little world was a land of enchanted discovery.

St. Estèphe found himself reformulating his preconceptions yet again. He had established the fact of a love match between these two, however ill-assorted their ages and temperaments. Now they were parents and most unusual ones at that—openly affectionate, both of them totally at ease with that damp bawling creature. He cast a covert glance at the Countess of Linton. She was engaged in an animated, laughing exchange with that idiot Englishman, Viscount Westmore. It was one thing to winkle a wife from the tight shell of her marriage, quite another to pin and withdraw a mother. The challenge grew more exciting. He would have the woman, renegade aristo, loving wife, and devoted mother, and he would break her before returning the pieces to her husband and child.

"What is it between you and St. Estèphe, Justin?" It was not until much later that night that Danielle had sufficient time alone with her husband to broach the subject that had been disturbing her thoughts all day.

Justin frowned. "I do not know exactly. He claims that our fathers were close friends, but my father never mentioned such a thing to me and he took me into his confidence on most matters. However." He shrugged. "It is not impossible that an old friendship slipped his mind. There is just something about the man that I do not trust, and I do not care for the way he looks at you. There is an intensity that makes me uneasy."

Danny chuckled. "You think he means to seduce me?"

"You will not find me a complacent husband if you succumb, wife," Justin warned, trying to sound playful but failing miserably.

"Oh, pah!" Danielle dismissed the comment with a careless wave. "He has the eyes of a fish and the face of a horse, so long and narrow. But he cannot help either of those misfortunes," she added kindly. "I find him sensible, my lord, and that is a most refreshing change. Also, he shows no indication to flirt with me at all, so I do not think you need worry." Suddenly, her conversation with Madame Cloury at the Tuileries popped into her head—strange how she had forgotten that story of St. Estèphe's checkered past. But then scandalous gossip was the mainstay of the French court and one could not believe more than a fraction of what was said.

"What is it?" Justin probed, seeing the changed expression that now showed no laughter.

"*Rien du tout.*" She shrugged easily—why bother Justin with tittle-tattle? "I was thinking of how best to impart some sense to those crazy hotheads."

Chapter 20

"What think you, Justin?" William Pitt held his wine to the May sunlight, turning the glass so that the rich claret sparked amethyst lights through the exquisitely chiseled cuts.

"The claret is superb," Linton observed. "Since Danielle took over the running of our cellars, we rarely have a poor vintage."

"I do not think Milord Chatham refers to the quality of the wine." Danielle spoke from the chaise longue where she sat on this sunny afternoon with her son, turning over the pages of a picture book while Nicholas clapped his hands gleefully and struggled to articulate his mother's careful definitions.

"What have you to say to this proposal then, Danny?" Justin regarded her gravely.

"I think that if the prime minister needs you to go to Russia, then you must do so."

The prime minister heaved a sigh of relief. He had come here today in considerable trepidation to enlist Linton's aid. In earlier days he would have asked the earl in private, assuming that he would make his own decision and then inform his wife. But Pitt was now well aware that he was dealing with no conventional marriage and if he asked the husband to undertake a potentially dangerous mission then he must also ask the wife's permission.

"I would have liked to see Czar Alexander's court for

393

myself," Danielle said wistfully. "But we have Nicholas to consider and the voyage could prove dangerous. I also have much work to do here." She turned to Pitt. "How long do you expect the journey will take, sir?"

"No more than three months, ma'am," he responded. "Hopefully less. Linton should not need to spend more than a month at St. Petersburg and as soon as he has an accurate impression of the czar's views as to the affairs in France and the war between France and Austria, then the sooner he brings them back to me the better."

"At least it is not winter." Danielle stroked her son's head thoughtfully. "The seas are quite calm and St. Petersburg will not be snowbound. How soon will you leave?" She looked directly at her husband.

How could he leave her for three months? Justin wondered. She was but twenty and yet evinced a quiet maturity and wisdom more suited to a woman ten years her senior. But she was still impulsive and inclined to recklessness when the spirit moved her. What would she do when he was not here to apply the checks and balances? And could he bear to be without her for three long months?

He had no choice, of course. His prime minister needed him and Danielle had given his answer. "Within the week," he said.

"If t'were done when 'tis done, then t'were well t'were done quickly." Danny smiled as she quoted *Macbeth*, a smile of complete understanding as she heard his thoughts. It would be no easier for her to live without the mainstay of her existence, to worry, sometimes needlessly and sometimes with reason, as he made the treacherous journey. But they were no longer private people who could conduct their lives according to their own whims and fancies. In this year of trouble, 1792, they had a part to play in the greater scenario and were both political animals who shared the same goals.

Justin left England five days later and a week after, on May 30, King Louis XVI's bodyguard was dismissed by the Assembly, who decided that they held an "unpatriotic spirit," being too royalist in their sentiments. Detachments of the

National Guard took their place and the path to dethronement turned the hill and began its inexorable drop to the river of blood.

"We cannot work *with* these imbeciles, so we must work without them," Danielle said forcefully to the small group of Englishmen augmented by D'Evron and the Comte de St. Estèphe.

"How do you propose doing that?" St. Estèphe asked, hooding his eyes over the spark of excitement. He sensed that his chance for revenge was approaching. He would take her as a flagrant betrayer of the revolution—to exact vengeance but also to perform the work that he had been sent here to do. Once she committed herself to action then he had his excuse, and he knew her well enough now to be sure that such action would no longer be confined to haranguing her despised compatriots.

"We must achieve a list of those in danger and go into France and issue the warning," Danielle said simply. "It will mean working in Paris but also in the countryside. There are many who still keep to their estates, but the villagers will move against them sooner or later. D'Evron, you will go?"

"*D'accord.*" The chevalier inclined his head.

"And you also, *comte*? It is best if those of us who are native Frenchmen go amongst our people. We will be more convincing." She smiled an apology to the young Englishmen.

"Danny, you are not intending . . .?"

"No, Jules." She interrupted him swiftly. "Not unless it is necessary. Whilst Justin is away, I must keep myself safe for Nicky for as long as I am able." She rose to her feet. "That reminds me of my promise to take him for a drive this afternoon. *Comte*, you will discuss plans with the chevalier, *n'est-ce pas?*"

"*Certainement.*" He stood up with the rest of the men and bowed to his hostess. "We will gather together the names and then formulate a plan. At this stage, it is necessary simply to warn."

"Yes." She agreed. "It may be necessary to facilitate their escape later. But if they are sensible now . . ." Her light shrug spoke all her lack of conviction in such an idea. "We shall see, messieurs. *Au revoir.*"

St. Estèphe and the chevalier went to France within a few days. While the chevalier sedulously performed his mission, the *comte* reported to his masters in minute detail, handing over the lists of names, urging their immediate proscription and imprisonment.

The chevalier was in the house of the Levandou when a detachment of National Guard burst through the front door, muskets at the ready. The family were taking tea with their guest in the salon. The *duc* spoke in dignified protest at this assault on his household as D'Evron was seized roughly, his hands bound behind his back and the accusation of treason proclaimed in ringing accents. He made no attempt to resist his captors although he pleaded energetically the innocence of his friends. To no purpose, however; the entire family from the youngest child to the elderly grandmother were bundled into the unmarked coaches waiting outside and hauled before the tribunal where their guilt as conspirators against the constitution was declared and proven.

D'Evron was taken to the Châtelet where, for a while, he had money enough to pay for a mattress beneath him as he slept. But when his resources dwindled to nothing, he joined the majority of the five hundred inmates and slept on filthy straw. The Levandoux fared better during their imprisonment in the aristocratic Abbaye where all had mattresses, there were only six prisoners to a room, and with their one meal came a bottle of wine a day. But on Sunday, September 2, 1792, they all shared the same fate. Carters, carpenters, cabinetmakers; hat makers and jewelers; cobblers and watchmakers with clubs, swords, and pikes massacred the inmates of the nine main prisons in Paris. Some thirteen hundred prisoners died in the violence inspired by the fear that the political prisoners would break free and join the counter-revolutionary armies threatening the borders of France. But the original motive for the mass murder was soon forgotten, and children, prostitutes, thieves, and debtors fell beneath the swords of the mob.

D'Evron died in the courtyard of the Châtelet where he had been dragged, a filthy, emaciated figure that Danielle would have had difficulty recognizing. His last conscious thought was of her and of his failure to warn her of the traitor who had given evidence with such complacence before the tribunal. The heavy club fell again and the chevalier found release in unconsciousness and mercifully felt not the ripping stab of the pike that ended his life.

But that blood-soaked weekend was some months ahead. In the meantime, St. Estèphe decided not to return to England once his reports were made and his standing as a faithful adherent of the revolution confirmed. He had two reasons for this. There was much politicking to be done with the fall of the Brissotin ministry and he could not afford to be absent as the wind changed. He also hoped that Danielle, in the absence of news from D'Evron and himself, would decide to take matters into her own charge. Once she made a definitive move on French soil, she would have played into his hands and he could have his revenge on the house of Linton while removing a traitor from active duty.

Danielle waited until the end of June, until news came of the mob's attack on the Tuileries. While D'Evron languished in the Châtelet and St. Estèphe insinuated himself among the power-holders, a crowd of demonstrators, now proudly bearing the name of sans-culottes, broke through the iron gates of the Tuileries intent on confronting their king. They flourished their banners, an old pair of gentlemen's britches, and the bleeding heart of a calf—*le coeur d'aristocrat*—as they poured into the courts at the rear of the palace. The royal family cowered in their apartments as they heard again the terrifying sounds of a mob attack—the wild shouts, the smash of doors, the pounding of feet coming ever closer. The Tuileries was under attack as Versailles had been three years previously. Louis, behind a phalanx of a few faithful guardsmen, took what protection was offered in the deep embrasure of a window. The red bonnet of the revolution was placed upon his head and he listened to the diatribe of a butcher and drank to the health of the nation as the mob gaped at this man who was their king, who, from the moment of their births had been deified, all powerful, a power given directly from God. But he was just a man, just like the rest of them—legs, arms, blood, and water, and capable of fear in spite of his apparent patient calm. In another room they found the queen—the hated Austrian—with her children and the king's sister. They stood behind a table and a group of guards, while the mob peered, would have poked and prodded had they been able to get close enough, and wondered again at the simple flesh and blood of this family who had known only riches beyond the dreams of avarice and the privilege of the supremely powerful.

Six hours after the invasion began, the palace was cleared of demonstrators and the royal family safe from the violence of the sovereign people. But it was to be a short respite and Danielle paced the drawing room in Grosvenor Square in an agony of indecision.

"We have heard nothing from D'Evron and nothing from St. Estèphe. We would have received a message by now if they were safe. We must then assume that they have been taken and plan accordingly."

"What do you have in mind, Danny?" Sir Anthony Fanshawe asked the question on the lips of every member of this small gathering. It was a natural enough question since she held undisputed leadership.

"Why, that we must assume they did not succeed in their mission and must try it ourselves," she replied simply. "It will be more difficult, of course, after this latest news and if our friends have been discovered . . . as they must have been." She sighed and tried to put out of mind the face of her friend and colleague these past three years.

"Danny, you cannot mean to go into France yourself," Julian protested, knowing the protest to be ineffectual but one he had to make for his cousin's sake.

"I do, Jules. But we will be a little more devious this time." She laughed suddenly, a laugh of pure deviltry that did nothing for Julian's disquiet. "We shall have some splendid adventures, *mes amis*. We will work from Cornwall to the north coast of Brittany. No one in Paris will suspect such an approach. I have played the urchin once and shall do so again. I do not think my figure has changed significantly with motherhood, do you?" She looked anxiously around the group who had recourse to coughings and shufflings of feet. "Oh, do not be such milksops," she chided. "Tell me directly. Do I have too many curves to wear britches undetected?"

"No you do not," Julian replied eventually, when it was clear no one else was prepared to venture an opinion. "But that is not the point. You cannot expose yourself to such danger. Justin would not allow it, and in his absence I . . ."

"You what, Jules?" Her eyes glittered dangerously.

"Oh, I meant nothing," he said hastily. "Except that you must think of your husband and Nicholas."

"And do you dare to think that I do not?" Her voice was a mere hiss and Julian blanched.

"Danny, we all share Julian's concern." Westmore stepped in briskly. "But we will pledge ourselves to your support. If you must go into France then we will go with you. But you cannot keep secrets from us and while you may formulate the strategy, you must allow us equal voice."

"*D'accord, mes amis.*" Danny smiled. "I did not wish to appear managing. Let me explain my plan."

The plan was essentially very simple. They would base themselves at Mervanwey and use the Earl of March's yacht, *Dream Girl*, to cross to the north Brittany coast. From there, they would travel to Paris along unfrequented country roads. "You will leave me to do most of the talking," Danielle instructed the attentive group. "I mean no aspersions on your French, but there is an accent . . . *vous comprenez?*"

"Danny, there will be times when we will have to speak," Lord Philip asserted.

"*Mais, oui.*" She shrugged. "I will teach you a regional accent that you may use in emergency and for a short conversation will provide adequate disguise."

"And just how do you propose to persuade your grandparents to lend both house and yacht?" Julian demanded, feeling as if he should provide a brake of some kind to his young cousin-in-law's blithe plans.

"Oh, *pas de problème*," Danielle responded confidently. "They will be happy to help once they understand the urgency.

And they will be there for Nicky whilst I am away. It will work perfectly, you will see."

The Earl and Countess of March in fact did what they could to dissuade their granddaughter, but eventually decided that if they did not support her plans she would find some other way to achieve her ends and it were best that they remain involved, offering some kind of family base in Justin's absence. They thought it highly likely that Linton would reject out of hand Danielle's schemes, but their own authority was nebulous in the extreme so they settled for providing a home and guardians for the baby viscount in his parents' absence.

St. Estèphe, unaware of these plans, fortunately for his own, made his next move before they left for Cornwall. A messenger arrived late one night in Grosvenor Square and his news confirmed Danielle's urgent determination. D'Evron had disappeared, presumably imprisoned, but all St. Estèphe's efforts to discover his whereabouts had failed. Many of those on the list had also disappeared as the National Guard increased its vigilance and the number of its raids on the houses of the aristocracy. St. Estèphe would remain in Paris, in hiding, doing what he could to persuade the others to take flight, but it was becoming almost impossible to leave Paris now, as the city gates were manned night and day and passports were no longer being issued. There was little that he alone could do, and the message ended with a desperate plea for reinforcements and precise instructions as to how he could be found once they reached Paris.

Danielle questioned the messenger minutely. His story of how he had slipped out of Paris through the *Barrière* St. Martin hidden beneath a pile of straw convinced her that he had indeed come in secret from the *comte* and that the *comte* himself was risking his life every day he remained in that beleaguered city. It was now more than ever imperative that they go to his aid and set up some organization for the safe escape of those who wished it. It was quite clear that groups of royalists would not be allowed simply to walk through the city gates with the

400

blessing of the people any more than Danielle and her friends would be able to leave freely once they were within the city walls.

On the long journey into Cornwall, Danielle and her four cavaliers discussed the situation endlessly. "We must find a small beach on the Brittany coast from which to base our activities," Danielle decided. *Dream Girl* can remain anchored offshore while we journey to Paris. I do not think we should attempt to bring more than four or five out with us at any one time. Apart from the increased danger of detection, *Dream Girl* cannot safely carry more than ten passengers."

"How the deuce are we to get through the gates anyway?" Westmore demanded.

"Ah, we shall use farm carts. The messenger from St. Estèphe has given me the idea. We will be French farmers, gentlemen." Danny smiled in smug satisfaction. "We will enter the city at dawn in the company of all the others with produce to sell and we will leave at sunset with that produce we were unable to sell. We can hide people beneath cabbages or some such . . . that is a mere detail." She waved an airy hand. "If we act our parts well, we shall go undetected. The guards cannot possibly search every farm cart; there are far too many of them passing through at those times of the day, and they cannot deny them leave to pass since the city would otherwise starve. It is simple, is it not?"

"To you, maybe," Jules grumbled. "How are we to find carts and cabbages, in the first place?"

"We will steal them," Danny informed him outrageously, her eyes twinkling. "Well, perhaps not exactly. We will take them at dead of night, and we will leave money in their place."

"You are quite mad," Julian stated definitively. "And so, clearly, am I."

Succeeding events did nothing to dissipate this conviction. *Dream Girl* sailed with the evening tide one Friday at the beginning of July under the command of a dour Cornishman who seemed quite unaffected by his extraordinary orders.

"Jake knows the Brittany coast like the back of his hand," Danielle informed her colleagues with a serene smile. "He will

401

find us a small beach where the rocks are not too treacherous and the surf not too high. One of the sailors will row us to shore in the dinghy and then return to *Dream Girl*. On the tenth day they will look again for us. We shall flash a light from the beach. If we have not done so by the thirteenth day, I have said that they should return to Mervanwey." She shrugged and they all fell silent, occupied with their own thoughts.

Three days and a hundred miles later, near the town of Brest, Jake found what he was looking for. A small inlet in the barrier of jagged cliffs that made up the wild rugged coastline of North Brittany. Dragon's teeth rocks rose high in the water on all sides and the white flecks of breaking water indicated to the wary the presence of concealed reefs. Only a small dinghy could negotiate these hazards, but a rower in such a fragile craft would not be able to handle the tidal streams ripping parallel to the coast. But at the point Jake had chosen, the rocks and reefs stretched only two miles from the unfriendly coast and *Dream Girl* could sail that far inland without danger, and the dinghy could be lowered beyond the riptide.

It was a black night when the brawny Cornish sailor ran the dinghy onto the tiny beach and they spoke in whispers as if danger lurked in the cove and on the cliff tops rising high above. There could be none, though, Danny reassured herself. They were too far from Paris and the Breton people were as reclusive as their Cornish ancestors. It was the main reason why she had picked this approach. The Bretons would be unaffected by the revolution; it was even possible that it had escaped their notice in these remote parts. Four men and a boy appearing mysteriously from the sea would perhaps cause a raised eyebrow, but these people were too busy wresting a living from the unfriendly waters and the wind-torn, infertile land to ask questions.

Horses were their first priority and those Danny decided they would acquire legitimately. For the right price, they could be found on the small struggling farms and if her plans worked they could return them at journey's end and use them again on the next occasion. But they could do nothing until dawn, so behind the shelter of a small rocky outcrop beneath the cliff they settled down, wrapped in cloaks, to wait out the night.

Danielle fell asleep almost immediately. She had learned to sleep by the roadsides, in barns, and under haystacks; to sleep with one ear cocked for the sounds of approaching danger, until the Earl of Linton had happened upon her and removed all need for such self-protection. Amazingly, though, the old habits reasserted themselves automatically as, once again on her own soil, once again faced with a long and dangerous journey, her real identity became subsumed by the simple needs for survival and secrecy.

Unused as yet to any form of discomfort, the others remained awake, saying little as they kept vigil until the sky began to lighten, at first imperceptibly and then with a pinkish tinge to the east. Danny woke instantly, sat up, rubbed her eyes, and grinned at them. "Breakfast," she announced. "*Allons-y*."

As she had expected, their appearance in the fishing village caused little remark. They were received in a manner that was neither friendly nor hostile. Their money was good and bought them breakfast and horses. Three days of hard riding and three nights of hideous discomfort in the primitive country inns along the road brought them to the outskirts of Paris.

"We must wait until night before we go in search of carts," Danielle stated, turning her mount off the road and into a wood bordering the pasture of a small, well-maintained farm. "They will fill the carts before retiring so that they may make an early start in the morning."

"How do you know that?" Sir Anthony wiped his perspiring brow with the bright checkered neckcloth that formed a part of his farmer's costume.

"Because, when I traveled from Languedoc to Paris, Tony, it was always the way." She dismounted, knotted the horse's reins, and flung herself on her back in the grass. "We will harness our own horses to the carts and take them back with us to Brittany." She chuckled lazily. "On our next visit, we shall find both horses and carts awaiting us and matters will proceed more easily. We can fill them simply enough from the village markets along the way so that we can enter Paris fully laden and as respectable as can be."

"Y'know, don't mean to be discouraging, Danny, but it seems to me there's a better way of managing this affair." Philip coughed apologetically. "I don't like this notion of stealing . . . I mean to say, why can't we just *buy* two carts? Bound to be somewhere around here where we can do so. Then, if they belong to us quite legitimately, if you take my point, we can do what we like with 'em."

"That, if I may say so, is about the first word of sense I've heard in a week," Jules declared. "No, don't rip up at me, Danny," he begged as she sat up indignantly. "I have no argument with the basic plan, but there's no reason to make it any more complicated than it has to be. Stands to reason. All this about sneaking into stableyards and stealing carts full of cabbages while every dog in the village goes berserk is a bit too fantastical to my mind. You stay here with Westmore and Tony. Philip and I will go off in search of carts. We'll fill 'em with turnips or something."

"Well, why can't I come?" Danny demanded.

"Because two of us can do it just as easily as five and we'll be a lot less noticeable. Besides, it's high time someone else had a say around here. I ain't denying you have it right most of the time, coz, but you do let your imagination run away with you on occasion." So saying, Julian chucked her beneath the chin in an avuncular fashion which left Danny gobbling with indignation and remounted. "Ready, Philip?"

"Well of all the . . .!" Danny stared, for once speechless.

"Now don't get on your high ropes, Danny," Westmore advised, leaning comfortably against the trunk of an enormous oak. "They have the right of it and Jules is not the one to accept a petticoat rule for too long."

"I'm not wearing petticoats," she said crossly.

"What difference does that make?" Tony inquired with some interest.

"I'm going for a walk." Danny stomped off into the woods but her annoyance faded rapidly. She *had* been ruling the roost and she *had* become so involved in the adventure that her plans were becoming unnecessarily convoluted. This was not just her adventure, it belonged to them all and if they couldn't work in harmony then they may as well give up immediately. The only hope they had of scraping by in safety was by relying absolutely on each other.

Danielle sat down on the bank of a small stream, pulled off her boots and stockings, and dabbled her toes in the cool water. It had been six weeks since Justin had left. He should be in St. Petersburg now. What would he say if he could see her here? With her hair cropped tight to her head beneath the woolen cap, her body sweaty after six days of travel and inadequate water, her britches and shirt rumpled. She peered disgustedly at her fingernails—the skin beneath was black with dirt and her feet even worse. Justin would not be best pleased, she decided as his face hovered in her mind's eye. She glanced behind her, listened carefully. There was no sound but the droning of insects, the chirp of birds, the rat-a-tat of a woodpecker; nothing to see but trees and the ground dappled with the evening sun filtering through the leaves.

With sudden determination, Danny stood up and stripped off her clothes. She could at least take a bath for her husband. The water was gloriously cold, too shallow for complete immersion but she splashed every nook and cranny, prised the grime from beneath nails of fingers and toes and dipped her head, emerging with a luxurious shake of curls.

"Danny? Danny? Where have you got to?" It was Tony's voice, his feet snapping twigs as he plunged through the wood in search of her. Danielle sat on the bed of the stream where the water barely covered her thighs and quite ridiculously wanted to laugh. At any moment Tony would appear and discover her sitting here like some guilty freshwater mermaid! She daren't run for her clothes, he was too close and would be bound to break through the trees just as she was streaking across the grass.

"Tony, I'm in the stream," she called softly. "Just go away. I won't be long."

"What the devil do you mean, you're in the . . . Odd's blood!" He stood gaping. "A thousand pardons . . ." Stammering, he turned away.

"It's all right, Tony," she said to his back. "Would you bring me my bag? I wish to change my shirt, you see, and can use the old one to dry myself."

Muttering something that sounded vaguely like an affirmative, Tony disappeared the way he had come and Danny sprang from the water, drying herself vigorously with her old shirt and dragging on the britches and thin camisole.

"Danielle?" It was Tony's voice coming cautiously from behind a bush.

"I am relatively decent," she called back, "but if you leave the bag there, I will fetch it myself." She washed the wet shirt in the stream. It would dry in the warm night air and would at least be fresh, if crumpled, when she needed it again.

Tony had some difficulty meeting her eyes when she rejoined them, but Danny chattered cheerfully about the pleasures of her bath, making no reference to his inadvertent intrusion and suggesting that they might care to follow her example while she watched the horses. They went readily and she unpacked their supper from the picnic hamper that they had stocked in a small market town that morning. This night would be their last of comparative safety until they left Paris far behind them on their return to Brittany. They could afford to spend no more than two days in the city, and Danielle, at this point, wanted only to find the chevalier in whatever prison he was held. She would leave the others to locate St. Estèphe, to gather together those who would make their flight this time, and prepare others for the next time. They should be able to manage at least one more trip before Justin's return and then, if he would join them, as he surely would, they could bring the *Black Gull* from Dover and start operating on a much larger scale.

Julian and Philip returned some two hours later, exulting in their success. They had paid a delighted farmer, who had no intention of questioning his good fortune, for two carts and their contents. The farmer was saved a day's work selling in the city and had been paid more than liberally for his potatoes, turnips, cabbages, and lettuce.

At dawn they passed through the St. Antoine gate in the

406

company of a hundred others, dressed as they were, driving a long procession of similar carts, and they received but a cursory glance from the guards.

Danielle had the reins of the leading cart and drove with unerring memory to Les Halles where once she had scrabbled beneath the stalls and carts for discarded fruit and vegetables, had begged for bread from amenable matrons, and held horses for a sou. They all knew what they were to do and spoke little as they placed the carts. Westmore and Philip prepared to sell their wares as Jules and Tony went off to find St. Estèphe.

Danielle vanished into the crowd, an urchin no different from the thousands of others roaming the streets, to begin her search of the prisons. She had little hope of success, but the effort had to be made. She tried La Force and the Concièrgerie. It was easy enough to gain admittance since little attempt was made during the daylight hours to segregate the prisoners from each other or from their friends outside. The prison guard was undermanned and should have been increased as the prisons filled under the vigilant activities of the *comité de surveillance*, but nothing had as yet been done and it took the people of Paris to deal with the situation. They chose murder as their means— by killing the prisoners they restored the ratio of guards to their wards. However, it was still only July and that massacre was not to take place until the beginning of September.

When neither prison yielded a spark, Danielle tried the Abbaye in the hope that the chevalier would have been accorded the minimal courtesies due to an aristocratic prisoner. By the time she gave up there, it was three in the afternoon and she had to return to Les Halles. The five of them had established an absolute rule of timing. If one member of the group failed to return fifteen minutes after the appointed time then the others would continue with the plan on the assumption that that member had been taken by the *sécurité*. In such an event, it was to be every man for himself, but Danielle strongly suspected that if she did not appear on time her friends would turn the city upside down to find her. In that case, they would probably all find themselves in La Force or the Concièrgerie, or even Châtelet, whose very name sent shivers down the back of the most hardened criminal. Accordingly, she made her way back to find them all waiting for her, together with St. Estèphe who at first did not recognize the Countess of Linton in the slight, grubby figure who appeared seemingly out of nowhere at his side. Her language was not that of a de St. Varennes either and he listened in amazement to the explicit argot, conscious that his attempts to respond in kind were but a poor imitation.

"We lodge tonight with the family of the Comte de St. Vire," Jules told her swiftly. "He will not leave here himself but wishes to send his wife and children to safety. While we are gone, he will organize others to come with us on the next journey and spread the word. Those who can will make their own way to the coast in our absence, and when *Dream Girl* brings us back, Jake can take them to Cornwall and then return for us. He can make the double journey in ten days during the summer months."

"*D'accord.*" Danielle nodded. "You have accomplished much in a few hours, Jules. I, on the other hand, have accomplished nothing." She turned sadly to St. Estèphe. "You have no way of knowing where the chevalier is held, *comte*?"

"None at all." He shook his head. "I have tried for two months, Danny. I will continue my search in your absence and will hope to have him safe and able to accompany you on your return." The promise would bring her back, of that he was sure. He would allow her to make this journey, to set up the means of escape, and he would listen to de St. Vire, find out who else was ready to abandon their native land, and with a grand coup snare them all and take the little de St. Varennes for his plaything.

"If we remain in Paris tonight," Danny said slowly, "we shall not be able to leave until tomorrow sundown. Why do we not take the de St. Vire family out now? It will allow us an extra day to make the journey to the coast, and St. Estèphe and de St. Vire can do as well if not better what little we could accomplish tomorrow. It is simply a matter of passing the word and making preparations."

"I own I'll rest easier once I'm out of this city," Jules

declared. "There is an element of hysteria in the streets that has me as jumpy as a cat with its paws in the fire. The sansculottes are everywhere, massed on street corners, parading the alleys, and I do not think they are any friendlier toward farmers than they are toward the aristos."

"No," Danielle concurred. "I have met no hostility, but then I am dressed as one of them. I think, on our next visit, it would be wise for you all to do the same."

"Lud!" Westmore sighed in resignation as he examined her appearance anew. She had contrived to collect a considerable amount of dirt in her journey through the city and wore her shirt hanging outside her ragged britches and her cap at a jaunty angle pulled low over her face. "What a repulsive thought." He sighed again. "But I daresay we must try."

"For now, we must make all speed," Danny said briskly. "The market is closing and if we are to mingle with the procession to the gates then we must do so quickly." It was true—all around them the farmers were closing their stalls, reharnessing the patient horses to the carts, and packing up unsold produce.

"I will go ahead and tell the de St. Vire family of your change of plan," St. Estèphe offered. "You will bring the carts to the alley behind the house where your passengers will be waiting for you."

"*D'accord.*" Danny agreed. "In a half hour then."

It was a petrified group waiting in the shadow of the high wall enclosing the St. Vire town house and Julian's heart sank when he saw the infant clutched in the *comtesse*'s arms. One inopportune cry from beneath the turnips and they would all be lost. There were two other children, white-faced, solemn-eyed tots of around four and five. The Comte de St. Vire stood with them and stared incredulously as Danny sprang from the leading cart and began to give swift instructions. This filthy little vagabond was going to take his family to safety! He looked helplessly at the four large farmers and one of them, as if reading his mind, winked and nodded.

For an instant the *comte* had second thoughts and then a drum roll sounded from a nearby lane and a great cry of

"Vivent les patriotes!" rent the air. He embraced his wife and children and helped to hurry them into the carts.

"Madame," Danielle said urgently, "you must contrive to keep the babe silent until we are through the gates."

They spread blankets over their passengers, then a layer of straw before arranging the remaining produce in seeming haphazard fashion.

"Next time you will come with us yourself, *mon ami,*" Danny whispered to de St. Vire. "Someone else can then continue your work and we will operate a chain in that manner."

The *comte* looked down at the small grime-encrusted face, the large brown eyes sparkling with intelligence, heard the authoritative cultured voice of one of his own kind and took her hand in a firm grip. *"Bonne chance.* You will find me ready on your return and the chain in place."

"Ça va. Au revoir, comte." She leapt into the cart and Jules clicked his teeth at the horses and they lumbered in the direction of the Barrière St. Antoine.

Danny, throughout the journey, hopped up and down on the slatted bench, yelling comments to the people in the street in the rough argot that came so easily to her lips. The comments were received with laughter and frequently returned in vulgar kind. As they mingled with the traffic moving slowly toward the gate, she kept up a stream of conversation with their neighbors, jumping in to answer any remark directed to Julian or to the three farmers in the cart beside them. Her four colleagues maintained a dour mien that aroused no remark—it had been a long hard day, after all. As they approached the gate, Danny made a particularly outrageous sally and Jules cuffed her with an exasperated inarticulate growl. Even the guards laughed and shouted friendly advice to Julian as the urchin poured out a stream of indignant protestation at this summary treatment—and then they were through.

"Eh bien, c'est possible," Danielle murmured almost to herself, and Julian shot her a startled glance. It was the first time she had given any indication that she had had doubts as to the success of their enterprise. In fact it was only her unfailing

410

confidence and unflagging spirits that had kept the hounds of discouragement at bay for the rest of them.

Julian made the silent resolve that this would be the last occasion she carried the full burden. They had played their parts, certainly, but except for the matter of the carts they had followed instructions and accepted her cheerful insouciance at face value. Justin would not have done so, Jules reflected. He would have seen beneath the surface to the fatigue and anxiety that now showed clearly in the drawn face and enormous smudged eyes.

"Climb in the back and go to sleep, Danny," he said quietly. "We cannot stop for the night until we are at least twenty miles from Paris. The horses are quite fresh after a day's rest and we will travel further if we are able."

"But you may need me . . ." She looked longingly behind her at the straw and the turnips.

"I do not wish to offend you, ma'am," Jules said dryly, "but I think we may do very well without you for a few hours."

At that she chuckled wearily. "Very well then. I own I am in need of a short rest, but no more than an hour and then I will be quite refreshed again." Danny scrambled into the back where she located the two bodies of the children and whispered encouragingly to them as she burrowed into the straw and slept.

Jules had a brief consultation with his friends and they agreed to press on until after dark, by which time they should be deep in the countryside, safely away from the environs of Paris that seethed with revolutionary ferment almost as much as did the city itself.

They could not risk an inn this close to the capital and when Danielle eventually awoke it was darkest night. She lay for a few moments recapturing her senses, looking up into the panoply of trees. Something was digging into her back and she located the offending object to find that it was a turnip. Memory came flooding back and with it the knowledge that she was ravenously hungry. She sat up blinking as her eyes accustomed themselves to the darkness lightened only by the moon filtering through the trees and the soft glow of a small

411

fire. Two little figures and a larger one cradling a tiny bundle slept wrapped in blankets at the mossy base of a tree. Beside the fire sat Danny's fellow conspirators. The most glorious aroma wafted from an iron pot resting over the embers.

"Ah, Danny, you are awake at last." Philip got up to swing her down from the cart. "We have made our bivouac, as you can see, and have saved you some excellent rabbit stew."

"But how long have I been asleep?" she asked, looking around this orderly scene that had somehow been accomplished without her. "And where are we?"

"Some forty miles from Paris and you have been asleep for six hours. We made good speed," Tony informed her. "Come and eat. Julian appears to have an extraordinary skill when it comes to cooking rabbits and we had no shortage of vegetables."

"How do you know how to cook rabbit, Jules?" She sniffed hungrily at the laden bowl Tony handed her as she joined them. There had been a time when she hadn't cared for rabbit stew—a time when it had been offered her by a friendly innkeeper's wife and Justin had insisted that his servant eat at his table . . .

"John of Danesbury," he responded with a chuckle. "I was something of a favorite of his in my youth, and while the man's a wizard with horses he can match that skill when it comes to the snaring, skinning, and cooking of rabbit."

Danielle nodded without surprise and scraped the bowl clean. How they had acquired cooking pot, bowls, and utensils seemed irrelevant. She failed to notice the satisfied exchange of nods amongst her companions when she finally sighed with repletion and stretched out on the grass, smiling in contented relaxation. *"Et la famille?"* she asked, dreamily staring into the night sky. "Are they at ease . . . in as far as they can be?"

"The countess is a sensible woman." Tony dropped his voice in deference to the sleeping bodies. "She is anxious for her husband's safety but sees her principal responsibility in her children."

Danielle said nothing. She too feared for her husband but she had left her child—their child—certainly in no physical danger but with the possibility of being orphaned. But how

412

could she have done otherwise? She was not like the Comtesse de St. Vire—wife and mother to the exclusion of all else. If those seeds had ever been sown in her, they had never been watered, nurtured to maturity. And so she stood alone, juggling priorities, embracing risks, fighting down the panic when she thought of what she was doing and the effect it could have upon her son and her husband.

Chapter 21

"*Eh, Nicky, tu seras tranquille, n'est-ce pas? Maman reviendra a bientôt.*" Danielle stood on the dock at Mervanwey holding her son as she prepared to go aboard *Dream Girl* and make the second foray into enemy territory. She was entering her native land now as spy and enemy—a subversive against a regime as tyrannical as the one that held sway under Louis XVI. She cared for this one as little as she had cared for the former but she was no longer too ignorant or too young to do her part for the victims of tyranny. It mattered not that today's victims were yesterday's oppressors. While there was suffering she would do what she must.

An imperative shout came from Jake and she handed the child to Lavinia. "With good fortune, *Grandmère*, Justin will return in my absence. We shall be home before the beginning of September."

The Countess of March took her great-grandson and kissed her granddaughter. There was nothing to be gained by further protestations and she could pray only for the early return of Danielle's husband and the safe passage of the five who now stood on the deck of the yacht waving good-bye as she sailed out of the sheltered harbor and made for the open sea.

This time when they made landfall on the Brittany coast it was an easy matter to retrieve both horses and carts. They found also a small party of would-be émigrés who had been contacted by the Comte de St. Vire on their country estates and had managed to make their own way to this remote coastal

415

corner of France. The laconic Bretons had received them with few questions and the dinghy, in response to a flashing light from the cliff top, returned to pick up the group and take them to safety in Cornwall.

The journey into Paris was again accomplished without difficulty and once they were ensconced in Les Halles, Danny set off to mingle with the crowds and learn what she could. Julian and Westmore went in search of St. Estèphe and Tony to the house of St. Vire.

There was even more excitement in the streets, Danielle noticed as she slipped through the throng, ears open for the news on every tongue. All five of them now wore the uniform of the sans-culottes—wooden pattens, dirty shirts and cut-off britches—and were indistinguishable from their fellows.

That evening she slipped unnoticed into an *épicerie* in the Faubourg St.-Honoré. A cask of wine had been broached and she took her share with the rest. It was the fateful night of August 9, the night when the National Assembly finally fell into the hands of the insurrectionist republicans. She listened as the excitement grew to fever pitch as breathless messengers brought the news, minute by minute, from the Assembly into the streets. Danny sat on an upturned barrel, kicking her heels nonchalantly until the cry went up: "*Au Tuileries, citoyens.*"

She joined the group, caught up in the tidal swell of hysteria. She sang the "Ça Ira" with the best as they marched on the palace, the crowds swelling to thousands, pouring through the streets in a torrent of humanity intent only on one thing—the removal of the king from the royalist garrison of his palace and into the hands of the sovereign people.

While the king and his family sought shelter in the parliament house the mob slaughtered his garrison of Swiss Guard who were instructed too late to lay down their arms. Danielle, sick to her stomach, moved amongst the assassins, stepped over the bodies being stripped by eager hands, watched as the emblems of royalty were torn down, and generally behaved as if she was one of them until the tumult died down. Then she was able to slip away through the dark streets where the cries of the mob's triumph faded in the distance and she reached the walls of St. Vire's house. The postern gate stood unguarded—an ominous sign, but after what she had seen this night it was not surprising. Their carts, piled high with straw, stood in the deserted courtyard and she nodded in satisfaction.

"We must leave here immediately," she said to the group waiting, grave-faced and talking in subdued whispers in the salon. "There is no time to waste. We must mingle with the crowds who will roam the streets 'till dawn and then attempt a daytime passage through the *barrière*. You will decide amongst yourselves who is to come with us."

"The decision is made already," St. Vire said. "You will take the women and children of these three families, the rest of us will remain and attempt to effect our own escape to Brittany."

"*D'accord*." She glanced at Julian who merely said, "All is arranged, Danny. While we have been waiting for you to make an appearance, we have been quite busy."

St. Estèphe gnashed his teeth in silent fury. All his carefully laid plans must again be postponed. He had intended to follow Danielle and her friends with a party of his own men and make his move in that remote fishing village far from civilization. He would take them all red-handed in the moment of flight, returning the aristos and the English spies in triumph to Paris as further evidence of his loyalty to the revolutionary committee. He would remain in Brittany amusing himself with the little de St. Varennes while he waited for her husband who would find her—and her captor—easily enough. And when he eventually returned to Paris, leaving his enemy dead, he would deliver Danielle to Madame Guillotine and mop up the rest of these traitors and all the others whose identities he held. It was a perfect plan and one that accomplished many things in a single throw. But now, after the mob's activities of this night, again he could not afford to leave the center of the power struggle that would inevitably take place in the next weeks.

He would have to wait until her next visit, and nothing would prevent her from returning; not now when the need had become so totally imperative and would become even more so by the minute. In the meantime, he would throw a few of these aristo fools to the lions, bait for the mob's appetite, and the panic that that would cause would run like wildfire, inevitably leading to carelessness as they made their plans for exodus, and he would pick them off one by one, with no one any the wiser of the traitor in their midst. Yes, it was a pleasing plan, St. Estèphe decided, looking around the anxious faces in the room. He must just be patient and remember that everything comes to him who waits.

Danielle was conferring in a low voice with her colleagues as St. Estèphe mentally revised his plans. "Our only hope is to approach the *barrière* boldly," she was saying. "This night's work can be used to our advantage. We will wear the *bonnets rouges* and sing the "Ça Ira" and will tell with much bloodthirsty detail of what we have seen. In fact," she paused with a shudder, "I think it would be more convincing if we carried with us some souvenirs from the Tuileries, and . . . and perhaps we had better look a little bloody ourselves."

There was short silence and then Tony said grimly, "Let us go then."

The five of them slipped from the house and then ran boldly through the alleys in the direction of the Tuileries. The streets were packed with shouting, singing hordes brandishing flaming torches, passing around flagons of wine. Impromptu dances were being performed on corners and in squares, and the scene in the Tuileries gardens came straight from the pits of hell. The crowd, intoxicated with blood and liquor had hardly diminished since Danielle had left. Some had collapsed beside the bodies of the Swiss Guard, others trampled heedlessly over the living and the dead, their voices rising in raucous triumph. Danielle smeared blood on her blouse and ripped a gore-stained shirt from one of the bodies before vanishing behind a tree to retch violently as the rough red wine that she had drunk earlier revolted in her stomach and spewed forth in a convulsive tide. The others, as filthy and bloody as she now was, found her there within a few minutes. They had shared too much intimacy for Danielle to feel embarrassment as they waited in silence for the spasms to pass before helping her to her feet.

"I am all right," she whispered, trying to stiffen her wobbling knees. "Please, let us leave now."

Dawn was breaking in eerie beauty over the hellish scene of horror as they made their way back through streets rapidly emptying as the night's excesses began to have their effect. "Danny, you must rest a while," Jules insisted. "We will leave in two hours."

"No, we must leave now. I cannot rest until we are through the gates. We will find somewhere to wash off this . . ." A tremor shook her slight frame and the four men looked at her anxiously. "Please, you must not worry," she reassured, intercepting the look. "I am really quite strong, you understand."

"Yes," Jules said with a dry twist of his lips, "we understand quite well, but I am very much afraid that Justin will not. I hope to God he will be at Mervanwey to put a stop to this."

"Oh, do not be absurd." The remark had the desired effect and brought a flash to the brown eyes. "He will do no such thing since he and I are now quite in agreement over priorities. I am sure that the next time he will accompany us."

"Well, he'll most assuredly not permit you to leave without him," Jules stated and Danny grinned, much in her usual manner.

"*Mais, d'accord, mon cousin. Ça c'est la pointe.*"

There was little traffic as they made their way to the gate, their passengers hidden beneath the layers of straw. About half a mile before they reached the *barrière*, Jules and Tony put their horses to the gallop and they all stood, singing the "Ça Ira" at the tops of their voices, flourishing the bloody shirts they had stripped from the bodies and waving a leathern flask of wine.

The guards who had spent the night at their posts, hearing the sounds from the city but unaware of what had transpired, rushed forward to stop them and the horses came to a plunging standstill. Danny leaped from the cart, offering her flagon and demanding that they drink to *La République*. The five of them were a fearsome sight with their gory talismans, the blood and filth streaking their exhausted faces—fearsome but utterly convincing. Danny poured out the story in an excited stream of gruesome, explicit detail while her companions nodded, grunted, and drank as the flagon was passed around and her audience shouted their enthusiasm. The three women and six children, packed like sardines beneath the straw, held their breath and huddled, paralyzed with fright as the party seemed likely to continue forever. And then came the sound of a whip crack and the carts began to move, slowly at first but gathering speed as the white dusty road to safety stretched emptily ahead.

"You have missed your calling, my friend," Jules remarked to Danny, who under the rush of adrenaline, appeared quite restored.

"And what is that?"

"You were clearly made for the stage," he told her, a tired grin cracking the caked filth on his face.

"Yes," she agreed, giving the thought all consideration. "I think I might have liked that, but then I could have been only Justin's mistress, so it would not have been at all *convenable.*"

Julian's laugh crackled in the still morning air and the other cart drew alongside. "Just what's so amusing?" Westmore demanded in French, using the regional accent that Danny had taught them. Jules shared the joke and their hilarity bordered on the hysterical as the aftermath of that horrific night took its toll.

Safe again at Mervanwey, Danielle appeared to move in an abstracted dream.

"She is herself only with the child," Lady Lavinia bemoaned to her husband as August became September and Danielle continued to postpone a return visit to France, waiting each day for the sight and sound of her husband.

"She sent the messenger to Pitt two weeks past," Charles said, idly turning the pages of his book, the words they contained conveying nothing to him. "There should be a reply soon."

Danielle was in the rose garden at the head of the cliff playing hide-and-seek with Nicholas as she kept watch over the winding path that climbed steeply to the house. She spent the most part of the day here, as it commanded the best view of the approach road, and Nicky was more than content to be in his mother's company during thet late summer days. Danielle talked to him constantly about his papa, showed him the picture she kept under her pillow every night before he slept, desperate to keep the image and memory alive for the child who now ran on tottering chubby legs and had mastered an impressive vocabulary of demand and description. The words came singly as yet, but they came in both French and English. Danielle ached for Justin's presence, sharing with her the excitement as their son developed in leaps and bounds.

This sunny late September afternoon she sat on the wall where an eon ago Justin had proposed to a hoydenish minx who had just held him up at pistol point for a joke that he had not shared. Nicky was blowing vigorously on a dandelion clock, chuckling delightedly as the white cotton wool puffs danced in the air. "*Un, deux, trois,*" he shrieked, running to catch the fluffy strands.

Danielle smiled absently, looking down the path. At the sight of the lone horseman her heart lurched and then sank. Even at this distance she could tell through the pores of her skin that the figure was not the one she sought. However, maybe it was the messenger returning from London and if so he would have news. Good or bad, it no longer mattered. Just something to make sense of the waiting. She scooped up Nicky and ran with him toward the house.

The messenger brought little comfort. Pitt had made no attempt to dissemble in his note to Danielle. There had been no news from Justin—it was too early to despair as he had been gone but five months, but there was cause for concern. More than that he could not say. He thanked her for the invaluable firsthand reports from Paris and begged that she take both care and heart.

"*Eh bien, mes amis*, are you ready to make another voyage? We have delayed overlong and there may well be people waiting for us in the village. If so, they will be losing heart rapidly." Danielle smiled with an effort across the dinner table that evening. "The news from Paris worsens, if that is possible, according to Pitt's message. The royal family are now imprisoned in the Temple, quite at the mercy of the people, and Madame Guillotine takes her victims with increasing fervor."

"Danny, let us make this next journey without you?" Julian asked quietly, knowing the request to be fruitless but shivered by the bleak look on her face.

"*Non!*" she declared. "I will go quite mad if I stay here! I beg pardon." She apologized for the rude exclamation. "I cannot walk the cliffs waiting for Justin," she explained in a more moderate tone. "We will go again to Paris and I will use my energies in that way. There is much work to be done and I can do it with more heart than I would have preparing for my widow's weeds."

The blunt statement contained only truth, clear-cut and invincible, and no one around the table could find the words of contradiction.

They set sail three days later and in nine days were again in Paris—the capital of the new republic of France. The abolition of royalty had been decreed on September 21. While Louis XVI and his family suffered the discourtesies and cruel deprivations of the sans-culottes guards, the tumbrils began to roll from the prisons to Place de la Revolution. D'Evron had been dead these last six weeks, spared the journey from Châtelet to Madame Guillotine where, with hands bound, hair cropped, and shirt collar opened, he would have placed his head upon the block for the blade that would have ended his life amidst the jeers of the *tricoteurs* who knitted the names of the aristos-come-to-judgment into the long scarves taking shape beneath their busy needles.

The Comte de St. Vire died in that manner, unaware that in the jeering crowd a small figure witnessed his death and prayed for his soul. Danielle ran beside the tumbrils as they moved to the place of execution, searching for familiar faces, pallid in preparation for their deaths. She could do nothing for them now, but had a desperate need that they should see a familiar face and die in the knowledge that there was still hope of escape for those they left behind.

This time they were to take three carts out of Paris. St. Estèphe had provided the third and *Dream Girl* would handle the extra passengers because she must. Once the winter storms set in, raging against that unwelcoming coast, not even Jake would risk the voyage, not to mention standing to at anchor for two weeks while he waited for the light to show from the cove.

They passed the *barrières* in their usual fashion, except that

422

this time Danielle wore the peasant dress and kerchief of a farmer's daughter and flirted outrageously with the guards, dancing around the guardhouse as the carts passed through unquestioned by the distracted sentries. She made her escape by the hem of a grimy petticoat, leaping back onto the seat beside Julian with a stream of invective that contained the promise of her return. The guards laughed heartily and promised her reception on the next occasion with much ribaldry.

"God damn it!" Jules exclaimed as they hit the familiar road. "Why must you take such risks? You become more outrageous every time."

"It is necessary," she replied calmly.

They reached the Breton coast in ample time, quite unaware that St. Estèphe and his men were following them, half a day's journey behind and by a different route.

St. Estèphe had hoped to make up the time, knowing that his chosen route was shorter and that on horseback they could travel faster than the laden carts. But he made a grave error of judgment in picking a path that, unlike Danielle's, took him through major towns where they were frequently stopped and held at the gates while their credentials were examined. In one place they were hauled before an excitable mayor prepared to suspect any party from Paris of being fleeing royalists. St. Estèphe fumed at the delays, raged at the officious bureaucracies that insisted on confirming his passports with meticulous care, and could not begin to understand why he was in such a hurry as they conferred at length before returning the papers and wishing him a pleasant journey. Thus his hopes of being on the beach, ready in ambush when the fugitives signaled for the dinghy, were unfulfilled and the careful orderliness of his plans thrown into disarray.

"The dinghy will have to make two journeys," Danielle whispered to Westmore as they stood on the small beach, shrouded in dark cloaks. "We should first send our passengers." She glanced at the pale shivering group huddled in the lee of the cliff, sheltering from the blasts of the late October wind. There were nine of them, seven women and children and two men, and the journey from Paris had been

y

423

arduous in the extreme, made even more miserable by constant complaints at the privations they all endured and the incessant challenges of the men who refused to accept the authority of the grimy urchin that was Danny, now back in her shirt and britches.

Westmore agreed. "I'll be monstrous glad to see the last of them," he muttered. "The voyage will be made wretched with their moans."

Danny laughed without much humor and shrugged, peering across the black expanse of foam-flecked water for the first sight of the dinghy. "It is coming," she said as her sharp ears picked up the soft splash of oars an instant before her eyes made out the dark shape.

They all ran to the shore to help beach the dinghy and the two monosyllabic sailors merely grunted when told that they must return. The boat could carry seven passengers if enough of them were small and the nine passengers argued amongst themselves, wasting precious moments, as to who should go first.

"Take the women and children; the men stay here with us," Philip ordered crisply. One aristocratic lady, clasping her child to her bosom, announced dramatically that she would not be parted from her husband. "As you wish, madame," Philip responded in frosty tones. "Let us just *hurry* for the Lord's sake!"

The husband in question began to bluster at this brusque manner of addressing his wife and Danielle, quite out of patience, whirled on him with a few well-chosen words that left him stammering with fury. But at last they pushed the laden dinghy off the beach, Danny and her companions soaked to their thighs while the French family stood high and dry on the beach, muttering indignantly at their rude treatment.

"*Merde!*" Danielle hissed. "Perhaps you would prefer the tender strokes of the guillotine?"

"Hush," Jules said, putting his arm around her. "They are frightened."

"And are we not all?" she muttered, thinking of Justin with a deep stab of lonely despair.

It was two hours later when the dinghy reappeared and this

time, in the interests of speed, waited in the shallows instead of running onto the beach.

"*Vous permettez, madame?*" Jules said politely as he swung the woman off her feet and carried her to the boat. Westmore carried the squawling child but no one offered to assist the stiff figure of the father who waded with a visible shudder into the cold black water. The rest followed and the oarsmen picked up their oars just as the child shrieked. "*Ma bébé. J'ai oublié ma bébé.*"

Danny swore, feeling the profanity quite justified, as she plunged back into the surf. "*Attendez!*" She ran across the beach to where the forgotten doll lay by a rock.

None of the watchers in the small craft were able to sort out what happened next. Men seemed to appear from nowhere, hurtling down the narrow cliff path, a musket shot exploded in the still air, but apart from that, for an eerie moment, there was no other sound. Jules and his three companions leaped to their feet setting the small craft rocking dangerously, the woman screamed, and the rowers put to their oars as rapid fire broke out anew from the beach, quite clearly directed at the dinghy. Danielle was a tiny figure, dodging from side to side, attempting to evade her captors and make for the water as the dinghy pulled away under the desperate efforts of two pairs of strong arms encouraged by the hail of bullets spurting the water around them.

Suddenly Danielle stopped running, recognizing the tall figure on the beach who had been watching her gyrations. She called the traitor's name with all the force of her lungs.

"St. Estèphe!" Jules exclaimed just as a scream of pain came from one of the Cornishmen. A bullet had caught him in the shoulder and he collapsed gasping over the oars.

"Take over, man, damn your eyes!" Jules, with a brutal foot, kicked the Frenchman cowering with his wife and child in the bottom of the boat. "If you do not, you will never reach safety. Quick!" he said urgently to the others. "Into the water, but silently. There are too many of them and our only hope is in surprise." He turned to the uninjured Cornishman. "Tell Jake to hold *Dream Girl* offshore until we signal again." The man merely grunted, all breath and energy devoted to his task, and the four discarded boots, cloaks, swords, and pistols, keeping only the wickedly sharp daggers, before slipping into the now deep water where the current ran strongly but the dark night hid them from the confusion on the beach.

St. Estèphe swore as he saw one-half of his prey make its escape, but there was nothing he could do. It was a moonless night and the boat had almost vanished, swallowed into the blackness long before it would have been out of range of the muskets. But he *did* have the most important object and, for a moment on the cliff top as he'd watched them pile into the dinghy, he had thought to lose that also. Why she had suddenly leapt from the boat and straight into his arms was of little interest—suffice it that she had done so. He walked toward her, withdrawing from his pocket the wad of cloth.

It had taken three men eventually to subdue her, but although her body was held imprisoned, arms bent painfully behind her back, her tongue was still virulent and the defiance glared from the brown eyes as she spat in the comte's face.

He smiled and wiped his cheek with the back of his hand. "You will pay for that later, *ma belle*," he said and suddenly clamped the wad of cloth over her mouth and nose.

Danielle smelled the sickly sweetness of the chloroform and struggled until a vicious jerk of her arms made her cry out in pain against the smothering cloth. The last thing she saw was the flat gleam of those fishy eyes and her last conscious thought was that the simile was wrong. They were the eyes of a cobra preparing to strike . . .

Her friends, cowering in the freezing water against the black overhang of a jutting rock, could see little detail of the events on the beach. There was nothing they could do at this point since they were hopelessly outnumbered and armed only with knives—good enough weapons in single, close quarters combat, but of no use at all against ten men with muskets.

They waited until the beach party had reached the top of the cliff before dragging their soaked bodies onto the sand of the small cove.

"What the devil has St. Estèphe to do with this?" Westmore led the way up the narrow path.

"Only the devil's work," Philip answered. "Why else would

426

he take Danny?"

Hidden behind the windswept scrub of the cliff top they watched St. Estèphe and his men mount and take off across the fields, Danny's limp body hanging across the comte's saddle bow.

"They are not going immediately to Paris then." Jules spoke for the first time. "We can be of little use without dry clothes and horses and now we know their direction we will find it easy to follow their tracks."

"And what of Danny?" Tony demanded.

"If St. Estèphe intended to kill her he would have done so already," Jules replied. He seemed to be now simply a cold thinking machine, all emotion banished. He was responsible for the safety of his cousin's wife and they could afford no hasty impulsive action. St. Estèphe would not himself have carried her dead body in that way, he would have left such a burden to a minion. So, whatever they had done to her on the beach had simply immobilized her. Their task was to find where she had been taken and effect her rescue—simple enough if one went about it in the right way. "Come, let us go to the village. We will retrieve the horses from the Legrands and find fresh clothes. If we succumb to the ague we will be of little use to Danny."

It was cold common sense and no one demurred. They now had friends in the village, fisherfolk who accepted them with undemanding hospitality and no questions, receiving more than adequate recompense for their kindness. In an hour or so, they would be able to follow the tracks of Danielle's captors—eleven horsemen could not disappear without trace in this isolated region where all strange occurrences would be noticed—and her friends had the advantage of surprise.

Danielle woke to hammer blows in her skull, rhythmic, regular, each one seemingly intended to split her head in two. A violent wave of nausea, the inevitable aftermath of the chloroform, left her retching into the pillow in helpless self-disgust as she tugged futilely at whatever it was that held her wrists fast above her head. Then the merciful black wave of unconsciousness swallowed her yet again.

The next time she awoke it was when something warm and soothing sponged her face and hair and the soiled pillow was removed, leaving her aching head to lie flat.

"She'll not vomit again," St. Estèphe said to the pasty-faced girl ministering to the still figure on the bed. There's no further need to keep her head raised. You may go now, and you will come in here only when I tell you—do you understand?"

The girl stammered her promise of obedience and stumbled from the room. The two guards outside the door caught her, their hands straying in gross familiarity over her body as she shuddered and begged them to leave her be. They laughed and let her go with a generous salting of coarse remarks and promises.

Danielle opened her eyes and looked into the snake eyes of St. Estèphe. Her head was pounding sickeningly and the candle he held shot sparks behind her eyeballs. She averted her head and the *comte* laughed. "You are not comfortable, *ma belle*?" he questioned, taking her chin and turning her face back toward him.

"I am perfectly comfortable, thank you, sir," she responded with a travesty of a smile. St. Estèphe chuckled in rich satisfaction.

"We will amuse ourselves," he promised. "You will become more amenable when you have experienced your position for a little longer." He left her, taking the candle and plunging Danny into pitch-darkness. She had lost all sense of time and lay still in the darkness until her eyes became accustomed. A thread of light indicated a closed window shutter, another filament showed her the door. Apart from that there was nothing except the sensation of her damp britches clinging to her thighs, an uncovered mattress beneath her, and the straps cutting into her wrists.

She slept again and awoke to the same darkness and the pressing demand of her body. But there was no way she could free herself. Her legs were unfettered but her hands were held fast. She opened her mouth to call out and thought again of the stories she had been told of St. Estèphe. If they were true then her humiliation and degradation was his object and to plead would only increase his satisfaction. Danielle gritted her teeth and bent her mind to the business of making some sense out of all this. If the comte was simply an agent of the revolutionary committee, why had he not betrayed them in Paris? It would have been easy enough. But he appeared on the scene long before she had begun this adventure, had talked to Justin of an old friendship between their fathers . . . had appeared in London, all charm and eagerness to offer his services. And Justin had disliked him and mistrusted him from the outset without knowing why . . . .

The door opened. For an instant bright daylight flooded the room and Danny took in her surroundings, such as they were, before the door closed again and the dim flicker of a tallow candle pierced the renewed darkness.

"Madame?" a soft anxious voice spoke. "I am permitted to release you if you wish to use the pail and take some food."

"Then in the name of charity do so," Danny groaned.

"You will please try not to . . . There are guards outside the door," the voice stuttered unhappily.

"*Je comprends*," Danielle reassured. "I will make no move to escape." The straps were undone. She rubbed her reddened wrists, and stretched the cramped muscles of her protesting shoulders and upper arms before making use of the facilities.

She looked at the bread, cheese, and pitcher of water with a frown. "When will you come again?"

"I cannot say, milady," the voice whispered. "When the comte tells me."

"I see." Danielle spurned the food despite her hunger pangs and slaked her thirst with but two sips of water. The less she put inside her at this point, the longer her body could resist nature's imperative calls. "Will you tell me what you know of this place?" she inquired gently, pacing the floor and swinging her arms as she flexed the muscles in her legs and feet. "Are we still in Brittany?"

"*Mais oui, madame*—but five miles from the coast. The cottage belongs to my father. The comte has paid him well for its use and my services." The girl's voice was very low now. "I dare not disobey. If I displease the comte my father will beat me and I cannot bear it another time." With a simple movement, the girl slipped her blouse off her shoulders and Danielle stared in horror at the crusted welts crisscrossing her back.

"Have no fear," she said quietly, "I'll not put you in further danger. What is your name?"

"Jeanette," the girl replied. "Milady, if you will not eat, I must . . ." She gestured toward the cot.

"*Bien sûr.*" Danielle lay down on the rough mattress and allowed the girl to fasten her wrists again.

"I dare not fasten the straps more loosely," Jeanette whispered in soft apology.

"No, I understand." With a supreme effort Danielle smiled and the girl left, taking the tallow candle and returning Danny to her dark prison. She knew now that it was a tiny room, no more than seven paces in length and perhaps five in width, containing the cot and a low table—nothing more. Outside there were guards and five miles away the coast. It was little enough to go on but she had to think of something constructive to blot from her mind thoughts of Nicky and Justin and the fear of her unknown destiny at the hands of St. Estèphe.

Her arms began to ache unbearably. She moved up the cot, trying to ease the pain, but there was little relief to be gained from the tiny adjustments she was able to make. The continuing darkness did nothing for her slowly despairing spirit, and hunger and thirst raged. Danny had faced many dangers, but never before had she been quite without resources and, as the long hours of confinement passed, she fought despair with every fiber of her strength.

It was six interminable hours later when St. Estèphe entered the disorienting darkness with a bright lantern that he placed carefully on the small table.

"*Alors, ma belle,*" he said, looking down at her. "Do you find that you are still perfectly comfortable?" His eyes mocked her as she blinked in confusion at the sudden light.

"Perfectly, thank you," she replied through dry lips.

"You cannot be comfortable in wet clothes," he argued, bending over her supine figure, patting her down with intimate hands. Danielle held her breath and bit back the scream of revulsion. As he began to unbutton her shirt, she curled her

430

legs and kicked him in the stomach. St. Estèphe drew back with a gasp of pain. "That was foolish," he said almost gently, and with quiet deliberation hit her across the mouth with his open hand.

Tears sprang in her eyes and she tasted the salty blood from a cut lip.

"Would you prefer that I have my men strip you?" he inquired casually as her shirt tore apart beneath his hands. "They would take much pleasure in the task, I assure you." He examined her breasts through hooded eyes and Danielle lay still preparing herself for what she knew was to come. When he stripped off her britches she made no foolish futile movement of protest and received her reward in the clear disappointment in her tormentor's eyes. "So, you will not fight me?" His hands stroked lasciviously over her body. "Eventually you will beg me to take you, *ma belle*. When you can no longer bear your discomfort."

"Just tell me why?" Danielle summoned her last reserves of energy. "What have I done to you that you should do this to me?"

St. Estèphe chuckled. "It is nothing that *you* have done, *ma belle*. You are merely the instrument of my revenge. Many years ago your husband's father dishonored my family and I am pledged to avenge the insult. Your husband will come in search of you and when he finds you, you will be my willing submissive plaything. And I will kill him after he has seen what you have become."

Danny licked her dry lips again. "You have overlooked one thing, comte. My husband is dead. I heard the news from Pitt before I left England. You may use me as you please, but Justin will have no knowledge of your revenge."

The second blow smashed her head sideways into the mattress and, without a further word, the comte took the lantern and her torn clothing and left her, naked and alone in the darkness.

Chapter 22

Justin's heart leapt as he rounded the corner of the steep path and at last saw journey's end. The long low house of Mervanwey glowed mellow in the afternoon light of this last day of October, and the trees bordering the path were a deep copper. One strong wind and they would lose the fragile leaves to the winter of gales and sea storms waiting in the wings. As he reached the head of the cliff he looked over the low stone wall into the rose garden and saw a sight that brought a glow of pride and love into his eyes. His son, turned sixteen months now, was running on sturdy legs across the grass, shrieking with glee, pursued by Maddy, the young nursery maid, growling like a lion.

Justin dismounted and vaulted over the wall. "Nicky?" Both child and girl stopped, and Maddy's rosy cheeks suddenly paled as if she saw a ghost.

"My Lord," she gasped. "Is it really you? You are alive then?"

"I certainly have that impression," he agreed with a smile. "My son, do you remember your papa?" Kneeling in front of the little boy, he took his hands.

"Papa?" Nicky looked at him seriously and then the small face split in a sunny beam. It had been six months since he had last seen this man but he still saw his picture every night before he slept, and everyone always talked to him about "Papa."

Justin laughed with pleasure and picked up the little figure, kissing the firm round cheek. "Come, let us go and find *Maman*."

433

"*Maman* . . . boat." Nicky pointed to the gray Atlantic ocean stretching into the distance.

"What?" His father frowned and looked at Maddy whose eyes were stricken. She gazed at the ground, apparently tongue-tied. "I will take Nicky with me up to the house," he told her and, hitching his son onto a hip, vaulted the wall again and remounted easily with one hand. Nicky squealed with delight at finding himself on the back of this great beast, an experience that he found not at all terrifying, held as he was by an iron arm against a broad chest. He babbled nonstop, a mixture of nonsense and baby words, pointing excitedly from side to side and bouncing up and down on the saddle. Justin responded with the right degree of interested encouragement although the prick of unease was rapidly becoming a cold stab of premonition.

There had been something in the prime minister's attitude that had puzzled him when he had made the detailed report of his mission immediately on his return. Pitt had appeared curiously evasive when Justin had asked him if he had news of Danny, and had said only that he believed her to be in Cornwall. Linton, in his eagerness to reach his wife's side, had hardly noticed the awkwardness until memory now came back with full force. Unconsciously he urged his mount into a canter as the path leveled off.

Nicky shrieked, and the earl instantly checked the horse, only to hear his son demand, "'Gain, 'gain." Definitely his mother's child, Justin reflected, obeying the instruction. Their arrival at the circular gravel sweep outside the house caused an extraordinary commotion. Justin tossed his son over his shoulder and swung to the ground in one movement, striding through the gaping gabbling throng of servants into the cool flagged hallway.

"Justin! Oh thank God! We have been certain that you were dead. There has been no news and . . ." Lady Lavinia flung herself weeping against his chest.

"It is a long story, ma'am," he said, patting her back helplessly as his son squirmed and wriggled in his upside-down position.

"Let the man get inside, Lavvy." Charles appeared from the

library and took his wife's arm. "It is such a relief to see you, Justin," he explained, seizing his hand in a hard grip that spoke volumes. "Come into the library before someone starts charging a fee to witness this spectacle."

"Oh, what can I have been thinking of?" Lavinia scolded herself as her husband's words took effect. "What an unseemly display, and poor Nicky is quite scarlet."

Justin righted the child who wriggled and said imperatively, "Down."

"I wonder how long it's going to be before you learn to say 'please'?" Justin mused, setting him on his feet.

"Oh, he does already," Lavinia put in hastily. "But sometimes he forgets. Danielle is most insistent that he . . ." Her voice faded.

"Where is she?" Anxiety rasped harsh in his voice.

"Not in front of . . ." Lavinia gestured toward Nicky, who was pushing chess pieces around on a board resting on a low table.

A cold shiver of apprehension raised the hairs on the nape of his neck. What news was there about the child's mother that they must keep from him? "Come, Nicky. You must go to Tante Thérèse for a short while." He scooped him up, ignoring the complaining wail, and bore him upstairs to the sunny nursery where Tante Thérèse evinced no apparent surprise at His Lordship's appearance and dealt with Nicky's incipient tantrum with serene firmness.

"Now." Justin faced the Earl and Countess of March. "What scrape does she find herself in this time?"

"If only it were just that," Lavinia moaned.

"Here, Linton, take a glass of sherry, and I will tell you the whole." Charles took over briskly, and Justin gave him a grateful if wan smile.

He heard Charles out in complete silence, standing at the window, gazing blindly at the late autumn garden and the unfriendly gray sea beyond.

"This is the third time, you say, that she has made this journey?" he asked finally, turning back to the room and absently refilling his glass.

"Yes, but they have never been away this long. It has been

well over five weeks and in another week, maybe less, the weather will turn and *Dream Girl* will be unable to make the return journey in safety. Jake is too good a sailor to risk his ship and he will have made it clear to Danny and the others that they must rendezvous in ample time. We can only assume that he is waiting until the last possible moment and therefore that something has happened to prevent their meeting."

"Yes," Justin agreed bleakly. "And it requires little imagination to think what may have happened in that city of mayhem and murder." He paced the room. "I should have foreseen this. I know well enough what she is like."

"We did what we could to prevent her," Charles said with a heavy sigh. "But I feel utterly responsible."

"Nonsense!" Linton cut him off abruptly. "You are in no way responsible, March. Stopping Danielle when she has her mind set is as impossible as halting the path of an avalanche. There is nothing we can do but await the return of *Dream Girl*. If what you say of your captain is true, he will return with or without them within the week. If he comes alone, then I must go myself. It will be possible to make landfall further up the coast throughout the winter."

How long had she been held in this way? Danny could no longer even estimate. St. Estèphe's latest move had been to bind her eyes so she could no longer draw comfort from the thread of light beneath window and door. But she took one small comfort—blindfolded as she was the comte could not see the fear in her eyes. She would be alone for an eternity and then the door would creak open and close and sometimes, for hours it seemed, she would sense his presence but he would make no move until she wanted to scream—tell him to hit her again, anything but this black silence as she lay, naked and spread-eagled on the rough ticking, her ankles now also bound to the posts at the foot of the bed. Sometimes he would laugh and she would hear the door close again, and other times he would run his hands over her shrinking flesh and tell her in a soft sibilant whisper what he would eventually do with her when she begged him for release and he decided to grant it.

436

Jeanette's appearances were infrequent and brief. The girl was not allowed to untie the blindfold and Danielle had to accept her help in tending to her physical needs. She continued to refuse all but a mouthful of bread and took only a few sips of water. She was allowed to wash and to brush her hair, however, and could only assume that St. Estèphe's interest in her body was genuine enough for him not to enjoy the sight of her dirty and bedraggled. It was bleak comfort, but at least she was saved the ultimate humiliation, although sometimes kept waiting for relief almost to breaking point.

The others would be safely back in Mervanwey by now, or at least on their way back. It was a three-day voyage but surely her captivity had lasted longer than that? She couldn't blame them for not coming to her rescue. Jake could not hold *Dream Girl* offshore for any longer than the last week of October as he'd explained bluntly on the voyage over. They had spent much longer in Paris than usual and the journey to the coast had been slowed by the moans of their passengers. They had reached the cove on the last possible day that Jake had declared to be safe and if any of them were to get out of France before winter set in then they would have had to have left immediately.

It was all quite reasonable and understandable, Danielle told herself, as the hot tears stung her eyes and soaked the blindfold. If she cried her nose would run and she had no way of wiping it. She sniffed vigorously as the tears ceased instantly at the thought that St. Estèphe *must not* see a sign of weakness.

In fact, it had been only thirty-six hours since Julian and his friends had watched the cavalcade of horsemen take off across the fields. In the meantime, they had found dry clothes (rough threadbare fishermen's garb that both parties were more than happy to exchange), retrieved the horses from the Legrand's pasture, and set off in search of information. The Breton folk were cautious about divulging anything to strangers, but the word had spread about these peculiar Englishers who came out of the sea and left by the sea, causing no trouble but leaving lavish expressions of friendship in their wake. The arrogant Frenchman, on the other hand, was a very different kettle of fish. He had first appeared some weeks previously with a group of henchmen who had paraded around the village, clear intent in their eyes as they looked over the young girls. As a result, every girl over the age of ten had been sequestered behind cottage doors and the murmurs of resentful hostility had spread.

Only the sour-faced miserly sonless widower Betrand Ville had listened to the Parisian, bloodshot eyes gleaming at the prospect of money that did not have to be torn from the seabed or wrenched from an unkind soil. He had three daughters, mewling whining useless creatures who had not the strength to fight the ocean with him, although they had learned to till and to sow the land, and they kept his house in the expected order; that they did so in constant fear of the studded belt he wore around his waist seemed only right and proper to Betrand.

He had offered the *comte* both the use of a small cottage on the outskirts of his land and his youngest daughter, fourteen years old and thoroughly obedient. St. Estèphe had been well pleased, and the negotiation had been accomplished in great amicability. But Betrand was less than amicable when accosted by four horsemen as he stood at the backyard pump swilling the dirt of the fields from his face and neck.

Jules and his fellows were not prepared to be put off by the rough curses and the threats to set the dog on them. They had been sent in this direction by reliable sources and nothing they had seen so far of this wretched farm gave the lie to their informants. Betrand Ville, under the astonished eyes of his two daughters, was held under the icy stream of the pump water until, gasping and shivering, he told what he knew.

"Danny has a name for that breed," Westmore remarked as they set off at a gallop across the fields. "Can't for the life of me remember what it was, though."

"*Canaille*," Philip reminded him. "Not good to use in Polite Circles, y'know."

"No, no, to be sure," Westmore agreed. "Wouldn't dream of it me self."

"Danny would," Tony stated. "Never one to mince her words."

They rode on in silence until the landmarks Betrand had been forced to produce came into view. "We go on foot from here." Julian broke the silence with quiet authority. "Counting St. Estèphe, there are eleven of them, armed with muskets, and the girl. We can't discount her, not if she's anything like her father."

They tethered the horses a half mile from the cottage and crept as close as they dared. "We wait and watch," Jules said and they did so for long hours. The *comte*'s men appeared to be housed in a long barn set at right angles to the cottage. Every four hours two of them went into the cottage and two others reappeared. A girlish figure in a shabby worsted gown and kerchief darted across the yard every so often to draw water from the well and to bring food to the barn. Ribald shouts greeted her when she did so and once or twice she was grabbed and mauled, her piteous pleas producing great gouts of laughter from the men. But they always let her go, unharmed, and the reason for this restraint became clear when St. Estèphe appeared in the yard, eyebrows meeting as he paced back and forth, snarled at the girl who dodged instinctively as if in expectation of a blow, and spoke in a low voice to the men who slunk back to the barn.

The *comte* was becoming impatient. That stubborn little fool was still giving hardly an inch and she was too perfect, too well honed for the crudity of plain violence to give him any satisfaction. He wanted her on her knees, unmarked. But naked, bound, alone in complete darkness, pushed to the limits her muscles could hold tenure, *still* she would not yield. The information about her husband's death had driven him into an icy rage of frustration but did nothing to change his plans for Danielle, who was now a total obsession with him.

He gave a sharp order and his horse was brought from the stable. Riding the cliffs, St. Estèphe decided, would clear his head of the anger that smudged the edges of his clear thinking. He took two of the ten with him as protection—these Bretons could not be trusted any further than one could throw them—

and rode out of the yard, leaving eight men and Jeanette to guard the prisoner.

"It has to be now," Jules murmured. "Four to eight are the best odds we will ever get. Six out here and two in the house.

"I used to think as a child that it would be monstrous amusing to set a light to a haystack," Tony reflected. "Not to endanger the horses, you understand, but just to see it burn. November 5th *par excellence*." He chuckled and waited for the idea to take root.

> "Remember remember the 5th of November,
> Gun powder treason and plot."

The old nursery rhyme rose easily to their lips. November 5th, guyfawkes day was a day of pure joy for the English child who gathered sticks for the bonfire weeks ahead and made effigies of the man who had attempted to blow up the Houses of Parliament. The guy was set atop the bonfire and burned amidst the gleeful shrieks of adults and the cascading crescendo of fireworks.

"You have the right idea, Tony." Jules chuckled. "We set fire to the haystack and see how many roaches crawl out from the woodwork . . ." And then he froze. The girl appeared in a doorway, cast a scared glance toward the barn, and was off and running across the yard to disappear behind a low wall. Philip went after her without further consultation, keeping his head low as he skirted the wall and then saw her running toward a small copse of stunted trees.

Jeanette heard the footsteps pounding at her back and ran like a small animal until a strangely accented voice said in her own language, "Stop, I mean you no harm. I wish to talk of the lady."

She stopped, panting for breath, and Tony came toward her, hands held open in friendship.

"What of the lady?"

Tony examined the white face, the wide candid blue eyes, the heaving bosom, and he gambled. "We wish to help her. Will you help us while the *comte* is absent?"

"They will kill me," the girl whimpered, her hands knotted

in anguish.

"No, because we shall take you with us." Tony was playing his cards with a cool desperation he had never needed in White's. There, if he made the wrong discard, he paid only with money. Here, in this scrubby copse on the north coast of Brittany in revolution-torn France, Danny's safety hung on his skill.

"Out of France?" Jeanette's eyes widened at the terrifying scope of such an idea.

"Yes, out of France. Have no fear, little one, you will be well looked after." He held out his hand.

Jeanette had known no gentleness in her fourteen years. Her mother had died before she was three and her older sisters had had their own battles to fight. She had scrambled to maturity amidst curses and the thwack of a belt, had learned that the latter at least came less often if she kept a still tongue in her head and obeyed without question, but always she had believed, as a fierce talisman, that there was a world outside this mean grubbing for survival and the brutality that informed her environment. And here was someone, with a soft smile and a promise on his lips, someone who looked and spoke like that poor woman bound to the bed in the dark chamber; a woman who had never given Jeanette anything but smiles and instant comprehension of the girl's dilemma.

"What do you wish of me?"

"Information only. You can tell us how to effect entrance to the cottage where the lady is held and we will decide what to do." Tony took her hand. "Come, you have little to lose and much to gain."

Jeanette went then willingly enough and answered the rapid questions. Milady was held in a chamber at the front of the house. There were two guards always at the door. She had not yet been harmed but she was weak because she had taken no food since her captivity and was bound in such a manner as to restrict all movement . . . . Her description of Danielle's captivity was accurate and matter-of-fact and the four men contained their fury and made their plans.

Jeanette gave them a detailed account of the layout of the cottage and the routine of the guards.

441

"Very well," said Jules when she had finished. "We can assume we have little time before the *comte* returns. You will set fire to the haystack and take the six guards. I will deal with the two on duty."

"Milord," Jeanette whispered. "I can perhaps help. I may distract the guards at the door . . . they have shown a certain interest . . ."

"Are you willing to do that, child?" Jules asked quietly.

"*Mais oui*, milord. You will be there also."

Julian nodded. "Three to six, my friends. You can manage?"

"Without doubt and with much pleasure," Westmore said. "I will fire the stack now and you and Jeanette will make your way into the house under the cover of the smoke."

Danielle, stretched supine on the bed, heard the clamor as a confused tumult of shouts and curses. Smoke filled the yard and the six guards hurtled from the barn to meet no mercy from the outnumbered three who could afford to take no chances.

The guards outside her prison, a few minutes before the tumult broke out below, found the little maid, soft and inviting, curling herself around them. The *comte* was away; why not take advantage of what was offered? And she was a taking little thing with those nubile curves that she knew so well how to flaunt. As they pawed and patted and Jeanette offered her body with titillating little murmurs, Julian moved. He had only one knife and used it carefully but without compunction—no time for delicacy when Danny lay beyond the locked door. The guards fell at his feet and Jeanette had the key almost before Jules could draw breath.

"What the devil . . .?" The figure on the bed writhed against her bonds, the voice amazingly strong. "*C'est toi*, Jules?"

"*Oui, c'est moi*." He tossed his cloak over her hastily, before unfastening the straps at wrists and ankles. "Keep still now and for once just do as you are bid." It was a strange thing to say in the circumstances but in his anxiety he could not have cared.

"I am incapable of doing otherwise." She laughed weakly. "But *please* . . . my eyes!"

"Damn!" Jules untied the blindfold. "We have little time,

Danny. I must carry you."

"*D'accord, mon ami.* But Jeanette, we cannot leave her here."

"*Je suis ici*, milady," the girl said. "I have a change of clothes, if you will do me the honor. They may be a little large but the winds blow strong."

"*Va, vite.*" Danielle swayed on her feet, smiling at the girl as she clung to Julian.

Julian turned his back as she scrambled into Jeanette's best petticoats and gown, and then he picked her up and ran down the stairs to where the others waited impatiently, horses stamping, nostrils flared at the smell of smoke and charred hay.

"Set fire to the barn," Jules clipped, handing Danny to Westmore as he swung astride his horse and then reached down for her again. "We are but five miles from the coast and the lights may perhaps alert Jake."

"And also St. Estèphe," Tony said, throwing Jeanette up ahead of him before mounting himself.

"He is now but three to our four," Jules reminded.

"Five," Danielle declared. "I am not as weak as I seem. If you have a spare weapon, I claim the *comte* for my own."

"We have not and you may not," Julian told her flatly. "You will keep your mouth shut, cousin, until we are again aboard *Dream Girl.*"

"If she has not already left," Danny said soberly.

"That is not a helpful remark! Will you please keep quiet."

Danielle took no offense at Julian's autocratic tone, sensing both his acute anxiety and his relief at finding her relatively unharmed. The days of her captivity must have been almost as horrendous for her friends as they had been for her.

Meanwhile, Jake had reluctantly made up his mind that he must sail on the evening tide. He had intended to leave that morning but perversely the clamoring insistence of his passengers that he wait not a moment longer had kept him on deck, straining his eyes desperately for the flash of the beacon. Why the devil anyone would bother to save this ungrateful lot, he thought disgustedly as a whining voice came up behind. They were concerned only for their own skins and quite happy at the idea of abandoning their rescuers in that inhospitable

443

land. Then something caught his eye, a bright scarlet glow coming from inland. It bore no relation to the signal of the beacon, but it was just possible . . . An accidental fire on this damp windy coast where material possessions were treated with all the desperate care of poverty was almost inconceivable, particularly one that had been allowed to get out of hand, judging by the brilliance of that light. He had nothing to lose at any rate, and if it were indeed a signal then everything to be gained by having the dinghy on the beach waiting for them. He gave the orders for the boat to be lowered and then resumed his impatient pacing, ignoring the excitable foreign babble as his passengers demanded to know what was happening.

"We will leave the horses here," Jules said as they reached the cliff head. "They will find their way back or someone will find them." He dismounted. "A thousand pardons, Danny, but I cannot carry you in my arms down that path to the beach." Danielle was about to say that she was quite capable of walking now, when she found herself draped over his shoulder.

"This is most undignified, Jules," she grumbled, bumping uncomfortably as he began to leap down the steep path.

"Well, I am sorry for it, but it cannot be helped. And I am telling you straight, Danny, if we come out of this one alive, none of us are making such a journey again."

Danielle said nothing. One of these days she was going to kill St. Estèphe *very* slowly, but since she was sure Jules would not approve of her bloodthirsty thoughts she kept them to herself.

"Odd's breath, there's the dinghy." Westmore crowed with delight. "Jake must have seen the fire and drawn the right conclusions. What a stroke of luck!"

"We are certainly due for some," Philip said with absolute truth. "*Viens*, Jeanette." He took her hand and ran with her to the shore where the two sailors held the dinghy against the crashing surf.

Danielle sat huddled in Julian's cloak on the thwart, watching the cove recede as the powerful arms of the oarsmen bore them away from the nightmare. In three days she would be back with her son and maybe there would be some news. Black spots danced before her eyes and the strangest sensation crept up her neck, like being enclosed in a gray fog . . . .

Tony caught her as she slumped sideways and began chafing the white face. But she was out for barely a minute and came to, muttering apologies even before her senses had fully returned. "It is perhaps because I have had little food," she mumbled, struggling upright.

"Lie still." Tony put her head back in his lap. "It will not be long now."

Half an hour later Jake had the anchor taken up with an overpowering sense of relief. Ominous clouds scudded across the evening sky and the wind was coming in unpredictable spurts that gathered strength as the yacht moved into open water. The coastline offered no safe shelter with its riptides and concealed reefs and, unable to hug the shore, they had no choice but to put to sea. It was going to be a very long rough voyage, Jake thought, wondering grimly how those refugee passengers were going to manage in their cramped quarters below decks.

Justin paced the long drawing room at Mervanwey, fighting the helplessness, the hopelessness of his frustration. He could make no plans until *Dream Girl* returned, could only renew his relationship with his son—an immensely rewarding process, but Nicky asked constantly for his mother and was happiest in the rose garden where his father held him as they sat on the low wall both gazing at the noncommittal sea, waiting.

Lavinia looked at the man she now loved as if they were tied by blood, as helpless to help him as she was to help herself. They had dined at five o'clock, keeping country hours as usual. Nicky had been brought down in his nightgown to eat sugar plums and almonds, nestling in his father's lap as they took dessert before Justin carried him to bed, told one of the stories from his own childhood that returned with amazing ease to memory. It was nine o'clock and the November wind battled against the windowpanes.

"D'ye care for a game of piquet, Justin?" Charles asked as his wife plied her embroidery needle.

"By all means." Justin came over to the crackling fire. "I am poor company these days. I beg pardon . . ."

"*Tiens*! You have tried my patience beyond bearing. I cannot help it that you are wet and that it is a steep climb from the beach. If you do not care for your hospitality, I suggest you swim back to France where I am certain Madame Guillotine will make you most welcome!" The unmistakable voice rose in exasperation from the hall and the three in the drawing room gazed at each other in wonder and disbelieving hope.

The door burst open. "*Grandmère*, I do beg your pardon. You must have been in such a worry but . . ." Danny stopped on the threshold. "Justin?" Six months hadn't changed him at all, except for the drawn look about his eyes.

"Danny, you wretched little vagabond!" It was the most extraordinary salutation from a man who hadn't seen his wife in six months and who, for the last week, had assumed that she was dead. For Danielle they were the most wonderful words. She sprang across the room and into his arms, heedless of the tiresome group crowding the doorway or the soft exhalations of relief from her colleagues.

Justin kissed her, hugged her, feeling the remembered pliancy under his hands, the firm yet soft lips beneath his own. He pushed the cap from her head and gasped in sudden outrage at her cropped head. "Brat, how *dare* you do that again!" Gripping her shoulders, he shook her with all the vigor of a terrier with a rat, giving vent to the pent-up fear of the last seven days.

"P . . . p . . . please! Do stop," Danielle stammered when her head seemed about to leave her shoulders, and with a muttered exclamation he hugged her to him again.

"Incorrigible urchin! Why are you so wet?" Justin demanded as his senses returned and he became aware of her sopping britches pressing against his thighs.

"The surf was too high for *Dream Girl* to make the dock. We had to land in the dinghy," Danielle explained. "And the dinghy had to make several journeys because there are so many of us, you understand. Jules, and Tony and Philip and I had to wade in to help beach it. It is quite simple. But what is most interesting, Justin, is that I am no longer seasick. It was a monstrous tempestuous voyage but I felt not the slightest need to puke."

446

A tired grin suddenly split her face. "I do beg your pardon for my vulgarity, *Grandmaman*. But you understand how things are at the moment." She left her husband to embrace her grandparents. "How has Nicky been?"

"He is well and asleep these last two hours," Lavinia reassured, holding her granddaughter in a fierce grip.

"I will go up to the nursery shortly. But first we must do something for these . . ." Danny gestured toward the miserable group of utterly bewildered French who had been unable to follow a word of the conversation and could not begin to understand the extraordinary reception this diminutive bully had met at the hands of the tall Englishman.

"We are all like to die of hunger," Danielle went on. "We have been living off salt pork and ship's biscuits for the last five days."

"You are more like to die of the ague if you do not get out of those wet clothes this instant." Lavinia expressed her relief in severity, belied by the warm glow in her eyes, and took charge. "Justin, look to your wife while I do what I can to make these poor people comfortable. The rest of you may look after yourselves," she declared briskly. "There will be a meal in the dining room within the half hour."

"Jeanette." Danielle turned to the young girl standing awkwardly, twisting her red chapped hands into impossible knots. "I will take you to Tante Thérèse. She will look after you and make you quite comfortable, and I can visit my son at the same time."

"No," her husband said, recovering at last from his bemused joy and deciding that it was time he took a hand in this affair. "I will take the child to Tante Thérèse and you, Madam Wife, will put yourself into a hot bath without further ado. You may see Nicky when you are in dry clothes." —

"But that is ridic . . . Justin!" She yelped as he grabbed the collar of her jacket and marched her to the door.

"It is quite clear that I have been away far too long," he told her. "You appear to have forgotten in my absence that I do not tolerate disobedience." His eyes teased in the old way and his voice carried that note of mock severity that was part of their private language.

"I thought you were dead, love," Danny whispered, standing outside the door, away from the eyes within.

"And I you," he whispered back. "I will never leave you again, my love. What we do, we do together in future."

She nodded. "Come to me quickly."

"As soon as I have taken your little Jeanette to Tante Thérèse."

He found her in the porcelain tub before a blazing fire, receiving Molly's relieved ministrations and the reproaches that her privileged position allowed her to make. But a strange thing happened when Justin's gaze slowly traversed his wife's naked body with all the wonder of remembrance. A panicky flash of pure fear shot into the wide brown eyes and an unmistakable shudder ran through the slender frame.

What the devil? He opened his mouth to exclaim and then closed it again and simply sat on the window seat leaving Molly to complete her work. The fear in the eyes became relief and his lips tightened. What had happened to her in those long months of their separation?

They talked into the early hours in the dining room that night as Danielle and her four colleagues told of their adventures. Jules and the others waited for her to bring up her ordeal with St. Estèphe and when she did not do so felt that her silence was in some way a command that they must follow. They now all knew the comte's motives and it was for Justin's wife to tell him at what time and in whatever manner she chose. Their delay in returning was easily explained by the mayhem in Paris, the difficult personalities of their passengers, and the storm.

Justin found it possible to laugh at Jules's description of Danielle's play-acting at the *barrière*, although he knew that the ghosts of horror at the risks she had taken would haunt him for many months. The camaraderie existing between the five of them was very clear in the way they teased each other, the way they were able to leave sentences half finished, thoughts uncompleted, and the meaning was immediately grasped. It was also clear that Danny was their chief planner, although she admitted, quite cheerfully when reminded, that on occasion her imagination got the better of her and it needed a more sober appraisal to make her plans at least safer if less imaginative.

Justin wondered if he were jealous of this easy relationship based on so much intimacy and terrifying danger. He was, he decided. But it was a mean-spirited emotion that must be repressed. What concerned him more was the brittle quality of Danielle's laughter, the ease with which she slipped over the description of the attack on the Tuileries, their return to the scene of the massacre, her earlier attempts to find D'Evron, and the days when she had run beside the tumbrils looking for a familiar face.

His own adventures had paled in comparison. The czar's court had received him kindly and it had been a series of misadventures that had delayed his homecoming—that and the czar's pleasure in the company of the Earl of Linton, pleasure that had become a royal edict which under that absolute rule could not be gainsaid.

It was Julian not Justin who told Danielle that she looked like the very devil and it was time she was in bed. As for the rest of them, they were too nerve-riddled to sleep and would play cards until exhaustion took over.

Danielle did not demur, saying only to Justin in a low whisper that he should stay up as long as he wished; she was utterly exhausted anyway. To her relief, he merely nodded and walked her to the door, tipping her chin to place a light kiss at the corner of her mouth.

She ran up the stairs, tore off her wrapper, and flung herself into bed. Something she could never in her wildest imaginings have foreseen had happened. Not only could she not tell her husband of St. Estèphe's violations, but she could not bear the thought of being touched, of being looked at. Her skin crawled in revulsion as she hugged her breasts beneath the sheet in fierce protection of her bodily privacy. What was she to do? Pretend to be asleep when he came to her bed, as he most assuredly would? Tonight, perhaps, it would work, but for how long could she maintain the deception?

Justin remained in the dining room for half an hour after his wife's departure and he learned much. He learned the full truth of their experiences in Paris and Danny's reaction to what they had seen and done, and he learned that something was being kept from him; something other—far worse than what he had been told. No one gave him the barest hint but the secret hummed in the air, lurked in their eyes.

"Well, gentlemen, I will bid you good morning. Enjoy your play. You have earned some relaxation, I think." He left them amidst chorused good nights and went upstairs, both thoughtful and determined. His wife by some miracle had been returned to him, but she was not whole and he would have her so.

The bedchamber was in darkness, except for the dying embers of the fire. He lit two tapers and carried both to the bed. "You are not asleep, Danielle, so do not pretend to be so."

Danielle muttered incoherently and curled more tightly beneath the covers, but they were wrested from her grasp and drawn back. "I wish to look at you," Justin said softly, sitting on the bed and turning her onto her back. She began to shake even as she tried to offer herself to his gentle hands, simulating the old eagerness.

It was such a pathetic attempt. The fear stood out in her eyes and shudders of revulsion crept over her skin as he caressed her breasts, rolling her nipples between finger and thumb in the way that had always drawn moans of pleasure from her.

"What has happened to you?"

"Nothing . . . *rien du tout*. It is simply that it has been such a long time and I am out of the way of . . . of loving." It was a poor offering and Danielle knew it.

He took her hands, palm against palm, holding them above her head and she cried out in terror. "No . . . no please, not in that way."

Once he had made the almost fatal mistake of allowing her withdrawal, gentling and courting her, hoping that she would recover, without intervention, from what was troubling her. But those methods had failed and Justin never repeated his mistakes. Now he stood up and reached for her discarded wrapper. "Get up." His voice was quiet.

Danielle had not the slightest idea what he was going to do and made no move to comply. Nothing had ever frightened her as much as this petrified reaction to Justin's touch and look and now she just lay there.

"Get up!" The voice this time was a lash and Danielle found herself on her feet without conscious thought. He pushed her arms into the wrapper, tied it securely about her waist, and then, without speaking, took her hand and led her back to the dining room.

Four startled pairs of eyes looked up from their cards. "Now," Justin said to his wife, "I am going to ask you the question again. What has happened to *you*?"

Four hands of cards slapped onto the table and her friends sat back in total silence looking into the middle distance, for once offering her no support and telling her husband all that he needed to know at this point.

"Thank you." Justin turned back to Danny. "Since it is now clear that something *has* happened, we will dispense with further prevarication, if you please. You may tell me here or in private. If you are unable to tell me yourself then I am certain someone else will oblige."

"They may be able to tell you the facts, Justin, but only I can tell you of the horror." Her voice shook. "I do not wish to."

"No," he said, suddenly gentle. "But sometimes one must do what one does not wish to do. Let us go upstairs now." Not a word had been spoken by anyone but themselves in the quiet dining room.

In their own chamber, Danielle crawled again beneath the covers and Justin undressed, blowing out the candle before slipping in beside her. "Now . . . ?" he asked softly.

She told him the whole as he held her close in the cloaking darkness as one would hold a child in the midst of a nightmare, and after she had at last fallen asleep in the arms that simply held and made no demands he lay awake and allowed the bitter rage full rein. He would not rest until he had hunted down St. Estèphe as one would rid the world of a rabid cur, and from Danielle's account that was a perfect description of their enemy.

Chapter 23

Viscount Beresford darted from his hiding place behind a rhododendron bush and scampered across the lawn, chuckling gleefully. He had managed to evade the watchful eyes of Tante Thérèse, Maddy, *and* Jeanette—some considerable achievement. His goal was the great barn behind the stables where, on one of his earlier escapades, he had discovered a litter of kittens. It was nearly his teatime and the hue and cry would start up at any moment, but *Maman* and *Papa* were out riding on this crisp March afternoon and so long as news of his flight was not discovered by either of them, there would be no uncomfortable consequences.

As luck would have it, however, his dash across the open ground of the stableyard coincided with the clattering of hooves on the cobbles and the return of his parents.

"Nicky?" his mother called and, with a pout, the small boy stopped.

Danielle dismounted unaided and marched toward him, the tawny velvet of her riding habit swinging around her. "*Méchant*," she scolded. "Where are you going?"

"*Les petits chats, maman.*" He grabbed her hand eagerly, eyes shining. "*Viens, vite.*"

"Kittens!" his mother exclaimed. "Where?"

"The barn." Nicky tugged on her hand.

"Just what are you up to now?" Justin strode across the yard. There was an ominous frown in his eyes that the little viscount recognized and he pulled anxiously on his mother's hand.

"Nicky has found some kittens, Justin," Danielle explained. "We must go and see them. Show us, *mon petit.*"

"Danielle," Justin expostulated. "Kittens or no, he knows he's not to be here alone, or anywhere else for that matter."

"Oh, pah!" She dismissed such rigidity with disdain. "Do not tell me that you were able to resist a litter of kittens at his age? It is no fun to be always doing things with one's nurse, and not at all *amusant* never to do things without permission."

"No," Justin agreed, struck by the truth of this statement. "Well, let us go and see these fascinating creatures." He held out his hand to his son and received the small trusting one with a smile and an admonitory headshake. Nicholas just beamed, quite unabashed, and trotted between them, chattering in his fluid mixture of French and English, interspersed with baby burble when his as yet simple vocabulary failed.

Danielle's pleasure in the kittens easily matched her son's and Justin watched as she sat on the dusty barn floor, her skirts spread to receive the furry parcels, as Nicky picked them up with exaggerated delicacy and deposited them in her lap.

The last five months had seen the execution of Louis XVI—a king who had died with dignity beneath the blade of Madame Guillotine amidst the jeering crowds of his erstwhile subjects and the Reign of Terror now gathered momentum. England had been at war with France since the beginning of February and it was now impossible for an Englishman to travel openly in that beleaguered country. Danielle's clandestine activities had been dangerous enough, but now the danger was increased a hundredfold.

Justin had controlled his impatience and devoted his attention to his wife and son, taking pleasure in the former's growing relaxation. It had been many weeks before she had responded with the passion and eagerness of the past to his gently determined lovemaking. But understanding had leant him compassion and the patience of Job. She was her old self again now, less tempestuous perhaps, and the months of wearing britches had given her an inordinate dislike of such attire, even when riding. Her hair had grown, the thin cheeks

454

had filled, and there was a seriousness in the brown eyes that denoted maturity rather than pain.

But the winter storms that had prevented safe passage from Cornwall to the north coast of Brittany were now on the wane and Justin was growing restless. Images of St. Estèphe hung on the periphery of his sleep, sometimes intruded in violent dreams, and it was time to begin the chase. How to tell Danielle that he wished to take his revenge alone?

He looked at her as she explained to Nicky that the kittens were still blind and could not be taken from their mother however well Nicky could look after one in the nursery. He must wait for at least another month before they would be ready to live without their *maman*. Nicky listened seriously, understanding the import if not every word. And how was Justin to leave them both—his wife and his son, dearer to him than life itself? But it was because they were so that he had no choice but to follow his obsession. If he did not take matters into his own hands, then St. Estèphe would be an ever-threatening presence in their lives. Until Justin was certain that the *comte* was dead, there would be no safety for himself, his wife, or his children. Danielle's description of the St. Estèphe that she now knew had convinced Linton of the cold, detached fanaticism, bordering on madness, of the man who had set his heart on revenge on the house of Linton.

"Come, children." He broke into their game with a broad smile and the brisk directive: "Tante Thérèse is waiting for one of you, at least." The kittens were returned to their nest and, laughing, Danielle allowed him to pull her to her feet.

"Not an appropriate sobriquet," she informed her husband with a mock curtsy.

"On the contrary," he replied. "There is not a pin to choose between the pair of you." He lifted his son onto his shoulders and Nicky crowed with delight, bouncing up and down, his chubby fingers twisted in his father's hair as they made their way back to the house.

Nicky had learned enough in his twenty-one months not to protest too vociferously as he was returned to the nursery with the promise that *Maman* and *Papa* would visit him after his bath. Danielle, on the other hand, showed no such self-

455

discipline when Justin broached the subject of his returning to France.

"We agreed that in future what we do we do together," she insisted. "I also claim St. Estèphe for my own. You are quite correct to say that we must make our move first, and he will not be expecting it for the nonce. If, as I suspect, he is playing politics with the tribunal, he will be too occupied preserving his neck to concern himself with us. He has the great gift of patience and will put aside what can wait. He will assume that I am safe and his spies will by now have told him of your safety. He will be content to watch and wait, assuming that we will use *la Manche* and the war as our protection. We will strike now while the cobra watches another prey."

"Danny, St. Estèphe is mine." Justin's eyes met hers in the dresser mirror as he fastened an emerald pendant around her neck.

"Very well," she agreed. "Yours or mine, depending how the hand is played. But I come with you, it is agreed?"

"And Nicky?"

"You know there is no choice." Her son would be safe, well looked after, with grandparents, cousins, and friends to see him to maturity. She could not allow her husband to go alone into a danger that they both shared.

"It is agreed then." Justin yielded without the fight that would achieve nothing in the long run.

"We must bring Jules and the others with us." Danielle stood up, patting down her skirts with a femininity quite at odds with their discussion. "This is not something the two of us can accomplish alone and we work well together."

"You and they," said Justin. "How will the five of you manage with a sixth?"

"Quite easily," Danielle responded, fastening an emerald bracelet around her wrist. "As long as you follow orders, *tu comprends, mon mari?*"

Justin caught her by the tiny waist and threw her, skirts, petticoats, emeralds and all, facedown on the bed. Planting a knee firmly in the small of her back, he demanded, "Say that again. I did not quite hear you."

456

"I do not remember what I said," Danny mumbled into the coverlet. "But it was of no importance."

"You are quite sure?"

"Quite sure."

"It is not, perhaps, something you may remember to say on a future occasion?" His voice was deceptively soft as he slid a hand beneath her petticoats.

"No!" Danny squawked. "It is quite expunged from my memory."

"That is most fortunate." He removed both hand and knee and Danny struggled upright, her face pink with laughing indignation. But she had provoked the attack and was not one to protest the consequences of her actions. They went down to dinner in smiling accord.

Jules and the others, who had eschewed the pleasures of the London Season this winter, preferring the simplicity of Cornwall after their adventures, heard the proposal with a considerable degree of enthusiasm.

"We have been waiting for you to decide when to make the move and so long as you are around, Justin, to keep a rein on Danny, you have my heartfelt support," Jules declared. "I am sure I speak for us all?" He looked inquiringly around the table and, while Danny spluttered indignantly, everyone pledged their support in the matter of St. Estèphe.

Four days later, *Dream Girl* set sail again for the Brittany coast. Danielle, her hair again cropped much to Justin's resigned annoyance, was back in her britches and full of strategies. There was no capacious master cabin on the small yacht and for the three day voyage Justin gained true insight into the close-quarters living of these five. He and his wife became simply partners, exchanging bunks automatically as the rested one went up on deck, taking turns at the wheel, putting to when sails needed reefing or unfurling. No one, least of all Jake, paid any attention to Danny's sex and she asked for no especial consideration.

When they made landfall, she was as wet as the rest, and as heedless of discomfort as they climbed the steep path to the cliff top. In the Legrands' farm house they explained their

457

return, their needs, and heard the story of subsequent events after they had fired Betrand Ville's barn and the *comte* had returned in a fearsome rage to find his plans in ruins and his victim fled.

"As we expected, then," Danielle said thoughtfully. "The *comte* returned almost immediately to Paris and no one has disturbed our friends since. They know little of what is happening in the country but will lend us horses again, and anything else we may need. The carts are still here, but I think we need only take one."

"How do we enter Paris this time?" Philip asked. "It will not be as easy."

"*Comme d'habitude*—in the usual way." Danielle shrugged. "It is how we leave that will present difficulties."

They made the journey to Paris exactly as they had done in the past. The countryside was alive with rumor now but no one questioned the passage of five ragged sans-culottes and a scrubby lad whose command of the insults left them torn between laughter and annoyance. The boy's companions appeared to do what they could to control his excesses and those who had seen the urchin were not those who saw the coquettish peasant girl in a grubby blouse and torn skirt who made flirtatious play with the guards at the various posts now sprung up along the road to Paris.

The five men kept their hands on their pistols at each *barrière* but never had reason to use them as Danielle danced them through and Justin decided, like Jules, that she had missed her vocation. On stage, she would have been superb.

They were through St. Antoine on the evening of the third day and, to their horror, found themselves caught up in a grim procession as the last tumbrils of the day moved through the crowds to Place de la Révolution. It was impossible, in the wildly yelling throng, to turn the cart in another direction, just as it was impossible for them to allow their revulsion to show. Danny hissed suddenly to Justin, "I will meet you in Les Halles." Before he could react, she had leaped from the cart and vanished as if she had never been.

"No," Jules whispered, seeing his cousin prepared to go

458

after her. "You'll never find her; she's as slippery as an eel and knows all the back streets, besides you will draw attention to us all."

Justin swore viciously, but there was nothing he could do but wait in a spiral of anxiety until the day's grisly business had ended and the last head rolled into the blood-soaked basket. The crowds thinned gradually as the spectators, exhausted by their day of shouting, jeering, and applauding, made their way back to the shops and hovels in the poverty-stricken faubourgs St. Antoine and St. Marcel from where they would crawl out again on the morrow, thirsty for more blood.

It was still an hour after the spectacle had ceased, however, before the cart with its five sans-culottes managed to reach Les Halles where the presence of one more cart would pass unremarked. Many of the peasantry from the surrounding countryside poured into Paris these days to witness the executions, sleeping in the streets or, if they were lucky enough to possess one, in carts loaded with straw as Danielle and the others planned to do themselves.

Danny's flight had been inspired first and foremost by the knowledge that she could not stand to see again the sights in Place de la Révolution that still haunted her dreams. Her jump from the cart had been purely instinctive but once lost in the crowds she decided to put her freedom to good use. St. Estèphe's previous lodging had been in a tall narrow house near the magnificent medieval edifice of Notre Dame. It would be as well to discover if he was still to be found there. With a stroke of luck, Danny found the concierge sitting in the courtyard with a flask of wine, taking the mild evening air. She was a slovenly, sour-faced woman who appeared to take her duties lightly, but she did not refuse the dirty urchin a glass of water, particularly in exchange for a lively description of the day's executions—a description Danny drew from memory and embellished lavishly. She encouraged the woman in her grumbles about her tenants—coming and going at all hours, quite prepared to wake her up if the gates were locked; as if she hadn't got enough to do keeping the stairs clean with the pains in her joints!

Danielle examined the swollen knees and ankles with much sympathy and mentioned some remedy that her grandmother had used. The concierge tutted and began a long description of everything she had tried and was kind enough to remark how unusual it was these days to find young people, particularly lads, prepared to listen to an old woman. Encouraged, Danielle broached the subject of the tenants again. It produced another diatribe but the names came out and Citoyen St. Estèphe's was one of them. The woman coughed and spat and imparted the information that that *citoyen* had some strange habits—the noises she heard sometimes coming from his apartment directly above her own . . . Then she recollected herself hastily. The *citoyen*, of course, was an excellent man, a member of the tribunal and a good friend of the Citoyen Robespierre. He worked tirelessly for the republic, ridding the land of the aristos, and Citoyenne Gérard meant no criticism.

Danny made the appropriate responses, praising the work of the tribunal and damning the aristos in rich language that drew an appreciative chuckle from her companion. The sun was very low in the sky now and Danny became fully conscious for the first time of the dangerous position she was in—sitting in the lion's den! Her disguise would not fool St. Estèphe for one minute, he was far too accustomed to it. With a hasty excuse, she darted from the courtyard just as St. Estèphe rounded the corner of the street, deep in conversation with another man. Danny darted into a doorway, her heart pounding, the sweat of fear misting her brow. Had he seen her? She would know soon enough—there was nowhere to run to. The door at her back was closed and she cowered in the narrow space as the loathsome sound of that remembered voice came closer and her skin felt as if an army of slugs undulated beneath her clothes, leaving a sticky trail in their wake.

But the voice faded. She kept to her hiding place for another petrifying five minutes before peeping around. There was no sign of St. Estèphe or of his companion so presumably they had gone into the courtyard. She slipped from her hiding place and walked down the alley, hands in her pockets, whistling the "Ça Ira" as she kicked negligently at stones and garbage littering the street. If she ran, she would draw instant notice, but as it was, she was just another Parisian street urchin with an empty belly and pockets to let.

Danielle, at this point, was blissfully unaware that she stood in more danger from her husband than from St. Estèphe. Justin was frantic and nothing his companions could say did anything to alleviate his fear or his fury. In fact, the more often they told him that they had grown accustomed to his wife's sudden disappearances, the more livid he became. The sights, sounds, and smells of this city disgusted him more than anything he had previously experienced and it was only now, he realized dimly, that he was experiencing the full emotional impact of the horrific risks Danielle had taken in those months of his sojourn in Russia.

Westmore spotted her first, wriggling like an eel through the crowd toward them. As usual, she was chattering nonstop, tossing off the light badinage that was perhaps the most effective part of her disguise. He nudged Jules and the four of them melted discreetly into the throng. Whatever was about to happen between husband and wife needed no witnesses.

"Where are the others?" Danielle appeared breathlessly at the cart. "I have made some most interesting discov—" She gulped at the sight of Linton's face and her heart plummeted to a resting place somewhere in the region of her toes. "Wh . . . what is the matter?"

For answer, he seized her upper arms, slamming her backward against the cart where he held her, imprisoned by his body. "You *dare* to ask what is the matter?"

Danielle stared into those eyes, burning like red hot pokers, and as she struggled for words her mouth opened and closed like a goldfish.

"If you *ever ever* run off like that again, Danielle, you had better not come back, because, so help me, I will ensure that you regret the day that you were born!" His fingers squeezed her arms as the words came with slow fierce emphasis. "Do you understand me?"

"I am sorry, I didn't realize you would be so frightened." Danielle, knowing her husband as she did, had no difficulty

461

understanding the reason for this blind rage any more than she doubted he would make good his promise.

"How could you *not* have realized?" he rasped, for the moment unappeased by the apology. "You disappear without a word in the middle of this hell on earth! It matters not that you are at home in this city, more so than the rest of us, you may *not* take unilateral action. Is that clear?"

"Yes . . . yes, please. It is quite clear," she stuttered. "I am sorry, I will not do such a thing again."

Justin drew a deep breath as the anger flowed from him and relief at having her safe again took its place. "You had better not," he said quietly. For some extraordinary reason he had a great desire to kiss her, and the thought of the absurd image of a scruffy sans-culottes kissing a disreputable urchin in the middle of a crowded marketplace in this revolution-torn city of terror brought a shout of laughter to his lips.

"Now what is amusing?" Danielle demanded, relief that the storm had passed mingling with annoyance at this bewildering volte-face that merely added to her disadvantage.

"I am not going to tell you," Justin declared. "And you may count yourself fortunate that you have escaped further reprisals."

"Is it safe to come back?" Philip's voice, deliberately plaintive, sounded at Justin's back.

"For the moment," Justin said, releasing his wife. "Until the next time my brat decides to do something outrageous."

"You do not quite understand, I think, milord." Danielle spoke with an assumption of dignity. "I could not bear to face the spectacle in *La Place* again. I ran without thought at first, and then decided that I should do something useful. I have some information about Citoyen St. Estèphe."

"I understand your explanation," Justin told her, "and while I respect it, it changes nothing of what I have said." He pinched her cheek, looking steadily into the brown eyes until satisfied that his point had been well taken. "Now, I think we should go in search of our supper. It will be less than adequate, I daresay, since we can hardly appear to have more than a few sous to spend."

462

"If you will follow me," Danny offered, "I will show you where we may eat quite well for a few sous. Unless, of course, you would prefer, milord, that we follow you?" Her eyebrows lifted fractionally. Jules turned away, hiding his snort of laughter under a spasm of coughing. Had she no sense of self-preservation? The thinner the ice, it seemed, the faster she skated.

Justin wished as he had so often done that he were alone with her, but since he was not he chose to ignore the challenge. "Let us go then."

Danny was as good as her word. In a small dark room full of bibulous customers they ate a rich vegetable soup, sausage, ripe cheese, and crusty bread, washed down with a rough wine that convinced Justin, at least, that his liver would never be the same again.

"No one seems at all interested in what I have discovered," Danny stated, wiping her mouth with the back of her hand—a gesture that caused Justin to wince reminiscently, even as he recognized its authenticity in the part she was playing. "I have also a plan—a good one, I think. It is perhaps not foolproof, but then what plan is?"

"We cannot talk here," Tony remonstrated.

"There is nowhere better," she said with a tranquil smile. "No one is interested in listening to our conversation." She gestured around the noisy room. "Why would they be? We are quite unremarkable."

"I think, as far as you are concerned, infant, that that is probably the wrong adjective," Justin murmured. "But enlighten us, pray."

She shot him a look so out of keeping with her disguise, a look radiating sensual promise, that his body rose, stirred in inconvenient response. "*Dépêche-toi!*" he insisted.

"Very well." She told them in a few words what she had discovered, prudently leaving out her near miss with St. Estèphe. "I think it will be possible to conceal ourselves in his apartment. Citoyenne Gérard took a kindness to me, and I think I may be able to draw her away from her post tomorrow. There will be an interesting spectacle in the streets nearby . . .

463

a lynching or some such." She shrugged carelessly. "So long as it is sufficiently violent it matters not what we invent. I will offer to take her place while she goes to view the excitement. She is lazy and bored and will accept such an opportunity with enthusiasm. St. Estèphe's apartment is directly above hers—that is how she hears so clearly the strange noises . . ." A look of pain scudded across her face. It was not hard to imagine those sounds as St. Estèphe played with whatever little *putain* had been unlucky enough to take his fancy. "Anyway," she went on, "it will not be difficult to identify the apartment. We overpower whatever servants he may have and await his return."

"And how do we gain entrance to the apartment in order to overpower the servants?" Jules inquired, taking another swig of wine with a grimace.

"Oh, but I thought I would leave some part of the planning to you." Danny smiled sweetly as she nibbled a crust of bread. "'It should be simple enough. There are few people around in the daytime and we watch until St. Estèphe departs for the Parliament House. There are four other tenants and it would be best to wait for them to go about their daily business, also. A servant or two should not present too many problems." She licked a finger and absently picked up the crumbs littering the stained planking of the narrow table. Just in time, Linton smacked her hand in the process of carrying the crumb-laden finger to her mouth.

"You do not know what has been on this table," he snapped. "It is not necessary to carry your part to quite such extremes."

"Oh, pah! You do not know what has been on the platters or in the tankards before they came to the table. It has not stopped you eating and drinking," she retorted.

"I think it is time we sought our beds, such as they are," Philip said diplomatically. The tension was affecting them all and Danny's continual provocation of her husband, while clearly simply reaction to strain, was not helping.

They all rose with relief. Justin surreptitiously took a firm hold of Danielle's belt as they strolled back to Les Halles and the cart of straw that would be their resting place for the night.

464

But when they rolled in their cloaks beneath the straw, she crept against him as if they were in their own bed in the privacy of home and whispered her apology with a soft kiss against his ear. He held her tightly as she fell, with all the ease of a cat, into a dreamless sleep where she hovered just below the level of unconsciousness but ready to wake, instantly alert, at the slightest hint of danger.

By seven o'clock the next morning the streets were again alive and the April sun, though still low in the sky, promised a good day. They breakfasted on warm bread and the bitter coffee of the working people and Danny maintained a steadfast cross silence. Justin had taken a not so playful revenge earlier, when she had made an inappropriately sharp remark, and held her head under the cold water of the pump in the center of the market square with the comment that it was the only appropriate treatment for hot-headed hoydens who were ill-tempered in the morning. Now she nursed her wounded dignity while the five of them, apparently sublimely indifferent to her fit of the sullens, made their plans.

Her naturally sunny temper could not be held down for long, however, any more than could her bursting need to participate in the discussion. "We cannot be too rigid," she broke in. "If strategies are not flexible, then they stand in danger of fragmenting at the point of impact."

"How true, *mon général*." Justin gave her a teasing conciliatory smile. "Where do you see the danger of rigidity?"

"I think it best to plan one stage at a time and adapt according to circumstance. We will remove Citoyenne Gérard without doubt, and we will gain entrance to the vermin's apartments, without doubt. What we then decide will depend upon what we find."

Justin regarded her thoughtfully. He knew that secretive, excited gleam in those brown eyes. Danielle had her own plans. "What is it that you have in mind?"

Danny pulled a wry face. "It is disconcerting that you can read my mind, Justin."

"Not your mind," he stated. "But I *can* read your eyes."

"Very well. I wish to confront St. Estèphe alone . . . No,

pray listen," she said urgently, seeing denial on every face. "Only initially and only if it is possible. If, perhaps, there are two rooms then you may conceal yourselves in one. I will have my pistol and the advantage of surprise. I have to see him just once more alone, when I am without fear," she explained simply. "Afterward, you may do as you wish."

"If it is possible," said Justin, "then we will act in that manner. If it is not, then you must also be flexible."

"*D'accord.*" Danny shrugged easily. "Shall we then begin, *mes amis?*"

No one remarked on the six sans-culottes mingling with the pedestrians in the street outside St. Estèphe's lodgings. They were quite undistinguishable from the rest except for the sword sticks concealed beneath their jackets, the pistols hidden beneath their shirts. They behaved in no unusual fashion as they hung around the cafés, and no one was aware that six pairs of eyes watched the comings and goings in the narrow house on the banks of the Seine, overlooking the crenellated cathedral of Notre Dame.

St. Estèphe came out at nine, unaccompanied, and walked briskly in the direction of the Right Bank and the Parliament House. Within the next hour, four others left the building, wearing the red, white, and blue cockade standing in proud declamation against their tricorn hats, its brilliance seeming curiously at odds with the somber jackets and britches of respectable citizens.

Tony wiped the sweat from his brow in a flamboyant gesture, the bright checkered neckcloth flinging its message to Westmore across the street. Westmore did the same and the message passed to Jules who waited on the corner.

Danny, engaged in idle conversation with a group of youths, heard the sharp report from the street corner. "*Tiens, donc! Qu'est-ce qui se passe?*" She was suddenly alone as her companions hared in the direction of Julian's firecrackers now creating a rat-a-tat of noise and smoke. A great shout of excitement went up from the excitable crowd. Danny ran into the courtyard of St. Estèphe's lodgings and hammered on the door of the concierge's apartment. Citoyenne Gérard appeared instantly.

"Citoyenne," Danny gasped. "There is much excitement. I think they have captured the aristo who escaped the guards this morning. It will be a great spectacle. *Venez vite!*"

"*Mais, la maison,*" the concierge said, even as her bloodshot eyes lusted for the sight so close to the door.

"I will watch for you," Danny said. "I have seen such sights many times and can go again to the executions this afternoon. *Dépêchez-vous, chère citoyenne.*"

"Ah, but you're a good lad." Citoyenne Gérard made haste to don her *bonnet rouge* and scurried off in search of food for her hungry soul.

Danny shot across the courtyard and through the main door, waiting at the foot of the stairs, whose littered condition bore ample witness to the concierge's housekeeping. The others joined her in minutes with Jules only a little later.

"It is amazing," he said. "There is nothing to see, but they are determined to find something. They are off on a wild rampage."

"It takes little to stir a mob," Justin said. "Particularly one with an insatiable appetite. Let us find what St. Estèphe's apartment holds."

The five men shrank against the wall on either side of the door as Danielle pounded with her fists. "*Citoyen, j'ai un message d'urgence de Citoyen St. Estèphe.*"

The door flew open and a burly manservant in a leather apron appeared. "*Qu'est-ce que c'est, garçon?*" She ducked beneath his arm and was into the room before he realized it, the excited words babbling from her lips. In the instant of his bewilderment, turning toward this bouncing urchin and away from the door, the hapless manservant found himself overpowered from behind. As he opened his mouth to shout, a clenched fist made contact beneath his chin and the star-shot blackness hurtled to meet him.

"That was well done indeed," Danny said admiringly to Tony. "Your left is quite as punishing as Justin's. I had not realized."

"Cease your comparisons, brat," her husband instructed. "Find something to bind the man. He will not be out for long and I think it unlikely that our quarry will return before the evening."

"Well, we must not make him too uncomfortable," Danielle demurred, rifling St. Estèphe's wardrobes and drawers. "We do not know what kind of man he is, and maybe he is not of the vermin's ilk."

"Unlikely," Justin muttered, catching the hank of rope she threw him. "But far be it from me to destroy your faith in human nature."

Danielle gurgled with laughter at the ironic tone and found one of St. Estèphe's cravats. "This will do for a gag, I think."

The manservant was bound, gagged, and rolled into a capacious wardrobe. The apartment yielded bedroom, parlor, a *cabinet de toilette*, and a slip of a room for the servant. Danny's plan was clearly feasible and her companions, despite their reluctance, agreed to hide in the bedroom while she waited for St. Estèphe, pistol in hand, in the parlor.

It was a long tedious wait. Citoyenne Gérard reappeared eventually, hot and flushed. The mob, set off by Julian's firecrackers, had careened through the streets and found a wine barrel toppled from a delivery cart. The bloodred liquid oozed from the cracked cask and was seized with yells of excitement by a crowd deprived of their expected diversion and anxious, therefore, for another. Shoes, hats, and hands were pressed into service in the absence of more utilitarian vessels to scoop the wine into eagerly open mouths. Those lucky enough to live in the area of this unexpected bounty filled pots and tankards as the cask split apart and the wine, in a crimson torrent, ran across the cobbles and into the kennels. Citoyenne Gérard was unable to do more than curse the absent urchin who had not fulfilled his promise to remain in her place, before falling onto her cot and subsiding into a stertorous sleep.

St. Estèphe left the Parliament House at six on that evening of Saturday, April 13. It had been a momentous day. The Jacobin, Marat, had been impeached by the Girondist majority in the Assembly and St. Estèphe's head now clung to his neck by a frail thread. At last forced to swing down from the fence, he had picked the Jacobins, the party of Marat and Robespierre. The Girondists for the moment held the majority

468

in the power house, but St. Estèphe had felt the strength of Robespierre, the quiet fanaticism that tugged an empathetic cord.

He had gambled and now it looked as if he had lost. With Marat's indictment the parliamentary strength of the Girondists stood undisputed unless the people of Paris decided to take a hand. Their voice in the Assembly was the most powerful and the tribunal *extraordinaire* before which the impeached Marat would appear was the voice of the sovereign people. If they supported the Gironde, then Marat and all his associates would lose their heads. If Marat were acquitted, then the Girondist would go to the guillotine. It was a black and white game, no compromise, no gray areas. Life and power versus death and St. Estèphe had declared his hand and could only wait.

But he was a past master at the waiting game and, besides, he had plans for this evening which would take his mind away from politics and events that, while highly possible, might never happen. The little Lisette would afford much amusement. She cringed in the most enticing way when he . . . His step quickened. Five men of the National Guard, loyal Jacobins, followed at a discreet distance, unwilling to impose their presence on the *citoyen*, but kept their eyes and ears open for the hint of attack.

Danielle, keeping watch over the courtyard from behind a curtain, alerted her companions as St. Estèphe strolled through the gate. He cast a disgusted glance in the direction of the powerful snores emanating from the concierge's apartment before mounting the stairs.

"Bernard!" He bellowed for the manservant as his key turned in the lock. Stepping into the room he found himself facing Danielle de St. Varennes. She was sitting on a low table opposite the door and held a small silver-mounted pistol. On the table beside her were two epées—his own, he recognized dreamily, as his mind fought to adjust itself to this extraordinary visitation.

"*Et bien, ma belle*," he murmured, "so the bird has come home to roost."

469

"Indeed," she agreed, unsmiling. "And I am going to see you dead, *Citoyen*."

"I think not," he said softly, moving away from the door. One shout would bring the men from below, but one shout could also precipitate that steady finger on the trigger.

"Ah, but you are mistaken," Danielle replied. "I do not think I will shoot you, though. You do not deserve such a clean death."

"Who knows you are here?"

"No one." She chuckled. "This is between ourselves."

"Linton?" He frowned.

Danielle shook her head and again gave that strange disconcerting little laugh. "You think, *Citoyen*, that I would tell my husband of what passed between us. I would die rather."

Looking at her, so calm, cool, and unexpected, remembering what she had done in the past, St. Estèphe had no difficulty believing this. Danielle de St. Varennes would never behave in a predictable fashion and would never disclose the humiliation she had endured at his hands.

"*D'accord!*" Danielle swung from the table. "We fight, *Citoyen*." She tossed him an epée as she took up her own.

"And the pistol?" He quirked an eyebrow, bending to pick up the sword that had fallen at his feet. "I do not care for the odds, you understand?"

Danielle placed the pistol on the table and faced him, her sword point resting on the ground in front of her. "Take off your boots, *Citoyen*. I'll not have you at a disadvantage."

St. Estèphe removed boots and jacket as if in some sort of trance. She surely did not imagine she could put up even a fair opposition? Then her sword flashed in a brief salute and St. Estèphe realized that he was engaged with no tyro. This slithery slippery creature whose bare feet on the oak floor had more purchase than his stockinged ones, was truly fighting him to the death. She feinted, thrust, parried, her eyes never leaving his as she outguessed his every move. Not only was she nearly twenty years younger, with all the stamina of youth, but she danced across the floor and handled the epée like a duelist, showing none of the punctilious niceties of the playful fencer.

Behind the half-closed bedroom door, five men took shallow, soundless breaths as they heard the clash of steel on steel, the soft thud of feet shifting on the boards. They could have interceded at any moment but Justin held them back, an arm across the crack in the door. It was a calculated risk he took, but one that in the long run paid off.

Danielle allowed St. Estèphe to deliver the attack, ignoring the lures that invited her to initiate. Her guard was constant and her opponent began to breathe heavily, sweat rolling from his forehead as his sword was caught time after time in a swift parry and the scrubby little creature laughed in soft mockery, inciting him to further attempts to break through her guard. But Danielle was also tiring, a dull ache spreading down her swordarm from shoulder to wrist. Soon she would need to call for support. She parried a straight lunge in high carte as St. Estèphe, nearing the end of his strength, bellowed, "*A moi!*"

The cry reached the National Guard in the courtyard and they pounded up the stairs, bursting into the room, swords in hand, to face five cold-eyed Englishmen.

Danielle knew now that she was fighting alone. Her husband and friends were fully occupied, one against one. Her own silent battle had to take precedence, however, and ignoring what was happening around her, she pressed the attack, becoming an automaton, fighting the ache in her arm as viciously as she fought her enemy. St. Estèphe wanted to wipe away the sweat dropping into his eyes but dared not as the attack, fueled by desperation, moved into the endgame. When she lunged, he parried too late and her blade slid over his to bury itself in his chest.

His point dropped as the bright blood spread across his shirt; he swayed and then fell. Danielle stood over him, making no attempt to pull free her sword.

The battle behind her was soon over. The guardsmen used their swords as best they could but were no match for the grim-faced English lords who had taken advantage of the minute's warning given by St. Estèphe's cry and had been prepared for their arrival.

Justin fought grimly, hearing Danielle's blade clash with St. Estèphe's, but he could do nothing to help her, not until he had immobilized his own opponent. In the deepest recesses of his mind he knew that she was a better swordsman than himself. She lacked brawn not skill and she had all the divergent imagination of the true artist.

Overpowered, the five wounded guardsmen lay on the floor to be bound and gagged as the manservant in the wardrobe.

Danielle continued to stand over St. Estèphe, her point as immobile as her body.

Justin went to her, placed his hands on the hilt of the sword. "Enough now, Danny."

"No." Her eyes glittered strangely. "I am going to kill him, but I have not decided how I shall do so, yet."

"Your race is run, my love," said Justin, his voice very quiet, as he looked down at the inert body, the glazed eyes, the blood welling from the pierced heart. "He is dead."

Her eyes carried a wild almost feral look and with the gentlest of apologies, Justin slapped her face. She gasped and stared at him in bewilderment. Then she became herself again, life and recognition dawning in the blank eyes.

"Julian," he said curtly.

Julian took her arm and led her into the bedroom, the others following.

"I do wish my stomach were not so treacherous," Danielle remarked a few minutes later, lifting her head from the chamber pot. "It seems most unreasonable, do you not think?"

"Most unreasonable." It was Justin's voice, Justin's hand dipping the washcloth into the ewer of cold water, bathing her face. "We have now to leave Paris, my love. You will simply close your eyes and do as I tell you. Do you think you can manage that?"

She nodded and said nothing as they bound her hands behind her back, stripped the guardsmen of their uniforms, and became themselves members of the National Guard. Citoyenne Gérard looked at their prisoner, the little thief who had been so convincing and was now caught red-handed in the apartment of Citoyen St. Estèphe. She spat and returned to her bed.

This time it was Danielle who hid under the straw as her companions, still in the borrowed uniforms, took the cart unquestioned through the *barrière*. But it was several days along the road before she was able to talk without stammering and the convulsive shudders left her body.

Epilogue
August 1794

The Earl of Linton strolled into the sun-filled nursery at Danesbury early on the morning of August 19, 1794. He was in search of his son. Viscount Beresford was three years and one month old and, as usual, had disappeared.

Tante Thérèse apologized in voluble French for the fact that she had mislaid *le petit* and Justin refrained as always from the caustic comment that it seemed just a trifle careless to mislay such a bundle of energy by eight o'clock in the morning.

"He will be in the stables, my lord." Maddy bobbed a curtsy. "We do not worry because John will watch over him. I will fetch him immediately."

"No, I shall fetch him myself," Linton said easily. "But was he not told to stay in the nursery until I came for him?"

"Yes, my lord," Maddy dropped another curtsy. "But . . ." She hesitated, reluctant to appear forward.

"But what, Maddy?" her employer encouraged.

"I do not think he cares for the idea of Lady Philippa."

"Ah," Justin said with total comprehension. "But he has not yet met his sister, so perhaps we can forestall the prejudice." He smiled—a smile that Maddy returned in full.

"Is My Lady well, sir?"

"Very well, thank you. And Lady Philippa is every bit as vociferous as her brother, four hours into the world."

Justin left the nursery and went in pursuit of the errant Nicky.

Four shire horses stood in the stableyard, tethered alongside each other, waiting to be shod. This breed was the pride of every farmer with their rippling shoulders, powerful hocks, necks that could take the strain of any dray, plough or cart, and Nicholas, Viscount Beresford, was fascinated by them. They came rarely into the stableyard and he awaited their arrival with an enthusiasm that far exceeded the news of a baby sister.

Linton saw a pair of sturdy legs in nankeen britches disappear beneath the belly of the first shire horse.

"Nicky?" he called, reaching the horse and laying a reassuring hand on the powerful rear. The animal's skin rippled in confirmation of the touch and Nicky, three horses away, contemplated an escape route in the hay bales stacked the other side of the yard.

"Nicholas!"

The child stood beneath the belly of the fourth horse. Experience had taught him that that note in his father's voice boded ill for further procrastination. With a resigned sigh, he made his way back through the living tunnel of heaving chests and bellies and huge hooves that with one kick could smash his fragile bones to pulp, and popped up at Justin's feet.

"*Bonjour, papa.*"

"Good morning, little ragamuffin." His father returned the greeting with an exasperated shake of the head. "You are quite repulsively dirty, child. Were you not told to stay in the nursery until I came for you?"

Nicholas said nothing, but examined his boots with a studious air.

"Mmm," Justin murmured, with a twitch of his lips. "Well, since today is your sister's birthday, I will grant you a dispensation. But you cannot make her acquaintance as dirty as you are. Let us go back to the nursery and clean you up."

"Don't want a sister," Nicky muttered, trotting beside Justin.

"Oh." His father's long stride shortened. "Would you have preferred a brother?"

"No," Nicky said definitely. "Don't want eiver of 'em."

Justin swung him into his arms, brushing back the fair curls from the child's brow. "It's a little late to do anything about that, my son. But I feel certain you will become accustomed to the idea eventually."

Justin waited in the nursery while Nicholas was washed and brushed. Danielle, of course, wouldn't notice whether he was grubby or not.

She was sitting up in bed, looking pale but incredibly fresh after her ordeal of the night. Lady Philippa, after her own ordeal, slept in the crook of her mother's arm.

"Where'd she come from?" Nicholas demanded, climbing onto the bed.

Danielle exchanged a look with her husband. "Nicky, love, I told you. She was growing in my stomach."

"Well, why can't she go back? She's all red and crinkly."

"So were you when you were just born, like Philippa." Justin sat on the bed and took his daughter so that Danielle could hold her son who settled against her breast, sucking his thumb, a dreamy look in his dark eyes.

She was twenty-two now, Justin mused in the quiet sun-filled room, but the events of the last five years seemed to have wrought little change on the heart-shaped face or in the eyes that were still as full of curiosity as ever. They had been five years marked with blood, violence, and terror and Danielle had experienced all three, side by side with her country struggling to free itself from the chrysalis of the past as she also fought to escape her own.

"What are you thinking, my love?" she asked with a soft smile.

"Of the last five years," he answered. "Of the day I first met you." He chuckled. "I do not think you are so very different now from that scrubby brat."

"Now that is not kind in you," Danielle protested. "I am a respectable matron with two children."

Justin shuddered. "You must promise me *never* to become a matron! If you must become respectable, then I daresay I shall adapt, but matronly never!"

"I do not suppose we shall have any further adventures," Danielle said with a mournful sigh. "I think I shall miss them, Justin."

He gave a shout of laughter. "You see you are not at all

respectable, my brat. Well, I regret to inform you that I have had enough adventuring to last for a lifetime and since I shall not permit you to have any without me, you must accustom yourself to the idea that you will no longer go adventuring."

"Quite so," she murmured. "As you command, my lord." Her eyes were lowered with the submissive docility that always set off every alarm bell in his head.

"Little devil," he said and, ignoring the presence of his children, kissed her soundly. "I do not think I will ever be able to manage you." It was said with a degree of satisfaction with which, judging by Danielle's fervent response to his kiss, she heartily concurred.

The same August sun that bathed the four members of the house of Linton shone that day on the Assembly in Paris as a city, sickened by blood, called a halt to the Terror and the great cry went up: *"Justice pour tout le monde."* It was a cry from the heart of France, the cry that began the revolution and opened the door for the butterfly of the future.

Put a Little Romance in Your Life With
Fern Michaels

__Dear Emily	0-8217-5676-1	$6.99US/$8.50CAN
__Sara's Song	0-8217-5856-X	$6.99US/$8.50CAN
__Wish List	0-8217-5228-6	$6.99US/$7.99CAN
__Vegas Rich	0-8217-5594-3	$6.99US/$8.50CAN
__Vegas Heat	0-8217-5758-X	$6.99US/$8.50CAN
__Vegas Sunrise	1-55817-5983-3	$6.99US/$8.50CAN
__Whitefire	0-8217-5638-9	$6.99US/$8.50CAN